THE KEEPER'S DAUGHTER

THE KEEPER'S DAUGHTER

"A Novel"

Leanne Denise Knott

iUniverse, Inc.
New York Lincoln Shanghai

THE KEEPER'S DAUGHTER

iUniverse books may be ordered through booksellers or by contacting:

iUniverse
2021 Pine Lake Road, Suite 100
Lincoln, NE 68512
www.iuniverse.com
1-800-Authors (1-800-288-4677)

ISBN-13: 978-0-595-38642-0 (pbk)
ISBN-13: 978-0-595-83023-7 (ebk)
ISBN-10: 0-595-38642-3 (pbk)
ISBN-10: 0-595-83023-4 (ebk)

Printed in the United States of America

To my mother, Dianne,

who gave me the courage to believe

A shipwreck,
the wild waters roar and heave.
The brave vessel is dashed all to pieces,
and all the helpless souls within her drowned;
all save one.

A man whose soul is greater than the tempest
And his spirit stronger than the sea's embrace.
Not for him a watery end, but a new life
beginning on a stranger shore.

—William Shakespeare, *The Tempest*

Acknowledgments

On the long journey to publishing this novel I have been blessed with support from many, including my mother, Dianne Gray, whose editing of this manuscript was transformational; my husband, Dan, with his sustaining patience and love; my sister, Shelley, for her inspired book cover art; my dear friend, Nancy Mikitta, who has stayed true and listened since the earliest drafts; Sue Narayan, for helping shape my narrative, and lastly my writing group at the Loft Literary Center (members past and present) including Jaime Wurth, Steve Sorenson, Carole Olsen, Doug Dorow, Carrie Wright, Wendy Watson and Jeri Youness. Without your insight and gentle criticism, I would not be the writer I am today.

If you wish to visit this book's Web site, you will find it at www. squarehousepublishing.com

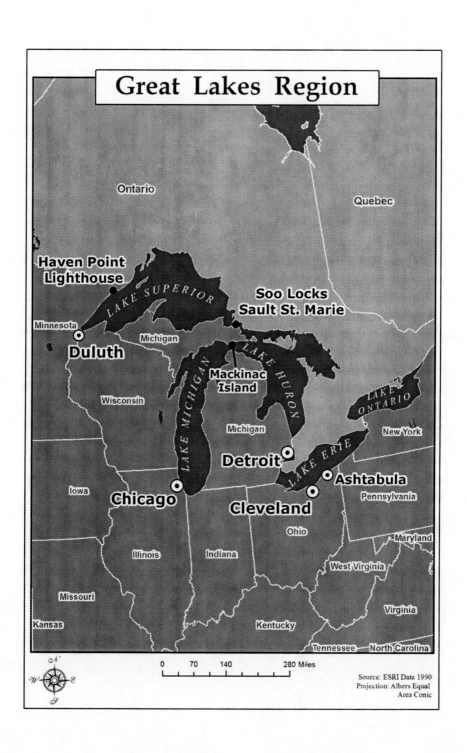

Great Lakes Region

Ontario

Quebec

Haven Point
Lighthouse

LAKE SUPERIOR

Soo Locks
Sault St. Marie

Minnesota

Michigan

Duluth

LAKE MICHIGAN

LAKE HURON

Mackinac
Island

Wisconsin

LAKE
ONTARIO

Michigan

New York

Detroit

LAKE ERIE

Iowa

Ashtabula

Chicago

Cleveland

Pennsylvania

Illinois

Indiana

Ohio

Maryland

West Virginia

Missouri

Virginia

Kansas

Kentucky

Tennessee

North Carolina

N
W   E
S

0   70   140   280 Miles

Source: ESRI Data 1990
Projection: Albers Equal
Area Conic

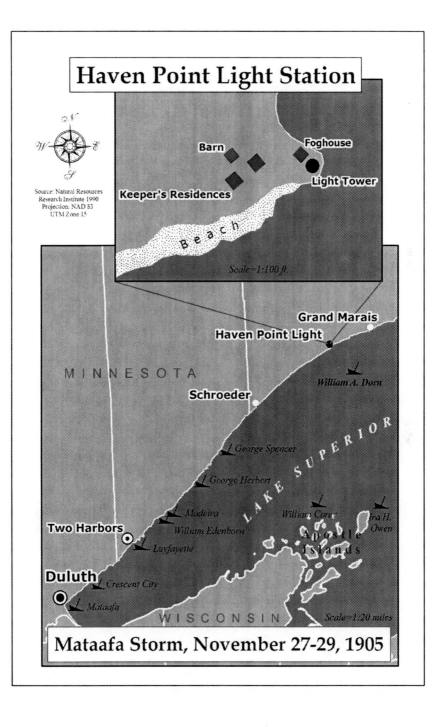

Haven Point Light Station

Barn

Foghouse

Keeper's Residences

Light Tower

Beach

Source: Natural Resources
Research Institute 1990
Projection: NAD 83
UTM Zone 15

Scale=1:100 ft.

Grand Marais

Haven Point Light

MINNESOTA

William A. Dorn

Schroeder

LAKE SUPERIOR

George Spencer

George Herbert

Madeira

William Corey

Ira H. Owen

Two Harbors

William Edenborn

Apostle Islands

Layfayette

Duluth

Crescent City

Mataafa

WISCONSIN

Scale=1:20 miles

Mataafa Storm, November 27-29, 1905

CHAPTER 1

▼

The Minnesota Coast of Lake Superior, 1905

Here I will build my dream. Here, I will build a paradise on the North Shore.

Eleanor Thompson paced out the dimensions of her future lodge with the care of a bride planning the details of her wedding. Long strides measured the lodge's north wall, the portico, the kitchen. It was a late afternoon in November, less than a week after her return to Haven Point Lighthouse. Under a leaden sky, water lapped the cobbled stones along the curved shore of the cove—stones as smooth as hen's eggs and colored every possible shade of gray. A brisk northeast wind whipped Eleanor's dark hair and pinched her cheeks until they shone red against porcelain skin. The bitter cold pierced her wool coat and mittens.

Poplar, birch, maple trees crowned the hill behind Eleanor. Jack pines and spruce swayed among them, still clad in soft green needles, while a thin layer of snow blanketed the surrounding forest and the half-decayed remnants of a fishing cabin.

A sudden wave broke against the shore, its sound blending with the *scree scree* of white-winged gulls as they wheeled and dived over the open waters of Superior. Far out on the lake, a cluster of schooners with their triangular courses sailed southward toward the harbor city of Duluth.

In Eleanor's mind's eye the lodge was already complete. Fifty dollars more and she'd have the full amount to buy the cove, the cabin, and homesteaded land surrounding it. Though her fingers stung from the cold, Eleanor withdrew a pencil and notebook from her coat to make a calculation. "Soon," she said, drawing a sigh full of both longing and satisfaction

When she looked up from her notebook, she saw another ship slowly plying southward, one of the newer steam freighters. Eleanor squinted to catch the name. "*William A. Dorn*," she said aloud, taking note of the metallic-painted smoke stack. A Zenith Steamship Company "silver-stacker," undoubtedly, one of several dozen that sailed past the rocky shoals of Lake Superior's North Shore each day.

Eleanor turned northward, toward Haven Point Light Station where her father, John Thompson, had been Head Keeper since before she'd been born. She couldn't see the tower, yet she felt its presence deeply. Haven Point Light stood in defiance of Superior, a punctuation of brick, metal and glass.

The stiffening wind brought a higher chop to the waves. *Time to leave*, Eleanor thought, moving toward the small skiff moored to the footings of an old fishing pier. Eleanor gingerly climbed over the skiff's gunnel, taking care not to snag her long skirt, and then shoved off with one of the oars. The hull scraped against the rocks before gliding free. She turned the bow into the waves and began to stroke for Haven Point.

It would be a half-mile of hard rowing. *Darn this change in weather, anyway*, she thought, frowning. She'd hoped to spend another hour at the cove, dreaming of things yet to come. But her mother, Adeline, was waiting, along with her father, the thirteen-year-old twins, David and Bridget, and the Assistant Keeper, Lars Berglund.

Worrisome thoughts needled Eleanor; Adeline had barely spoken a civil word to her these last few days. Their running argument over twenty-year-old Eleanor's decision to remain in the northlands had only worsened since her return from the Grand Hotel on Mackinac Island. *Mama's stubborn and spiteful as ever*, Eleanor thought, taking a firmer grip on the oars.

Eleanor rowed past weathered high cliffs and knifing peninsulas. Superior churned and foamed over huge crags and splits of broken rock. The waves came up a little higher in the wind, breaking over the stern, and Eleanor bent to her rowing, as Lars had taught her.

Lars had been acting so strange of late, by turns overly talkative and attentive followed by periods of silence. This confused Eleanor, made her feel almost uncomfortable. In the five years that Lars had served at Haven Point, the two had been fast friends, fishing together, gathering summer berries in the woods, sailing on the lake. He'd insisted on teaching her to row the skiff, something her mother still vehemently disagreed with. "Why has Lars changed?" Eleanor murmured, even as she rounded the final headland before home and the light tower came into view.

Haven Point Light was a moderate-sized lighthouse for a Lake Superior station. Its tower, built of white-painted brick, rose seventy feet from its base. The beacon slept at the moment, awaiting dusk and the keepers who would maintain its precise rotation throughout the night.

Eleanor rowed past floating chunks of ice as she neared the dock and boathouse. A narrow path wound upward from the rock-covered beach to a high ridge, beyond which stood both keepers' residences. Each house was built of pale yellow brick and was topped with a red tile roof. Smoke curling upward from the chimneys spoke of the welcoming warmth inside.

Lars emerged from his house and descended the snow-covered path toward the dock. He appeared younger than his thirty years with his dark blonde hair, weathered face, and easy smile. He wore a lined cap, heavy coat, wool trousers, and sturdy work boots. Lars smiled and waved. Eleanor felt a small start when their eyes met, but then brushed it off.

"Good rowing, Eleanor?" Lars asked as she cast out the skiff's line.

"Worse on the way home." Tired from the cold, Eleanor took an unsteady step up to the dock, where Lars caught her arm. Eleanor, cheeks tingling, pulled it away at once. "Thank you, Lars," she said, and then quickly walked away.

"Eleanor!" Lars called, hurrying to catch up with her. "What are you running from, *flicka*?" he asked with a laugh, withdrawing a small, tissue-wrapped package from his pocket. "I made this for you."

Eleanor accepted the package cautiously. "Open it," Lars encouraged, smiling. "Please."

Eleanor tore away the paper to reveal a carved red cardinal. "How beautiful," she said, holding it close to admire the detail. Everything about it was perfect, down to the feathers on its folded wings. Lars had clearly spent a great deal of spare time carving and painting it.

When Eleanor looked at Lars, his face was shining. "Why did you give this to me today?" she asked.

"A Christmas present. I've been working on it for the past two weeks."

"Christmas is a month away, Lars."

"I know. But I wanted to surprise you."

He stood watching her, not speaking. Eleanor hesitated, then thrust out her hand and said, "I thank you for your gift, but now I must be heading home."

Lars seemed crestfallen as she shook his hand. Eleanor turned on her heel and made her way up the pathway to her father's house. As she approached the two-story brick home, she saw her mother's glowering face in the front window.

Eleanor, jaw clenched, hid Lars' gift in her coat pocket before mounting the steps to the kitchen door. As she placed her hand on the knob, she caught a glimpse of herself in the window. Eleanor frowned at her reflection: too thin, too tall, cheeks too high, that brooding stare she'd inherited from her mother's side of the family. Her broad shoulders she especially disliked, for they were wider and straighter than those of the women in the *Ladies' Home Journal* clothier advertisements. Her father always said they were the shoulders of someone who could work as hard as a plow horse, but Eleanor hated them. What man would want her anyway, so far out here in the wilderness?

Not the kind of suitor she envisioned, certainly. Eleanor's beliefs about love had been nurtured by the romance stories abounding in the magazines. She longed for a heroic man, larger than life and yet who wooed her with tenderness. She'd recognize him when he appeared, she told herself. Love would be mutual and instantaneous, just like in the stories.

As Eleanor let herself inside, she noticed her father sitting at the round oak table in the center of the kitchen, smoking his pipe as he read a back-issue of the *Duluth News-Tribune*. John Thompson was a hale man with graying brown hair and moustache, and was dressed in wool trousers and a blue chambray shirt.

"Hello, Tomboy," John said in his kindly, resonant voice. *Tomboy* had been his nickname for Eleanor since she'd been old enough to climb a tree. "Been out to the cove again?"

"Yes, Papa." Eleanor removed her mittens and coat at the door, and then went to hold her hands to the Monarch cook stove. A fragrant stew bubbled in a large, speckled-enamel pot. Eleanor stole a glance at John. His face looked tired that day, tired and older than usual. *How much longer will he last as Head Keeper?* she wondered, not for the first time.

Bridget roller-skated into the kitchen, wearing a brown wool skirt with a frilled shirtwaist much like her older sister's. Eleanor envied Bridget's golden, upswept hair, her serene blue eyes and lovely, curving brows. Mouth like a bow, cheeks soft and round as a peach. Perfect child. Perfect as far as Adeline was concerned.

David appeared next with his sketchbook and tin box of pencils. Tall and ungainly as a colt, David had their father's dark hair and eyes. David was already outgrowing last winter's knickers and wool sweaters. A smile lit his freckled face. "I drew a picture of the lighthouse," David said, opening his sketch book for Eleanor to see.

Eleanor studied the carefully drawn lines and proportions. "This is the best one," she assured him.

"You really think so?"

"I do." Before Eleanor could say more, Adeline appeared, causing David to close his sketch book.

"You've done a splendid job making us wait for supper, Eleanor," Adeline said with barely veiled sarcasm. "How kind of you to join us."

"I'm sorry, Mama," Eleanor said as she turned to face her mother. Tall and austere, Adeline radiated an icy calm. Her graying blonde hair was brushed high into an impeccable coiffure. There was a touch of hauteur in her pinched expression and hooded eyes, belying an iron will that sometimes frightened Eleanor.

"Set the table, Eleanor, while I take out the corn bread," Adeline said. "And Bridget, take off those dreadful skates."

"Yes, Mama," Bridget said, sitting in her chair to remove them.

Eleanor placed bowls and silverware on the table. "Do we have any butter in the ice-box, Mama?"

"A little, yes. We're running low on everything, it seems," Adeline replied. She opened the oven door and withdrew the steaming pan of corn bread.

"Won't the *Amaranth* be coming any day now?"

"It'll be a week yet before the supply ship arrives," John answered. He tapped his pipe. "Sometimes it feels more like a year."

His tone caught Eleanor's attention. "Is something wrong, Papa?"

"There's news to share, but let's wait until we're all seated."

They hurried to put supper on the table. After bowing for grace, John said, "I received new orders from the Lighthouse Board in this week's mail bag. The light will continue to run until mid-December."

"What about school?" Bridget asked. "What if the lake freezes over before the *America* can take us to Grand Marais?"

"Both you and David will keep up your home studies, then return to regular school when we move back to town," John said. "Nothing will change from before."

Eleanor cast a quick glance at the Hoosier cupboard in the corner of the kitchen. "Papa, we're almost out of flour—"

"We'll make due with the cornmeal in the bin," Adeline interrupted. "And we've plenty of meat yet; there's the side of ham out in the smokehouse, along with the Thanksgiving turkey. So you see? We've nothing to worry about."

The brittle cheerfulness in Adeline's voice unnerved Eleanor. "Do you know why the season has been extended, Papa?"

"Truth is, I think the shipping companies want to make up their financial losses from the fall storms."

"They're making a mistake," Eleanor said. "Almost eighty sailors died in the September and October gales alone."

"I know, I know," John said, shaking his head. "I wish it were otherwise. But the Lighthouse Board has made their decision. The ships will continue to sail."

"What does Lars have to say?"

"And why does his opinion matter for anything?" Adeline asked, her tone arch.

"Lars was a sailor and a surfman for years," Eleanor argued. "His opinion should count for something."

"*Tsk.* Any fool can be a sailor. Not that any of this should concern you personally, Eleanor," Adeline added. "Once the light station closes, you'll be taking the steamer to Duluth and then the train to St. Paul."

Eleanor stiffened. "I'm not going to St. Paul, Mama."

"Of course you are. It's all been arranged." Adeline dipped her spoon into the stew and took a sip before continuing. "Uncle Casey's law firm has been flourishing, and Regina hinted in her last letter that several junior partners are anxious to meet you."

Beneath the table, Eleanor's left hand closed into a fist. "I'm not leaving the North Shore. I'm going to buy that cove between here and Little Nesna for a vacation lodge."

"Oh, that nonsense," Adeline said with a dismissive wave. "The old Nielson homestead probably sold over the summer."

"No, it hasn't. Papa checked at the Land Survey office the last time he was in Marais. Isn't that so, Papa?" Eleanor said, turning to her father.

"That's right," John said with a nod. "No one's asked about the cove since before last winter."

But Adeline was not so easily deterred. "Tell me, Eleanor, what makes you think yourself qualified to run such a place?"

"I learned all about lodge operations working as a cook at the Grand Hotel these last three summers. I'm not afraid of hard work, Mama." Eleanor paused, then said, "I have almost enough money to buy the land and get a start on the construction of the main building. Just one more winter cleaning houses in Marais, and a few months doing laundry for the Norwegians at Little Nesna next spring, and then I should have all I need."

"I see." Flustered, Adeline's expression grew tight. "Well, don't expect any help from your father or myself. If you cannot buy the land by next summer, then I'm packing you off to Regina's." Without another word, Adeline rose and left the kitchen.

Everyone ate in silence, except Eleanor, who pushed her food around in her bowl with her spoon. John touched her arm and said, "Don't listen to her, Tomboy. She's all just huff and bluff, you know."

Tears stung Eleanor's eyes. How could he defend Adeline after the misery she'd made of his life? Eleanor grabbed her coat before fleeing out the back door.

Wind off the lake froze the tears on Eleanor's cheeks as she walked to the ridge overlooking the lake. Did she dream in vain? Was she strong enough to maintain faith in herself, or was she acting a fool, like some wayward child building castles out of sand?

Determination steeled inside her. She would show them. She would prove to everyone that she didn't need their help, that she could accomplish whatever she wanted to on her own.

At the shore, waves rushed against the rocks unceasingly, a force of water against the anvil of land. It reminded Eleanor once again of the terrible autumn season and lives lost on Superior. How long until another violent storm churned the lake? "Probably just a matter of time," she murmured.

At least staying near Superior was preferable to living in St. Paul. Eleanor stifled a bitter laugh; why should she marry at all when her mother had made such an unhappy alliance with her father? John was a dear man but wedded with an almost single-minded devotion to keeping the light, while Adeline, frustrated, dreamed of the city and high society.

Eleanor wiped her face. Her mother could go hang, for all she cared. The lodge would be her own personal masterpiece, her legacy on the North Shore. Eleanor hugged herself; only six more months of enduring her mother, and everything she'd labored for these last three years would finally come to fruition.

*   *   *   *

"Get your hide out of bed now, Liam MacLann, or I'll throw your arse overboard myself!"

Liam, resting with his eyes closed in his ship's berth, lay still despite Chief Mate Klassen's threat. Liam heard the tap of a cudgel in Nathaniel's palm, and he tensed, readying for the blow.

"I said *get up!*" Nathaniel snarled. Liam rolled to his feet and grasped the cudgel just above Nathaniel's hand. Liam, well over six feet tall, towered over the smaller man.

"If you threaten me with this again, I'll have no choice but to bust your head with it," Liam said. Their eyes locked, will striving against will, until Nathaniel slowly released the cudgel.

"Suit yourself," Nathaniel said. He was stocky man with thinning brown hair, dressed in navy-blue trousers and a work shirt. "Chief Wright wants you down in the firehold as soon as possible. The winds have freshened this afternoon."

Liam, himself wearing long underwear and trousers, looped his suspenders over his broad shoulders. "Go down yourself, then, if it's so fucking important."

Nathaniel's eyes crackled with spite. "All you Irish are alike, you lazy, ignorant bastard."

Liam ignored the insult. "Where's Nicky?"

"In the galley, having an early supper. Did his work already. That one attends his business, unlike some I know," Nathaniel said before turning for the hatch.

"You forgot your club," Liam said, holding it out. Nathaniel grabbed it and then stalked outside, slamming the thick metal door behind him.

"And to hell with you, you rotten Yank!" Liam shouted after him. With a grunt, he sat on the lower bunk and pulled on his leather work boots. Raking a hand through his hair, his thoughts moved ahead to the coming work-day. Another shift of shoveling coal, same as that morning, just the same as the last eight months. *Well, no use shirking anymore*, Liam told himself. Time to get to work.

Liam washed his face in the small sink opposite the bunks. After patting dry with a towel, he combed his hair, trying in vain to make his cow-lick lie down. He stared at the small mirror hanging above the sink. At the age of twenty-five, he strongly resembled his father: wide forehead, blue eyes, light-brown hair, a prominent nose bridge that had been broken in fistfights on more than one occasion.

He looked out at the lake through the tiny porthole beside the hatch. Having spent most of his life on the sea, Liam felt the weather by the pitch and roll of the freighter, heard it in the conversational creak of the ship's platings.

Waves rolled along the riveted hull, spraying the window and the rail outside the door. Wind rattled the lines as a few stray flakes of snow blew past. "Look at those whitecaps, God's curse on 'em," he muttered.

Liam sighed as he pulled on a heavy knit sweater. The day was sure to be cold and inhospitable. *Damn these end-of-season-hauls anyway*, he thought with a scowl as he swung open the metal hatch.

He paused for a moment and stared down the length of the 450-foot deck, past the twelve covered hatches filled with 6,000 tons of coal. The *William A.*

Dorn was a typical freighter, with two raised towers, fore and aft, connected by a lengthy spar deck. The captain and his officers navigated the ship from the forward pilothouse, a semi-circular room: the pilot at the wheel, the second mate manning the engine-room telegraph, the watchman observing the steering pole, the captain bending over charts or sitting on the mate's stool and staring through the bank of front windows. It was a world apart, completely different from the stern tower where the men of the engineering department lived and labored.

If the forward pilothouse at the bow was the brain of the ship, the stern power plant was the muscle. Four coal-fired reciprocating pistons powered the *Dorn's* twelve-foot wide propeller, making possible the transport of massive cargo loads along the Great Lakes. After-cabins provided housing for the Chief Engineer, his assistants, the firemen, and coal-passers. The galley and mess hall were also located in the aft, along with quarters for the steward and his porters. A life-raft was stored near the galley cabin, while the ship's two lifeboats hung atop the poop deck from a set of curved davits beside the slim, silver-painted smokestack.

Liam raised his arm to shield his face from the wind. Granite sky blended into the agitated lake, and Liam frowned. "Just me luck," he grumbled as his boots slipped on the ice-coated deck. "Lord spare me from the wrath of this wicked lake."

He unlatched the galley hatch and stepped inside. A long table ran the length of the room, lined with stools bolted to the steel deck. The aroma of roasted turkey, sourdough biscuits, and creamed corn beckoned to Liam, and he went to join his best friend and bunkmate, Nick Bryant.

"Sit down and have some coffee, Liam," the dark-haired, wiry Nick invited. They had served together aboard Zenith Steamship freighters the last four seasons, where each man held one of the rotating positions as ship's fireman. Nick had just come off the noon-to-four watch, and Liam was to be his replacement.

Liam nodded and took a seat beside Nick as the watchman, Tom Gustnor, poured a cup of coffee. Of the three friends, Tom was the only man with a wife and children.

"Me thanks," Liam said as he took the cup from Tom. "Rough day below, Nicky?"

"We've had worse. Chief Allen had a sour face, though he'd never admit his nerves."

"A right he has, now," Liam said. "Him being the only one among us who's survived a November shipwreck."

Tom mopped the creamed corn on his plate with a slice of turkey. "Aboard the *Lewis Hutton*, right?"

"Back in '95," Nick replied. "She was caught in a real bad blow, then went down with all hands except Allen near Isle Royale. Still won't talk about what happened that night, not even if you ask him directly." The three men grew silent as their dinnerware shifted slightly under the rocking of the heavy seas.

Liam broke the tension with a snort. "Sure now, trying to put off my appetite, are you?" He watched as the portly steward, Charlie Eberlien, approached the table with a plate of food.

"Burnt again, eh, Charlie?" Liam asked with a grin.

"Only the stuff you're getting," Charlie replied. "Why is it you micks eat twice as much as the next man?"

"I starved as a child on Aran," Liam answered. "Seaweed stew and half-rotten potatoes aren't much to keep a family of ten alive."

"What did the last letter from home say, Liam?" Tom asked as Charlie returned to the galley.

"Mam wrote that my father has the rheumatism something fierce, though he still sets his fishing nets whenever he can."

"Any other news?"

"Och, just the usual gossip: who has died, who has married, another child born, poor soul, how nobody likes the new priest. Five years I've been gone and yet Mam still writes as though 'twas yesterday."

"Maybe she wants you to return home," Tom observed.

"That will never happen," Liam said, frowning. He glanced out the porthole at the passing shore. "Sometimes I wish for a little peace and a bit of land." Liam chuckled and shook his head. "There, now, I'm starting to sound like my damn fool brother, Conall, again."

"But what about your sister, Maeve?" Nick asked. "Did she marry that man who was courting her?"

"Ah, now, the day any man marries Maeve MacLann will be one he regrets forever," Liam replied. Tom snickered, but Nick leaned forward.

"Why won't she marry, Liam? In America she'd be an old maid already."

Liam shrugged. "Irish men are not always big on marrying. There's an old saying what goes, 'Tis better to spend your life wanting what you don't have than having what you don't want.'" Liam swirled the coffee around in his cup. "Anyway, the only woman a man loves is his dear mother."

"I can't say I entirely agree with you," Nick said. "Maeve should come to Minnesota, her being such a handsome woman and all." Nick kept a photograph of the shapely, red-haired Maeve above his bunk.

"Handsome or no, she'd not set foot off of Inishmore, even for you, Nick." Liam finished the remains of his meal. "Catch some sleep, boyo, and I'll see you later tonight."

"About time you showed up, MacLann. I was ready to send Klassen beating for you."

The sonorous tones of the bull-necked first-assistant engineer, Hans Schneidermann, rolled from the deep shadows of the firehold. He was a thick-bodied man, dressed in dungarees stained with coal-dust, oil, and sweat. His skin was ruddy from long hours working in front of the furnaces.

The engine room itself was suffocating, with the smell of hot grease and oil hanging heavy in the air. Everything was in constant motion: rods, pistons and crossheads pummeling, rocker arms and cranks flying around and around. The massive machinery was both muscular and yet startlingly precise in its movement. To Liam it almost seemed that, once set in motion, the engine might run forever.

Hans wiped the sweat from his forehead with a greasy rag before handing the shovel to Liam. "Waiting for supper in bed this time, MacLann?"

"Very funny." Liam studied the familiar glow of the coals inside the furnace. "Any problems?"

"*Nein*, none on the afternoon shift."

"When are we to arrive in Duluth?"

"Later tonight. Captain Graling is hoping for a quick turn-around. He wants the iron ore we'll be loading to arrive in Ashtabula before Thanksgiving." Ashtabula was a town on the southern shore of Lake Erie.

A half-smile twisted the corner of Liam's mouth. "The Old Man's an optimist, I'll say that much."

Hans tipped a drink from the water jug. "I'm heading upstairs. You can expect me back in a few hours."

"I won't have moved, I promise," Liam said. He was soon joined by his coal-passer, Ransom Hoyt, a burly lad of fourteen who had signed aboard ship that summer. He had reddish-blonde hair and cheeks spattered with freckles.

"Ready to fire her up, Rannie?"

"Whenever you say, Liam."

"To work, then. The day's not getting any shorter."

Ransom hefted the handles of the wheelbarrow and pushed it toward the coal bunker, where he shoveled black coal to haul back to the furnaces.

Liam's thoughts wandered as he began stoking the fires. He was grateful that the season was nearly finished; by mid-December the hard work would be just a memory. The crewmen were all anxious to leave the ship and return to their lives ashore. Sailing the freighter for months at a time with the same twenty-eight men put a strain on even the seasoned veterans.

Tempers were up. Those who were married and had families waiting for them were irksome and spoiling for a fight, while the bachelors were eager for liberty, ready to blow the season's earnings on liquor, cards, and women. Liam smiled at the thought, along with the chance to loaf away the winter at a comfortable boarding house in Duluth.

Liam's shovel made a harsh scraping sound against the steel deck as he filled the furnace. With the sound came troublesome thoughts, chief among them Captain Graling's recent offer to promote him from the firehold next season. "You're a man with good instincts, the kind of sailor who knows how to read a sea," Graling had confided during the course of their meeting. "I want you to sign aboard as my new third mate next season."

Liam paused to wipe the sweat streaming down his face. A third mate's position would mean better pay, but more responsibility as well. Did he want a long-term career on the Lakes? Would he become a respected and prosperous gentleman like Captain Graling, or a heavy-handed, conceited ass like Nathaniel Klassen? Moreover, was he setting himself up for failure, engaging in the sort of dreaming which had ended with the catastrophe of Conall's death?

Conall had been dead from scarlet fever five years now, buried in a prairie cemetery on the outskirts of distant Graceville, Minnesota. It was to have been a new beginning for the two brothers, a refuge from the vengeance that had driven them from their island home. Their flight began with the latest round of tenant evictions in 1899, when the wealthy landlords, who lived on the Irish mainland, had taken every last possession of the defaulters and then directed the authorities to burn their cottages. Was anyone to blame if the potato harvest had been worse than usual, or the winter sea too storm-tossed for fishing? But the landlords didn't care if the islanders were starving. All that mattered was their rent payments.

Liam never knew where Conall had gotten hold of that pistol, and there were times when he still regretted what happened afterward. An informer among the islanders, one Francis Flaherty, had ratted out the debtors for his own financial gain. Conall, with his grim sense of justice, put a bullet in Francis' head one night. So much for the informer. But when the sheriff came for Conall, Liam took matters into his own hands and shot the sheriff dead on the cottage steps, thereby sealing his own fate. With the help of local families and money from their father's cousin in Minnesota, Conall and Liam escaped to America to begin anew among the Irish emigrants of Graceville.

The echoes of Liam's native Irish Gaelic faded before the clamor of the engine room. He took a long gulp from the water jug before asking, "Hot enough for you, Rannie?"

"Not even close," Ransom replied, grinning. White teeth contrasted sharply with the black dust staining his face.

Roaring flames and smothering darkness surrounded them, baking their senses and dulling their thoughts. Liam barely remembered the year after Conall's death, when he'd forsaken Graceville and wandered from town to town, taking work where he could and drinking himself into oblivion any chance he had. At last he'd arrived in the port city of Duluth, where the sight of Superior revived memories of the sea. He'd signed aboard his first ship as fireman, work he continued to perform daily in the Stygian depths of the *Dorn*.

Muscles limbered and drenched in sweat, Liam used his strength to stoke and spread the fires. He was an expert at what he did, and the close friendship of his mates eased the pain of his brother's death and his vague yearnings for Ireland.

But in his heart he knew that he would not make his living on the freighters forever.

CHAPTER 2

▼

"Up for a game of cards, Liam?"

It was late evening. Liam had come to the galley in search of something cold to drink after his shift in the firehold. The steward kept apple cider in the icebox, and Liam lifted the bottle for a long pull. He sauntered over to the galley table where Nick, Tom, and the wheelsman, Harry Renek, sat playing poker.

Liam shook his head when he saw the pile of money heaped between them. "I'm not ready to lose that much tonight, lads."

"Come on! Don't you feel lucky?" Nick badgered. "I'm always telling everyone you're the luckiest man I know!"

"Not interested," Liam said. "I'm trying to save up to buy some new boots."

"Your loss, Liam," Nick said, shifting the stub of his cigar from one side of his mouth to the other. "You'll have to settle for the cheaper whores the next time we get into Buffalo, those skinny ones who're missing some of their teeth."

"Says you," Liam growled in mock menace. He swung out playfully to cuff Nick, who ducked the blow with a grin. Laughing, Liam said, "I'm going deck-side for a smoke—I'll be back to the cabin before too long."

"I'm heading there myself after this next hand," Nick said as Liam grabbed his wool pea-coat from the row of hooks along the bulkhead. Swinging the hatch open, Liam stepped into the darkness.

Though the winds had grown calmer, the air was still bitterly cold, and Liam pulled up his jacket collar. Starlight glittered overhead. Waves lapped against the hull as the *Dorn* slowly cut through the water. Night blended into the ebony waters of Lake Superior, with no sight of land or another ship for miles. Liam strolled along the rail and then paused as he withdrew a rolled cigarette from his coat pocket. He struck a match against the heel of his boot before lighting up.

Liam took a long drag off the cigarette and then looked toward the far lights of the pilothouse. The captain's offer. Third mate. Conflicting thoughts crowded into his head and piled into an ache at the base of his neck. Should he accept the position? And if he did, how would it change his friendship with Nick and the other men of the engine-room crew?

"I just don't know," he said as he tossed the cigarette into the water. Liam shivered as a feeling of desolation settled over him. He was no good at thinking about such things. Who was he, after all? A poor Irish *gaelach* with the charge of murder on his head.

He needed to make a decision but had no idea where to turn for advice. Suddenly the latent Catholic inside him stirred, and he closed his eyes as he murmured a prayer. "Heavenly Father, please help me to choose what's right."

There was no audible answer, nor had he expected one. But a peculiar feeling crept over Liam, a horrible, crushing dread.

Choking, drowning, with spikes of icy pain piercing his limbs...
His face rubbed raw on a life-raft's hull...
The muffled report of an underwater blast...
Clumps of ice frozen in his hair...
Towering waves...
"MacLann...!"

Liam's eyes flew open as he jumped back from the rail. To his shock, he saw the lake flat and placid as before. "Jesus and Mary!" he stammered, his hand flashing the sign of the cross. Disoriented, he stumbled along the deck until he reached the galley bulkhead. Planting his back against the steel wall, he stared into the night sky.

Premonitions had come to him before, as a boy on Inishmore. Once, when Liam was climbing the fortress ruins at Dun Oghill, he looked to the ocean and saw old Cathal O'Malley's *curragh* boat swamped in the waves. Liam never told anyone of this frightening vision, and he had quite forgotten all about it until the following winter when the O'Malley boat was lost in a tremendous storm.

Liam knew what his mother would say. "You have seen a window into the future, my son. Get ashore the first chance you have, for the warning was a gift. Do not lay it aside, Liam."

But Liam did lay it aside. "I'll have no part of it," he muttered. He deserted the spar deck then, anxious for the familiar safety of his cabin.

Nick, in his upper bunk, set aside the book he was reading when Liam arrived. "What's wrong, Liam? You look as though you've seen a ghost."

"Nothing. 'Tis nothing at all." Liam's hand shook as he filled a water glass at the sink and then took a gulp. "It's this stinking ship. I need time on land, aye, that'd be the cure of it."

"Sure enough," Nick said as he settled back and resumed reading.

Liam, a little calmer now, moved closer. "What have you got there, boyo?"

"Melville's *Moby Dick*. Ever read it?"

"No. Where'd it come from?"

"Captain lent it to me, last week."

Liam cocked a brow. "Since when did you become such a bookworm, Nicky?"

"Well, I did spend a whole semester in college before coming up north to work the ore boats," Nick reminded him. He flipped back to a previously marked page. "Melville's a wordy bastard, but he gets your attention, I'll say that much. Listen to this:

> Now, gentlemen, in their interflowing aggregate, these grand fresh-water seas of ours—Erie, and Ontario, and Huron, and Superior, and Michigan—possess an ocean-like expansiveness. They contain round archipelagos of romantic isles. They have the fleet thunderings of naval victories. They are swept by Borean and dismasting waves as direful as any that lash the salted wave. They know what shipwrecks are; for, out of sight of land, however inland, they have drowned many a midnight ship with all its shrieking crew."

Nick whistled. "Goddamn, but he tells the full truth, Melville does. 'Shrieking crew'—I like that, don't you?"

"I guess so." Liam stretched out on his berth, still haunted by his deck-side vision. After staring at the bottom of the metal bunk for a few minutes he asked, "Do you ever feel like you'll never get off this ship, like you'll never see your home again?"

"Sometimes," Nick replied, leaning over the mattress' edge, his spiky bangs hanging over his eyes. "Why do you ask?"

"No reason." Liam sat up and unlaced his boots. "I'm turning in," he said as he covered himself and snuggled onto the mattress.

"I'm on again at midnight, so I'll just keep reading 'til then," Nick said. The whispering turn of pages overlaid the familiar throb of the *Dorn's* engines, and the two noises gradually became one as Liam drifted into an uneasy sleep.

*   *   *   *

"Mama, why did you decide to marry Papa?"

It was the next day at Haven Point, and Eleanor and Adeline were setting the table for the noon meal. "Why would ask such a thing, Eleanor?" Adeline questioned in return.

The sad arc of her parent's marriage had consumed Eleanor's thoughts since the last argument she'd had with her mother. "Well," Eleanor began, "you're always talking about how I should marry soon, and I started wondering what it was like between you and Papa. The courtship, I mean."

"Well, you know already that my father ran a logging camp in northern Michigan, and that Mother, myself, and my older sister cooked and did laundry for the lumberjacks there. John Thompson had just come from Massachusetts by rail, seeking his fortune in the 'Great Northwest.' I still recall the day he arrived at the camp, looking for work. John was about the skinniest, most unpromising young man my father ever hired.

"The way John tells it, the moment he set eyes on me, he just knew we were going to marry. He courted me, but I refused him."

"Why, Mama?"

"I didn't think he was the one for me, I guess." Adeline settled herself into one of the chairs. "You see, my sister Regina and I had been proposed to a hundred times before by any number of those foul-mouthed, lice-ridden woodsmen. We never accepted, of course, which suited my mother just fine. She wanted better for us, to marry a rich man who would free us from a life of endless drudgery."

"But why Papa, then? Was it for love?"

"I didn't love him at all, at first. I was actually in love with another of the jacks, the man Regina eventually married, Casey Darland." Adeline's gaze grew distant. "Sometimes I wish things had turned out differently. Regina lives in a house on Summit Avenue in St. Paul with servants and fine clothing, and here am I, still stuck in the woods, pumping water from a cistern, cooking and cleaning day and night."

"Papa tries his best."

Adeline quickly rose and began bustling about the table again. "Sometimes that's not enough, Eleanor. I've had to live with my mistake, but you still have a chance at comfort and security. The important thing, above all, is money."

"I will marry for love, or not marry at all."

"The second is more likely, if you persist in the notion of wasting your youth in this god-forsaken wilderness." A thin smile stretched Adeline's lips. "At least you won't have to worry about Lars Berglund pestering you. He told your father last night he's considering resigning at the end of this season."

"Resigning? But why?" Eleanor asked, purposely ignoring her mother's barb about the assistant keeper. "Lars has always been so happy here."

"It is not your place to wonder. Now, go tell Lars that dinner is almost ready, and I'll call Papa and the children."

Eleanor put on her winter coat before heading across the yard to Lars' house. She shielded her eyes as she scanned the lake's horizon, which was table-smooth in the tranquil weather. Her face tingled in the chill air, and she inhaled the sharp smell of wood smoke and pine needles.

She knocked firmly on the kitchen door, knowing that Lars was deaf in one ear. He appeared in the entrance a few moments later, and Eleanor was surprised to see his face half-lathered in creamy white soap.

"Come warm yourself inside, Eleanor. I'm almost finished shaving," he told her, holding the door wide. Eleanor lingered on the threshold, a little uncertain of the propriety of entering his house alone. "Come along, it's freezing out there," Lars insisted. She stepped inside as he shut the door behind her.

The place was a mess. A cast-iron pot, half-full of day-old pork and beans, sat on the cook stove. Unwashed dishes lay piled in the sink. Lars' faded denim work-jacket hung from the back of a ladder chair, while his mud-encrusted boots rested on the floor beside the wood box. It was a bachelor's home, and the disorder gave the room a sense of the exotic.

"I overslept today, so I'm a little behind schedule," Lars explained as he returned to the basin of hot water by the sink. "I'll just be a minute."

"That's all right," Eleanor told him. "Dinner can wait."

As Lars lifted the straight-edged razor and scraped the stubble from his cheek and jaw, Eleanor's gaze was drawn toward two photographs hanging on the wall. "Who are those young men in the picture?" she asked.

Lars rinsed his face and patted dry with a towel. "That's me and my brother, Erik, on our family farm in Iowa. That was taken the year before I left to join the Merchant Marine Service."

"You look so much alike," Eleanor said. The resemblance between the brothers was striking, with their wavy dark-blonde hair and almond eyes. Both were built broad and muscular in the manner of their Viking forefathers.

Lars came beside Eleanor, smelling strongly of the soap's residue. "And that's another bit of personal history," he explained, nodding to the other picture. "From my days as a surfman at the Ottawa Point Lifesaving Station."

"Where's that?"

"In Michigan, near Tawas City off Lake Huron." He tapped a finger on the glass. "There's me and the other crew members, with the station keeper." Seven men in lifejackets sat inside the lifeboat, oars at the ready while the keeper stood in the bow.

"That's you?" Eleanor's eyes widened. "You look so young! How old were you then?"

"About twenty." Lars cleared his throat. "That *was* ten years ago—"

"Do you ever miss it? I mean, the danger and excitement of being a lifesaver?"

"The excitement part I wouldn't know about. The danger, no, though in our day we were considered the best surfmen on the Lakes." Lars' eyes gleamed. "We saved many a sailor from certain death, in conditions so terrible it still gives me bad dreams."

She turned to face him. "Why did you leave it, Lars?"

"Once or twice I came near to drowning myself. It's always a risk going out when the sea puts on a nasty face and the waves come calling." Lars sighed. "We'd better get along now, or your mother will scold me for holding everything up."

"She'll scold you anyway," Eleanor said quietly.

Lars sat in the chair and slid his feet into his boots, and had just begun to tighten his laces when Eleanor said, "Mama told me that you're thinking of leaving."

He leveled his gaze at her. "I don't think I can stay."

"Where will you go?"

"Not sure yet. Erik has written and asked me to join him down in Iowa, to help out on the farm. Problem is, I don't care too much for farming."

"Then why not stay? You're the best assistant keeper we've ever had."

Lars opened his mouth to speak, but then frowned and shook his head. "I have my reasons. The main thing that's decided me is that I can't take the loneliness any longer. I'm wishing for a wife and children of my own, and, as you pointed out, I'm not a young man anymore."

"Oh," Eleanor said. She closed her eyes in momentary self-reproach. Lars' plans were his own private business, and she had no right to convince him otherwise.

Lars shrugged into his coat and then held the door open for her. As she neared the door, he asked, "How much time do you spend each day at the cove, Eleanor?"

"An hour or two, if it's not too windy and cold."

Concern deepened the lines on Lars' face. "Beware the lake, Eleanor. After I quit the lifesaving service, I spent years sailing every type of vessel on the inland seas, and Superior is the meanest of all her sisters." He stood over her for a moment, and Eleanor caught her breath before stepping out the door.

"I won't forget, Lars. I promise."

*   *   *   *

The *William Dorn* arrived in Duluth later in the evening, where she was given orders from the dockyard tug to drop anchor and wait to deliver her payload of coal. It was close to nine o'clock at night, and the men were gathered in the galley for coffee and sandwiches.

Night deepened around the ship as the sailors' talk turned to the telling of tales. Some shared personal stories, while others retold well-known yarns passed down through the years from crew to crew. Chairs had been drawn in from officers' mess to accommodate the overflow. Liam was content to sit near the galley hatch. He smiled to himself as Nick thrust his way into one of the stories.

"No, no, you've got it all wrong!" Nick objected as he waved his hands, interrupting the grizzled oiler, Jim Rehbein. "Now, *this* is the true story of the sinking of the *Western Reserve*—"

"True story my arse!" Jim sputtered, his face flushed. "What the hell would you know about it?"

"I know plenty, that's what! Why, I berthed with her sole survivor, Harold Stewart, when we sailed together aboard the *Queen City*." When no one challenged this outrageous claim, Nick pulled his chair to the front of the room to spin his version of the oft-told story.

Abruptly, Chief Engineer Allen Wright rose from his seat and made his way toward the door. On impulse, Liam grabbed his arm. All heads turned to watch. "What's the matter, Allen?" Liam asked.

The blonde-haired, spectacled man stared down at Liam. "Curse him and curse the lot of you!" Allen growled, and then glared at Nick. "Thinks he can talk about things he's never lived through himself!"

Allen tried to pull his arm away, but Liam tightened his grip. "It's about the *Lewis Hutton*, isn't it?" Liam asked. When Allen nodded, Liam said, "Then tell us the truth of what happened, Chief. Tell us about the shipwreck."

Allen hesitated, staring into Liam's eyes before twisting free of Liam's grip and striding to the front of the room. A few moments later Nick yielded his seat to Allen, who waited for the room to fall quiet before he began.

"It was the night of November 17th, 1895, and I was serving aboard the schooner *Lewis Hutton* as first mate. The ship's master was a newcomer to the Lakes, a young fellow named Roland Jacobs." Allen hunkered forward, his elbows resting on his knees. "Jacobs only got that job because his uncle was the chairman of the company that owned the *Hutton*, the Duluth and Georgian Bay Transit. That greenhorn had no business taking on the responsibilities of a Great Lakes captain.

"We sailed from Port Arthur, Ontario, fully loaded with two tons of Canadian wheat and bound for Chicago. The ship hadn't hardly stuck her nose outside the protected bay waters when we ran smack into high seas and whipping, gale-force winds, a real nor'easter. The officers begged Jacobs to heave to and drop anchor at Fort William, but that mule-head refused to listen. 'Chicago must have her wheat, and I intend to deliver it to her at the contracted time, gentlemen!' he told us. He was nervous about going against orders, you see."

Liam nodded. He knew that concern for the lives of ordinary sailors figured far below the shipping companies' drive for profits. "So on we sail," Allen continued, "until the schooner is rolling and wallowing so bad that a couple of times I almost tumbled over the rail.

"'Captain,' I says, 'it's a terrible blow! We've got to reef up the sails and turn into the storm!'

Down to his cabin he goes to check his charts. 'We'll beat for Isle Royale and lay up in the lee of the island 'til the storm passes!' he orders after coming back on deck, and the helmsman does his best to set the new course. But we were doomed already. We had no idea what our position was, though I had a strong feeling we were near the tip of the Isle. Suddenly we heard the crash of shattering timbers.

"We'd hit the southerly reef of Canoe Rocks, and the *Lewis Hutton* immediately took water into her hold and listed to port. I remember someone yelling to swing out the lifeboat, but it was too late, with the angle of the sinking ship and those twenty-foot seas.

"You can't believe how quickly the ship was swallowed up. Ten, maybe fifteen minutes, and then we were all in the water. Huge waves swamped those who were at the surface, and I guess they either drowned or froze to death. I never saw Captain Jacobs or any of my mates again."

Charlie Eberlien brought out a cup of coffee for Allen. "How did you survive?" Nick asked.

"I climbed aboard a piece of wooden deck that was floating on the surface. Shortly after, I washed ashore on the island itself, where I huddled alone near the shore. I survived three days and was hungrier than a spring bear, but at last I was rescued by the *Santee*."

There was a general murmuring and shuffling of feet at the story's conclusion. Allen quietly made his way toward the exit.

Liam, his heart filled with emotion for the older man, followed Allen out the hatch. "'Twas a good tale, Chief," Liam said, "and no man but you has the right to tell it."

"Aye," Allen answered, "though I have paid heavily for the privilege."

It was almost eleven o'clock before the *Dorn* was cleared to unload her coal. Liam and Nick both lay awake in their berths as Liam smoked a cigarette and pondered Allen's story. Would he have done as well himself? Was the knack for survival something that slept inside, untapped until the critical moment, or was it simply a matter of luck?

The cabin's quiet was interrupted by the clank and scrape of massive, metal-toothed Hulett unloaders. The noise was accompanied by the low thrum of the resting engines and the occasional creak of the upper bunk as Nick read the final chapter of Moby Dick.

"Liam, why not take a look at that new letter?" Nick asked. "You've had it ever since the mail bag was thrown aboard at the Soo Locks."

Liam sat up and stubbed out the cigarette in a tin can that was overflowing with butts. "I suppose I might." He opened his dresser drawer and withdrew the letter from atop his shirts. It was postmarked October 12th.

Liam sat on the edge of his bunk before tearing along the top of the letter. "Jesus," he grunted.

"What? What'd you find?"

"'Tis from Maeve." As Liam withdrew the letter, a metallic object slid from the envelope and fell onto his lap. "Now what do we have here?" he asked, lifting what looked to be a small medallion.

"A gift, apparently. Go on, read what she has to say."

Liam sat up a little straighter. "My dear brother Liam," he began, "I send greetings to you from Ireland. I hope this letter finds you in good health and still happy in your pursuits. I am writing to share the joyful news that I am now a wedded woman. The name of my new husband is Paddy Donoghue, and he owns a bicycle shop in Dublin city."

"Dublin?" Nick repeated. "How the hell did she get to Dublin?" Inishmore and Dublin were on the opposite coasts of Ireland.

Liam shrugged and continued reading. "Paddy and I met at the Galway country fair last year where I was selling our sister Fiona's sweaters. He came for the fishing, but caught me instead." Liam chuckled at this last part; Maeve always had a wry sense of humor. "Married life is all that I hoped it would be, and I am more glad than I can say to be away from the poverty of Inishmore. I understand now why you left, brother, and I do not begrudge your life in America.

"In token of my affection, I am sending along a St. Brendan's medal, that patron saint of mariners whose very bones lie buried on our island home. I hope one day we will meet again. Know that I pray daily for your protection. Your devoted sister, Maeve Donoghue." Liam's eyes traveled over the final postscript, which read, "P.S.—Mam says to tell you that Rose O'Malley sends her regards."

"Rose O'Malley?" Nick asked. "Who's that?"

"Ah, well, just a girl I once knew back home."

"Just a girl?" Nick reached down and gave Liam's head a shove. "Why haven't you said anything about her before, you hold-out!"

"'Tis none of your damned business, for one. And for another, we were only childhood sweethearts and nothing more. Good Catholic girls like Rose were not ones for doing more than strolling together down the country lanes."

"All right then, keep your secrets," Nick said. "There's one thing I don't understand, though. I thought you said that Maeve would never leave Inishmore."

Liam set the letter aside and examined the medallion. "A lot has changed since I left home, I guess. It *has* been five years." Liam slipped the thin chain around his neck and tucked the medal inside his undershirt as Nick returned to his reading. Liam called up to his friend. "Almost done with that book, boyo?"

"Just finished, in fact. Here, let me read the very last part:

> The drama's done. Why then does any one step forth? Because one did survive the wreck. And I only am escaped to tell thee."

Nick closed the book. "And there you have it—'I only am escaped to tell thee.'"

"Sound's all right. Maybe I'll read it meself sometime," Liam said. He climbed beneath his blanket. "I'm going for my forty winks."

"I guess I will too. You can turn off the light."

When darkness had settled, Liam spoke to Nick in a low voice, asking, "You don't mind it so much, Nicky, that Maeve is married?"

"Why should I? She's half a world away."

"But you did like her, at least a little? I mean, with you keeping her picture and all?" Liam asked.

"Maeve's a fine lass. Much better in looks than your average American girl."

"But—?"

"Maeve is in Ireland. The sporting girls are in Duluth and Buffalo. That's the difference."

"Goodnight, you old fornicator."

"From one to another."

Liam lay on his berth for a long while thinking about Maeve and her letter. For some strange reason, the news of her marriage brought an ache to his heart. Maeve was settled; at long last, she'd found her place in the world, while he himself was still searching, still wandering.

His thoughts drifted to Rose O'Malley. Liam remembered her as a shy girl with strawberry-blonde hair and an upturned nose. She was a few years behind him in school, the same age as his younger brother, Christy. Almost from the day they met, Liam knew she was the girl he would likely marry. But the incident with the sheriff had changed everything.

Liam searched his feelings for Rose. He'd been fond of her, taking pleasure in her quiet laughter, the way she'd bring over the new spring lambs to show to him, the flash of her white stockings when she rode her bicycle along the country road. A fine lass, but one for whom he'd never really formed a deep attachment. He wondered why she'd never married, and hoped that one day she could find another man to build her life with in his absence.

Liam closed his eyes and rolled onto his side. *No use dwelling on the past,* he told himself. Rose's sweet face faded as sleep finally overtook him.

Liam fell into hard dreaming that night. Images of home, fleeting memories of his old life on Inishmore. He saw himself and his brothers and father walking down to the beach with oars in hand, rowing into the maw of the Atlantic to fish, emptying their nets at day's end, and then enjoying a humble supper beside the hearth. His father gathering the family and telling of the Irish hero, Fionn Mac Cumhaill, his Gaelic a softly spoken murmur in the gloom.

The dream changed, assumed a new shape as Liam became a bird of the sea. He sped onward across the foaming waves until he came to a far golden shore lined with gemstones and pearls. *Hy Brasil*, the island of Heart's Content, that mythical land waiting always just beyond the western horizon.

A small figure stood on the island's shore, far below. It was Liam's brother, Conall.

"Conall, Conall!" Liam cried.

The tall, fair-haired Conall raised a hand as if to beckon Liam closer. Liam squawked and beat his wings. "I have thought on you everyday, Conall, and missed you so."

Conall made no reply. Heart-torn, Liam said, "I wish that you had lived. I would have died for you instead, if I could have. Why were you taken away?"

At last Conall spoke. "'Twas my fate, Liam. I've learned that much since long I have dwelt here. Mortal men may not know, but the dead know many things."

"You're speaking in riddles, *dearthár*. I don't understand."

"Someday you will. Now, it's time for you to wake up, Liam boy."

Liam resisted the sudden tugging sensation. *No! Not yet!*

"Awaken now, sleeper—"

"Conall!" Liam shouted as he sat bolt upright in his berth. A granite sky cast dismal daylight through the porthole. Someone pounded urgently on the hatch. Liam swung his feet out and called, "Come in!"

It was Ransom. "Rannie," Liam said, rubbing his knuckles against his bleary eyes.

Ransom shut the hatch and peered down at Liam. "No disrespect, Liam, but you look as though Klassen has been scrubbing the deck with your face all night."

"Nice," Liam muttered. "What time do you have?"

"It's almost ten. We sail in two hours. Nick sent me to make sure you were awake."

"Ten o'clock? They've only now finished loading the ore?"

"That's what I was told. Nick's over in the mess. He said you were sleeping like a dead man. You hungry, Liam?"

"Maybe some coffee, I guess." Liam waved the boy off. "I'll be along shortly."

Liam was deck-side when the *Dorn* blew her farewell signal at noon on Monday the 27th. He stood alone at the rail and gazed at the towering Missabe Ore Docks, their pitch-stained wooden trestles and rusty steel chutes rising from the black water like cathedrals of industry. Deck hands hosed the reddish iron-ore dust that coated the hatches. Steam was up, and it was time to begin the thousand-mile journey to Ashtabula, Ohio.

Harbor tugs moved the ship slowly astern. Liam heard the watchman call off the distances to the pilothouse as the vessel maneuvered through the crowded harbor. On the opposite dock, the steamer *Mataafa* and her barge consort, *Nasmyth*, were just beginning to load. The day itself was unusually balmy for November, the water a mirror. The only ripples on the surface came from the gentle plowing action of the departing ship.

The *Dorn* was riding low and heavy, filled beyond capacity. This would be what the crew referred to as a "money run," a way to pad their profit ratio at the end of the season. Shipping rates skyrocketed the closer they came to December, especially for heating coal.

The year had been a difficult one between the labor unions and the shipping companies, especially for the *William Dorn's* parent company, Zenith Steamship. Zenith's president, Sumner Russell, had done his best to break the sailors' demands for higher wages and greater job security. A strike had narrowly been averted that spring, and only because of the threat of bringing in strike-breakers. It had been a bad business, and resentment still lingered, especially among the unrated deckhands and firemen.

Men with power and money will always take advantage of those beneath them, Liam thought with a sense of disgust. He wondered what Sumner Russell was like and what sort of life he led. A fancy house, servants, probably even a motorcar to drive. No hunger, no want, and no risk to life or limb. Just the desire to build an even greater fortune on the backs of working men like Liam and Nick.

Liam shook his head. No use in speculating on someone whose path he'd never cross. Liam turned to face the pilothouse and decided he'd make good on the captain's standing invitation to watch the officers at work. "To get a feel for the duties you'll assume as third mate," Graling had assured him.

Well, and what would be the harm? Lunch first, then a shower and shave and a clean change of clothing.

Anything to keep his mind off Conall.

CHAPTER 3

▼

In the yard outside the kitchen door, Eleanor pinned wet laundry to a line that was stretched between two towering oaks. The trees loomed over her in silent grandeur, their dried brown leaves clinging stubbornly to gnarled, knuckly limbs. Watery sunlight shed an incandescent glow across the snow-clad hills and cliffs. Superior was flat and impotent in the late-autumn afternoon. No birds sang, no creature stirred. To Eleanor it felt as if the world was holding its breath, waiting.

Eleanor, her fingers numb with the cold, shoved a wooden clothespin onto the corner of her father's undershirt. She cupped her hands and blew on them. A whoop of laughter carried through the stillness; it was David, sledding down the ridge on his Flexible Flyer. *What I wouldn't give to join him*, Eleanor thought, as she reached into the hanging cotton sack for another pin.

As Eleanor lifted one of Lars' plaid shirts from the pile of laundry, her thoughts returned to their conversation in his kitchen, to the tension she'd felt when she'd brushed past him. Was it possible that he felt a romantic attachment to her, and, if so, was she part of his decision to leave? She considered Lars a good man, kindly, honorable, and devoted. But he was not the suitor she dreamed of.

She gritted her teeth and dug out a dripping wet petticoat. How she hated Mondays, laundry day. But Wednesdays were also laundry day for Eleanor, when she washed and dried clothes for the Norwegian fishermen who lived to the south of the light station. She'd made an arrangement with these men several years earlier, agreeing that, whenever she was home from her position at the hotel out on Mackinac Island, she would do their laundry. The fishermen's camp was named Little Nesna, after the Norwegian village of their birth. Nils Finnesgaard had the best grasp of English among them, and he was the one who paid her a dollar for each of the men. Six dollars a week made the hateful, back-breaking labor worth-while, and Eleanor saved every penny she earned in a hat-box she kept under her bed.

The laundry was already stiffening in the cold. Eleanor shook out her hands and then gazed toward the house. She felt dull and languid, as though the day's somnolence had crept into her bones. How nice it was going to feel when she finally went inside and warmed herself at the woodstove.

Afterward, if she had the time, she would write to her two friends from the Grand Hotel, Gracie and Allison. Eleanor smiled to herself, thinking of the fun they'd enjoyed together over the summer.

Though it had only been a few weeks since they'd seen one another, to Eleanor it already felt like long months. Both Gracie and Allison had planned to travel to Duluth in search of employment as housemaids with one of the many wealthy families living there. Eleanor hoped her friends had found work, and that they would forward their address to her as soon as they could.

A stick snapped behind Eleanor. She turned around but no one was there. She felt a shift in the air, a perceptible tightening. Her pulse raced as she hurried to the ridge.

A bank of clouds met the lake. A slender line, just a stroke of charcoal across gray canvas. Wind ruffled the dried oak leaves behind Eleanor, whispering to her of a coming change in the weather.

She hurried along the path, thinking, *I must tell Papa at once.*

*   *   *   *

"And how are you today, MacLann?"

Captain Edward Graling nodded toward Liam, who stood in the pilothouse door. Captain Graling was tall and gaunt and wore the wearied expression of a man who never slept. Piercing eyes gazed from beneath a high forehead capped with white hair. Graling looked disheveled, his uniform wrinkled, his collar unbuttoned, his master's insignia slightly askew. But his authority was palpable; Captain Graling's mates served him with unerring devotion, seldom questioning his seamanship or ability to command.

"I'm fit, sir, thank you," Liam replied, looking at Nathaniel Klassen from the corner of his eye. Klassen's expression was carefully composed, though Liam noticed the lines deepen around the mouth. Captain Graling crossed the bridge to shake Liam's hand before inviting him to take a seat on the mate's stool.

"I was wondering when you'd come to the pilothouse, MacLann. Perhaps this means you've accepted my offer." Graling's face broadened into a smile. "Don't wait too long to give me your answer. There's paperwork to file and arrangements to be made if you're to train under me directly."

"You'll have an answer before the end of the month, sir, I promise," Liam replied. "A fine day for sailing."

"Yes." Captain Graling clasped his hands behind his back. "We'll put the *William Dorn* through her paces and see if we can set a record for this late in the season."

The wheelsman nodded toward the barometer. "It's a high glass, Captain."

Graling checked the gauge himself. "All the better. One, maybe two more trips like this, and we should be ready for lay-up."

"I think the men will welcome it, sir," Liam said.

"Who wouldn't? I myself am looking forward to a rest, a chance to see Matilda and play with my grandchildren in Cleveland." Captain Graling's smile faded. "Until that time, we have our duties to attend."

Liam made himself comfortable on the stool, pointedly ignoring Nathaniel. The ship had long since passed the harbor canal entrance and was already steaming across Superior. A feeling of expansiveness settled over Liam as he watched the shore slide by. Too seldom did he see the end results of his labors, this forward motion through the world of sky and water.

By the same time the next day the *Dorn* would pass through the Soo locks, and the crew would be one day closer to the end of the '05 shipping season.

The thought cheered Liam as the ship continued to steam onward.

*   *   *   *

Eleanor opened the double doors to the fog house and stepped inside, where Lars was at work with the twin air-compressors. Flywheels whirled as the gas motors rattled noisily. Exhaust hung in the air, despite the fact that all eight of the double-hung windows had been opened. Lars' expression turned from concentration to pleasure when he saw Eleanor from across the room.

"Is Papa still in the tower?" Eleanor yelled above the din.

"Last I saw him!" A frown wrinkled Lars' forehead. "Is something wrong, Eleanor?"

"I think a storm is coming," Eleanor said, pointing to the window.

Lars looked for himself and then cursed in Swedish. "Go tell your father that I'm heading down to the boathouse to pull the skiff up the beach. We can't afford to chance losing it, especially if the supply boat is delayed. Go along, now, he's up on the lantern deck."

"I'm on my way," Eleanor said. Back outside, the wind had begun to play in little gusts between the buildings. She passed through the lighthouse's annex before entering the tower's base. Wrought-iron steps spiraled up to the lantern deck. Fifty steps. The soles of her shoes made a quick tapping noise as she hurried upward.

John was polishing the massive, clam-shaped Fresnel lens when Eleanor entered the light room. "Papa, there's a storm—"

"Yes, I see it. I've been watching it for about a half-hour," John said with an air of calm. "Nothing to get excited about. We'll meet it head on, just like everything else."

She joined him on the lantern deck and gazed out anxiously as the clouds continued to build. "Lars went down to the boathouse to haul in the skiff, Papa," she said, her face close to the window.

"That's what I was going down to do myself, in just a few minutes." John tucked the polishing cloth in his coat pocket. "I'd better go down and make sure we've got plenty of kerosene stocked from the storehouse. It could end up being a long watch tonight, from the looks of it."

"I'll go help Lars with the skiff if you like, Papa," Eleanor said.

John gave her an appreciative smile, and then, to her surprise, rested a hand on her shoulder. "My grown-up girl. Not much of a tomboy any more, eh? You know I depend on you, Eleanor."

Eleanor's throat tightened. "Of course, Papa," she said, then stood on tiptoes to kiss his cheek. "I'll always be your brave soldier, no matter what happens."

After helping Lars pull the skiff up the shore, Eleanor returned to the house and broke the news of the coming storm. Adeline sent the younger children out to haul in more wood, then considered what to do with the hanging laundry. "We'll leave it out as long as possible and then string it through the kitchen just before the storm hits," she told Eleanor.

"I'll help bring them in when you're ready," Eleanor said. The scent of nutmeg and cinnamon teased her nose. "What's baking?"

"Gingersnaps. Your father asked for them when he woke before dinner. The first batch is almost ready."

Eleanor wandered into the parlor and sat in the rocking chair. Through the front window she saw that whitecaps frothed the lake. Slowly Eleanor rocked, the chair creaking in the stillness. Daylight began to fail as thick clouds spanned the sky.

Adeline carried a plate of cookies into the parlor and offered them to Eleanor. "I know these are your favorite."

Eleanor was surprised by her mother's sudden kindness. Why was she acting so friendly all of a sudden? "I'm not really hungry, Mama. Save them for Papa and Lars."

Adeline turned toward the window. "Wind seems to be picking up some. Good thing your father bought the Thanksgiving turkey from the Grand Marais butcher shop last week."

"Three days away. Seems like it will never come," Eleanor said just as John came inside.

"Berglund says it going to be a blizzard-maker. That Swede's got a nose for weather, I'll say that much about him."

Adeline nodded, her expression grave. "Is everything ready, John?"

"As ready as it'll ever be. Put some coffee on, Adeline. Lars and I are going to both keep the watch together tonight." John gave Adeline a quick kiss, and Eleanor saw the brief look of displeasure on her mother's face before she pushed him away.

Now it comes, Eleanor thought, rocking faster as John left to prepare for the coming battle.

Now it comes.

*   *   *   *

Liam was eating supper in the mess when the steward pointed to the window and said, "Look at it snow!"

Hard ice-pellets clipped against the portholes, erasing the last of the day's light. The freighter lurched and shifted, a clear sign of the worsening weather.

"So much for Captain Graling's record run to Ashtabula," Liam commented as he took another bite of roast beef.

"What did you say, Liam?" This came from Tom Gustnor, who was sitting across the table.

"I was saying that we'll be a mite longer to the Soo with a storm coming on." A gust of wind clattered snow and ice against the bulkhead. "She promises to be a gagger, too, or I'm no seaman."

"Quartering on the starboard. I hate these nor'easters," Tom said as he shook his head. "Captain will haunt the bridge all goddamn night now."

"Maybe you'd prefer a shift shoveling coal in the firehold, hmm?"

Tom grimaced and shook his head. "I'll leave that to you and Nick. I don't envy you fellows, keeping her at steady steam through this mess."

"I just hope Schneidermann gets everything tied down before the boat starts riding rough." Liam pushed his plate away. "I'm going out to have myself a look."

"Good luck," Tom said. Liam pulled on his pea-coat and a wide-brimmed, sloping sou'wester hat. A burst of snow blew in behind him as he passed through the galley hatchway.

Heavy snow swirled around Liam the moment he stepped outside. The lights of the pilothouse were barely discernable in the heavy squalls, while the lakeshore itself was hidden from sight. Sheets of water, sheared loose by the driving bow, flung upward as heavy spray against the wheelhouse windows. Large combers crashed and rolled along the spar deck, the steel hull groaning in protest under the assault.

Suddenly the deep-throated ship's whistle tore through the wind's screech, startling Liam. Three short blasts, once a minute: the fog signal of the Great Lakes.

"Bloody old bitch!" Liam cried, shaking his fist at Superior. "Haven't you given us enough already this year? Why are you acting so high and mighty now?" A strong gust nearly tore his cap away.

"All right, all right, your Royal Highness! Have your way, then, and be quick about it!" Liam shouted before sliding off toward his cabin.

"Are you ready to dance, Liam?"

Nick, coal dust ringing his bloodshot eyes, grinned as he leaned against the handle of his shovel. Liam had just arrived in the engine room for the four-to-eight shift as the ship climbed and plunged in the even-growing swells.

"Bellyaching again, eh, Nicky? You complain more than me baby sister," Liam said. "'Tis nothing more than we've seen this season already."

"That's what you think. I'm heading up for a quick bite, and then I'll check on Dan. He told me earlier that his stomach was acting up," Nick said, referring to Dan Gilberg, the *Dorn*'s third fireman.

Liam shook his head. "Still prone to seasickness after all these years, poor Dan. Well, off with you, then, Nicky, and let a real man take over."

Ransom appeared in Nick's place. "It's blowing up a real gale out there, Liam. I was just in the galley, and the second mate came in and said that he'd never seen the barometer fall so fast."

Liam took the youngster's arm. Though Ransom often tried to act tougher than the other coal-passers, Liam knew how much he feared rough weather. "Stay on duty," Liam said, looking squarely at Ransom. "The Old Man knows his job."

Ransom's face smoothed. "The *Dorn* won't make much headway, will she?"

"Not in this dirty fucking weather. But standing here having a grand discussion won't change what's ahead. That wheelbarrow isn't likely to move all by itself, now, is it, lad?"

As the *Dorn* rose to meet the ten-foot waves, the ship rode high on the crest and then listed forward, causing Ransom's wheelbarrow to tip again and again. Swearing like a seasoned sailor, Ransom did his best to keep the coal from scattering all over the deck, though it was a losing battle.

Liam calmly fed the fires, balancing against the rolling action, dancing with the ship as Nick had predicted. Scoop after scoop, numbering in the dozens, then hundreds, one shovelful of coal after another. After a few hours there was no longer conscious thought, only action and reaction, the shovel becoming an extension of Liam's body. His entire universe narrowed to heat, fire, and the darkness of the hold.

The din was tremendous. Everything that was moving, and a few things that weren't supposed to, slid from one side of the room to the other. A wrench flew off the wall and clanked along the steel deck, narrowly missing Ransom's boot. Liam grabbed it on the next up-swell and secured it without comment.

Toward the end of the shift, a new and ominous vibration ran through the freighter. "Throwing her wheel out," Liam hissed. Conditions on the lake were worse than anyone had anticipated.

From the third level of the engine room, the chief engineer bellowed down to his assistants, "Shut down the engine! Propeller is out and racing!"

Liam's stomach clenched as the ship throttled down. "She must be riding high and heavy," he muttered. The tossing of the vessel had become so forceful and regular that the stern was rising above the water. The propeller whirled dangerously in the free air, then smacked the water again with a sickening thud.

Liam and Ransom climbed the ladder to the upper deck. Chief Engineer Allen Wright was barking orders to Hans Scheidermann, the second assistant engineer, and the oiler, Jim Rehbein. "No one's to touch the throttle but me!" Allen told the men. "Keep the boiler pressure at one-eighty, and pray that we can heave to, and soon!"

"There's nothing out here, Chief!" Jim argued. "The leeward of Isle Royale is miles away!"

"That's Captain's concern, not ours! Liam, roust Nick and Dan. No one sleeps 'til we're safely through!"

"Aye, sir." Liam mounted the stair leading to the outer door, and then braced himself for the walk to the firemen's cabins.

The sight on deck made Liam's heart sink. Monumental waves rolled from fore to aft along the hatches before exploding like fists against the stern. Layer upon layer of jagged ice coated the freighter's decks and lines. The ship itself heaved upward and shook in the heaviest water, then crashed forward on the sloping down-swell. As the *Dorn* plunged into each new trough, Liam watched the steel mid-deck twist and shudder in a way that frightened him deeply.

Liam slid the short distance to the cabin where he threw open the hatch. "Nick, the Chief has invited you to join the party downstairs."

"Can't sleep anyway." Nick dressed quickly, then asked. "Should we take the lifejackets?"

Liam hesitated. Was it a sign of bad faith, or even cowardice? And what would the other men say?

The roar of the waves battering the ship decided him. Nothing else mattered if the worst should come to pass.

"Bring 'em with."

*   *   *   *

Eleanor slept little that long night. She twisted beneath her quilts, troubled by a strong sense of unease. Regular blasts of the light station's fog signal filtered into her shallow dreams. Wind gnashed at the windows as bitter cold seeped into every crack of the house.

A sharp crash brought Eleanor fully awake just after dawn. Bridget jumped from her bed, and for a moment the sisters stared at one another. "Did the barn roof blow off?" the younger girl asked.

"I don't know." Eleanor went to the window, but thick frost blocked her view. "I can't see a thing."

David, white-faced, opened their door and asked, "What was that?"

"Let's go see if Mama knows," Eleanor said before wrapping herself in her flannel robe. The younger children followed behind her as she descended the stairs.

They found Adeline alone in the kitchen. "Mama," Eleanor began, "there was a terrible noise—"

"I know. It was one of the oak trees in the yard, the one that was struck by lightening last year. Papa figured it might blow down." Adeline clutched a cup of coffee in her hands. "Lars came in to warm up a short while ago. He said the thermometer is reading below zero, and he's guessing the winds are up to fifty miles-per-hour."

"Fifty?" David repeated. "Will the wind damage the house, Mama?"

"I don't think so, David. But the ships on the lake are another matter."

Bridget drew near Adeline. "No one would be on the lake in this storm, would they, Mama?"

"Probably some are, yes. We'll do our best to warn the ships from the shoals." Adeline gave Bridget's arm a pat. "Go upstairs now and change while I make breakfast. Eleanor, we'll haul in more wood after you've dressed."

"Yes, Mama." Eleanor followed behind the children, her thoughts lingering on the ships riding the storm.

The wind continued its unceasing shriek all through the morning. Eleanor kept returning to the kitchen window every few minutes, though all she saw was a curtain of white. Gusts of snow raked the panes. Neither John nor Lars had returned.

Eleanor knew in her heart this was a fierce storm, even for a Lake Superior November gale. Something about the pitch of the wind stretched her nerves unbearably taut. Filled with restless energy, she longed to join the men in the tower or fog house, just to have something useful to do. *It isn't fair*, she thought, pressing her fingertips to the frosty window. She knew almost as much about running the light as either Lars or her father.

Eleanor returned to the table where Adeline and Bridget sat reading. David was drawing another building in his sketchbook. Eleanor glanced at the picture briefly before asking her mother, "Why did Papa ever agree to be a lighthouse keeper anyway?"

"It was the only thing he ever wanted to do, really," Adeline replied. "I've never told you this before, but Papa's father worked on a whaling ship out of Boston harbor. He died in a shipwreck when Papa was a small child."

"Why didn't Papa ever tell us?" Bridget asked.

"He doesn't like to speak about it. But I know it's what drives him to stand the watch, night after night, year after year." Suddenly Adeline slapped her magazine closed.

"What's wrong, Mama?" Bridget asked.

"It's this screaming wind," Adeline answered, then strode to the door, where she drew on her coat and mittens. "I'm heading out to the smokehouse," she announced

"Ham for dinner?" Eleanor guessed.

"Yes. Hopefully the men will take a break at noon and come inside for a bite to eat. They've been at it for eighteen hours straight, and I've a feeling we haven't seen the tail end of this storm yet."

Eleanor was setting out the dishes in the dining room for the noon meal when John and Lars finally came inside. They stamped their boots and complained bitterly about the cold.

She rushed to greet them but then halted in the kitchen door. Ice had formed on John's eyebrows and mustache, and there were gray patches of frostbite on his cheeks. Lars seemed little better; his skin was blistered, his eyes glazed and sunken.

"I want you both to take off those wet things and come close to the stove," Adeline told them.

"Coffee, please," Lars said as he dropped into a chair.

"I have some right here on the stove," Adeline replied. "Dinner will be ready soon. Warm yourselves while Eleanor and I take care of everything." Soon Adeline placed two cups of steaming coffee on the table.

"How much longer will it blow like this, Papa?" David asked, coming to stand beside his father.

"Could be one hour. Could be forty." John leaned back in his chair and slapped his hands on his knees. "I've never seen anything like this in all my years at Haven Point."

Lars nodded. "The waves at the beach are easily topping twelve, fifteen feet. I'm not holding out much hope for the dock and boathouse."

"They can be replaced. It's those poor devils who are caught out on the lake that have me worried," John said before wiping his dripping mustache with his sleeve. "Good thing we pulled that skiff way up the beach, or that would have been lost, too."

"We might just need it if any ships crack up near the point." Lars withdrew a handkerchief from his pocket and blew his nose. "How soon until that ham is done, Mrs. Thompson?"

"Right now, in fact. Go ahead into the dining room. There's bread and creamed corn as well."

"Sounds dandy," John said. "With your good cooking and that fog horn blasting away, we might just beat this gale yet!"

*   *   *   *

In the bowels of the *Dorn*, the blackened gang of the firehold had stoked the furnaces without pause for almost twenty hours. Dan Gilberg was by now so sick and weak that he could barely stand. Liam and Nick continued to shovel with short, mechanical motions in an effort to shore up their waning strength. Ransom and the other coal-passers stuck to their stations with dogged determination, the leaden fear in their bellies long forgotten in the face of their crippling fatigue.

But the most courageous man in the engine room that day was Chief Engineer Allen Wright. He stood at the controls, patiently nursing the engine along, shutting it down when the stern rose from the water and then opening it up after they had breached the crest. Limited instructions had been telephoned down from the pilothouse during the overnight watch. Nathaniel Klassen had called at 3 AM to say that they were driving toward the shelter of the narrow straight between Isle Royale and Thunder Bay.

The ship's furnaces had devoured enormous quantities of coal, and a bone-weary Liam wondered how far they'd progressed since daybreak. The electric clock on the wall read two o'clock in the afternoon, though it felt to Liam as though a week had passed, the longest, most punishing week of his entire life. But he refused to quit; his mates were counting on him to stay on task, and he did not intend to disappoint them.

This was how it had been since Liam's earliest days. "Men must show courage in the face of their fear," his father, Joseph, had often told him. "Strength is born of character, *mo buachaill*. The staunchest heart can accomplish miracles."

Liam clenched his jaw and redoubled his efforts. Before long his self-awareness dwindled to almost nothing, replaced by this singular, driving purpose. They had to reach safety or the ship and their lives would be forfeit.

"I'll bet the officers have frozen arses by now," Nick said from Liam's side.

"Not like us down here in the sweat-box, though I'm plenty damned starved," Liam answered. "I'm ready to eat anything that's not moving."

Nick grinned. "Hey Liam, remember that time we docked in Sandusky, and Tom's wife met him at the pier with that whore who'd had his baby? I thought Tom was going to jump right into the water, by the look on his face!"

Liam laughed out loud. "Poor Tom. I don't think he was ever the same after that."

"Or remember that time aboard the *Elysium* when the skipper found a woman in the cook's cabin? I'd never heard anyone cuss like that before!"

"Captain docked his wages for a month, that much I recall." Liam knew that Nick was telling these stories to take their minds off their fatigue and boost their morale. It might have worked, too, if Liam hadn't lifted the water jug and found it empty.

His temper blazed. *Fuck the officers and their orders*, he thought. "I don't care what the Chief says," Liam said. "I'm going up to the galley before I pass out."

"You should. You're starting to look as bad as old Dan," Nick said, looking toward the doubled-over fireman. "Let me know how things are up top."

The stokers and their assistants paused as Liam propped his shovel against the bulkhead. He looped his arms through the cork-filled lifejacket and then spoke to Ransom, asking, "Rannie, can you tie it for me? My fingers have gone numb."

"Yes, Liam." Ransom's expression was somber as he tied the stays.

"No slouching now. I'll be back shortly," Liam promised before he climbed the steps. He took one last look at his friends before opening the outer hatch.

CHAPTER 4

▼

As Liam stepped outside, a mountainous wave smashed him to the deck. Green water washed over him as it curled along the stern. Liam grasped at the rail in desperation as a monstrous hand dragged him out and back, the water sucking at his legs and feet. Ice-water bit into him like shards of broken glass, the cold a tremendous shock after the sweltering heat of the firehold. It was an unimaginable force of water: *he must not let go, hold fast, hold fast, his strength sifting away*...Then the wave cleared and the ship plunged forward, as it had countless times before.

Instinct took over as Liam groped his way toward the galley hatch. The next wave washed over the bow and along the deck, cresting as it surged toward him. Liam fumbled with the latch and managed to squeeze inside only seconds before the wave passed.

Liam was greeted by chaos. Waves had broken out the starboard portholes, and two feet of lake water sloshed through the galley. A cupboard-door latch had banged loose sometime earlier, coughing out dishes which now floated haphazardly between the table and stools.

Charlie Eberlien poked his head out the kitchen entry. "Liam! Have you seen Uno?"

Liam stared blankly at Charlie. "What—? Who—?"

"Uno Toivanen, my porter! I sent him forward a couple of hours ago with food for the pilothouse crew, and he was supposed to hurry back and help me with the bailing!"

"Uno's gone! No man could survive on deck with those waves!" Liam shouted. "How could you send a man to his death like that?"

"It wasn't my fault! Klassen ordered it himself—"

A deafening *bang* interrupted the steward's defense, followed by another, even louder. The two men gaped at one another, then waded their way to the hatch. Liam took a tentative step onto the deck, bracing himself in the frame.

"Oh my God," Liam said, his voice barely a croak. A stress fracture had opened amidships, and the stern section had taken an undeniable list. Water streamed inside the hull breach, and though the lights still flickered atop the smokestack, the bow was completely dark.

"She's hogged, Liam! She'll go to the bottom!" Charlie cried. "What should we do?"

Liam didn't answer. He'd retreated into a bizarre world of disconnect, as if everything was happening to someone else, and he wasn't really there at all. He saw Charlie's mouth moving but could hear no sound, the waves continued to thrash the foundering ship but the wind and water seemed far away. There was only the beating of his heart and the wonder of the widening gap in the mid-deck.

Panic choked him. They were going to die, all of them, drowned in the watery graveyard of Lake Superior, like the thousands gone before them. It had come to this, then. He would die a young man, as he had always feared.

A voice cut through Liam's thoughts, a voice that sounded very much like Conall's. *Get to the life-raft, Liam boy*, the voice whispered. *You don't have much time.*

"We've got to untie the life-raft before she lists any further!" Liam cried, throwing off his torpor. "Hurry!"

Liam and Charlie exited the galley and slid their way toward the life-raft, both men cursing as another mammoth wave rolled past. Liam tried to untie the laft-raft's lines, but the ropes were stiff and frozen.

"Look!" Charlie pointed as the ship began to tear apart at her riveted seams. Inch-thick steel plates ripped as steam from the severed pipes rushed forth. Huge sparks flew as the stern shuddered and began to sink.

Liam worked feverishly to unhook the raft. He thought briefly about his ship-mates below but knew there was no time to help them. Everything depended on freeing the life-raft. He gritted his teeth as he bent his will to the lines.

The *William A. Dorn* was caught in her death throes. Millions of gallons of ice-water poured atop the iron ore tonnage, exerting incredible pressure on the failing ship. The bow nosed downward at an absurd angle, exposing the open mouth of the cargo hold.

The raging sea hammered Liam to the deck, and the pressure nearly yanked him over. He managed to regain his feet, though he was drenched from the freezing water. "I've almost got it free, now, Charlie!" Liam yelled above the hurricane-force winds, turning toward the steward.

But Charlie was gone.

The stern continued to sink, trembling and wiggling under the influence of the still-rotating propeller. Liam clawed at the lines, desperate to release the raft.

And then he too was in the water.

*   *   *   *

A tremendous gust shattered the front window in the Thompson's parlor. Adeline and the younger children ran in from the kitchen as sub-zero wind howled through the room. Eleanor, who'd been reading in her bedroom, threw her book aside and hurried down the stairs.

"Get your father!" Adeline cried. Eleanor ran into the kitchen to grab her coat, and then counted to three before opening the door. A ferocious gust tore it from her hands and slammed it against the outer wall. Eleanor forced the door closed before turning toward the light tower.

Needles of wind-driven snow pricked the skin on her face. Her breath came hard and smothered, and her toes grew numb as cold shackled her ankles and then her knees. The wind was like the hand of a giant creature, spiteful and hurting.

Eleanor slipped on a patch of ice and fell flat on her back. She gasped as she stared all around. *Where am I? Where is the tower?* The sky, the land, the lake—everything was lost in the blowing whiteness.

As Eleanor struggled to stand she heard the moan of the fog horn. "Not much further now," she whispered. Head bowed, she shouldered her way through the storm.

She found John and Lars in the fog house, huddled beside the pot-bellied Franklin stove. "Come quickly!" she cried. "The parlor window's broken out!"

"Both of you stay here until I return!" John ordered before disappearing into the storm.

Lars made room for Eleanor near the stove. "That wind gust had to be near seventy miles per hour," he said, shaking his head.

Eleanor covered her ears as the rooftop horn blasted. "What about the beacon?" she asked during the interval.

"We've been running it all day, just in case," Lars replied. "There's just no way to know who's out there and where they ride. Superior has never seen a storm like this before, God's truth."

Lars and Eleanor stood in silence for several minutes, soaking up the wood-stove's heat. Eleanor studied Lars' tired face, and, as she did, she became aware of his closeness, how alone they were together. Lars seemed to notice it as well, and his cheeks grew flushed. "I'm glad you're here, Eleanor," he said. "I've been want-ing to talk to you about something for a long time now—"

He was interrupted by John's appearance in the doorway. "Get the tools from the tower, Lars. We've got to board up that window right away."

Lars hesitated as he threw a glance in Eleanor's direction. She stood com-pletely still, a little breathless over what Lars might have intended to say. But it never came, to her vast relief.

"Yes, sir," Lars replied, "we're coming."

*   *   *   *

Liam bobbed at the surface of the colossal waves, fighting to keep his head free of the churning surf. Wind sheered off the tops of the waves in horizontal bands of white spray. Black masses of water bore down on him with startling speed, carried him on the rising crest, then dropped him behind as they rushed onward. Liam gasped as the cold water squeezed his chest in its iron vice. Snow fell in furious sheets, and he was only able to see a few yards away.

He heard rumblings from a nearby explosion; the steam-driven boilers had made contact with the icy lake water, further destroying the fast-sinking stern. Liam, in despair, cried out for his friends. "Nick! Tom! Harry! Ransom!"

A cry pierced the storm's wail. "MacLann!"

Who was that? "Over here!" Liam called back.

Soon Nathaniel Klassen drifted near, wearing a life vest. "Quick! I thought I saw the life-raft over in that direction!" he cried to Liam.

"But I can't swim!" Liam said, his words lost to the wind. He felt his strength ebbing in the crippling cold. Another wave surged over him, certain to drag him under, and then, miraculously, the life-raft floated within reach.

"Grab a hold!" Nathaniel shouted.

Using the life-raft's trailing lines, Liam pulled himself over the side while Nathaniel boarded the raft on the opposite end.

But not for long. A tremendous swell flipped the raft over, throwing both men into the water.

Liam, his lifejacket waterlogged, plunged below the surface. Downward he was dragged, far downward into the endless depths of water. *Just like in the vision*, a corner of his panic-stricken mind screamed. Darkness enfolded him in a deadly embrace, merciless, inescapable, overwhelming.

But Liam refused to accept death. He followed the upward rise of air bubbles and kicked as hard as he could, breaking the surface just as his breath gave out.

Wind blasted from the lake and slammed against Liam. He cried out from the unbearable pain, a cry which saved his life.

"Liam!" Nathaniel yelled. The chief mate had regained the raft, now righted and sea-worthy, and he lunged over the edge to haul Liam from the water. Liam's teeth chattered as he collapsed inside the raft.

"We'll tie ourselves together," Nathaniel said, lashing the trailing line from his wrist to Liam's. "Now, wherever one goes, the other will too."

"E-even if it's t-to the b-bottom?" Liam stuttered through chattering teeth.

"Damn your mouth, MacLann." Nathaniel ducked his head and flattened himself tight against Liam as they crested the next wave.

"F-flares?"

"Gone, along with the oars and emergency provisions. We ride until we make landfall, or…" Nathaniel's words faltered.

"G-graling?" Liam asked next.

Nathaniel shook his head. "I tried to get him to jump when the bow rolled under, but he wouldn't leave the wheel. Thought he could buy the rest of us a little more time. Old fool."

Liam turned away. So far they had seen no one else. "H-how l-long?"

"'Til we die? Can't tell for sure. Don't talk, it'll only drain your strength. Our last position was five miles off Haven Point Lighthouse, so keep your ears open for that fog signal."

Liam willed his chattering to stop as he took a hard look at Nathaniel, a man he despised more than anyone. "Tell me this, Nathaniel: why do you hate me so much?"

"I hate all Irish, not just you."

"How is that so?"

"I'm the bastard son of an Irish sailor. He left my mother before I was born and never returned."

Liam passed a hand over his face. All these months, filled with words of bitterness and misunderstanding. "I can see why you feel as you do."

"I said don't talk!" Nathaniel reprimanded. They both fell silent amidst the gale's roar, neither man daring to guess when or how their suffering would end.

*   *   *   *

John and Lars finished boarding over the broken windowpane, and then closed both sets of sliding pocket doors to shut the parlor from the rest of the house. The wind continued to build through the course of the afternoon, even as the men, taking shifts, attended the light and fog-horn.

Eleanor dragged the rocking chair into the kitchen and placed it beside the stove, whose fire barely kept the cold at bay. She took up her knitting then, hoping for distraction. For Bridget and David, it was time for school-work and reading. Bridget fetched her father's inkwell from his desk in the dining room. Upon returning, she unscrewed the lid and then frowned. "It's frozen Mama."

Adeline took the jar from Bridget. "I'll heat some water so we can thaw it in a shallow bowl."

David, sitting at the table, was reading *Twenty Thousand Leagues Under the Sea*. Eleanor held a skein of flax-colored yarn in her lap, picking up dropped stitches on the new mittens she was knitting for her father.

Doubt gnawed at her as she envisioned the waves breaking against the shore. Was the skiff safe? Or had Superior stolen away their only mode of transportation from the isolated light station?

The gale ranted, the fire crackled, Adeline chatted with Bridget, the tea kettle whistled for attention, but these sounds faded as Eleanor listened to the clock in the dining room. The wall clock pendulum swung back and forth, back and forth, its aggravating click echoing in her mind.

*Tick. Tock. Tick. Tock…*Eleanor dropped the knitting needles and covered her ears.

Adeline gave her a sympathetic look. "I know, Eleanor. Those winds are driving me to the edge of lunacy."

"I just wish it would end," Eleanor said, her words a half-whispered prayer.

*   *   *   *

Father in Heaven, please spare my life.

Liam and Nathaniel had been riding the storm-tossed seas for more than two hours, though time was meaningless. Exposed to the elements, covered by the whipping spray, Liam's body temperature was dropping gradually, but with sure effect.

First he shivered and then he shook, and then he lay still as sensation left his limbs. The skin of his face was scratched and chafed from rubbing against the life-raft's hull, the motion worsened by the snap-rolls of the pitching vessel. Liam eased in and out of consciousness, and as pallid daylight yielded to obsidian night, he knew his only salvation lay in prayer.

And so he prayed. He spoke to the Lord of Hosts in English and then in Gaelic, just to be sure. He prayed for deliverance from his torment, but also begged for mercy for his lost shipmates.

He hallucinated that Nick was beside him, smiling as he offered Liam a sandwich and a cup of coffee. But Nick was gone, as were all the rest. *Sweet Christ,* Liam thought, *Nick is dead, dead, they're all of them dead!*

He and Nathaniel bumped together in a frostbitten stupor. The ache of Liam's cramped muscles grew distant and dim. Ice matted his hair and clothing. Over time, he grew very sleepy. *How grand 'twould be to sleep forever*, he thought. *Just sleep and forget this useless suffering.*

Liam roused after nightfall, thinking he heard voices crying to him on the wind. "Nick? Tom?" he groaned, unable to raise his head. There was nothing but the turbulent waves and endless snow, and his sole companion, Nathaniel Klassen.

"Nathaniel." Liam shook Nathaniel by the wrist. "Are you still alive?"

At first there was no answer. But then Nathaniel stirred, answering, "Yes, Liam?"

"What will you do after we get out of this?"

"Don't know. Don't care," Nathaniel said in a barely audible voice.

"I'm going to sleep a week, eat everything I can, and stay drunk the rest of the time," Liam said. He felt feeble as a new lamb, but talking kept him from sinking into the nightmarish sensation of being half-awake.

Nathaniel groaned. Foam bubbled from the sides of his mouth as death overtook him.

Long minutes passed. Liam closed his eyes and stopped struggling against his own inevitable passing. It came with a tug and whoosh, a release from his earthly body. Pleasant warmth radiated throughout his limbs as he was lifted away from his prostrate form. Once again, he became a bird of the sea, winging through the winds to soar high above the coverlet of storm clouds. Soon he escaped the shadows of the world, sailing aloft to the golden island of *Hy Brasil*.

As before, Conall stood at the shore. "Brother, I have come to stay!" Liam declared.

Conall shook his head. "This place is ready for you, chieftain of the MacLanns, when your time comes," he replied as Liam fluttered just above the glittering sands. "But you are not meant to die this day. You must go back, Liam."

"For the love of Mary, no! 'Tis only a yoke of pain and sorrow, and I've had my fill of both!" Liam cried, flapping his wings.

"The choice is not yours to make. A future of great possibility awaits you, brother: do not shirk your duty, nor despair of love." Conall turned his back and began to walk up the beach.

"Conall! Don't send me back!" Liam hurtled through space and time before landing with exquisite agony inside his body.

"Conall," Liam whispered. It was then that he heard the triple-blast of the fog horn and the slam of waves against the rocky shore.

"Nathaniel! Nathaniel, wake up!" Liam cried as he tugged on the limp arm of the first mate. There was no response.

Grinding and clattering, the life-raft crashed against the jagged reefs just off Haven Point. The raft smashed to pieces under the weight of the great wave, and both men were plunged underwater once more.

Another surge propelled Liam's helpless body toward the toothy rocks. The weight of Nathaniel's corpse dragged him in the opposite direction. Liam felt as though he was about to be torn to pieces, ripped, clawed, mangled, shredded, slashed…

Finally the water hurled Liam onto the beach. He felt the line snap between his wrist and Nathaniel's as the back-surge pulled them toward the lake.

Have courage, Liam, Conall's voice said. *She will come.*

While Superior spewed her rage, Liam fought to drag himself free from the surf. Moments later, he lost consciousness beside the Haven Point skiff.

*   *   *   *

Supper at Haven Point consisted of cold ham sandwiches and pickled cucumbers. John came inside to eat first, then Lars took his place when John returned to the tower. Gathered together in the warmth of the kitchen, their talk centered over when the storm would finally break.

Eleanor continued to worry over the skiff. If the boat washed out to sea, there'd be no way for Lars or her father to row up to Marais for supplies and no possibility of her making the trip to Little Nesna for laundry. They'd be cut off completely, at least until the supply ship arrived. But what if the storm delayed the *Amaranth* indefinitely?

"Eleanor, would you mind cutting more bread?" Adeline asked. "I see that Lars is ready for another sandwich."

"All right." At the work table, Eleanor took up the bread knife and began to saw through the thick-crusted loaf. Suddenly, inexplicably, she heard an unfamiliar voice whisper, "*The beach.*"

"What?" Eleanor said aloud, turning to glance over her shoulder. No one had moved from the table, no one was addressing her. She shrugged and returned to cutting.

He comes.

The knife fell from Eleanor's hand. Adeline, who'd risen from the table to refill the water pitcher, startled at the knife's clatter and asked, "What's wrong, Eleanor?"

Eleanor blinked and roused herself. "I'm going down to the beach," she announced.

"What? In this weather? Under no circumstances are you to leave this house!"

"Something. Someone." Eleanor shook her head. "I need to check on the skiff, that's all," she said as she dressed in her coat and mittens and then lit one of the lanterns. A few moments later she was out the door.

"Eleanor! Wait!" Adeline turned to Lars. "Go with her, and make sure she comes back safe."

"Yes, ma'am." Lars drew a heavy sigh. "And just when I was beginning to thaw out."

When Lars caught up with Eleanor, he grabbed her arm. "You're going to wait in the fog house while I go down to the beach!" he shouted above the storm's howl.

"No! You don't understand!" Eleanor yelled back. "Let me go! You have to let me go!"

"Eleanor, it's too dangerous! Listen to me!"

With a supreme effort, Eleanor wrenched free and sprinted away. Something was driving her on, something she couldn't explain. But it was commanding, undeniable. It simply had to be obeyed.

She slowed just short of the beach, astounded. Twenty-foot towers of water detonated on the cobbled stones and against the cliff base, following one after another in devastating procession.

She faltered, almost turned back. But the memory of that mysterious voice compelled her onward. She pressed ahead, seeking the skiff.

Eleanor bumped into the skiff's bow before she actually saw the wooden vessel, now lying at a cant at the edge of the surf. She heard Lars running up behind her in the darkness, and then, strangely, the sound of a loud moan somewhere near the ground.

Adrenaline shot through her. She dropped on all fours and began crawling, searching for something, anything. Her hand brushed against the ice-stiffened canvas of a lifejacket, and quickly she felt along the stranger's torso. Sweater, neck, face. Mouth. Shallow breathing. Still alive, though barely.

"Eleanor! I've found a body!" Lars shouted from a few yards away. There was a long pause. "I think he's dead! No heartbeat, no breathing, nothing!"

"I've found another one, and he's still alive!" Eleanor called back.

Lars knelt by her side, his hands traveling over the stranger's unmoving body. "Christ, I wonder where they came from," he said.

Eleanor, lantern in hand, quickly searched the beach and found a few shards of lumber from the smashed life-raft. "Here's your answer." She held up a piece bearing the name *Wm. A. Dorn.*

"Probably from a wrecked steamship. This is bad, very bad." Lars took Eleanor by the arm. "Stay here until I return with your father."

In Lars' absence, Eleanor crouched beside the unconscious sailor and tried her best to shelter him from the wind. She removed her coat and carefully tucked it around him, whispering, "You will not die, I will not allow it."

Time stretched away from her while she hovered over him. Her heart grieved as sickening fear twisted her stomach. Had there indeed been a wreck? And if so, then how many had died?

The voice. Where had it come from, and why? "It was because of you," she whispered, looking down at the stranger. Suddenly she wanted to wrap herself around him completely, do anything to save him.

A familiar voice cut through the wind. "Eleanor! Where are you, child?"

"I'm here, Papa!" Eleanor lifted her face when John found her.

"Papa…"

CHAPTER 5

▼

Adeline was waiting at the kitchen door when Eleanor returned to the house. "Thank God, at last!" Adeline exclaimed. "I was so afraid you'd gotten lost out there—"

"Mama, listen to me!" Eleanor said, cutting Adeline short. "We've got to start up a fire in the stove in the spare bedroom, right away!"

"Why, for heaven's sake? What are you talking about?"

"A ship wrecked on the lake and a life-raft crashed ashore." Eleanor pulled the ice-encrusted mittens from her stiffened hands, and then held her fingers to the woodstove. "Two sailors, one of them dead, but the other man is still alive."

"A shipwreck?" David asked, wide-eyed. "Can you see it from shore?"

"It's too dark to see anything," Eleanor told him, brushing her windblown hair from her face. "Papa and Lars are carrying the sailor to the house right now, so get the kindling and matches. Please, Mama."

"Yes, yes of course," Adeline said, stirring to action. Both women lifted an armful of wood from the wood box and carried it to the spare bedroom just off the dining room. This room was seldom used for anything other than storage, though a bed was kept for visitors.

Frigid air rushed out the moment Adeline opened the door. Wooden boxes sat beside a rack of hanging clothes. Adeline's cedar chest stood at the foot of the narrow bed. A single window gazed out over the yard. Eleanor moved quickly to load wood into the small metal stove.

Adeline lit the lantern on the dresser, while David and Bridget watched from the doorway, their eyes bright with excitement. "Bridget, turn down the blankets," Adeline directed as she struck the match inside the stove. "David, wait at the kitchen door and tell us when they arrive."

Eleanor went to the window. She took a deep breath and then exhaled, trying to calm her shattered nerves. Those men, those sailors, one lifeless, the other nearly so…With shaking hands she smoothed her skirt. *Slowly.* That was a little better.

"They're here!" David shouted from the kitchen. Eleanor hurried through the dining room and watched as John and Lars struggled to carry the sailor's comatose body inside.

"Like hauling a trough of cement," John said with a grunt. He held the sailor by the armpits while Lars grasped him by the knees. "Where to, Eleanor?"

"The spare room. We've started a fire in the wood stove." Eleanor skirted ahead as the men carried the stranger to the bedroom.

They maneuvered the limp body through the doorway. "Adeline, pull that bed right next to the stove," John said. "All right, that's better. Lars, lay him down gentle."

Gingerly, they placed the man on the bed. John and Lars stood together for a moment, catching their breath as they stared down at the sailor. He was a big man, broad through the shoulders and well-muscled. He reminded Eleanor of the blacksmith in Grand Marais, only larger.

David bent to examine one of his hands. "His fingers are blue, Papa."

"Frostbite. His face is bad with it, too. Thank goodness nothing has gone black yet, at least not what we've seen."

Eleanor leaned near the sailor's mouth and listened. "Shallow and gurgling. There's water in his lungs."

"He's had a rough time of it, certainly." John frowned as he felt along the man's chest, legs, and arms. "I'd say the left arm is broken."

"We must get his clothes off, sir," Lars said. "He'll never thaw out until he's dry and covered."

"I know, I know." John rubbed the back of his neck, his brow furrowed in thought. "Eleanor, bring the sewing scissors."

"Yes, Papa, right away." In the parlor, Eleanor rummaged through the sewing cabinet drawers until she found the scissors.

Returning to the spare room, Eleanor placed the shears in her father's hand, then stood back as John cut away the sailor's lifejacket, sweater, and undershirt. Adeline stood at John's shoulder, critically eyeing the young man's injuries.

"Those ribs look badly bruised, John," Adeline said. "We'll need to wrap his midriff and then make a splint for that arm."

"Yes, it'll have to be set. But first we strip him."

"If you must. Eleanor, Bridget, come with me." Adeline led her daughters back into the dining room before closing the door. "Bridget, set the tea kettle to boil on the kitchen stove. Eleanor, go upstairs and take down a bed sheet and the extra quilts from the linen closet. Be quick about it, but knock before you go back in the spare room."

"Of course, Mama." As Eleanor approached the foot of the stairs she paused, leaning against the square newel post. A wave of grayness passed through her as the floor threatened to tilt beneath her feet; this was really happening, it wasn't just a fireside story, all those other sailors drowned or dying, and only this one, *this one—*!

Stop it, she thought angrily, biting down hard on her lip. The sailor needed her help, not hysteria.

Eleanor returned to the kitchen a short while later, her arms loaded with blankets. The water in the kettle steamed as Adeline snapped off splinters from two kindling sticks. "Not exactly what I wanted, but they'll have to do." Adeline took Bridget by the hand and led the girls to the spare room. Adeline rapped on the door, asking, "Is he covered?"

"You girls can come in!" John replied. As Eleanor entered the room, she noticed the sailor's trousers and socks had been draped over the cedar chest to dry.

Eleanor paused at the look on her father's face; something was wrong. "What did you find?" she asked.

"He's badly frostbitten on his right foot. Two of the toes have gone black," John answered. "Don't know if we can save them."

Eleanor's stomach knotted at the thought of amputation. "We should try, at least," she said in a low voice.

"We'll see what we can do about it after we set that arm. Lars, you ready?"

Lars swallowed hard and nodded. "Support his shoulder while I give the quick jerk," John instructed. He passed a hand over his face before lifting the sailor's arm. "Lord help me to do this right the first time."

Eleanor held her breath. John grasped the stranger's wrist with both hands and then yanked back hard. The stranger groaned but did not awaken.

Adeline gently felt along the damaged arm. "The bones are in place now, John, but what about his ribs?"

"If and when he awakens, we'll wrap him then. Best not to move him too much."

Eleanor placed a hand over the sailor's covered foot. "His toes, Papa?"

"I'll leave that to you and your mother. Right now Lars and I need to haul that other fellow up from the beach."

"Are you going to bring the body into the house?" David asked.

John shook his head. "The light tower annex should be good enough for now. We'll be back shortly."

The kitchen door slammed just as the tea-kettle whistled on the stove top. "Go and pour some water into a basin and let it sit out and cool a bit while I make a splint," Adeline told her.

"What are you going to do, Mama?"

"Warm water is best for severe frostbite. I remember the time at the lumber camp when one of the jacks stayed out too long in the cold and his pinky toe turned that same color. He was crazy with fear that we'd have to cut it off, but my mother managed to save it."

"I hope we can save this man's toes, too," Eleanor said, staring at the stranger. Pity filled her heart. His face was battered and swollen, with red abrasions covering his jaw and cheekbone. She reached down to smooth his hair when she noticed something around his neck. "Mama, what do you suppose this is?"

Adeline glanced at the medallion. "A saint's medal or something," she replied as she began to tear the bed sheet into long strips. "Bridget, hold his arm while I wrap it."

Bridget carefully supported the arm. "His skin feels clammy, Mama, just like the belly of a dead trout."

"Never mind about that." Adeline bound the arm tightly. "There. It's set and wrapped and that's all I can do for the broken bone. Now, let's take a look at his toes."

Adeline lifted the blankets to reveal the stranger's feet. Eleanor winced at the sight of his blackened toes.

"Bridget, bring the lantern near. Eleanor, hold the basin while I sponge, and David, I want you to bring in more wood from the wood box and pile it on the floor beside the stove."

Ten minutes passed, maybe fifteen, it was hard for Eleanor to tell. No one spoke as they worked. The only sound came from the soft splash of the water as Adeline bathed the damaged toes. The quiet was broken by the sound of the kitchen door opening and closing, and a few moments later Lars appeared, snow draping his shoulders in a white shroud. "The other sailor's in. Mr. Thompson has gone up to the tower to wind the gears, and says he'll come inside in a few hours." Lars gestured toward the patient. "How's he doing?"

"As well as can be expected," Adeline replied. "In a few minutes I'll bandage his foot, and then we'll tuck him in tight."

Lars gave him a sympathetic look. "He's got a good chance of surviving, with the fine care he's receiving."

"Are you hungry, Lars?" Adeline asked. "I could heat up something from the ice box."

The Swede shook his head. "I've no appetite, what with the goings on we've had." He shuddered. "That man what froze to death—there's no worse way to die than at the hands of this cursed lake."

"He's starting to shiver, Mama."

The time was ten o'clock. Bridget and David had gone up to bed while John and Lars continued their watch in the fog house. Eleanor sat in the rocking chair, having carried it in from the kitchen and placed it beside the sailor's bed.

Adeline laid the back of her hand against the stranger's forehead, which was beaded with sweat. "He's warming too fast. Loosen those quilts a bit."

"Yes, Mama." Eleanor peeled back the top layer of blankets.

"I'll bring some cold water and a cloth," Adeline said. "Call me immediately if he starts to convulse."

"Convulse?" Eleanor repeated. She stared down at the sailor, her heart tripping. This was all a mistake. What did they know about saving a man's life? By all rights he ought to be in a hospital in Duluth. Anywhere would have been better than an isolated light station with no medical supplies of any kind.

"Here we are," Adeline said as she spread the cloth across his brow. "Poor, poor boy. He doesn't seem very old, does he? Twenty-four, twenty-five at the most."

"Where do you suppose he's from?"

"With any luck he'll come out of this by morning, and then he can tell us himself," Adeline answered, then said, "Do you want to take the first shift with him tonight, or shall I?"

"I'll stay. Go on ahead and get some sleep. I know how tired you are, Mama."

"Is it that obvious? I'm worn to the roots, as they say, so yes, I'll catch a few hours' rest."

"Should I waken you at three, maybe?"

"That sounds fine. Goodnight to you." Adeline paused in the doorway. "One more thing, Eleanor. How did you know to go down to the beach?"

Eleanor gazed at Adeline in the flickering lamplight. She didn't dare tell her mother about the voice that had compelled her to go to the beach. "Just a feeling, I guess," she finally answered.

"Much longer in that cold and he'd have frozen to death, just like the other. How very strange, all of it." After Adeline closed the door, Eleanor settled in the rocking chair. She watched as the stranger's shivering grew stronger.

"Peace, peace," Eleanor said, rinsing the cloth before spreading it out once more. She rested her hand on his chest and was surprised at the softness of his skin.

He's tall and strapping, she thought, her hand riding the shallow crests of his breathing. Sandy brown hair shot through with streaks of gold, fair skin, full lips. A handsome face, despite his scars and bruises. Bold features, a clean jaw, shoulders like granite. Very interesting.

Defined muscles flexed beneath her palm as his body twisted in delirium. Fear almost forced her back, but she held herself at his side. "What did you do, stranger, aboard the *William Dorn*?" Eleanor asked in a soft voice. "Were you a deckhand, perhaps, or maybe even ship's captain?"

The sailor jerked his face from side to side, eyes clamped shut, sweat glistening his neck and chest. "*Deartháir, deartháir*," he mumbled. "Conall, *deartháir*."

Eleanor quickly withdrew her hand. What was he trying to say? Did it mean he was going to live?

Who was this man?

By the time the dining room clock struck midnight, Eleanor struggled to keep her eyes open. The sailor's fever had passed, and he'd fallen into an unmoving sleep. Eleanor had watched him from the rocking chair, rising on occasion to stir the glowing embers in the stove and add more wood. Warmth filled the bedroom, making her feel thick-headed and drowsy. The wind's shriek and the foghorn's blasts faded before the sound of the stranger's labored breathing.

Her thoughts drifted. Visions came to her, of the ship lying at the bottom of the lake, of the men trapped inside the flooded hull. Eyes without sight, faces pale and haunted. Silence. A single tear ran down her cheek as she closed her eyes.

Eleanor slept.

*   *   *   *

Warmth.

In the vaults of Liam's consciousness, the sensation began as a singular point in the blackness, slowly enlarging until it was an enormous, shining orb. Liam basked in its sultriness and swam in its depthless pool, drinking from it like a horse that has run many miles without pause.

Gradually his euphoria was replaced by a new awareness, an insistent, throbbing pain radiating from his arm and toes. He felt, but could not move or speak. Motion. Voices. A light. People surrounding him, doing things to him. Was he alive or dead?

A woman's voice, her hand touching his skin. Liam wrestled against his paralysis, crushed by a feeling of helplessness. *I want to see, I want to know, I have to tell them what has happened...*Then, for a long while, he remembered no more.

A clock chimed. One, two, three. Three o'clock. *Morning or night*, he wondered, still trapped in a coma-like state. There was no voice, no sound at all. Alone. Was this his fate, then, to be caught in limbo, a death worse than actual dying?

Rest, Liam boy, Conall's voice assured him. *Soon you will return.*

∗   ∗   ∗   ∗

Eleanor was awakened just after three AM, alerted by the voices of John and Lars in the kitchen. She blinked and rubbed her eyes. The bluish-gray cast of the sailor's skin had warmed to a peachy pink, and his breathing seemed more settled. Eleanor smiled; he was going to live.

Her pleasure faded as she picked up the thread of conversation in the nearby room. The men were arguing, and Eleanor tiptoed to the door to listen in.

"I say no. Even after the storm breaks, it's just too risky," John said.

"Sir, we have a duty to take the skiff out if there's even the chance of other survivors," Lars countered. "Those freighters are equipped with two lifeboats apiece—"

"It's a long shot at best. We'll wait until our sailor wakes up before we plunge headlong into some sort of rescue operation."

"I must disagree," Lars said firmly. Then, after a long pause, Lars added, "It's a hard-hearted thing, Mr. Thompson, to turn your back on those in need."

"It hurts me to hear you say that, Lars, but my decision stands." The wood floor groaned beneath the men's boots. "Get some sleep, and we'll see how things look in the morning."

Lars said nothing, and a few moments later they were gone. Eleanor turned from the door, troubled by her father's decision. Great was the risk if they rowed out in the storm's aftermath, yet how could they refuse when other survivors might be waiting and watching, desperate for rescue?

Eleanor stirred the fire before adding another log. The time had come to rouse Adeline, but instead she lingered. It was pleasant to sit alone with the stranger, to feel cozy and safe while the storm raged outside. She rearranged the blanket over his chest and shoulders. He was her responsibility now.

His presence filled the room. Calm stole over her as she watched his face, memorized the details of his profile, breathed in the faint musk of his body. What sort of man was he? He must be very strong, she decided, to survive both the wreck and the passage across the stormy lake.

She settled back into the rocker. Her lids drooped as she meditated on him. Here he would find rest, a quiet to ease the pain of his injuries. Nothing would trouble him as long as he was in her care.

It was her promise to him.

The storm was rolling eastward when Liam awakened near dawn. Snowfall tapered off as the sky began to lighten with the approach of coming day. His eyes fluttered open, and he found himself staring at a white-painted ceiling.

Liam blinked. Had he died and gone to his reward, then? Where were St. Peter and Gabriel and all the blessed saints? But then his eyes traveled from the ceiling down the wall where he saw a counted cross-stitch hanging on the wall beside the bed. For a moment this struck him as funny. *In Heaven there's no such thing*, he thought. *I never heard of the archangels doing needlework.*

Realization swept over him; *Alive, and God be praised.* Liam lay for a few moments and reveled in the thick blankets, the soft mattress, the wondrous warmth. Pearl-gray light slowly expanded in the small room. His tongue felt dry and swollen, his lips cracked. Liam heard the catch of someone's breath, not his own, and his heart began to thud with wonderment.

With great effort he moved his head to the side, and it was then he caught sight of a sleeping young woman. *Ah, now, who was this black-haired colleen?* Her chin was resting against her chest, her hair was slightly disheveled, her features indistinct in the dim light. He tried to move to his side for a better look, but, as his muscles contracted, a spike of pain raced up his arm. *Bedad, but it must be broken*, he thought with a grimace. *And who lit a fire under me toes?*

Liam shifted once more, but the pain was so sharp he groaned aloud. The woman startled, her eyes flying open.

He whispered to her, rasping, "Water."

"Forgive me, of course!" she said. "I'll be right back!"

She disappeared from the room, and a few moments later Liam heard the frantic up-and-down creak of what sounded like a hand-pump. She reappeared in the doorway with a glass of water in hand. Liam attempted to raise himself and gasped aloud from his damaged arm and ribs.

"Have a care, now, you've been hurt," the young woman explained as she set the glass on the dresser. "Your left arm is broken."

"Och, and well I know it!" Liam said. "It bloody fucking hurts!"

Her eyes flashed, and there was a look of reproach on her face. "Let me help you to sit," she said. Liam reached out with his good hand and took hers. "Are you ready?"

Liam nodded, clenching his teeth as she hauled him into an upright position. A rush of dizziness threatened to topple him, but he let it pass before releasing her hand. Suddenly he realized all his clothes were gone, and self-consciously he hiked the blanket to his chest.

The young woman pressed the glass into his hand. Liam, his arm shaking with exertion, drank it with long, gulping swallows. "Thanks," he said as he handed the glass back to her.

"Would you care for more?"

"Not—not yet. Where am I?"

"You are in the home of Keeper John Thompson. This is Haven Point Light Station. Assistant Keeper Berglund and I found you on the beach last night."

Recollections of the shipwreck came rushing back to Liam. "Where's Nathaniel?"

"Nathaniel? I'm not certain who you're talking about," she replied.

"Chief Mate Nathaniel Klassen, that other fellow!" Liam snapped. "I know he was with me when the life-raft crashed ashore!"

"Oh. I see," she said. "Yes, we found him too." Her face paled. "I...I'm so sorry..."

"He's gone then? Nathaniel?"

"Yes, your friend had already passed by the time we found him."

Liam slumped forward. *All of them, every man and boy. Gone.*

She grabbed his shoulder to steady him. Their eyes met. "You've not told me your name," Liam said in a husky voice.

Crimson bloomed across her cheeks. "I am Miss Eleanor Thompson, the lighthouse keeper's daughter. And your name is—?"

"Liam MacLann. From Inishmore off the coast of Ireland."

"Well, Mr. MacLann, you are very lucky to be alive now. What happened to your ship, the *William Dorn*?"

"The *Dorn* split apart," he answered. "She's at the bottom of the lake now. My best guess is she took the all the rest of the crew with her, save myself alone."

"All?" Eleanor repeated. "How many?"

"Twenty-eight souls."

She took a step back. "I'm sorry," she whispered, tears glistening in her eyes.

Liam looked away. He swallowed and asked, "Miss Thompson, where's your father now?"

"Papa's out in the fog house. Can't you hear the signal?"

Liam paused. "There now, I do. The same that let me know I was close to land aboard the raft."

Eleanor seemed to brighten. "Are you hungry? I could make some pancakes for your breakfast, or hot porridge, or whatever you like."

"I have nothing of the hunger on me, but I will ask you for two things: some clothes to wear and a drop of whiskey."

"I'll have to ask Papa or Lars about some spare clothing. As for the whiskey, I'm sorry, but liquor is not allowed on light station premises."

"A pity," Liam said. "More water then, if you would, Miss Thompson."

"Right away," Eleanor said, going at once to refill the glass. After Liam finished it, she helped lower him on the bed, gripping his hand as she supported his shoulders with the other. She was so near he caught the scent of her, rose-water and starched linen.

"You should sleep if you're able, Mr. MacLann," Eleanor said. "I'll bank the stove and leave you alone to rest." She stifled a yawn.

"Are you tired, Miss?"

"Yes. I was at your side all this night."

"I owe you and your family a debt of gratitude, then."

"Think nothing of it. I only wish we could have saved your companion as well." She filled the woodstove and then paused in the doorway. "I'll stay in the kitchen until Mama comes down. Call me if you need anything."

Liam closed his eyes after Eleanor shut the door. The pain in his arms and toes was a throbbing firebrand, but he pushed it aside as he rejoiced in his rescue.

My prayers have been answered, he thought before drifting off to sleep.

CHAPTER 6

▼

"Eleanor, why didn't you wake me sooner?"

Adeline spoke to her daughter from the kitchen doorway. An hour had passed since Eleanor had left Liam's side. Eleanor was mixing a small batch of dough for cinnamon rolls with the last of the flour. A pot of fresh coffee percolated on the stove.

"I didn't want to bother you, Mama," Eleanor replied, wiping her flour-dusted hands on her apron. She felt remarkably energized despite her lack of sleep.

"I would not have minded. You should not have sat alone with him the whole night," Adeline said. She peered out the window. "Have you seen your father?"

"Papa and Lars came in around three o'clock," Eleanor said before pouring coffee into two cups. "Papa sent Lars off to bed, and I haven't seen either of them since."

Adeline opened the door a crack and peered outside. "The storm is moving on, there's no question about it." She paused. "Listen!"

"What?"

"The fog horn—it's silent!" Adeline shut the door against the cold. "That means the worst has passed. Papa can finally come in and get some sleep."

"He and Lars deserve a week of it after what they've been through," Eleanor said, then went to listen at Liam's door. There was no movement on the other side, and Eleanor smiled. "Still quiet," she said when she returned to the kitchen. "Mr. MacLann seemed to be doing a little better when I left him earlier."

"Mr. MacLann?"

"The sailor. He woke about six, and I gave him some water to drink. He was in an awful lot of pain."

Adeline blinked. "He was awake?"

"That's what I said." Eleanor felt a flicker of annoyance. "He's not some two-headed monster from the lake, Mama. He's just like you or me."

"I doubt that," Adeline muttered. "Did he mention anything about the wreck?"

"Liam told me that the ship split in two and sank to the bottom."

"Mercy!" Adeline exclaimed, her hand fluttering to her throat. "Can you imagine, Eleanor? It must have been terrifying!"

Eleanor looked away, her heart still aching with the heavy toll of the disaster. "I think it's dreadful," she said.

John appeared at the door. "Is the storm over?" Adeline asked, helping to remove his coat and hat.

"Looks to be that way. You won't believe the drifts out there. Some are half-way up the side of the barn."

"What about the livestock, Papa?"

"They're fine. Only one hog and a few chickens left now, and we'll butcher 'em off this week or the next." John dragged his hand through his hair and said, "I'm heading up to bed now."

Adeline spoke to him, saying, "Our sailor was awake this morning, John. Eleanor was with him when he came around."

"What sort of fellow is he, Eleanor?"

"It's hard to say, Papa. He told me he's from Ireland."

"An Irishman! They're a tough lot, the ones I've known, anyway. What about his ship?"

"The *William Dorn* is at the bottom of Superior. Liam believes he's the only survivor."

"Sole survivor." John said. "I don't know if I'd call him lucky or cursed, coming through something like that." John made his way toward the stairs. "Adeline, wake me at noon for dinner, and make sure Berglund's up then as well."

Eleanor fell asleep the moment she crawled into bed. She didn't stir when Bridget rose and dressed, and even the aroma of baking cinnamon rolls didn't penetrate her sleep.

Her mother's hand awakened her. "Dinner is almost ready, Eleanor. Did you manage some sleep?"

Eleanor rubbed the drowsiness from her eyes. "I could have slept longer, I guess. Is Papa awake?"

"He's next. Bridget and David were outside all morning clearing the walkway while I cooked up a kettle of chicken soup." Adeline brushed a speck of lint from her sleeve. "Mr. MacLann is awake, Eleanor, and has asked for you."

"How's he doing?"

"Quite well, considering. His toes have shown improvement, but I think his ribs are giving him the most trouble. I'll have John wrap him tight before we eat." Adeline removed one of Eleanor's dresses from the closet. "Now, hurry and change."

Eleanor slid from her bed, wincing as her feet touched the hard coldness of the floor. Off came the flannel night gown, on went her binding corset, petticoat and dress. "What about a shirt for Liam?" she asked her mother, who stood waiting near the door. "Papa cut his sweater to pieces."

"I want you to go over to Lars' house and see if he has any to spare. I don't think Papa's shirts would fit." Adeline folded her arms as her gaze rested on her daughter. "Eleanor, I want you to keep your distance from Mr. MacLann. Your father and I will attend his needs until he can manage for himself."

Eleanor halted just short of the door. "Why? Is something wrong with him, Mama?"

"We know nothing about Mr. MacLann or his past, and I think the less you see of him alone the better."

Eleanor, unimpressed with her mother's logic, lifted her chin and said, "I'll do as my conscience bids me, Mama. Mr. MacLann deserves the best care we can give, and I intend to do everything I can to help him." Without waiting for a reply, Eleanor sailed past her through the doorway.

A short while later, bundled in her coat, Eleanor stepped outside the kitchen door. She paused on the back stoop and shielded her eyes from the sunshine's glare, amazed by the transformation to the landscape.

Sculpted drifts had buried the wood pile and chopping block. The ax handle poked through the white crust at a perfect forty-five degree angle. Wind-scoured ground exposed withered nubs of frozen grass, while, in the drifted areas, snow sparkled with the brilliance of a thousand tiny diamonds. The oak tree lay collapsed and broken, like the corpse of some ancient beast. Hearty chickadees tittered in the pine trees and aspens, their music a counterpoint to the ice-stiffened groan of swaying branches.

As Eleanor hurried along to the assistant keeper's house, her thoughts were on the conversation she'd just had with her mother. There'd been no mistaking her mother's tone of reproach when she'd spoken about Liam. How typical for her mother to think only of her strong distrust of strangers rather than the pressing needs of the moment.

Lars met her at the door. "Saw you coming," he said with a tired smile. Eleanor went inside to wait, her cheeks stinging from the wind.

"Did you sleep at all last night, Eleanor?" Lars asked.

"Well, I didn't actually go to bed until after Papa came in, maybe around seven," she replied. "I must have dozed off for part of the night while I sat watch over Liam."

Lars gave her a penetrating look. "Liam, you say? How much did he tell you about what happened to the ship?"

"Some. He's awake right now, so you should ask him about it yourself. I'm supposed to ask you for a spare shirt or two for him to wear."

"I'll have to get them from upstairs. What's he like?"

"I really couldn't say just yet." Eleanor sniffed and dabbed at her nose. "Liam believes the entire crew was lost in the wreck, all his shipmates. I'm amazed he survived at all."

"You two must have had quite a talk," Lars said as he stuffed his mittens inside his coat pockets. "Wait here while I head up for those shirts."

Lars' boots pounded up the narrow stairway and creaked the floorboards of the second story. On the table, near where Eleanor stood, lay a half-completed letter. She bent to read the words, written in Lars' firm script. "*I would feel glad to come and join you down in Iowa, brother, since there is little future for me here—*"

She pulled away, a heated flush spreading across her face. Lars was truly leaving, after all. That meant a new assistant keeper in the spring, a new man for her father to train. Eleanor brushed her fingers across the letter, saddened at the thought of losing Lars' friendship.

Lars reappeared with two flannel shirts tucked in the crook of his arm. "This should see Liam through until the light station closes. Tell your mother that he's welcome to stay here when he's up and around."

The thought hadn't occurred to Eleanor. "Let's just see how quickly he recovers before we make any decisions," she said as Lars pulled his coat on. "Have you told Papa yet that you're leaving Haven Point?"

The question brought a startled look, and then Lars noticed the letter laying in full view. "Not yet," he said quietly. "I will today or tomorrow."

"Still planning to go to Iowa?"

"I'll give it a try." Lars smiled. "After all the excitement these last few days, I don't think I'll mind the life of a farmer."

Eleanor said nothing. She carried an awareness that, on some deep level, Lars cared for her. But she just couldn't return his feelings. His leaving was probably the best decision for the both of them.

Lars drew on hat and mittens and then stood at the door. "Come along, *flicka*. We don't want to keep anyone waiting."

Eleanor found John seated beside Liam in the spare bedroom. Eleanor hesitated in the doorway, feeling as though she were intruding on a private meeting. Her father's smile reassured her, however, and she stepped forward to hand her father the shirts.

"Mr. MacLann and I were just getting acquainted," John explained. "Adeline and the children were in to visit a short while ago. Now everyone has said their 'hellos' except for Berglund." John fingered the checkered flannel shirt. "You've been over there, I see."

Eleanor nodded, and then turned her attention to Liam. "How are feeling, Mr. MacLann?"

"Sore. And hungry." Liam answered, his gaze unwavering. "The last time I had anything in my stomach was days ago."

"We'll fix that shortly," John promised. "My wife has cooked up a pot of the best chicken soup you'll taste this side of Grand Marais. I'm going to wrap those bruised ribs and then help you get dressed, Mr. MacLann. Afterward, I'll send Eleanor in with your bowl of soup."

"I'd like nothing better." A smile turned up the corner of Liam's mouth, drawing Eleanor's attention. *What a beautiful man*, she thought, hurrying from the bedroom without another word.

She joined the others at the dining room table and ate her soup in silence, listening as Adeline spoke. "I went down to the beach this morning," she said to Lars. "The dock and boathouse are completely destroyed, and the ice has extended out twenty feet at least. How is the launch from the *Amaranth* supposed to make landfall through all that?"

"The men will pull the launch across, don't worry," Lars told her. "And if worse comes to worse, I'll row up to Marais and stop in at Johnson's Mercantile."

"That's ten miles, Lars," Eleanor reminded him.

"No problem for an old mariner like myself." Lars' attempt at levity fell flat as Eleanor and her mother exchanged worried glances.

John emerged from the bedroom. "Is he ready, Papa?" Eleanor asked.

"Wrapped and dressed and waiting to be fed. Go on now, but take your time feeding him. He's still pretty weak."

Eleanor felt the weight of her mother's eyes as she rose and entered the kitchen. Steam curled off the golden, aromatic liquid as she ladled soup into a bowl. Chunks of carrot and onion floating among the bits of chicken. Nesting the bowl inside a kitchen towel, she carried it to Liam.

Liam was sitting upright, his back cushioned by the pillow. He wore Lars' flannel shirt, the red plaid color warming his skin. Someone, either Liam or John, had made an effort to comb Liam's hair.

Eleanor didn't realize she was staring until Liam smiled and said, "Will you feed me that soup now, Miss, or must I sit here and be tortured by the smell of it?"

"Sorry," she mumbled before taking a seat in the rocking chair. She moved closer to the bed. "Can you use your good arm?"

"Aye, I can feed myself. But you'll have to hold the bowl." Liam lifted the spoon and sipped. "Ah, 'tis fine, thank you."

"Have as much as you like, Mr. MacLann. There's plenty more," Eleanor said. A flash of silver from around his neck caught her eye. "That necklace you're wearing. Where did it come from?"

"It's a St. Brendan's medal, from my sister Maeve in Ireland. She sent it in the last letter before the storm."

"What's she like, Maeve?"

"Proud. Stubborn. She's a tongue that'll cut you to ribbons when her temper's up. But she was always my favorite sister, the one who stood up for me against my brawling brothers. More than once she tended my cuts and dried my tears." Liam paused. "I never thought I'd miss her so, truth to tell."

"How many in your family?"

"Five boys and three girls all together. Conall was the eldest, little Deirdre the baby. Five years it has been since I've seen any of their faces." Liam sighed and then turned his attention to the soup. He swallowed spoonful after spoonful until some of the broth accidentally dribbled on his chin.

"Allow me," Eleanor murmured, lifting the towel to dab his skin. She did it without thinking, but as she touched him the air between them grew suddenly charged. His eyes darkened as he dropped the spoon and grasped her slender forearm.

Eleanor stiffened from the heat of his touch, from the scent of fresh sweat on his skin. The whirlwind moved through her, a shuddering that pierced the depths of her soul. She felt as though all her bones were turning to water. "I want—I would like more soup, Miss," Liam stammered before releasing her.

Eleanor drew a ragged breath. "Of course," she said, lowering her eyes. "I'll return shortly."

After Liam finished the second bowl of soup, Eleanor fluffed the pillow and then helped him to lie down again. "More sleep now, Mr. MacLann. It's going to be a long while before your injuries heal."

Pain coursed through his arm as he shifted into a more comfortable position. "Tell me something I don't know," he said through gritted teeth. "Miss Thompson?"

"Yes, Mr. MacLann?"

"You won't go too far, now?"

Eleanor tucked the quilts around his shoulders. "Someone will be nearby. I'll be in and out with chores and helping to clear the snow. Lars and Papa are both outside right now, checking the storm damage."

"I see." Liam swallowed. "Miss Thompson, will you do me the favor of thanking your mother and father for their hospitality?"

"Of course, Mr. MacLann. Rest now," she added with a smile. "We'll see one another later." Eleanor closed the door with a click.

Liam listened to a succession of muffled voices on the other side of the wall before hearing the bang of the kitchen door. A sense of loneliness crept over him in Eleanor's absence, a hollow, gaping void.

She seemed a kindly girl. In fact, she reminded him quite a bit of his sister, Fiona. Quiet and gentle, but with an inner strength. Eleanor's conversation and attentiveness had helped anchor him in this new setting. Liam no longer felt as though he were in a chaotic free-fall of uncertainty.

Liam closed his eyes as the soup's warmth filtered through his battered body. From outside the window came the rhythmic chop of an axe against wood. It lulled him to sleepiness, and soon the he drifted into a dreamless slumber.

When Liam awoke, it was late afternoon. The room had grown cold in the waning daylight. His stomach snorted and growled, and he lay still for a moment, considering what to do next.

He felt along his bandaged arm and along his sheet-wrapped ribs. Pain answered him, pulsing and familiar. Years earlier, he had broken his collar bone after taking a fall from a rock crevasse that spanned one of Inishmore's beaches. Conall had dared him to jump the gap, saying, "Only a *big boy* can go that far!"

And so Liam had jumped and lost his footing, landing flat on his back ten feet below on the sand. The bone had snapped like a brittle twig.

Liam smiled to himself; how his mother had beaten Conall with the cane when she found out! Later that night, Conall turned his back on Liam as they had lain together under the sheepskins, listening to the keen of the Atlantic wind against the cottage rafters. Liam, only four, had snuggled against his brother and begged forgiveness, promising never to do anything to bring harm to him again.

Conall. Gone away forever, and yet Liam knew his brother's spirit had ridden with him on the life-raft. "Stay with me Conall," Liam whispered to the stillness. "Don't leave me now, when I am so weak and given over to the care of strangers."

A knock at the door. "Come in," Liam called, wondering if it would be John or Eleanor.

A man with thick blonde hair appeared instead, carrying a load of wood in his arms. He nodded deferentially as he came inside. "I'm the Assistant Keeper, Lars Berglund. Thought the stove might have burned low."

Liam pushed himself upright against the headboard. "You know my name," he said, bracing himself against the wave of pain.

Lars stirred the remaining coals before loading the grate. "MacLann. From Ireland, I understand."

"Aye," Liam said. Wood popped and crackled from the depths of the stove, and soon the sweet smell of burning birch wood filled the room. "What about yourself?"

Lars sat himself in the rocking chair before answering. "My family sailed from Sweden to settle farmland in Iowa. I was only seven at the time, so I barely remember anything of the old country." He gave Liam a long look. "How are you feeling?"

"Empty, to be honest. As though I'll never eat enough to fill up inside."

"You've lost a great deal of weight, I'll wager. How long were you in the lifeboat?"

"'Tis hard to say. A few hours, at least."

Admiration filled Lars' eyes. "More than twenty minutes would have killed most men," he said, leaning forward slightly. "What happened to the *William Dorn*?"

Liam's mouth tightened. "Didn't Eleanor tell you that the *Dorn* sank in the gale? What more can you want to know?"

"Plenty. I used to work as a surfman on Lake Michigan. I wanted to take the light station's skiff out to search for survivors after we found you on the beach. Keeper Thompson decided against it, and I have to know if he made the wrong call." Lars' expression was grave. "This is very important; Mr. Thompson's job might be at stake."

"I don't believe there were any other survivors, God's truth. We saw nobody in the water, nor any other boats. The ship fell to pieces..." Liam's words died away. "As far as I know, 'twas just myself and the Chief Mate, Nathaniel Klassen that made it ashore. And you know what happened to him."

"Then Mr. Thompson guessed right, though at the time it was only a guess. Well, it'll make the report about the incident much less damaging."

"Report? To whom?"

"The Lighthouse Board and the superintendent, Jamieson Greer. It's part of my duties, to supplement the head keeper's daily log whenever unusual circumstances arise." Lars' chuckle was dry and humorless. "I'd say this situation qualifies."

"As long as there's no trouble for John Thompson or his family," Liam said. He felt himself growing defensive on John's behalf. "I'll fight any penalty the Lighthouse Board imposes. 'Twas no man's fault what happened."

"It won't come to that, at least not based on what I'm planning to write. Don't worry yourself, MacLann; the last thing I'd want to do is any harm to the Thompsons, or Eleanor." Her name fell flat between them, and Liam glanced quickly at the assistant keeper's face. Lars cleared his throat and then asked, "Would you like to try walking? We could make a sling for your arm and see about getting something for you to eat."

"Sure, now, that sounds fine. I'm bloody well sick of playing the invalid. But I'll be needing your help, Berglund."

"Call me Lars." The assistant keeper brushed his hands on his trousers before reaching for Liam. They clasped hands, and then Liam nodded. In one smooth motion Lars pulled Liam to his feet.

Stars danced before Liam's eyes as he almost lost his balance. But then Lars looped his arm around Liam's shoulders, halting his head-long pitch forward.

"Take short steps," Lars said as Liam began to shuffle forward. The pain in Liam's frostbitten toes was a burning agony, but he blocked it from his mind. He was determined to prove to himself that he was no cripple.

Slowly they made their way through the dining room and into the kitchen, where everyone in the Thompson family looked up. Lars eased Liam into one of the kitchen table chairs. "We thought it was time to try walking," Lars explained.

"Of course, of course," John said, puffing his pipe. The tobacco smell filled Liam's nose, its fragrance reminding him of his own father. Adeline offered a cup of coffee.

"Me thanks," Liam said, trying to ignore the spasms cramping his leg muscles.

Bridget and David were playing checkers at the table. John was filling out the daily log book. Eleanor stirred the soup at the stove, her back toward Liam.

"Allow me to fit this towel for a sling, Mr. MacLann," Adeline said. Gingerly, she drew a towel, made from a flour sack, under the splint and tied the ends together at the nape of Liam's neck. "Is that comfortable? Do I need to make any adjustments?"

"No, 'tis fine. A grand improvement." To Liam's chagrin, his stomach growled loudly.

Bridget smiled and said, "We'd better feed him, Mama."

"Would you care for soup, Mr. MacLann, or a ham sandwich, or maybe even a plate of leftover chicken pot pie?" John asked. "Not much of a Thanksgiving feast, but it's the best we've got."

"How's about a little of each?" Liam answered.

Eleanor removed a bowl from the cupboard and filled it to the brim with soup before setting it down in front of Liam. Their eyes met for a brief moment, and he was riveted by the frankness of her expression, a reluctance mixed with curiosity. Then she turned away, and he lifted his spoon, somewhat bemused.

David moved his chair closer to Liam and asked, "What did you do aboard the ship, Mr. MacLann?"

"I worked as a stokerman. I shoveled coal into the engine room furnaces, which heated the water for the ship's Scotch boilers. My helper was a boy named Ransom Hoyt, not much older than yourself."

Interest kindled in David's eyes. "Maybe I could take a job like that someday. I'll bet it's quite an adventure."

"Why David, what a dreadful thing to say! Sailing, indeed," Adeline said, stabbing her needle forcefully into the woolen sock she was darning.

"How many seasons did you sail on the *Dorn*?" Lars asked.

"Only one, though in the four years since I signed my articles, I've always worked Zenith Steamship boats. 'Tis well-known that they employ some of the best captains on the sweet-water seas."

"What cargo was she carrying?" Lars asked next.

"Iron ore, downbound to Ashtabula." Liam shook his head. "A small fortune, to be sure, now scattered along the lake floor."

John tapped his pipe pensively. "We've no way of getting out the news of the wreck until our supply ship the *Amaranth* comes. Zenith Steamship will have to be notified, along with the Lake Carriers' Association and the families of those lost."

"When do you expect the *Amaranth*, Mr. Thompson?" Liam asked.

"Hopefully it'll be soon. She was scheduled to stop in yesterday, but—well, we're hoping for tomorrow or the day after."

"We might not see anyone until the *America* comes to take us to Grand Marais," Bridget said. "Haven Point is scheduled to close mid-December."

Liam looked up as Eleanor placed a ham sandwich next to the soup bowl. "Will you go to Duluth for the winter, Mr. MacLann? Or maybe return to Ireland?" she asked.

"Not Ireland. Never Ireland. Most likely I'll go to Duluth for the winter."

"This will be your home until then," Eleanor said, brushing a hand against his shoulder. From off to the side, Liam heard Adeline's sharp intake of breath.

Lars reacted as well. "Time to go up for my shift," he muttered, and then drew on his coat. He slammed the door behind him.

Liam ate his sandwich in silence, wondering. Did Lars have some claim over the girl? The notion bothered Liam, though he couldn't say why. Eleanor Thompson was his caregiver and meant little to him beyond that.

And yet what of her touch, so light and familiar? Liam's ears reddened from the thought of it, and from the memory of what had passed between them when he'd taken her by the arm earlier that day.

No point in thinking on it, he told himself. The situation here was temporary at best; all that mattered was returning to Duluth to report the shipwreck and finding a place in town to board for the winter.

As soon as he felt well again, he'd focus his thoughts on future plans, plans which would take him far from Haven Point and Eleanor Thompson.

CHAPTER 7

―――――――――― ▼ ――――――――――

As the two sisters prepared for bed that night, Bridget asked, "What do you think about Mr. MacLann?"

"What do you mean?"

"You know, what do *think* about him?" Bridget sat on the edge of her bed and began to draw a brush through her hair. "He's quite the savage, don't you agree?"

"I don't like that word at all, 'savage,'" Eleanor said, snuggling beneath the blankets. "I don't think it describes him in the least."

"You can't be serious," Bridget said. "I mean, with the way he looks and talks, he's just like those men that Mama always tells about at the lumber camp. He's not a nice man, not like Papa."

"And how would you know, Bridget? You've only just met him!"

"First impressions count. That's what Mama says." Bridget winced as she encountered a particularly difficult snarl. "And besides, you haven't answered my question."

Eleanor stared at the rumpled hills and valleys of her quilt. "I think—I think he's remarkable," she said. "I can't imagine the horror of what he lived through."

Bridget paused. "So you *do* like him!"

"Now, I never said—"

"Don't argue, Eleanor. I know you too well." Bridget placed the hairbrush in the dresser drawer and took out the latest issue of the *Ladies' Home Journal*. "Liam certainly is mysterious, no matter what Mama says."

Eleanor stared hard at her sister. "Just exactly what did Mama say?"

"What do you think?" Bridget placed a crooked finger on her chin in an attitude of contemplation. "Let's see, Mama considers him an uncultured oaf, a man of great misfortune who should have known better than take a job on that doomed freighter. Oh, and the sooner he returns to Duluth, the better."

"It's beyond reason, her attitude toward him!" Eleanor said, exasperated. "Poor Liam, after all he's suffered!"

"Poor Liam," Bridget agreed. Eleanor, restless, threw back her covers and went to sit beside the younger girl, who was leafing through the periodical. Bridget paused over a photographic spread of New York society debutantes. "Look at them, Eleanor: Vanderbilts, Rockefellers and Carnegies, each and every one."

Eleanor gazed at the young women in the photograph. They were dressed in expensive gowns, resplendent in their jewels and furs. "Daughters of privilege, all of them," Eleanor said.

Bridget nudged her shoulder. "You'll be like one of them, someday, hmm? When you go to St. Paul and marry one of Uncle Casey's lawyer friends?"

"I never agreed to going. It was Mama's idea anyway," Eleanor explained, fidgeting with the blanket's edging.

"But why not go? The men around here are nothing but hicks and back-woodsmen."

Eleanor's grip tightened. "Better that than some rich city snob." She shook her head. "Not much good someone like that would do me anyway, with my plans for the cove."

Bridget gave her a searching look. "Still dreaming of the lodge, hmm?"

"Of course. By next summer, if all goes well."

"You're not going back to the Grand Hotel?"

"I hadn't planned on it. I want to stay close to home, to make sure no one else buys the cove." Eleanor returned to her own bed. "Can we turn down the lantern now? I'm dead tired."

"All right." Bridget extinguished the light, and then crawled beneath the blankets. "Eleanor?" Bridget asked in the darkness.

"Yes?"

"I'm sorry about what I said about Liam. I like him the same as you."

"Go to sleep, now," Eleanor admonished gently. She turned to her side and stared out the window at the night sky. From where she lay, she saw the pin-prick glitter of stars in the blackness.

Eleanor's thoughts turned to Liam. He was so completely different from any man she'd ever known. Coarse and discourteous at times, certainly, yet she sensed something more beneath his bluff exterior. A poignancy, a sadness that went deeper than the calamity of the wreck. He seemed like a man who had lost his way in the world.

She'd never known this feeling herself, having lived at the light station all her life. What would it be like to not know who you were and where you were meant to be? *Like living in exile*, Eleanor decided. A sentence sometimes reserved for criminals and those without honor.

Eleanor wished she could learn more about Liam and his past, to help her understand him better and aid him in his recovery. Yet she knew their time together was short, that it was unlikely they would ever have the chance to truly know one another. Liam would leave after the light station closed for the winter, and then their lives would continue in separate directions.

When Eleanor approached Liam's door the next morning, she was surprised to hear David's voice coming from inside. "What's next?" David asked.

"Form up the lines, like so," Liam answered. "There, now, you've set the Fenians aright against the English cowards."

Eleanor rapped on the half-opened door. "Come in!" David called. The storage trunk had been pulled near Liam's bed, and an array of tin soldiers formed lines on the trunk's lid. David placed another of the tiny, painted recruits on the imaginary battlefield.

"Hello, Mr. MacLann," Eleanor said, settling herself into the rocking chair.

"Good morning to you, Miss Thompson. How are you this day?"

"I'm well, thank you."

"Eleanor, Liam's been telling me about the Fenian uprising of the Irish patriots against the English," David explained. He grasped one of the soldiers, placing the figure so that its gun faced point blank at the chest of the opposing general. "Here's the brave Fenian, Thomas Kelly, fighting against an imperialist English pig!"

"How interesting," Eleanor said, stealing a look at Liam. He shrugged sheepishly.

"'Twas what I was taught as a lad. My grandfather fought in the Uprising of 1867, you see."

"I've never heard anything about it," Eleanor confessed.

Liam's eyes grew wide. "Don't you know anything about English oppression in Ireland?"

"No. Perhaps you could teach me."

"I can tell you a little. Her Majesty's troops have been garrisoned among my people for seven-hundred years now, and we are governed by those not born on our native lands. For years we were forbidden to practice our Catholic faith, under penalty of death. During the Famine, the English barely lifted a finger to ease our suffering. And even today our children are taught by English school-masters who punish any child caught speaking in the Irish." A fierce light burned in Liam's eyes. "I hate the English, or any who deny a man his freedom and rights."

"But in America it's different," Eleanor said. "We worship in any church of our choosing, and no one is punished for their heritage."

"Is that so?" Liam said, lifting his brows. "And what would you say if I told you that 'tis as much of a curse to be Irish in America as it was back home?

"Here I am considered ignorant because of the way I speak. People think me superstitious, or expect that I only eat potatoes, or that I'm some fanatical Papist here to terrorize honest God-fearing Protestants. They can't believe that an Irishman has anything else on his mind other than getting drunk, or that he might have ambitions for a better life in the future."

Eleanor regarded Liam in silence for a few moments before asking, "And what kind of plans do you have in mind, Mr. MacLann?"

"The truth is, Miss, I don't really know."

"Then why did you come to America? There must have been a reason."

"We had to leave, both me and my brother Conall. There was trouble back home, is all," he replied evasively. Liam paused, and Eleanor sensed that he was holding something back. "There was nothing left for us on Inishmore. Just poverty and hardship."

"How did you travel to America, Liam?" David asked.

"Me Da's cousin, Tim Pat, who lives in Graceville, Minnesota, sent us some money for the passage across. And both Conall and I worked aboard the ship to help cover the cost. When we arrived in New York, we had just enough left to pay for our train tickets west.

"Tim Pat let us stay at his house, and we helped work his wheat fields. For the first time in my life I had enough to eat every day and warm clothes on my back and shoes for my feet. I felt like a king in a new land, sure."

"What happened to your brother?" Eleanor asked.

"The scarlet fever took him that first winter," Liam answered. He said no more, and Eleanor did not press him. It was evident by the look on his face that his grief still lingered.

"I'm sorry," she said. "I didn't mean to—"

"Ah, 'tis nothing, lass." Liam made a visible effort to brighten. "Enough of the sad talk, now. Conall had a lust for life, he did. He loved to fight and drink and tell stories by the hearth. I never knew anyone braver or more willing to stand up for what he believed in."

"What kind of fighting?" David asked. "Boxing, you mean?"

"Oh, aye, pub-fights and prize-fights both. See, there was this one time at the Galway fair when Conall went up against one of the most famous boxers in all the west of Ireland. Ah, 'twas a fine match, almost thirty rounds, with Conall the last man standing. Jesus and Mary, he almost beat the life out of the other fellow."

"Sounds perfectly barbaric," Adeline said, sweeping in with a breakfast tray. Eleanor moved aside, making room for her mother to set the tray on Liam's lap.

"The oatmeal is hot, though there's only a little sugar left for sweetening," Adeline explained. Her arch gaze rested on Liam. "How are you feeling today, Mr. MacLann?"

"A little better." Liam nodded at David. "And the lad has been keeping good company with me this morning."

David smiled. "Liam has promised to teach me how to play poker later, Mama."

"Cards," Adeline said with a scowl. "Come along, David, I need you to haul in more wood."

"Yes, Mama," David replied glumly. He followed his mother to the door, then stopped and said, "See you later, Liam."

Liam nodded. As Adeline ushered David along, she added, "Are you coming, Eleanor?"

"In a few minutes." Once again, Eleanor caught the clear look of disapproval on her mother's face before she left the room.

Liam saw it too. "She's a cold woman, your mother," he said.

"You must understand that she's used to having everything go her way. It's her only reward for living so far from town."

"Ah, then, she ought to leave. No use in staying if it makes her so unhappy."

"Mama wouldn't dream of it. Proper women do their duty to their husbands, or so she's told me often enough." Eleanor paused, and then asked, "Can you manage the oatmeal on your own?"

"Oh, aye." Liam shifted so that he was able to reach the spoon with his good hand. He took a tentative taste. "'Twill be fine," he said after swallowing.

"I'll leave you to your breakfast, then."

"Don't go," Liam said. "You're bonnie company," he added.

Eleanor considered. "I'll stay for a short while," she said. Liam ate slowly as Eleanor fell quiet, content to rock and watch him eat.

This silence stretched between them, past discomfort to the point where it seemed the most natural thing in the world. After Liam was finished eating, he spoke to her, asking, "Miss Thompson, there's something I've been wanting to know. Why did you go to the beach the night of the storm?"

The question set off inner alarms. "You wouldn't believe me if I told you."

"You might be surprised what I would believe."

"I just can't say," Eleanor insisted. She wasn't ready to tell Liam or anyone about the voice she heard.

Liam reached out to touch her skirt. "I want you to tell me," he said. "'Tis very, very important that I understand what happened."

His plea penetrated her reluctance. Liam deserved to know the truth, she decided. "A voice told me," Eleanor said at last. "A voice told me that you were down on the beach."

"A voice? You mean, like a funny little feeling inside, like when you know someone is talking about you just outside of earshot?"

"No, not like that. A real voice, like someone speaking to me."

"Ah," Liam said, a look of understanding dawning on his face. "That would have been Conall, then."

"Conall?" Eleanor ceased rocking as a chill spread down her limbs and made her shiver. "I thought you said that Conall is dead."

"Aye. But his spirit abides." Liam's voice was eerily calm. "Don't take on so, Miss Thompson. The love my brother bore for me now lives beyond the grave, somehow. Conall must've known you would listen to him."

"I don't believe in ghosts," Eleanor insisted.

"But what really matters, girleen, is that Conall believed in you." Liam chuckled. "In Ireland, such things are not so hard to understand."

"I thought you said you weren't superstitious."

"There's a difference. It can't be explained, but there is a difference." Liam nodded at the empty bowl. "I'm finished with the soup, and would very much like something to drink."

"I'll send Mama in, if you don't mind. I have chores to do."

"Aye, then." There was no mistaking the sound of disappointment in Liam's voice, but Eleanor had no desire to continue their unnerving conversation.

She paused just outside the door. *Ghostly voices? The dead watching over the living?* It was too otherworldly, too impossible to accept.

But the idea of it clung to her as she went about her tasks. Did a spiritual connection exist between her and Liam MacLann? She thought about her own vague stirrings concerning the lake at times. Was this something he felt inside as well?

"We're both of us crazy," she finally muttered. There were no such things as ghosts, and the only common bond between them was the fact that he was still a guest in her home. It was downright silly to imagine otherwise.

Mama was right. The sooner everyone left Haven Point, the better.

At chore time, Eleanor went out to the barn to feed and muck out the remaining livestock. In the barn, the air was strong with the smell of animals, straw and dung. Eleanor emptied the kitchen slop bucket into a trough just inside the fenced pen, which brought the spotted hog waddling and grunting. Chickens clucked from with their coop built along the barn wall.

She'd just reached for the mucking shovel when she saw Lars standing in the barn door. "I was coming out to the woodpile when I saw you," he explained. "Why don't you let me help you with that?"

"All right," she said, handing him the shovel. "There's not much to clean with only the one hog left."

"And by this time tomorrow he'll be a fresh carcass hanging in the smoke-house," Lars said. "Your father wants me to help him with the butchering later this afternoon."

"We don't have much of a choice, I guess, since we're almost to the end of our meat supply. Although we still have that Thanksgiving turkey."

Lars pitched a shovelful of manure into the wheelbarrow. "I'm sure we'll be cooking it sometime real soon. Especially with another mouth to feed," he added, glancing at her from the corner of his eyes.

Eleanor scattered handfuls of yellow corn for the chickens. "What do you think of Liam?"

"He seems all right. He reminds me of the men I used to sail with years ago."

"But there *is* something different about him, don't you think?"

"I don't know what you mean, Eleanor," Lars said, a stubborn set to his jaw.

"What I mean is, when you talk with him, when you're sitting next to him, there's an air about Liam, something quite extraordinary."

Lars leaned the shovel against the barn wall. "Don't put too much of a shine on Liam," he said, opening his pocket knife. "Sailors live a pretty rough life."

"In what way, exactly?"

Lars cut the wire on a fresh bale and scattered the straw around the pen. "Well, let's just say it wouldn't surprise me if your Mr. MacLann has visited brothels."

Eleanor paled. "Brothels? You mean he—? With prostitutes?"

"Most likely. Drinking and whoring are the favorite pastimes when sailors get liberty." Lars faced her directly. "I'm sorry to tell you all this, Eleanor. Believe me, I have nothing personal against the man. But the truth is none of us really know that much about him."

"You sound like Mama," Eleanor muttered. "Do you really think Liam pays women for—for that?"

"Why don't you ask him yourself, if you're so darned curious about it?" Lars snapped.

Her face burned with embarrassment. "I wouldn't dream of it," she said, dropping the subject at once. She stamped the ground with her shoes, her toes completely numb. "Mercy, it's freezing. Are you ready to go inside?"

"Nearly so. Almost finished with the straw, and then I'll dump it in the brush."

"I'll wait for you," Eleanor said. Later they walked together, pausing at the juncture between the two houses.

"Lars," Eleanor asked, "the night after we rescued Liam, I heard you and Papa arguing in the kitchen about taking the skiff out to search for more survivors. Could Papa get in any trouble for his decision?"

"He might. Superintendent Greer doesn't care too much for your father. I know there was an incident when the last assistant keeper fell to his death from the top of the lighthouse."

"But that wasn't Papa's fault! The assistant had been drinking before he went up to clean the windows, against orders!"

Lars held up his hand. "I'm not arguing with you. But I know the whole incident caused some trouble with the Lighthouse Board. Superintendent Greer told me before I came here to work that John should have dismissed that man long before." Lars shook his head. "He has an axe to grind against your father, I guess."

"Jamieson Greer is a fool," Eleanor pronounced. She briefly touched Lars' arm. "Thanks for your help in the barn, and for your advice as well. You've always been like a brother to me."

Lars scowled. "See you tomorrow, Eleanor," he said, then disappeared inside his house.

*   *   *   *

Liam awoke with a start in the darkness. He'd drifted off to sleep after supper, a difficult, shallow sleep marked by a vivid nightmare of the shipwreck. *Walls of black, foaming water, Charlie hanging on his arm, the ship tearing in two, oh Jesus, oh God…* Liam willed his heart to slow, his sense of terror to recede. "'Twas only a dream," he muttered.

Someone was playing piano in the other room. Liam sat up, disoriented by the juxtaposition of cheerful music with his ghoulish dreams. *They must have re-opened the parlor,* he thought. Probably one of the girls was playing.

Liam's thoughts turned to Eleanor. Their time together that morning had been both pleasant and revealing, especially concerning her news about Conall's voice. Was it truly possible Conall had communicated with Eleanor?

There was something about this girl that drew him strongly. She burned with a quiet intensity, evident by her willingness to defy her mother and her devoted care of both him and her family. Her keen spirit stood in sharp contrast to his own sense of physical weakness, a feeling worsened by the cold, dead place inside him where he grieved everything he once held dear.

Ireland was lost to him. Conall was dead. The ship and all his mates were likely gone. What more did Liam have to live for? He could always return to Graceville and find his place among his cousin's people. But this choice Liam rejected; the western prairie was simply too vast and unforgiving.

Liam rose and tested his weight on his bad foot. Still sore, but less so than before. The frostbitten toes would probably always bother him, though he felt grateful not to have suffered their amputation.

The piano continued to play, and Liam decided he would see for himself who had the musical talent in the family. When he opened the door, he saw that the parlor had indeed been reopened. He limped toward the dining room. John sat on the red-tufted sofa, drawing on his pipe and reading a newspaper. Adeline was dusting the mantel, while Bridget and Eleanor sat at the piano. David was nowhere to be seen. Bridget, who was playing, paused when she caught sight of Liam. Everyone looked at him, making him feel especially self-conscious.

"Go on and play," Liam said. "I came out to listen."

"Come and have a seat, MacLann," John told him with a nod. Liam shuffled toward the sofa, careful to avoid Eleanor's glance as he passed by the piano. He was ashamed of his infirmity, and just at that moment he couldn't abide the eagerness in her eyes.

"Continue playing, Bridget," Adeline said. Bridget opened her songbook and began to play a familiar song. It was an old mariner's hymn, called "Brightly Beams Our Father's Mercy."

Eleanor sang the words so dear to the heart of sailing men:

"Brightly beams out Father's mercy
From His lighthouse evermore,
But to us He gives the keeping
Of the lights along the shore."

Then came the chorus, and gooseflesh pebbled Liam's skin.

"Let the lower lights be burning!
Send a gleam across the across the wave!
Some poor fainting, struggling seaman
You may rescue, you may save."

Anguish tore at Liam. By all rights he should be dead now, either cast to the bottom of Superior or a lifeless corpse like Nathaniel.

"Dark the night of sin has settled,
Loud the angry billows roar;
Eager eyes are watching, longing,
For the lights along the shore."

Eleanor shifted in her seat. Her steady gaze bore into Liam in silent expectation. He held it, even as his heart was squeezed by a feeling of wretchedness. How could she or anyone else ever understand what he'd endured on the lake?

"Trim your feeble lamps, my brother:
Some poor sailor tempest-tossed,
Trying now to make the harbor,
In the darkness may be lost.

Let the lower lights be burning!
Send a gleam across the wave!
Some poor fainting, struggling seaman
You may rescue, you may save."

Sweat covered Liam's back like frost. He desperately needed to get outside and escape the cloying atmosphere of the Thompson household. Liam rose abruptly from the sofa and limped as fast as he was able to the door.

"Where are you going?" Eleanor called after him. "Mr. MacLann?"

Liam did not answer. He threw open the front door and stepped outside, where he took an enormous breath of bracing night air. Oh, how good it felt, especially after having been cooped up inside for several days. Liam closed the door, then took a few more tentative steps to the edge of the stoop before lifting his gaze to the tower.

The light swept across the seemingly endless miles of Superior. Waves rushed against the shore, a lonely sound, filled with all the yearning of the sea.

The door opened behind him. It was Eleanor. "Are you all right?" she asked.

"Yes. No." He wished she'd stayed indoors. "You wouldn't understand."

"It was that song, wasn't it?"

"Aye." Liam looked away. "I—I never knew what it really meant until now."

She touched his arm. "Why don't you come inside and let me make you some fresh coffee, hmm? It's very cold out here."

"Not yet. Maybe in a little while." Liam winced at the look of disappointment on Eleanor's face.

She moved toward the door. "I'll have it ready for you when you decide to come in."

"Eleanor," he said, "why did you follow me?"

"I was worried about you. I don't want anything bad to happen to you, Liam." The conviction in her voice brought an ache to his throat.

"You're a *brea cailín*, a fine girl," Liam said. He was rewarded by the hint of smile on Eleanor's full lips. She went inside the house without another word.

As before, Eleanor's absence felt like more than just being alone. Light and warmth had vanished with her, leaving him to confront the bleakness of his circumstance. Was he cursed, then? Was it his fate to always lose those whom he cared for?

The sound of the waves called to him, beckoning for him to join his shipmates. How easy it would be to pitch himself off the nearest cliff and surrender to Superior. Liam quivered on the edge of decision, his pain almost overwhelming him. But then he thought of Eleanor, thought of the devastation it might bring her if he took the coward's way out. He turned back and let himself inside the house.

For now he would wait and rest, he told himself, and once he returned to Duluth he would find out whether there might have been other survivors from the wreck. If even one other man had lived, he could bear what had happened, bear the guilt of his survival when the others had died.

For the moment, it was the only thing worth living for.

CHAPTER 8

▼

When the *Amaranth* had not arrived by December 4th, Lars rowed the skiff northward to Grand Marais. He returned late in the afternoon with a load of supplies. Supper that night was a feast: pork roast with sour cream gravy, corn bread with blackberry preserves, baked squash rings, followed by Adeline's specialty, frosted carrot cake. A festival atmosphere pervaded the Thompson household; Liam ate so much he collapsed into bed with a drum-tight belly.

He'd mastered the art of walking without assistance, though a slight limp marked his gait. Thirty pounds had dropped from his normally robust frame, and there were times when Liam felt like a mere shadow of his former self. But his strength slowly began to return, and after a hot bath and a shave he felt almost human again. He slept as often of he could, long, forgetful sleep, the likes of which he hadn't enjoyed since Conall's death so many years earlier.

The morning after the feast, Liam woke with a burdened conscience. He'd been thinking about Nathaniel Klassen and the months they'd served together on the *Dorn*, and Liam realized it was time to be reconciled with the man who'd saved his life. It galled Liam to think he must pay homage to someone who'd treated him with such contempt, but there was nothing to be done about it. For Liam it was a matter of honor.

He sat on the bed, brooding over his present circumstance. John and Lars were polite but distant, Bridget hardly ever spoke a word, David pestered him for stories and card games, Adeline treated him with glacial reserve, and Eleanor continued to offer assistance whenever necessary.

Liam was thankful that he could feed himself and move about on his own, for the time he spent alone with Eleanor fed an awakening hunger he recognized only too well. *How long had he been without a woman?* he wondered to himself. His last visit to Fitzgerald's Saloon, and the sporting girls in Buffalo, New York, seemed months ago.

Eleanor was a dark beauty, there was no question about it. The more they often were together, the more he noticed her gracefulness, her soft grey eyes, the rich tones of her voice. With each passing day his desire for her grew, though a part of him resisted. Eleanor Thompson was an innocent, while he'd consorted with sordid women in many ports of call. He wasn't fit to touch her, he told himself, much less dream of bedding her.

Liam pushed these thoughts away and went in search of Eleanor. He found her in the kitchen, pressing laundry on a board. The smell of starched linen hung heavy in the air. Her back was to him, and he watched her in silence as she smoothed the wrinkled fabric with the iron, humming absently to herself as she placed the iron on the stove-top and then neatly folded the shirt.

The slight twist of Eleanor's slender back and the flex of her arm riveted Liam. Her shirt sleeves were unbuttoned and rolled up to the elbow, revealing skin white as bisque. Eleanor's black hair shone in the sunlight that was streaming through the window. Liam swallowed hard, battling the sudden impulse to bury his hands in that sable abundance.

Eleanor burned her finger as she re-clamped the wooden handle atop the iron. "Ouch," she said, dropping the iron on the stove top with a heavy *clunk*. She turned for the sink, and Liam smiled at the look of surprise on her face. She reddened slightly and said, "I'm sorry, I didn't know you were there."

"Nor would you. I didn't announce myself."

Metal creaked against metal as Eleanor pumped water over her finger. "Is there something I can help you with, Mr. MacLann?"

"I want to see Nathaniel Klassen."

"Papa and Lars buried him yesterday."

"I guessed as much, but I still want to pay my respects. I wouldn't be standing here today if it weren't for him."

Eleanor re-buttoned her sleeves. "You'll have to wear Papa's spare coat."

"Fine by me, though I might need some help getting into it."

Eleanor held the wool coat as Liam gingerly inserted his good arm into the sleeve. He stared up at the ceiling, discomfited by their closeness, while Eleanor buttoned the front of the coat as far as the sling would allow.

"Take a seat at the table while I bring your boots," Eleanor told him. She disappeared through the dining room door and returned a few minutes later with the boots. Tendrils of pain raced up his calf as Liam shoved his sore foot inside the stiff leather. Eleanor knelt to tighten and tie the laces.

After putting on her own coat, Eleanor held the door open for Liam. Sunshine greeted them, with only the slightest of breezes stirring the air. Liam's eyes were immediately drawn to Eleanor as she led him down the steps and along the path.

"Papa and Lars had a tough time digging out that frozen ground," Eleanor explained. "But Papa just didn't have the heart to leave Mr. Klassen in the light-house annex until spring."

"Your father is a decent soul, God bless him," Liam said.

By now they had abandoned the brick path and were making their way along a trail cut through the drifted snow. As he followed behind, Liam gazed at Eleanor, alerted by her stride, the way her hair curled behind her ears, the mad-dening sway of her skirt. *Oh, and what would Nicky have said about a long-legged stunner like you, Eleanor Thompson?*

Dirt and wet brown leaves lay disturbed where the men had excavated the ground. A simple wooden cross stood at the head of the grave. Eleanor stayed back a few paces as Liam folded his hands and whispered a prayer in Gaelic.

He closed his eyes and summoned the picture of Nathaniel's face. Angry, vengeful, always with a flash of malice in his eyes. But he'd been a resourceful man, undoubtedly, and, in the end, Liam's salvation.

The *caw caw* of a blackbird split the air. When Liam opened his eyes, he saw that Eleanor was beside him. "He was your friend," she said politely.

"No. We had nothing but hatred for one another. 'Twas a strange fate that threw us together in the final hours."

Confusion clouded her face. "Then why do you honor him now?"

"Because we were mates on that ship. Sailing men are brothers, bound by their lives on the water. In that way, Nathaniel was the same as my close friends on the *Dorn*." Liam's expression darkened. "But in another way he was as different from the others as could be, for Nathaniel tormented me at every turn for my Irish-ness."

"Tormented for being an Irishman? I don't understand."

Liam looked to the side. He was tired of having to explain everything to her. She was just too inexperienced, too naïve. "What do you know of the wide world, girleen, and how men mistreat one another?" he said, exasperated.

The blood drained from her face. "How dare you speak to me that way!" she cried. "Just who do you think you are?"

"A wicked man, do you hear?" Liam said, grasping her shoulder with his good hand. "I've seen the ugly side of life, been places you couldn't imagine in your worst dreams! Don't try so fucking hard to take care of me! I don't want you for a nursemaid!"

"Oh? And what *do* you want me for?" she challenged hotly.

His lips twisted into a snarl. "Can't you get it through your head? I don't want you for anything! All I want is to be left alone!"

He half-expected her to run off, but to his surprise she stood her ground. "I was the one who found you, and I was the one who covered you while I waited for Lars to return with Papa!" she said. "And I'm the only one who gives a damn about what's going to happen to you when we leave Haven Point!"

Suddenly Eleanor's expression changed as her anger seemed to melt away. "Liam, why can't you accept that all I want is to help you?" she pleaded. "You're not alone, I'm here now, everything will turn out for the best, you'll see—"

"Don't say things like that," Liam said in a hoarse voice. "I don't want to care for you. I just can't take the risk." He hung his head. "Everyone's been taken away from me, everyone and everything that I ever cared for. I'm cursed, I tell you, cursed!"

Liam's eyes locked onto hers, and something broke loose inside him, something he'd been fighting since the first time he'd touched her. She was so beautiful, so passionate. He was overcome by the urge to kiss her, crush her against him and never let her go. Yet even as he leaned closer, a shout from the house interrupted them.

"Eleanor, Eleanor!" Bridget cried, running toward them. "The *Amaranth* is here!"

The tender ship, *Amaranth*, stood anchored several hundred yards off the shore, a stream of black smoke rising from the slim stack. It was a mid-sized ship with two spars, a pilot house, and an after cabin. A launch chugged across the bay toward the damaged dock.

Eleanor, Liam, and Bridget were the first to arrive. Lars and the rest of the Thompson family joined them a short while later. John and Lars moved forward to help as the launch grounded on the beach, where six crewmen stepped from the boat to haul it up onto solid ground.

Eleanor carefully composed her expression, worried that Adeline would see how upset she was. Liam's burst of emotion had shocked her. Why had he been so angry with her? Worse yet had been the heart-stopping moment when his anger had turned to desire and she'd felt him drawing close. Eleanor had half-dreaded, half-longed for Liam's kiss. But Bridget's arrival had severed the tenuous thread between them.

A stout man with a skipper's cap and a brass-buttoned wool coat approached John. "Keeper Thompson?"

"I am Keeper Thompson," John replied.

"Will Krenshaw, captain of the *Amaranth*," the ample-figured man announced as he shook John's hand. "Sorry about our late arrival. The ice along the North Shore has stiffened up quite a bit since the storm."

"We guessed as much," John said, nodding. "What supplies have you brought?"

"Fuel and foodstuffs. A short load, for this light station will be closing next week."

"Next week?" Adeline questioned. "Are you certain?"

"Here's your orders from Detroit," Captain Krenshaw answered, withdrawing a telegram from his coat pocket. "The *America* will be making her final scheduled run to Grand Marais on December the 14th, and I advise you to have your things packed and your place readied for closure by the time she arrives."

John read the telegram before handing it to Adeline. Captain Krenshaw looked past Eleanor to Liam. "I wasn't aware that Haven Point Light had been assigned a second assistant keeper," the captain said.

"He's not my assistant," John explained. "This man came to Haven Point aboard the *William A. Dorn* life-raft."

Captain Krenshaw's eyes widened as he stared at Liam. "You were on the *William Dorn*? Hells bells, man, the company officials in Duluth have been crazy to learn what happened to her!"

"The *Dorn* is gone," Liam replied. He took a few steps toward the captain. "Can you tell me, has there been any word about other survivors?"

"None. No one knew what happened to the ship, until now."

"I see." Liam's expression grew stony. "Well, then, she went down with all hands."

"With the exception of Mr. MacLann," Eleanor added. She remained firmly by his side, feeling a sense of protectiveness toward him.

"I see," Krenshaw said. "Just exactly what happened?"

Liam's eyes narrowed. "I won't be telling any tales on the beach. 'Twould be disrespectful to the memory of my shipmates."

John stroked his moustache thoughtfully. "Captain Krenshaw, why don't you and your men stay for supper? Then we'll have a chance to discuss everything in detail."

"Yes," Krenshaw agreed. He eyed Liam like a greedy merchant. "I want the whole story."

As the men began to unload the launch, Eleanor touched Liam's sleeve and asked, "Do you wish to stay here or return to the house?"

He gave her a cursory glance. "I think I'll stay."

Adeline drew Eleanor to the side, saying, "We'd better get busy if we're going to feed that crew. The turkey hanging in the smokehouse should be big enough, don't you agree?"

"If you say, Mama." Eleanor followed close behind her mother, her footsteps heavy. In less than a week they'd be back in Grand Marais. Real school for Bridget and David, church socials, a chance to see her old friends, sledding and skating parties, everything.

She should be happy, but Eleanor felt torn inside. The memory of Liam's unbridled rage hit her with an almost physical force. In those few minutes she'd sensed something inside of him, the core man, filled with pain and loss.

Though surrounded by the other sailors, Liam seemed so alone on the beach. She knew what it was like to be isolated, to feel as though no one understood your struggles and dreams. Yet Liam's choices were his to make. Who was she to disagree if he wanted to push her away?

If only I had more time, she thought, and then turned again toward the house.

*   *   *   *

"You look like you could use a smoke, sailor."

One of the *Amaranth*'s crewmen approached Liam and held out a cigarette. Liam scrutinized the other man's face before accepting the gift. "What's your name?" Liam asked.

"Shamus O'Rourke." Curly red hair and a spray of freckles confirmed Shamus' Irish heritage.

"From the homeland, boyo?"

Shamus struck a match and lit the tip of Liam's cigarette and then lit one for himself. "No, born in America. Spent me childhood in the slums of Boston. And you?"

Liam took a long, heavy drag. "Inishmore Island, off the Connemara Coast."

"How long in America?"

"Sure now, only five years." Liam gestured toward the tender. "How long have you worked the Lakes?"

"Three seasons. Last year I crewed a packet freighter, but I like the *Amaranth* better. I get to be home with my family more often."

"You have a family?"

"Oh, aye. A wife and three copper-headed wee ones, down in Duluth. In the winter, I work on a plowing crew for the city. No family for you, Liam?"

"Not here. I emigrated with my brother, but he died of scarlet fever the first year. Since then I've worked the ore boats."

Their conversation was interrupted by the captain. "O'Rourke, lend a hand, you lazy roundhead!"

Liam snorted as he flicked his ashes onto the rocks. "'Tis always the same, wherever we go. You'd better put your shoulder to it, Shamus."

Resentment smoldered in Shamus' eyes. "Krenshaw's a bloody *eejit*. Thinks he owns me, he does." Shamus thrust out his hand. "I'm honored to meet a man who survived a wrecked ship."

"Och, 'twas God's mercy spared me life, and nothing more."

"To be sure. I'm after hearing your story, Liam."

"Boyo, you're not alone."

The turkey came out of the oven by late afternoon, filling the house with its mouth-watering aroma as the women bustled between the kitchen and the dining room. Two leaf sections had been added to the cherry-wood dining room table, with extra chairs brought in from the kitchen. Covered dishware began to appear on the linen tablecloth: corn bread, stewed cabbage, green beans with onion and bacon, pickled herring, and butter-laden mashed potatoes.

Both John and Lars had changed into their formal lighthouse keeper uniforms. The crewmen and keepers gathered in a tight knot to smoke and discuss the storm. From where Liam stood between Shamus and Lars, he kept an eye on Eleanor as she busied herself about the table.

Captain Krenshaw dominated the conversation. "We gave heed to the storm warning flags hoisted in Duluth harbor and kept in port during the storm. I stayed aboard ship, and was there when the *Mataafa* wrecked on the pier head."

"The *Mataafa*!" Liam exclaimed. "I knew one of her firemen, a fellow by the name of Tom Woodgate."

Krenshaw shook his head. "Sorry to say, MacLann, but he was one of 'em listed among the dead. Most of the aft crew either washed overboard or were frozen in beds of ice. The only survivors were in the pilothouse."

Liam shuddered and crossed himself as the captain continued. "We passed some bad wrecks on our trip up the shore—*Crescent City*, just north of Duluth, the *Lafayette* off Encampment Island, the *Edenborn* at the mouth of Split Rock River, and the *Madeira*, just a little ways further up the coast. Many ships were still overdue when we steamed from Duluth yesterday."

The first mate, a preening, blonde-haired man named Jean Trenet, sucked on the long stem of his pipe. "I was at Lanigan's eatery when the ships' masters started coming in, clutching the newspapers with their lurid headlines. The stories those men told would raise the hair on the back of your neck."

"The *Ira H. Owen*, the *Western Star*, the *William E. Cory*, the *Bransford*, the *George Spencer*, the *Vinland*—just a few that were damaged or destroyed." Krenshaw shook his head. "And now we'll be adding the *William Dorn* to the list as well."

Adeline called for their attention. "Gentlemen, if you would come to the table, please. We'll be a tight fit, but there should be plenty of food."

It was a memorable meal. Liam's enjoyment of the delicious food was heightened by the company of the other sailing men, for they reminded him of his mates from the *Dorn*.

About the time everyone was scraping their plates, Adeline spoke to Eleanor, asking, "Would you bring out the coffee pot and refill the cups?"

"Of course, Mama." Soon Eleanor emerged from the kitchen with the coffee pot in her hand. She walked over to where Jean Trenet was holding up his cup. Liam watched as she poured the coffee and handed the cup back, when, to Liam's chagrin, the first mate deliberately brushed against Eleanor's arm.

Liam set his fork aside, angry thoughts buzzing in his head. Who did that man think he was, touching Eleanor like that, a fine, decent young woman, he'd smash Trenet's face to a pulp—!

"There's apple pie if anyone cares for dessert," Adeline announced after she and Eleanor had cleared the dinner plates from the table.

Liam's mouth watered at the sight of the flaky lattice crust covering the cinnamon-spiced apples. Adeline cut the pies into equal shares before dishing them out. The men ate in silent reverence, and then Captain Krenshaw said, "This is the best pie I've tasted in a long while, ma'am." This brought a blush of pleasure to Adeline's cheeks, who seemed to be thoroughly enjoying her role as hostess.

Later, as Bridget and Eleanor cleared the dishes, Liam watched Trenet's gaze follow Eleanor. Beneath the table, Liam's hand clenched into a fist.

"Come now, Mr. MacLann, we're all waiting for your story," Captain Krenshaw prompted.

Everyone turned toward Liam. It struck him that this would be his first sea tale, and how ironic that it should be his very own. "Look to your courage then, for it is a grim account," he began. "No machine made of man, nor a great many years behind the pilothouse wheel, could have saved us from the wind-driven perdition which was the height of that gale. Superior had marked us all for death, though I alone survived."

No one stirred as Liam spun out his narrative, starting from the afternoon the ship departed Duluth harbor and ending with his rescue on Haven Point's beach. Those gathered listened in awed, respectful silence.

Liam was transformed. His voice assumed a dramatic rhythm reminiscent of the Irish *shanachies* who traveled from the pubs to the cottages of his island home. Liam drew his listeners into the depths of the firehold, brought them deck-side to battle the icy waves, held them at his side as he rolled within the life-raft. Shamus, in particular, was mesmerized by Liam's description of the crew's heroic efforts in the final hours before the wreck.

Eleanor stood in the doorway between the kitchen and dining room, riveted by every word. "I was close to death, and ready and glad to go to my eternal reward, but Providence had other plans in mind," he said. "I crashed ashore here at Haven Point, where I was found and rescued by Miss Thompson and Assistant Keeper Berglund. My companion, First Mate Nathaniel Klassen, froze to death before we made landfall, and all the *Dorn*'s crew went down with the ship, including her master, Captain Edward Graling." Liam leaned back in his chair. "That is my witness, and all of it true."

A mournful solemnity hung over the table. "Remarkable," Captain Krenshaw said, taking a sip of coffee. "You'll need to make a report in Duluth, MacLann. The top brass at the Zenith Steamship offices are hot to know what's become of their ship."

"Will you go to Duluth, Liam?" Shamus asked.

"Aye, that's my plan. I've banked most of this season's earnings there, and I'm needing a long rest."

"Well-deserved, of course." Krenshaw stood and motioned his crew to follow. "Mr. and Mrs. Thompson, you've honored us with this fine meal. We'll be returning to the *Amaranth* now, as we're scheduled to sail up to the Rock of Ages lighthouse in the morning."

As John escorted the crewmen to the front door, Shamus came beside Liam and pressed a piece of paper into his hand. "This is my home address," he explained. "Look me up when you come down to Duluth, and I'd be proud to show you some decent Irish hospitality."

*   *   *   *

"Eleanor, why don't you go up to bed and get some sleep? You look like a candle burned down into a pool of wax."

John spoke to Eleanor just as she was finishing drying the last of the dishes. It was near eleven o'clock, and everyone had gone off to bed, save Lars, who was in the tower.

"I'm almost done." Eleanor saw her reflection in the darkened window above the sink; shadows puffed beneath her eyes, and her cheeks looked pale and hollow.

John, sitting at the table, lit his pipe. "Quite a crowd today, hmm?"

"I'm not sure I liked them very much," Eleanor said with a sniff, thinking about the man who had touched her so rudely. "They seemed low-class and vulgar."

"That's what most men are like, taken as a whole," John said, puffing reflectively. "You're just not used to them, not like your mother was when she was your age."

"At the lumber camp, you mean." Eleanor dried her hands on her apron. "How did Mama stand it? The noise, the smell, the profanity?"

"Truth to tell, she hated every minute of it, mostly. I had to sweet-talk her good to get her to come around." John leaned back in his chair. "You should have seen your mother then, Eleanor. Talkative and spirited. A woman with looks who knew it, too. Like a ship in full sail, she was."

Eleanor gazed at her father. "You really love Mama, don't you?"

"Like my own life. Oh, I know she can be difficult sometimes, and Lord knows we've had our differences. But I wouldn't trade a day of our life together for anything."

Eleanor untied her apron before hanging it on the peg. "I don't think I'll go to bed just yet."

"Down to the lake, is it?"

"Yes. I haven't spent any time alone there since before the storm."

"I'll place the lantern in the window for you, then." John came over and gave her a quick kiss on the forehead. "I'll be upstairs reading if you need anything."

*   *   *   *

"A toast to health and happiness, Liam boy, on this, your wedding day!"

Liam, asleep, wandered through the constructs of a vivid dream. It was the eve of his wedding, and all his fellows and friends were on hand to wish him well: Nick, Harry, Tom, even Conall. The whiskey and champagne flowed as the men sang bawdy songs to bless his union, swaying in drunkenness while Liam bragged about the many sons he would father.

She was waiting for him. As he entered the bridal chamber, no lamp shone in the darkness. He threw open the window shutters, allowing moonlight to reflect off a white dress and veil draped across a velvet chair. Liam smiled to himself, anticipating the pleasures of the marriage bed. Fumbling for a match, he struck it and lit the candle on the bed stand, wanting to see all of her.

But she was not there.

"Eleanor," he rasped, his tongue thick inside his mouth. She'd vanished, and, worse yet, there was no sign she'd ever been there. "Eleanor!" he cried, louder this time, frantically rifling through the room. *Where had she gone, how could this be happening, where the hell was she—?*

The kitchen door banging shut awakened Liam. He rose from the bed and looked out the bedroom window, catching a glimpse of Eleanor before she disappeared into the night.

He stood at the window, bewildered by his dream. How could he even consider such a possibility? Eleanor Thompson was an educated young lady, well-mannered, and in all likelihood a Protestant. And who was he? An Irish-Catholic, a stranger in a foreign land, no job, no prospects, not even his own clothes on his back. He was not a marriageable man: Eleanor was as far beyond his reach as the captaincy of a steam freighter.

But he wanted her more than anything he'd ever wanted in his life. And nothing was going to stop him.

CHAPTER 9

---▼---

An arctic breeze caressed Eleanor's cheeks as she stood near the ice-clad shore. Superior spread before her in the blackness, vast in its broad distances, its vaulted depths, the waves a constant song against the rocks. Overhead, the Milky Way cut a swath across the sky, startlingly clear in the cold night air. Eleanor smiled to herself; it had been far too long since her last visit to the lake.

Impulsively, she loosened her chignon and let her hair flow to her waist. Eleanor surrendered to the lake's grandeur, holding her arms wide to the night.

The sound of footsteps startled Eleanor, and she turned, half-expecting to see Lars Berglund. But instead she saw Liam.

She waited in silence as he approached. He halted before her, and she looked into his face, into the eyes of a man with an ancient soul. She did not pull away as he reached out to touch her.

For a moment, all the certainties of her world quivered. Eleanor trembled as Liam's fingers stroked her hair, his breath warm on her face. He leaned down and covered her mouth with a kiss.

She tensed. His lips hardened over hers, and Eleanor answered his kiss with one of her own. She softened and pressed her body closer to his, even as his tongue darted inside her mouth and roved with brown-sugar sweetness. Male musk, the smell of arousal, rose thick-scented in her nose. Her hand traveled over rough wool and fleecy flannel, felt the rhythm of his heartbeat.

Liam encircled her waist with his good arm. Eleanor drew back, feeling overwhelmed and a little frightened. "Liam—"

"Shhh, now, girleen, do not speak," he whispered. "Do not speak."

His grip tightening, his mouth claimed hers again and again. The shock of him ran through her body, heated her blood and sent her heart racing. She reached up to explore the planes of his face, comb her hands through the tangled thickness of his hair, feel the pulse raging at the base of his throat. Fingertips skated across the broad expanse of his chest, traced the longitude of his shoulders. Eagerly Liam began to unbutton the front of her coat.

Eleanor gasped as Liam cupped one breast through the fabric of her shirtwaist, and then, leaning down, he rained kisses along its curve. Eleanor arched to him, closing her eyes as he pressed himself against her.

"Give over to me, now, girleen, he whispered in her ear. "God, how I want to lie with you—"

The sound of Liam's voice jolted Eleanor back to reality. He had no right to touch and kiss her this way, not yet, not this soon. She tore herself from his embrace and took several steps back, staring at him with a mixture of outrage and reproach.

She sprinted up the pathway to the house, her chest heaving.

Nothing of herself would she give to him.

*   *   *   *

Liam stared after her, feeling as though someone had just punched his stomach. Why had she run from him? They'd been warming up to one another just fine, pleasurably so, in fact, when suddenly she'd turned cold as the wind off the lake. What wrong had he done? He'd been gentle with her, restrained, respecting the fact she was so young and sheltered.

He hadn't forced her in any way. Eleanor had returned his kisses, held herself against him; he knew when a woman was a willing partner in the dance of desire.

Maybe it was too soon, he reasoned as he began to walk along the beach. Maybe it should never have happened. Liam closed his eyes; how was he going to face her the next day?

"It's a fool you are, Liam MacLann," he muttered as he climbed the path toward the Thompsons' house.

*   *   *   *

Eleanor lay beneath her quilts and listened as Liam entered the house. The echo of heavy footsteps was followed by silence. She rolled to her side, staring at the filigreed brass knobs on the nearby dresser. Why had this happened between them, and how could she have allowed it?

She twisted in the blankets. He'd kissed her, laid hands on her, asked her to do things she wasn't prepared to do. Worse than this, she had responded to him in kind. Eleanor closed her eyes as she relived the moment; the taste of him, the urgency of his mouth against hers, his hand stroking her hair before pulling her tightly against him. Heat. Desire. The lust of a man for a woman. All of it wrong, she knew, and yet it also felt natural, as though she intuitively recognized him as her mate.

Absurd. It was pure chance that had landed Liam at Haven Point. She was not about to change everything for the sake of a man she'd known for little more than a week.

How would she feel when they met in the morning? Could she deny her attraction, behave as though she didn't care for him? Beyond all this was the fact that she couldn't very well allow him to take liberties with her. She shuddered, thinking of the consequences if her mother ever learned what had happened on the beach.

In the morning she would speak to Liam and remind him that he needed to treat her with the respect she deserved.

*   *   *   *

When Liam took his place at the kitchen table the next morning, he noticed that Eleanor was acting as though nothing had happened. He stared at the table top, wondering if she would denounce him to her mother. Sweat broke out on his forehead at the thought.

"How did you sleep, Mr. MacLann?" Adeline asked as she placed a cup of coffee before him.

"Well enough," Liam replied. He kept his expression guarded as Eleanor set a plate of eggs and toast before him. Their buttery aroma rose up to meet him, but he had little appetite. He broke one yellow yolk with his fork and let it puddle on the plate before taking a tentative bite.

David, sitting across from Liam, asked, "Would you like to go squirrel hunting with me and Mr. Berglund after dinner, Liam?"

Liam was about to answer when Eleanor said, "I'm afraid that won't be possible, David. Mr. MacLann is going to accompany me when I row down to Little Nesna to deliver the fishermen's laundry."

A frown line puckered Adeline's forehead. "How can you be certain those Norwegians are still there? Maybe they've gone south to their winter home in Duluth."

"Nils Finnesgaard told me himself that they're planning to stay at camp until the *America* makes her last stop for the season."

"I doubt you're strong enough to push the skiff onto the lake, Eleanor. Why not wait until Lars or Papa awakens, and ask them to help you?" Adeline argued.

"Liam can help me," Eleanor said as she threw him an expectant look.

"Liam?" Adeline said, lifting her brows. "Why, he's still half-crippled from his injuries. I think this most unwise—"

"Maybe you should ask Mr. MacLann what he wants to do," David suggested.

All eyes came to rest on Liam. He took another bite of his egg and swallowed before answering, "Aye, I will go."

"Then it's settled." Eleanor said. "After I've finished my chores, we'll head down to the beach and be on our way."

The winds were calm, the waves little more than dimples on the water. Columns of mist rose from Lake Superior. Rosy pink and muted blue washed across the wintry sky. Sea gulls shrieked and called to one another from the adjacent cliff-tops. Snow blanketed the beach. Jagged pieces of wooden board jutted out from a snow drift. Liam shuddered as he passed; these were the remains of the *William Dorn*'s life-raft.

Eleanor moved toward the skiff's stern. "This was where we found you," she murmured. After a moment she shook her head and settled the laundry basket inside the boat. Trousers, chambray shirts, long underwear and socks all lay nestled within the basket. "Thirty feet to the shore, and then almost as far across the ice," she said. "Do you think I can manage it?"

"I've no doubt you'll accomplish what you set your mind to," he answered evenly. Liam could only watch as Eleanor tugged and yanked on the skiff's bow line. His broken arm felt unbearably heavy in its sling.

Though Eleanor pulled in earnest, huffing and red-faced, the skiff wouldn't budge. "It's locked in the ice," Liam told her. "You need to break it free."

"Finer said than done," she snapped.

"I can help push it out, if you like."

Eleanor paused. "Are you certain? I don't want you hurting your arm."

An ironic smile twisted Liam's lips. "Didn't you tell your mother that I'd be a help if I went along? Or was that just the talk of a headstrong daughter?"

Anger tightened Eleanor's face momentarily, and then she laughed. "Your point is well taken. Do as you like, Mr. MacLann. I'll not stand in your way."

Liam positioned himself behind the skiff. "The trick is for the two of us to work together, you pulling while I push. My arm might be useless, but I can still throw weight behind my shoulders."

Eleanor took hold of the skiff's bow line again and doubled it around her hands. Liam hunkered down and placed his shoulder at the stern. "Give the signal," he said, bracing his boots against the rocks.

"Now!" Eleanor cried. Liam closed his eyes against the onslaught of pain as he pushed with his legs. Sweat bathed his neck and back as he gritted his teeth; he would make no sound, he would suffer like a man, he'd pass out in a heap before he showed any weakness.

A quiver ran through the skiff, and then it crept forward an inch, two inches, a foot, several feet, and then yards. Before long they'd pulled the skiff to the where the beach met the ice field.

"Rest," Eleanor panted, grinning. Liam straightened up and inhaled deep, staring up at the sky. He had never known such pain, but Christ, how grand it felt to be of use again!

Eleanor rested her hand on his sleeve. "I can pull it the rest of the way myself if this is hurting you too much."

"'Tis nothing. Pain can be ignored, controlled. Don't ask me to quit, not when we've come this far." Gamely, Liam squared himself to the stern once again.

"If you insist," she answered. They heaved and pulled across the ice, making slow but steady progress until they came to a halt just a few feet short of open water.

"Climb aboard, and then I'll ease her in," Liam directed. Eleanor did as she was told, hiking up her skirt as she straddled the gunnel. One final shove, and the skiff's bow dipped into gray lake water. Liam climbed inside before settling onto the stern seat.

Eleanor positioned herself on the centerboard, holding one oar in each hand. Deftly she maneuvered the boat into its proper heading. Eleanor rowed with rolling, even strokes.

Peninsulas jutted out to meet them, thick with majestic dark-green jack pine and Douglas firs. Snow frosted their branches, their limbs bent almost to the ground. Surf-spray coated the rock cliffs at the shoreline, forming sheets of ice that flowed like a toothy skirt to the water's edge. An eagle soared overhead, so near that Liam was able to see its flashing eyes and count the feathers in its tail.

He closed his eyes for a few moments, attuned to the sensation of water beneath him. Apprehension gnawed at him; this was his first time on Superior since the storm. *Heave and lurch, wind and water, Jesus and Mary I'm going to be sick*...Liam blew out his breath before opening his eyes.

He realized that Eleanor was watching him. Liam broke the silence, saying, "It's surprised I am, your asking me out with you today."

"I wanted a chance to talk with you alone." Eleanor paused, then asked, "Why did you follow me down to the beach last night?"

Heat flushed Liam's face. "Must you make me say it? I thought—that is, I mean, wasn't it obvious?"

"Yes. But why me? Why here, at Haven Point, with a girl you barely know? Because you don't know me, Liam, not really."

Liam's mouth went dry. He thought about the implications of the dream that woke him before he followed her to the beach. God, how he'd lusted for the sight of her in their marriage bed...! "I might not know you, Eleanor Thompson," he said, "but I've seen things about you. About us. Like with Conall's spirit, or with my vision of the shipwreck, I just know." He coughed self-consciously. "Only don't be after telling anyone. 'Tis a private thing."

"I won't tell, I promise," she told him. "What exactly *did* you see?"

"Never mind," he muttered, shuffling his feet. The last thing he wanted was to share the lurid details of his dream.

Eleanor continued to row steadily. "The truth is, Liam, you frightened me. I've never even been kissed before, not once," she said.

"Never kissed?" he said, incredulous. "Why, are the men in Grand Marais blind or something?"

A smile tugged at Eleanor's lips. "You'd have to ask them, I guess." The smile vanished. "You shouldn't have asked me to compromise myself as you did. Even if I'd wanted to, it would have cheated both of us." She hesitated before saying, "I'm not like those girls the sailors visit in the ports of call."

Liam's mouth fell open. *How did she know—?*

"So it *is* true," she said, a fleeting look of hurt passing over her face. "Lars warned me about that, about the sailors and their, um, 'ladies of the night.'"

"He did, did he?" This news confirmed Liam's own suspicions about the Swede's attachment to Eleanor. "And what business is it of his, or anyone else?"

"I don't condemn you for what you've done. As you said before, I know very little of the world. But I cannot plant my affections so easily, especially with a man who pays women for—for those kinds of things."

"Och, you make it all too complicated. I've no notion of tomorrow, or what will happen to the both of us. I just want to be with you, and can I help it if I want to put my hands on you? Or kiss you, as I want to right now?"

Now it was Eleanor's turn to blush. "When you talk that way I can't think, when you look at me like that I just plain forget all the important plans I've made!"

"You must tell them to me, then, for pity's sake! I'm no reader of minds!"

"I'll do better than that, I'll show you!"

The protected cove was situated at the mouth of a shallow, tree-lined river. The beach extended inland a hundred feet from the shoreline. "This is the land I intend to purchase once I've saved enough money," Eleanor announced, raising the oars from the water. "This is where I am going to build my future business on the North Shore."

Liam examined the beach. Aside from the sheltered waters he found it unremarkable. "What do you see, girleen?"

"A lodge. My lodge. A place for travelers to rest on their journey. My hope is that it might serve as a destination for travelers from Duluth, or even St. Paul and Minneapolis." Eleanor stared longingly at the shore. "People will come, Liam. I just know it."

Liam rubbed his chin. "But so far in the wilderness? 'Tis true that city folk long for fresh air and solitude, but with only the boat traffic during the shipping season—"

"You forget the stage route, Liam. One day there'll be a real road cutting through the north woods. We might even see motorcars as far north as Grand Marais."

"Well, 'tis a grand idea, girleen. But running a lodge 'twill mean a great deal of work. Even for someone with your energy and talents," Liam added with a smile.

"I'll figure that out after I've purchased the property. The asking price for the land is three-hundred and fifty dollars."

"Three-fifty!" Liam exclaimed. "It might be years before you can afford it."

"I'm less than fifty dollars short that amount. I've been saving for quite a while, you see."

Liam nodded, suitably impressed. "Everything seems to be going to plan, then."

"It should be, but time has grown short, I'm afraid. Mama is threatening to send me to live with my Aunt Regina in St. Paul if I can't come up with the purchase price by next summer." Defiance glowed in Eleanor's eyes. "I'll work my fingers bloody before that happens." She took the oars then, and began rowing toward the open lake. "We'd better get moving," she said. "There's still a half a mile to go until we reach Little Nesna."

The Norwegian fishery was little more than an odd collection of log and tar-paper shacks hunkered along the frozen shore. Three sturdy boats perched atop wood-rung slides. Ice entombed the twin docks. Beyond the dock stood two A-frame sheds, so flimsily constructed they looked as though the oars propped along their sides were the only things holding them upright. Smoke drifted from the chimney pipe of the nearby cabin. A layer of snow covered empty boxes, unused barrels, and several four-sided net reels. Bulging, hundred-weight herring sacks lay piled near the foot of the dock.

One of the fishermen emerged from the cabin. He was young and blonde, a giant with square shoulders and a rambling stride. "Hello, hello!" he called, waving as Eleanor eased the boat alongside the dock. More men appeared, dressed in wool and flannel, so similar in appearance Liam guessed they were members of the same family. They were clean-shaven and bright-eyed, with hair like burnished gold.

The men gathered at the dock. "Grab the line!" Eleanor called, tossing out the bow rope. Nils Finnesgaard secured the skiff while Eleanor shipped the oars.

"Miss Thompson, I see you have brought a friend," Nils said. He smiled and nodded at Liam, who returned the nod impassively. Liam studied Nils, trying to gauge the type of man he was. Nils had a humorous, good-natured face that also managed to convey a sense of hidden strength. Liam felt himself relax a little: this was a man after his own heart.

Eleanor lifted the laundry basket from the boat and then handed it up to one of the fishermen. Another fisherman gave her a hand out of the boat. Liam climbed to the dock unaided, grateful for the solid, reassuring feel beneath his feet. Nils approached Liam with an outstretched hand. "Nils Finnesgaard, and welcome to Little Nesna. These are my companions: Jens and Johan Svarre, my cousin, Sollie Pedersen, Gustav Mindstrom, and our cook, Karl Skadberg."

"Liam MacLann." He politely shook hands with each man.

"It's good to see you all again," Eleanor said with genuine warmth. "I apologize for the lateness of my return. The storm—"

"*Jah*, she was a bad one," Nils agreed. "We lost equipment, lost some of my best nets. The roof collapsed in the fish house, and we spent the whole week boarding it over. But enough of that. Come, come, we have just put the coffee on. You must tell us the news from Haven Point."

The cabin was a simple affair, with woodstove, table and chairs, bunks for six, and an odd collection of miscellany hanging on the walls. Liam was enveloped by the cozy interior smells: freshly brewed coffee, smoke from the stove, pine pitch from the wood box. His eyes sharpened on several bottles of whiskey, arranged neatly on the shelf.

Nils pulled out two chairs from the table. "How is your family, Miss Thompson? No problems since the big blow?"

"Everyone is well, thank you," Eleanor replied as she and Liam took their seats. "We lost our dock and boathouse, unfortunately." She glanced across the table to Liam. "Other things were lost as well."

Nils, sitting opposite Eleanor, nodded gravely. "There was a wreck out on the lake, we know. The *William Dorn*. Some pieces of the ship floated ashore the day after—"

"What?" Liam interrupted. "What did you find?"

"You were on that ship?" Nils asked. Liam nodded, and Nils spoke a rapid stream of Norwegian to Johan and Sollie, who immediately went outside. Gustav brought cups of coffee for Eleanor and Liam.

Awkward silence filled the room until the men returned. "I found these the morning we went to look at the fish house," Sollie explained. He was older and heavier-built than the others, with permanent smile lines creased at the corners of his eyes. "First the life ring, then the rest. So very little." With reverence he placed the life ring in Liam's lap.

"*William A. Dorn*," Liam whispered, running his fingers along the black letters printed on the canvas surface. "What else did you find?" he asked.

Now it was Johan's turn to step forward. "Bits and pieces." He emptied the box of salvage onto the table top. "Part of a wooden chair. A medicine bottle. A broken plate. A shaving brush. A pair of spectacles."

Liam touched the twisted, dirtied eyeglasses, amazed that both lenses were still intact. He lifted them to the daylight filtering through the cabin window. "I know the man who wore these," he said. "'Twas Chief Engineer Allen Wright, God have mercy on his soul."

Liam felt Sollie's hand clasp his shoulder. "There's more. Bigger pieces of the ship, a short distance down the beach. You should have a look before you leave."

"I'm obliged to you," Liam said in a choked whisper. He stared at the flotsam and jetsam before covering his face with his hands.

"Give the man a shot of whiskey," Nils said. Liam looked up and accepted the glass in silence.

"Were there any bodies?" Eleanor asked.

"No, we have found none." Nils added more whiskey to Liam's glass. "You were the only one that lived?"

"Aye, I think so." Liam tipped the cup to his lips again and grimaced at the trail of heat that drained down his throat.

"Then your life is your own to live," Nils said as he settled back in his chair. "In Norway, the fishing folk say that the man who lives where all others were lost is hallowed, sanctified. A second chance. Don't waste it, MacLann."

"I don't think he intends to," Eleanor said. She spoke to Nils, asking, "Are you all returning next April?"

This brought a collective grunt from the men. "Except for Gustav," Nils replied. "He's leaving us for a regular job in Duluth."

"I've had enough of the Big Lake. I quit now, before she becomes the end of me," Gustav said. He held out his scarred hands. "What else can a fisherman do, when he's lost his love of the sea?"

Conversation ebbed and flowed around Liam, but he didn't listen. Gustav's question echoed in his thoughts. Had he lost his nerve as well? What kind of man could he count himself, he, Liam Joseph MacLann, a proud mariner who'd ridden in the prow of his father's *curragh* even before he was old enough to walk?

It was a question he dare not answer for himself just yet.

*   *   *   *

On their return trip to Haven Point, Eleanor felt the weight of Liam's silence. He refused to look at her, seeming distracted as he held the glasses and life ring in his lap. The wind had come up a little, causing the waves to make a slapping noise against the hull. The boat breached one of the crests, and she heard him gasp out loud.

"Is everything all right, Liam?"

"Och, no." He looked straight at her, and she was startled by the raw fear in his eyes. "'Tis the water, the waves."

Eleanor slowed her rowing. "You're frightened, aren't you? Because of the wreck."

Liam nodded. "It's been a whole week, but to me it feels like yesterday." He closed his eyes and swallowed. "I should be down there with the rest of 'em: Nick, Tom, Ransom, Captain Graling, the whole crew. 'Twas only the chance of my coming on deck as what saved my life. That and being hauled into the life-raft by Nathaniel."

"I think Nils was right, Liam, when he said you survived for a reason. Nothing happens by accident. But I understand why you feel as you do. It must all be very unsettling."

"Aye, in spades," he muttered as Eleanor increased her pull on the oars. Gliding past the entrance to her cove, Liam asked, "Tell me, girleen, why does your mother want so badly to send you away to St. Paul?"

"Her pride, I suppose. Mama was once in love with my Uncle Casey, before she ever met Papa."

"How was that so?"

"Uncle Casey was a lumberjack at my grandfather's logging camp. Casey worked there before he began law school in St. Paul. He married Mama's sister, Regina, instead. Now Casey is a man of wealth and importance, while Papa barely ekes out a living here in the wilderness. I think Mama wishes she'd married Casey instead."

"But life is good here, aye? Your father seems contented."

"He is," Eleanor agreed. "I love the north too, the trees, the lake. I can't really imagine living anywhere else."

"What has it been like, girleen, growing up at the light station all these years?"

"It was very lonesome, sometimes, especially when I was a girl. But there was always something to do and places to explore. I was quite the wild child; some days I'd disappear in the woods from breakfast to supper time. Climbing trees, gathering wildflowers, catching frogs, swimming in Superior." Eleanor chuckled. "It took quite a lot of starch and temper for Mama to mold me into her idea of a young lady."

"But I still don't understand why your mother is so unhappy. She ought to feel proud of you and the hard work you do."

"I think that, in her heart, Mama wants to dress up and parade around town in an expensive carriage just like Aunt Regina. And if she can't, then I suppose I must, for her sake." Eleanor shook her head. "It will never happen."

"I can't see you anywhere but here, girleen. 'Tis in your face, your eyes, that wildness you must have had as a child. It's a part of your soul, sure."

Eleanor blushed at his words. She saw something in Liam's eyes, something which caught her breath. Liam cared about her, was genuinely interested in her. Not just because he thought her desirable, but because of who she was and what she valued.

She thought about their argument prior to the *Amaranth*'s arrival. Anger she could deal with, but his passion had been another matter. His desire threatened to overwhelm her, and she realized she'd run from him out of fear. Fear of giving him what he had demanded, fear of wanting it just as badly for herself.

She redoubled her rowing. Haven Point and the refuge of home beckoned. A place of safety where confused emotions could be sorted out in peace. The assurance of this drew her more strongly than any possible alliance with Liam MacLann.

CHAPTER 10

▼

Lars met the skiff at the edge of the ice field. "There's hell to pay at the house, Eleanor," Lars warned as he grabbed the line. "Your mother has moved Liam out of the house."

"What?" Eleanor cried, as she and Liam disembarked. "Why?"

"It all started with an argument between your parents at the dinner table," Lars said. "Seems Adeline disapproves of all the time you two have been spending alone together. She was yelling something about 'indecency' and 'strangers taking advantage of her hospitality and goodwill.' She made us move Liam's bed to the spare room in my house, and that's where he's going to stay until the *America* comes next week."

Eleanor, upset at her mother's decision, was about to march up to the house when she caught the look of exhaustion on Liam's face.

"Liam," she murmured, moving quickly to his side and looping an arm around his waist. He leaned heavily against her as they continued across the ice. Lars paused to watch them, and then renewed his efforts with a violent tug on the line.

When they'd forded the beach, Liam begged for a rest. Eleanor peered into his pain-etched face. "I'm so sorry, Liam. I'll get Mama to change her mind, don't worry."

"No," Liam said. "I won't stay where I'm not welcome."

Eleanor made an appeal to Lars. "You can help me to change her mind, Lars."

"I don't know, Eleanor. Maybe it's for the best if Liam bunks at my place for a while. I'll be glad to have his company."

Eleanor fumed in silence all the way up to the house. David was in the yard building a snow fort. He paused and yelled out a greeting and waved as the three adults approached. John was at the woodpile chopping the remains of the fallen oak.

Eleanor sought him out. "Papa, how could you allow this?"

John set the axe aside. "You know how sensitive your mother is about strangers, Eleanor. It's not that I don't like Liam. I think he's a fine fellow. But, in the meantime, I think it's best if he stays with Lars."

"I care for him, Papa," Eleanor said. "I just want to make certain he's going to be all right."

"I know, I know. You've done your best taking care of him, and you're worried about his injuries. It's not hard to see why. But before you think about running off with Liam or doing something equally foolish, remember your mother and I only want what's best for you. You will remember that, won't you, Eleanor?"

Eleanor hesitated before answering, "Yes, Papa, I promise. But I still hate the way Mama acts toward Liam."

The back door opened just then, and Adeline called, "Mr. MacLann, I'd like a private word with you."

Eleanor made to follow after Liam, ready to intervene on his behalf, but Lars stopped her. "Let your mother have her say, Eleanor, and be done with it."

Eleanor brushed past Lars and quietly entered the house through the front door. She stood in the entry and listened to Adeline, whose clipped tone was painfully familiar to Eleanor. "Mr. MacLann, when we rescued you from the beach the night of the storm and brought you in as our guest, it was done with an open heart and in the spirit of charity. We've offered you hearth and home in the hopes it would help in your recovery. Since that time, however, you've done precious little to warrant the trust we placed in you, and in fact have done everything in your power to earn my contempt. Lars mentioned to me that he saw you follow Eleanor to the beach last night, and I can well imagine what the two of you were doing down there together."

"What happened between us is our business alone," Liam said, his voice thick with resentment.

"That's precisely my point. It not only affects the two of you, it affects my family and the plans I've laid for Eleanor's future. It is my intention she become acquainted with an eligible young gentleman, someone who can afford her the best advantages when she settles into the role of wife and mother—"

"I'm not proposing marriage, if that's what you think!" Liam growled. Eleanor closed her eyes, horrified to be the topic of such indelicate conversation.

"That can hardly be what I think, Mr. MacLann. The matter is out of your hands. You may join us for the noon meal each day, if you wish, but beyond that I must insist you stay your distance from Eleanor." There was a pause, and Eleanor envisioned Adeline's righteous smirk. "Do I make myself clear?"

"Aye, clear enough. You're a stone-hearted woman, Mrs. Thompson."

"It's a pity you see me that way. I'm only a mother who cares for her daughter's happiness."

Suddenly there was the scuffling of feet. "Oh, and would you be saying these things to me if I weren't a penniless sailor, and an Irish-Catholic to boot!"

"Think what you like, Mr. MacLann. One way or the other, you will never be acceptable to Eleanor."

*   *   *   *

A weary Liam crawled into bed immediately after he entered Lars' house. He was in a state of near-collapse after the unnerving trip to Little Nesna and his confrontation with Adeline. Restless dreams troubled him throughout the afternoon, of his shipmates, of the wreck, of Conall in the grave.

When Liam awoke it was past nightfall. The house felt cold and unearthly quiet, and for a moment he panicked, thinking he'd been abandoned. But, as he went to the window, he caught a flash of sweeping light, and he guessed that Lars was on his watch at the tower.

Liam put on coat and boots and then went to the tower in search of the assistant keeper. He found Lars at work on the lantern deck. "Sleep well?" Lars asked as he descended the ladder to join him.

"No, not really." Liam peered upward at the rotating lens. Brilliant and massive, it turned with unexpected gracefulness. "How does it work?" he asked with a nod toward the apparatus.

"The kerosene is vaporized as it passes over the Bunsen flame, then drawn up into the mantle where it incandesces. The light is pure white in color, visible for at least twenty miles."

"How does it rotate?"

"A series of counterweights, which we wind by hand every two hours. Kind of like the workings of a giant grandfather's clock, if you think about it."

"And the light flashes every ten seconds, without fail?"

"It better. As you know, the reefs off Haven Point are very dangerous."

Liam considered the enormous lens. "Many times I spied this light from the decks of the freighters I sailed on."

"Do you think you'll sign aboard a new steamship in the spring?"

"That's my plan. But only if I can work up the nerve."

"It won't be easy," Lars said, and then motioned Liam to follow him. "Let's go down and sit on the annex steps for a while. There's a fine set of stars out tonight."

The night air was cold but tolerable. Both men sat on the steps without speaking for a long while, for which Liam was grateful.

Lars tilted his head back and scanned the clear night sky. "A jeweled crown for the queen," he said.

"What do you mean by that?"

"It was something Eleanor said to me once. That the lake was the queen of the northlands," Lars replied. "I sometimes think Eleanor knows more than anyone gives her credit for."

Liam gathered his courage for the next question. "You're in love with her, then?"

Lars stiffened, and Liam steeled himself for whatever confrontation might follow. But then all the tension seemed to drain from Lars.

"She doesn't know, and I've never told her. To her I'm just nice, friendly old Lars. She's never looked at me the way she looks at you," he added grudgingly.

"I only came into her life a week ago."

"I know. And I've had five years, and so what was I waiting for, right? Well, as you know, her mother is a very protective woman. Adeline took me aside one afternoon not long after I taught Eleanor how to row the skiff. She told me I was a man with no future, with nothing to offer a girl like Eleanor. She told me to back away." Lars sighed. "I didn't have the guts to fight her on it."

Liam nodded, thinking of their similarities. "And what of Eleanor herself?"

"Hard to say," Lars said as he stood and stared out over Superior. "I don't know if any man can make her happy." He offered Liam a hand and pulled him upright. "You're welcome to stay on watch with me as long as you like."

"I'll keep your company, then. And thanks."

A week crawled by, colorless and difficult. Battle-lines had been drawn, emphasized by lengthy silences at the dinner table and by the fact that Liam made any excuse to quickly absent himself from the Thompson household. For Eleanor, her entire day began to revolve around the twenty minutes when she and Liam shared the noon meal, cast eyes on one another, breathed the same air.

She'd spoken barely a dozen words to her mother since Liam's ejection. Adeline continued as usual, seeming particularly occupied with the task of packing their travel trunks for the fast-approaching moving day.

The only news of Liam came to Eleanor through David, who often sought the company of the two bachelor men. Eleanor watched through the window each afternoon as the three companions set out on tramps through the woods with hunting rifles in hand.

A snow storm descended over Haven Point the day before the *America* was slated to arrive. Snow fell fast and furious, though no breeze stirred the clumps of wet flakes. The hunting trip that day was postponed, and David sulked around the house, acting cross and irritable. He picked on Bridget relentlessly, as he often did when bored.

Their bickering continued through the early part of the afternoon, until Eleanor could stand it no longer. She'd bundled up and was about to leave for the light tower when there came a loud knock at the door.

John, who sat filling out the daily log book, leaned round from his desk in the dining room. "Now, who do you suppose that is?"

More knocking, firm and insistent. Adeline and the children emerged from the kitchen just as John opened the door. Two men came inside, their coats covered in snow. The sounds of barking dogs filtered in from the yard. Peering outside, Eleanor saw a dog team and sled near the tower annex.

Both visitors stomped their boots on the entryway rug. "Bless you for a king of a man!" the taller of the two men exclaimed. "Thought maybe we'd made the trip for nothing, until we saw the smoke in your chimney!"

The taller of the two pulled his brown leather gloves from his hands one finger at a time. "Devil of a time making it up here, with this rotten weather, but nobody beats Fairfax to a story!" He removed his beaver hat and wool muffler to reveal slick dark hair and a boyish face graced by a fashionable mustache.

"Allow me to introduce myself. I am Hudson Fairfax from the *Duluth News-Tribune*, and this is my photographer, Jim Collins." Jim, a blonde-haired man with ruddy cheeks, smiled and nodded and then began shrugging out of his coat. "We've just arrived by dog sled in search of an interview with Liam MacLann."

John extended his hand in greeting. "Keeper Thompson, and welcome to Haven Point Light Station." John glanced at Eleanor, who stood beside the door, still dressed in her coat. "I'll send my daughter to fetch Mr. MacLann. Why don't you gentlemen make yourselves comfortable while we wait?"

"Marvelous idea," Hudson said. At a nod from her father, Eleanor went off on her errand, eager for the chance to talk to Liam.

Lars answered their door. "Whose dog team is that?"

"Come to the house at once, both of you!" Eleanor exclaimed. "Two reporters from Duluth have arrived to interview Liam!"

Liam poked his head over Lars' shoulder and asked, "Why are they after talking to me, now?"

"The reporter didn't say. It must have something to do with the *Dorn*."

"Why the big rush on getting my story?" Liam said with a scowl. "I'll go to the Zenith Steamship offices and tell 'em what they want to know, but the death of my shipmates is no commodity for strangers to bandy with!"

"I think you should talk to them, Liam. They've traveled a very long distance to see you."

Liam hesitated, then said, "I suppose I might." Both men disappeared inside the house and then came out a few minutes later in their coats and boots. The air rang with the dogs' excited barking as Lars went over to have a look at them.

Liam gently laid a hand on Eleanor's shoulder. "I've been missing you, girleen," he confided.

"I've been missing you, too." Precious seconds were flying by, and Eleanor wanted nothing more than to talk with Liam about her thoughts and feelings. But their brief moment of privacy ended at the steps to the front door.

Everyone was seated at the dining room table. Adeline emerged from the kitchen with a pot of fresh coffee and a half-empty pan of chocolate cake. Hudson rose from his chair when Liam and Eleanor walked in. "Hudson Fairfax of the *Duluth News-Tribune*. I'm pleased to meet you, Mr. MacLann," he said, vigorously pumping Liam's good hand. "Just the man I imagined, from Captain Krenshaw's description. Now, have a seat. I'd like to ask you a few questions regarding the wreck of the *William A. Dorn*."

Both men sat down, and Adeline poured the coffee while Bridget served up portions of cake. Lars came inside and joined the group at the table. Hudson took a sip of coffee before beginning. "We arrived by train in Two Harbors the night before last, then hired a dog team to carry us overland to Haven Point. The snow on the stage route is packed solid, and we made splendid time. I know for a fact that at least one reporter from the *Duluth Daily News* is close on my heels, though he doesn't have my resources." Hudson grinned. "My commission will be double if we get the story into print first."

"What makes you think I'll tell you anything?" Liam asked, suspicion edging his voice.

"Mr. MacLann, I'm prepared to offer you thirty dollars for exclusive rights to your story."

Liam's bluster vanished. "Thirty dollars?" he said. "Thirty. Aye, that'd pay for my passage south on the *America* and then some." He stared at his hands for a long moment. "All right then, you'll get your story. But if you misrepresent anything I say, I'll find you myself and bloody that uppity nose of yours."

A shadow fell across Hudson's face. "Nothing of the sort will happen, I assure you."

Liam straightened up in his chair. "Well, then, let's begin."

The snow had ceased by the time the interview wound towards its conclusion. Liam had given every detail, including his rescue by Eleanor on the beach. Hudson wrote in furious shorthand while the photographer tinkered with his thawing camera equipment. "In your opinion, Mr. MacLann, what caused the wreck of the *William Dorn*?" Hudson asked.

"The waves tore the ship apart. We shouldn't have been out on the lake in that boiling mess of a storm."

"Then you don't believe it was negligence on the part of the captain, Edward Graling?"

"Not in any way, and whoever says so is a damned liar."

"Isn't it true, Mr. MacLann, that Captain Graling had a penchant for overloading his cargo holds?"

"What master didn't? They were all expected to ride heavy, to increase the company's profits."

"Hmm." More scratching of lead against paper. "Now, explain to me again why the *Dorn* didn't stay in Duluth harbor when the gale warning flags were raised."

"I told you already, all was clear when we sailed. Captain Graling had no mystical ability to see into the future, any more than the other ships' captains whose boats were damaged in the blow!"

"Calm down, MacLann." Hudson shoved the pencil behind his ear. "The reason I ask is because I heard a rumor that the company is planning to pin this one on the captain. Zenith Steam is looking for any excuse to lay responsibility elsewhere, because of possible lawsuits from the victim's families. I think it important to get your side of the story, since you were the only person who was actually there."

Liam pounded the table with his fist, making the dishware jump. "Zenith Steam can go to blazes if they think Graling was to blame! If anything, it's the bloody LCA's fault, extending the season like they did!"

"Gentlemen, gentlemen," John said, holding up his hands. "No harm was meant. The storm was an act of nature and nothing more, and it's a tragedy that lives and property were lost. We can't change what's happened, and no one is responsible."

Hudson twitched his mustache dismissively. "Getting back to your story, MacLann—there's one part I still don't understand. How did Miss Thompson know you were on the shore? I mean, it was past sunset when you made landfall, with the storm still raging at full tilt, was it not?"

All eyes shifted to Eleanor, who shrunk in her seat. "I—I'd rather not say," she stammered. She glanced at Liam, who had a warning look in his eyes.

"Come now, Miss Thompson," Hudson prompted. "Your actions show you to be a heroine, risking your life to run down to the beach. My lady readers will want to know what drove you to leave the safety of your home."

"I had my reasons, Mr. Fairfax, none of which would make sense to you or anyone else."

"Don't be cryptic, Miss," Hudson insisted. "Can't you elaborate?"

"Impossible. It is a private matter between Mr. MacLann and myself."

Inspiration animated the reporter's face. "Oh, I see! 'Two Hearts Joined by the Hand of Fate! Sailor Plucked from the Jaws of Death by Dashing Mistress of the Lighthouse!' What a headline it would make!"

Adeline shook her head in distress. "No, no, I think you go too far—"

"Wait, wait; a picture! Yes, a photograph of the two young people, down on the beach where she found him." Hudson stood and nodded for the photographer to follow.

Adeline glared at John. "No harm, wife," he said.

The small party waded through the fresh snow to the shore. "Ah, perfect! This will really set the scene!" Hudson exulted.

While Jim unfolded his tri-pod camera, Hudson stood back and framed the shot. "That must be the place where you found him, right beside the skiff. Now, I want you to stand side by side." He pushed Liam and Eleanor shoulder to shoulder.

"This'll take just a minute," Jim explained as he adjusted the lens.

With their shoulders touching, Liam leaned to Eleanor's ear and whispered, "How beautiful you are to me right now, girleen, how fine, how grand, the best girl I've ever known—"

"Hold it! Look at the camera!" Jim interrupted. The shutter clicked, and then Hudson rubbed his hands together. "Another, this time with the board you salvaged from the life-raft."

Eleanor held one end while Hudson placed the other in Liam's good hand. "Wonderful. That'll be all," he pronounced after Jim snapped the picture. Hudson reached inside his coat pocket and withdrew a roll of crisp bills. "I appreciate your cooperation, Mr. MacLann, and wish you luck in your future endeavors."

"Just remember what I said. Tell the truth, or you'll regret it." Hudson waved Liam aside as he went to help Jim repack the camera.

"We're off now," Hudson declared when the sled was ready. "Our plan is to reach the town of Schroeder before nightfall. Hopefully, the story will be printed in the *News-Tribune* Sunday edition." He smiled at Liam. "Say, I'll mail you a copy, if you like."

Liam rummaged in his trouser pocket and pulled out the wrinkled paper bearing Shamus O'Rourke's address. "Send it here. I'll catch up with it, sometime."

The Thompsons' belongings were packed and everything was ready for the *America*'s arrival. That night, December the 13th, marked the last that the beacon would flash for the 1905 shipping season. When the steamship dropped anchor at noon the following day, Haven Point Light Station would be officially closed.

Eleanor lay beneath her blankets in the darkness and stared out the window, agonizing over whether or not to make a final visit to the shore. The house was so still that she could hear the tick of the clock down in the dining room. The sound was a torment, for with each hour that passed, her and Liam's separation drew nearer.

Since the reporters' departure, Eleanor had closeted herself in her bedroom, refusing supper. Her thoughts revolved obsessively around Liam. What would happen to him when they parted ways? Who would make sure he was getting enough to eat and was resting properly?

Eleanor sat up in her bed and gazed across at her sleeping sister. A tide of resentment welled inside Eleanor; all her life she'd put other people's needs ahead of her own. Taking care of the twins, doing her mother's bidding, working long hours at both the Grand Hotel and for the Norwegian fishermen. Once, just once, couldn't she claim something for herself? True, the lodge at the cove would one day belong to her, but this new need went deeper, was more primal, somehow. Eleanor craved an emotional connection with Liam that tore the hazy veil of physical desire. She belonged to him, and he to her.

A tear trickled down her cheek at the realization. Her pain was so palpable, she had to stifle a sob.

Misery, ache, desolation. Unable to change what was going to happen, she rose from her bed and dressed in silence.

She would seek comfort from Superior.

Eleanor slowed when she saw someone standing at the frozen shore, and for a moment she faltered, caught in the grip of uncertainty.

"Eleanor!" Liam called to her. Joyfully, she crossed the beach and was soon enfolded inside the warmth of his jacket. "I prayed you would come," he told her. "I would have waited 'til the dawn."

"Liam," she said, placing a finger on his lips. "Liam, I want to come with you to Duluth or wherever you're planning to go. I can't leave you, Liam."

He stared at her in the gloom. "'Tis not possible, girleen. The truth is, I can't support you, not with these injuries. I've money enough to live on through the winter, but not for the two of us."

"But I can work," she argued. "I can do housecleaning, find a position at a factory, anything, just as long as we can be together—"

"No." Liam's tone was firm. "For one thing 'twould mean abandoning your dream for the lodge on the cove. And for another, 'twould be a disservice to your family. Though I've no love for your mother, I hold a great deal of respect for your father."

"Don't you want me to come?" she asked, her lower lip trembling.

"Want you? Jesus, more than anything!" He pulled her closer. "But I could never hurt you, Eleanor, or take from you what isn't mine. You were right before, when you said 'twould be cheating us both."

She turned from him. "This is it, then. There's nothing between us."

"No. You're mistaken." Liam gently drew her around, and when she looked at him there was only tenderness in his eyes. "I will come back, someday. When the time is right, I will return." He reached inside his coat pocket and withdrew his St. Brendan's medal. "I want to give you something to remember me by, to remember my promise. It's not much, but it's all I have."

"You should not, Liam," she said as he strung it around her neck. "It's from your sister, your only connection with home."

"'Tis nothing compared to your value and worth, and all I want to give to you, my darling girl." He gave her a final kiss. "Promise me that you'll not forget."

She rested her face against his chest. "It will be as you say, Liam MacLann."

CHAPTER 11

▼

The winter solstice came and went, the sun traveling in a low arc from one near horizon to the other. Winter was a mean business in the northlands. Mornings crackled with cold so intense that breath froze the moment it was exhaled; cutting winds howled down from the Canadian provinces without heed for geographical boundaries; snow grew so deep that it buried and erased all that was familiar. The north was a wasteland of snow and whiteness and cold.

Daily life fell into a new routine for the Thompsons after their arrival in Grand Marais. The house in town was reopened, the coal furnace cajoled to life, bed sheets washed and mattresses aired, the dust swept from each corner of the two-story dwelling. Gone were the long night watches and the vague insecurities over unforeseen storms; banished were the wrenching isolation and dependency on the tender ship for supplies.

John found work at the Cook County Manufacturing Company's sawmill, where he operated the gasoline-powered lathes. Adeline offered her services as seamstress, while Eleanor did housecleaning for several of the wealthier families in town, work which helped to fatten her savings for the cove. Bridget and David returned to public grade school, renewing friendships with children they'd not seen since the previous spring.

When Eleanor arrived home each afternoon, she kept a sharp eye open for the twice-weekly mail delivery. During the winter months, dog teams carried the mail by sled to the hamlets nestled along Lake Superior's shore. But no letters arrived with her name written across the front, and her hopefulness about Liam began to falter.

She'd passed along her address at their moment of parting on the deck of the *America*. Just as the gangway was lowered to the Grand Marais slip, Eleanor had gone to Liam and offered him a formal farewell. In full view of her mother, she'd clasped his hand in what seemed a mere gesture of friendship. "Goodbye and best wishes, Mr. MacLann," she said, as bright and cheerful as if he was nothing more than a fond acquaintance.

She'd pressed the folded paper into his palm, and he'd taken it, squeezing her hand before slipping the note inside his coat pocket. When Eleanor disembarked with her family, her last picture of Liam was that of a solitary man standing at the rail.

This image she cherished, yet his lack of contact jarred her. Didn't he care for her? Hadn't his true feelings been there in his touch, his glance, in the alertness that marked him whenever they were alone together? And, more importantly, in the promise given to her at the beach?

Her misgivings were compounded by a lack of social opportunities that winter. Most of her friends had either married or gone off to college, and Eleanor often found herself watching through the parlor window as sleighing parties of young people paraded up and down the snow-covered streets without her. Worse, her one-time best friend, Mari Lindquist, seemed to be snubbing her.

The reason for this became apparent one day near the end of January when Adeline returned from the post-office with a package in her arms. "What have you got there, Mama?" Eleanor asked as she followed Adeline into her parents' bedroom.

"A new project." Adeline unwrapped a bolt of pearl-white material and spread the shimmering fabric across the quilted blanket.

"A wedding dress?"

"What else?" Adeline replied. She ran her fingertips across the silky surface. "The Lindquists spared no expense."

"The Lindquists? Who's getting married?"

"Why, Mari, of course." Adeline glanced at Eleanor as she overlaid the white satin with lace for the veil. "I thought you knew."

Eleanor stood silent for a moment before asking, "Who's the lucky fellow?"

"Ernest Ulvestad. He accepted a position as clerk at the First National Bank in Duluth, beginning next week. Eloise Lindquist thinks it a brilliant match, and she speaks of little else at our ladies' meetings."

"Ernest Ulvestad?" Eleanor wrinkled her nose. "That boy who bullied everyone when we were all in school? I can't abide him, Mama!"

"Apparently Mari doesn't share your feelings. That's probably the reason she hasn't invited you over more often this winter." Adeline patted her daughter's arm. "Don't fret yourself, Eleanor. You'll outshine all your former classmates once you strike gold among the rich young bucks of St. Paul."

Eleanor stiffened. "Is that all I'm good for? A showpiece to attract the attentions of the highest bidder?"

"And why not? You're meant for a better life than this. I knew it from the day you were born," Adeline replied. "There's no advantage in this world for the impoverished. I saw enough of heartache and broken lives at the lumber camp."

Eleanor stared at Adeline, thinking, *She's ashamed of what I want to do with my life.* "What if I could prove to you otherwise?"

"Prove otherwise? You mean with that Irishman, don't you?" Adeline folded her arms. "As close a call as any I've had to contend with, worse even than that Swede—"

"You mean Lars?" Eleanor interrupted, her anger growing by the moment. "Just what are you implying, Mama?"

Adeline busied herself repacking the satin. "Don't act so innocent, Eleanor. We both know Lars was infatuated with you."

Though Eleanor knew this was the truth, still it galled her to hear her mother say so. "Lars was nothing more than a friend," Eleanor insisted.

"Believe what you like. Anyway, he'll not bother you again. Lars wrote to your father and mentioned that he's been courting a nice young girl. There might even be a wedding sometime this summer."

"So soon?" Eleanor found this news unreasonably upsetting. "Why, Lars has been down in Iowa for only a few months now."

"Consider him fortunate, Eleanor. And as far as your smitten sailor goes, you should be thanking me for the trouble I've saved you. You'd have had nothing but unhappiness from a man like that."

Eleanor jerked her chin. "You don't know everything! I could leave today and find Liam if I wished!"

"Truly?" Adeline said with a laugh. "And what kind of life could he offer you, hmm? He'd be gone for months at a time, sailing from one end of the Great Lakes to the other, and there you'd be, home alone in some port, probably with a baby to care for before the first year was out. Is that what you want for yourself? Because that's exactly what would happen!"

Eleanor, furious, went to the window and stared at the frozen harbor beyond. "Liam cares for me and will return as he promised." She turned to face Adeline. "And nothing will change my belief in him."

"I pity you, then, I really do. Weeks and months will pass, and you will never see him again. Why would he come back to Haven Point, after all? No work, no place to live, and certainly no welcome." Adeline spoke as though making a pronouncement on the dead. "Mark my words, Eleanor. Liam will never return."

*   *   *   *

"Get that Irish swine out of here! I'll not have him passed out on that table all night again!"

It was a late Friday night in Duluth, and the crowd inside Hanson's Saloon was as raucous as usual. Liam sat face down at a table in the corner. Rough hands grasped his elbows; he lifted his head and fixed bleary eyes to the right and then the left. It was the two eldest Hanson boys.

"Lay off, you horse's arse," Liam muttered, then reared, pitching the smaller of the two to the floor. Gerta Hanson came flying out from behind the bar, brandishing a long-handled broom. Her hair hung in greasy strands, and one of her front teeth was missing.

"Touch my Peder again and I'll bust you in the face, Liam MacLann!" Gerta said. She grabbed Peder by the arm. "Throw him out! His money ain't good here no more!"

At the mention of Liam's name, a head swiveled from the far end of the long bar. Shamus O'Rourke set down his pint of beer before calling out, "Pardon, ma'am, but did you say Liam MacLann?"

"Yes, I did." Gerta folded her beefy arms as her oxen-like offspring dragged Liam to the door. "And good riddance to him, no-good, drunken mick!"

Shamus jumped from his stool. "Stop!" he shouted, striding over to Peder. "Put him down. I'll vouch for him."

Peder glanced from Shamus to his mother. Gerta hemmed and hawed until Shamus reached into his pocket and fished out a coin. "That should cover everything," he told Gerta.

"Get the hell out, the both of you!" Gerta ordered before returning to her position behind the bar. Shamus bent to Liam's ear.

"Liam, 'tis your friend, Shamus O'Rourke." Shamus gently shook Liam by the shoulder. "Can you hear me, Liam? We're going for a bit of a walk, now."

Shamus. The name penetrated Liam's stupor and jostled his memory. "Shamus?" he croaked. "From the *Amaranth*?"

"Good, good, you're not too far gone." Shamus hauled Liam to his feet. "Up with you now, you great tree of a man. I'm taking you home."

When Liam awoke the next morning, he could not recall where he was or how he'd come to be there. The bed he was lying on undoubtedly belonged to a child, for his feet hung far off the end. There was another bed, shoved in the corner, and a crib. The room itself was cluttered and small.

Fly-blown wallpaper was peeling off the wall, there were brown water stains spread out along the ceiling, and the window pane was cracked. *Whoever lives here must be poor as church mice*, Liam thought.

Liam sat up and ran a hand over his face. His head pulsed, his stomach heaved, and he swallowed against the urge to vomit, the taste of raw whiskey scouring his mouth. *Whiskey.* Oh, aye, a shot would take the sting out of his suffering.

Liam, hunkered at the edge of the bed, rested his throbbing forehead in his hands. He remembered Gerta Hanson arguing with him over the second bottle, and the black look on her face when she finally set it on the table. Then there he sat, slamming down the contents one tumbler at a time, until he came to that blissful place where a man forgets all his troubles.

This was the worst bender he'd ever been on, he realized. But his nightmares about the wreck during the past week had been especially vivid and torturous.

More than anything he wanted to die. Drink would hasten his end, give him the release he craved.

But someone had reached out to him, had stopped his free-fall into squalor and self-pity. Liam recalled being dragged to the door, and then a voice had pierced his drunken fog. He recalled a kindly face with curly red hair and abundant freckles. Shamus? Liam smiled. Blessed Savior, his rescuer had been Shamus O'Rourke!

Liam crossed the hall to the washroom. After relieving himself he twisted the tap on the faucet and then dipped his hands for a cold drink of water. Liam splashed water on his face and neck and then groped for a towel. Using his pocket comb, he slicked down his straw-stack hair. He looked in the mirror and decided he was almost acceptable. At last he felt ready to find either Shamus or the woman of the house, Mrs. O'Rourke.

Liam made certain his footfalls on the stair were heavy enough to announce his arrival. Two mop-haired boys, four or five years of age, met him at the bottom step.

"And who are you?" Liam asked. "Lords of the realm?"

The tallest boy fixed steady brown eyes on Liam. "Sure, I'm the chieftain all right. I'm Flynn, and this is me brother Patrick." Patrick performed a short bow. "Baby Katie is with Mother."

"Where's your father?"

"He went out a while ago. Do you like tea?"

"What Irishman doesn't?" Liam answered with a smile. He felt immediately drawn to Shamus' young sons.

"Then come along. Mother's been waiting," Flynn said. Liam followed the children down the narrow hallway into the back kitchen.

A woman sat at a table in the center of the room. Overhead, a bare bulb hung from the cracked ceiling. The faucet dripped into the rust-stained sink, while the pungent odor of dirty diapers soaking in a pail met Liam's nose.

The woman had just finished feeding the baby, and was wiping her cheeks. "I'm Jennie O'Rourke," she said after placing little Katie on the floor. Jennie was short in stature and wore a plain homespun dress, with ginger red hair pulled tight into a knot.

"Pleased to make your acquaintance. I'm Liam MacLann."

"So I've heard. Shamus has told me a great deal about you. Sleep well?"

"Yes, ma'am," Liam replied. He rubbed his lips. "Have you got a bit of whiskey? I'm under the weather, you see—"

"Not a drop," Jennie said, her tone brisk. "Tea is the order of the day, Mr. MacLann. Have a seat."

Liam did as he was told, somewhat stung by her refusal. Jennie set a faded china cup before him and poured steaming tea from the tea pot. He inhaled its aroma before taking a sip. "Ah, how I have longed for such as this!" Liam said.

A smile curved Jennie's lips. "Orange Pekoe. My grandfather from Donegal sends it each month."

Flynn and Patrick had taken seats across from Liam and were watching him intently as he sipped the tea. "Where's Shamus now?" Liam asked.

"Shamus should be here any time," Jennie replied. "He's over at that hole you call a boarding house, to fetch your things."

"What?" Liam's cup clattered to the saucer. "And why the hell for?"

"Shamus has decided that you're to stay with us until ice-out."

Heat pulsed across Liam's face. "I call that a lot of nerve!"

"And I call that a helping hand! You'll never find the answers to your problems at the bottom of a whiskey bottle!"

Before Liam could object, Shamus appeared in the kitchen door. He dropped Liam's duffle bag to the floor with a resounding thud. "Good to see you awake,

Liam. As our guest, you can have use of the parlor sofa for sleeping on at night. I'll charge you no rent, though 'twould be much appreciated if you'd help with buying food."

Liam glared at Shamus. It rankled Liam that Shamus had done this without asking him first. "And if I refuse?" Liam challenged.

"Why, then, you can go back to relying on the good graces of Gerta Hanson!" This was said with a thin smile, but Liam knew that Shamus was serious.

Damn their logic, Liam thought, suppressing the urge to march out the door. His suffering was his own business, after all.

"Why not just stay?" Shamus asked, lifting Katie into his arms. "There's worse you could do."

True enough, Liam thought. He slumped in his chair, completely disarmed by the kindness of the O'Rourke's.

By evening, Liam was thinking with a clearer head. Jennie had served corned beef and cabbage soup for supper, satisfying both Liam's appetite and Irish spirit. They shared a long conversation, a comforting cadence about nothing in particular but which reminded Liam that he was again among his own.

Jennie was bathing the children in the upstairs tub when Shamus invited Liam onto the back porch for a smoke. Outside, the night was alive with the sounds of the city, the clip-clop of horse-drawn street traffic, the distant clang of the incline railway, dogs barking to one another. They stood in silence for a few minutes as they enjoyed the spectacle of the city at night.

"Fairest jewel of the Great Lakes, eh, boyo?" Shamus observed, flicking his ashes over the porch rail and into the snow.

"Duluth has no match," Liam agreed. "Buffalo and Cleveland might out-muscle her, but they're filthy beggars by comparison."

Shamus took a drag, the tip of his cigarette glowing orange in the darkness. "You're not overly resentful that I brought your things here, are you, Liam?"

"No, I suppose not. The truth is I needed a kick in the head."

"Tell me what happened."

Liam stared at the lights along the harbor. "When I arrived here in December, nothing seemed changed from the year before. I rented a room at the Union Boarding house, ate three square meals a day, saw the doctor about my arm and ribs and did little else. Week by week my bones healed and my toes got better, though they'll never be the same again. Other than that, I'm well and whole."

"But—?"

"Well, first there was the Board of Inquiry on the shipwreck, all those lawyers with their insulting questions and high-handed manners." Liam spat on the wooden porch floor. "Then there were the bad dreams. Some nights I was back aboard the *Dorn*, screaming to Charlie to free the lifeboat. Other times I watched as Nick and Ransom and my mates were covered with lake water as it poured into the engine room, Nicky begging me to save him. Some nights I awoke to find the ghost of my dead brother sitting beside me, saying nothing but just watching me."

"Och, aye. Any man would turn to drink from all that," Shamus said. "They never found anyone else alive, eh?"

"Not a one. No survivors, not even bodies, except for Nathaniel Klassen. 'Twas as if they all vanished without a trace."

"Tough, that," Shamus said, nodding grimly.

"But not the worst of it." Liam tossed his cigarette stub into the alley. "When I started dreaming of Eleanor, that's when I felt like my mind was slipping away."

"You mean that dark-haired colleen at the lighthouse, don't you?" he said, removing a newspaper clipping from his pocket and handing it to Liam.

Liam ran his fingers across the picture of him and Eleanor standing together. "The very one."

"Why not go to her, Liam, if you have it so hard?"

"Complications. The time isn't right." Liam stared at his boots. "I'm not ready to take on the responsibility of such a woman."

Shamus clapped a hand on Liam's back. "Let me give you a piece of advice; if you're waiting for just the proper moment, you'll be an old man before it comes. Pride can kill a man. I can't imagine my life without Jennie and the children. Nothing would keep me from that happiness."

Liam chuckled. "You're a persuasive fellow, O'Rourke. Maybe you could do the asking for me."

"No chance! 'Twas hard enough the first time with me own girl." Shamus opened the porch door for Liam. "Jennie and I want you to call this place home, until the ice breaks in April and you can sign aboard a new ship."

Liam nodded, deeply touched by Shamus' generosity. "Aye, I'll stay, if you can stand me. And thanks."

*   *   *   *

It was the near St. Valentine's Day when Eleanor finally received a letter, though it wasn't from Liam. The letter was addressed from her friend, Gracie, in Duluth.

Eleanor carried the letter home from the Mercantile, eager to read how Gracie had been faring over the winter. As Eleanor entered the house, she was surprised to find her mother absent, although the two younger children were already home from school. Eleanor removed her hat, muffler, coat, and mittens, and then gave her shoes a stomp on the entry rug.

"Eleanor, Eleanor, I have good news!" Bridget said, rushing up.

"Hello to you too, Bridget."

"Oh, well, hello," Bridget said as a second thought. "Anyway, we're doing a school play next month, *Little Women*, and I've been chosen to play the part of Jo." Bridget's eyes shone. "Isn't a wonderful? I've always wanted to be an actress."

"You'll be the best in the play, I'm certain of it," Eleanor said with an indulgent smile.

"Will you promise to help me practice my lines?"

"Of course. We can begin tonight, if you like." Eleanor frowned as she heard a hacking cough from the kitchen. "Is that David?"

"Yes. He's been like that since the noon bell at school." Bridget shook her head. "I told him to go straight to bed when we came home, but he won't listen to me."

"Where's Mama?"

"At Mrs. Lindquist's. I think they were going to discuss the bridesmaids' dresses or something. She said she'd be home before Papa arrives."

"I see." Eleanor went into the kitchen, where David sat drawing at the small round table. He looked up as Eleanor came inside, his face pale, a tell-tale rattle to his breathing.

"David, why aren't you in bed?"

"I've been working on something since this morning at school, and I wanted to finish it before you came home." David pushed the paper across the table. Eleanor bent to examine it. It was another of David's drawings, though this one was different than the others. It was a log structure, large and rambling, with many windows and a sweeping portico.

"It's your lodge, Eleanor," David said. "The one you've talked about building at the cove."

Eleanor gazed at the drawing, transfixed. Her eyes traced the strong lines, the romantic sweep. It was uncanny the way David's inner vision so nearly matched her own. "You did a wonderful job, David," Eleanor told him. "Just exactly as I imagined."

His cheeks pinked with pleasure at her compliment, but then he was seized by another coughing fit. "All right now," Eleanor said, "off to bed with you. I'm going to make you some honey tea and mix an onion and linseed oil compress for your chest."

"Do you have to? I hate the way those smell—"

"No refusals. Upstairs, young man," Eleanor said with an air of authority. After David left the room, Eleanor filled the tea-kettle and then stoked the wood-stove with kindling.

While waiting for the water to heat, Eleanor mixed milk, bread, onion and linseed oil together in a bowl on the stove. Only then did she take a few moments to open Gracie's letter.

It was a short note, as usual, though filled with interesting news. Gracie and Allison had taken new positions as housekeepers with a wealthy family in Duluth, just before Christmas. "Oh good," Eleanor murmured, relieved to finally hear some word of Allison, who hadn't written for some time now. Eleanor searched the letter for their new employer's name, but Gracie had forgotten to include it. Gracie went on to write about her latest beau, and had included a photograph taken shortly before she'd mailed the letter.

Eleanor gazed at Gracie's likeness, so much like the coveted Gibson girl image of the day: heart-shaped face, doe-eyes, upward-swept hair, lips like a small bow, and a gleam of mischief on her face. Eleanor smiled, recalling her friend's happy-go-lucky attitude toward life. She wished Allison had included a picture as well. Dear, loving, ethereal Allison. Eleanor had always felt protective toward Allison, who'd spent her childhood in a county orphanage.

Eleanor was returning the letter to the envelope when Bridget came inside. "The kettle's whistling," Bridget said.

Eleanor had been concentrating so intently on the letter that she hadn't heard the kettle's shrill call. "Take it off the stove while I get the tea," she told Bridget.

"Phew, what's that smell?" Bridget asked.

"A poultice for David. You know how easily his chest colds turn to pneumonia if we don't nip them in the bud." Eleanor happened to look out the kitchen window just then, and saw that it was starting to snow. "Why does this seem like the longest winter ever?"

"They always do. It's just that each summer we forget," Bridget answered. "Who knows? Maybe this time next year you'll be in St. Paul."

"Or on the cove with my lodge under construction." Eleanor showed Bridget the drawing. "David's drawings show real promise."

"I guess so, though he's still a pest at times." Then, much to Eleanor's surprise, Bridget gave her a hug.

"What was that for?" Eleanor said with a laugh.

"I'm going to miss you when you leave, wherever you go."

"I'll miss you too, though, hopefully, I won't be too far away. Now, fetch me some flannel for that poultice, and we'll bring it upstairs for our patient."

The creep of days slowed even more near the end of March, when an early spring storm dumped two feet of snow over Grand Marais. Arctic winds blasted the windows of the Thompson house. School was canceled and all work was delayed until the town roads were finally cleared.

This was followed a week later by the gift of an unseasonable thaw. Water dripped from the spiky icicles hanging from the eaves. Rivulets of melting snow turned the bare ground to mud. Blue jays hopped from leafless branch to leafless branch. Spring was coming, and the shipping lanes would be open soon.

Liam still had not written, causing Eleanor to waver between anger and uncertainty. Why had he turned his back on her? A simple letter would have been enough to set her at ease, even just a little note saying *"Everything is fine, still looking for work, I miss you."*

A host of winter-time illnesses had spread throughout Grand Marais. Had the same been true for Duluth? Had he contracted a winter cold or influenza? What if he were lying in some hospital, delirious with fever? The list of possibilities made Eleanor's time in Grand Marais pass with excruciating slowness.

As April neared, the Thompson family eagerly awaited the all-important letter from the Lighthouse Board, announcing the opening of the shipping lanes. Impatient to return to the lighthouse and resume his duties there, John grew more cross with every passing day.

John himself arrived home with the letter. Haven Point was scheduled to reopen on April 10th, while the *America* would arrive in Grand Marais on the 9th to ferry them southward to the light station.

"That's not much time," Adeline said after hearing the news from John. "I still have a few sewing projects to finish."

"Better get to it, then. The shipping fleets won't wait."

Eleanor touched her father's sleeve. "Papa, does it say anything about the new assistant keeper?"

"Yes. A fellow by the name of Cameron Russell, from Duluth. He'll arrive at Haven Point via the *Amaranth* on the 12th."

"Russell, Russell," Eleanor said, thinking. "Where have I heard that name before?"

"Maybe he's related to the Zenith Steamship Company owner, Sumner Russell," John said.

"I can't imagine that a company president's son would be sent to work at a lighthouse," Adeline remarked, withdrawing a shirtwaist from her sewing pile. "It must be someone else, surely."

"Well, he can be the King of Siam for all I care, as long as he does his job, though it beats me why the Board would send a city kid."

"It might be pleasant, actually, to have someone with a little polish and refinement for a change," Adeline said as she began to work the sewing machine treadle.

Eleanor took a seat at the kitchen table. She re-read the telegram and tried to imagine the new assistant keeper. Cameron Russell. What if he was indeed the son of the wealthy steamship company owner? A man like that might have a hard time adjusting to their rustic life at the light station.

Eleanor pushed the telegram aside. Her father was right; it mattered nothing at all, as long as Mr. Russell performed his duties and did his best to get along with her family.

CHAPTER 12

▼

When Liam awoke that morning, he felt especially tired and sluggish. From the sofa in the O'Rourke parlor, he heard the morning sounds coming from the kitchen: the rattle of a pot lid, the whistle of the kettle, and the boys' boisterous chatter. Outside the parlor window, the sky was a flat, unremitting gray, the same as it had been for the last several weeks. Liam slid from under the blankets to stretch the muscles in his arms and back, and then drew on his trousers and sweater.

Shamus descended the stairway, already dressed for work. "*Dia duit ar maidin,* good morning to you," Shamus said. He paused at the foot of the stairs. "Don't mind my saying, Liam, but you've looked better."

"Aye, and I've felt better too. Maybe it's the sickness or something, I don't know."

"The grippe has been going around, sure."

"I don't think it's that. It's the winter gloom. I just feel like I want to get out or get away."

"Ah now, you're no different than the rest of us. The winters in Boston were never so cursedly long." Shamus nodded toward the door. "Maybe you should go out and take a walk today, get some fresh air."

"Aye, maybe. Or maybe I should just leave altogether."

"Go back to Ireland, you mean?"

"No, I was thinking of Graceville. Though I miss Inishmore, sure and I do. The wind off the Atlantic, the smell of wild roses in my mother's garden." Liam's eyes grew distant. "I'll probably never see any of it again."

"Talk to Jennie. She's been missing Ireland something fierce of late."

Jennie came into the parlor just then. "I heard my name spoken. Is it some trouble I'm in?" she asked jokingly.

"No, Jennie darling, just a bit of talk about old Erin," Shamus answered. "Liam has the homesickness."

"Ah." Jennie turned her eyes on Liam. "I dream of Ireland too, Liam. But there's no sense in pining over something you can't have. Why not come into the kitchen for breakfast?"

"No thanks. I'm thinking I'll take that walk, after all."

Liam pulled on his boots, and then, as he was slipping into his coat, Jennie said, "Don't forget your hat and gloves. There's a stiff wind off the lake this morning."

"That's my Jennie, a regular mother hen," Shamus teased, though there was a note of appreciation in his voice as well. Liam gave them a nod before stepping out the door and descending the steps to the street below.

Liam wandered the frozen avenues for most of the morning. He passed by children in woolen coats on their way to school, past housewives on their way to the market, and day-laborers waiting to ride the incline railway. Liam kept his eyes fixed doggedly ahead, untouched by the humanity surrounding him. Dark thoughts plagued him; his hatred for winter, his guilt at living on the O'Rourke's charity, his own disgust at failing to write Eleanor. These thoughts carried him all the way downtown, where he found himself walking past old haunts, the boarding houses and taverns from his days before the shipwreck.

Liam paused before one of the places he often visited on shore leave, a bordello with red-fringed drapes hung at the window. Sally was the madam, a woman with a generous figure and coppery blonde hair.

Liam stood at the foot of the terra cotta steps that led up to the bordello's ornate wooden door. Sweat slicked his palms. It had been five months since he'd been with a woman; too long for a red-blooded fellow like himself. Maybe a tumble in the sheets would cure his malaise.

He was about to climb the steps when the door opened. A man staggered out, dressed in a black pea coat and a night-watch cap. He was obviously drunk, and, as he staggered down the steps, Liam caught the reek of tobacco and cheap perfume. Liam stepped away, revolted. *Oh, Christ*, he thought. *That could have been me.*

Liam broke into a fast walk, cursing himself. What a fool he'd been to come this way!

Liam paused in front of Hanson's Saloon. The door stood open, as if beckoning to him. Tobacco, whiskey, the sound of men talking. Liam's mouth watered. Jesus, how he needed to get drunk.

But then he remembered what Jennie had said about solving his problems with a whiskey bottle. Liam walked past the saloon entrance, moving faster and faster until he came full circle, arriving at the O'Rourke's row house.

Jennie, who was sweeping the front entry, startled at Liam's sudden appearance. She straightened her back with broom in hand. "Liam, you frightened me for a moment!" she told him. Liam said nothing, only stood staring at her. The cold had pierced his limbs, leaving him stiff and numb.

"Here, let me help you off with your things," Jennie said. She led Liam into the parlor and pulled up a chair for him beside the stove.

"I warned you not to stay out so long," she chided, stirring the fire with a metal poker before adding another scoop of coal. "There now, we'll thaw you out nicely."

"Where's Katie?"

"Asleep in her crib," Jennie replied. She frowned at the ceiling. "Though how she can rest through the noisy shenanigans of her brothers I'll never know." Jennie pulled up the other chair. "Where have you been all this long morning?"

"Here and there." Liam refused to meet her eyes. "Down to Superior Street, not far from where I used to board."

"Ah. That explains it," Jennie said as she settled back into her chair. "You've been fighting the lure of drink."

Liam grimaced. "I wanted to soak my head with whiskey, but I couldn't. Other things were bothering me worse than that."

"The thought of a woman?" Jennie shrewdly guessed.

Liam opened his mouth to speak, but then closed it as he nodded. "A sporting girl I used to visit, back when…" His voice trailed away as he squirmed in his seat. "Och, I shouldn't be talking to you about such things, Jennie girl!"

"Don't feel ashamed," Jennie said. "I know the temptations that face a sailor when he's far from home." She brushed a stray strand of hair from her face. "I trust Shamus with all my heart, but he is, after all, only a man."

Liam breathed a sigh of relief. Jennie had guessed, and taken pity on him despite his shortcomings. "Not that I really want to see Sally again, you understand, but I've been feeling so fidgety of late."

"What about that girl at the lighthouse? The one Shamus mentioned?"

"Eleanor? Sometimes I can't stop thinking about her, but then other times she seems so far away. It feels like a lifetime since I saw her."

"What does your heart tell you?"

"How am I to know?" Liam answered. "The only girl I ever courted was a shy colleen from the farm down the lane. So there's my childhood sweetheart, and then, well, the girls that know how to give a fellow what he wants for the right price. And Eleanor Thompson is a far cry from both, truth be told."

"What's she like, this Eleanor?"

"Kindly. Strong-willed. Tenderhearted." A smile lifted the corner of Liam's mouth. "And not too hard on the eyes, either."

"She sounds a fine girl, the kind you should settle down with. Does she have the same feelings for you?"

"I think so. I was supposed to write to her over the winter, but I haven't." Liam's smile vanished. "I just plain lost my nerve."

"Well, maybe it's not too late. You should write and let her know how much you've missed her."

Liam leaned closer to the stove. "But what do I say? I've never had a silver tongue."

"That part you'll have to figure out for yourself," Jennie said. "But remember, she's a lady, your Eleanor. Not a girl. Not a whore. A real woman."

Liam's gaze rested on Jennie. She reminded him of his sister Maeve, and not just because of her red hair. Jennie saw to the heart of things and was not afraid to say what needed to be said. "Shamus is a lucky man to have such a wise woman for his wife," he said, feeling a sincere affection for her.

"Shusha, now, save your charms for your sweetheart," Jennie scolded. "Just trust to tomorrow, and know that the answers will come."

Another week passed, and soon a buzz of excitement swept through Duluth. Shamus, returning home from the docks, made the big announcement. "The ice is breaking on the lake, Liam! The *Amaranth* sails tomorrow!"

Liam, sitting at the kitchen table, looked up from his newspaper. "Captain Krenshaw is fitting her out as we speak," Shamus explained, reaching for Jennie to dance her around the room. "No more clearing snow for a few miserable dollars! Isn't it great news, Liam?"

Liam was slow to answer. "Aye, 'tis grand." He stared at the floor for a moment before excusing himself.

Shamus and Jennie followed him into the parlor. "What's wrong, boyo?" Shamus asked. "Aren't you anxious for the work?"

Liam clenched his jaw and continued to stare out the window. Jennie nudged her husband and said, "Don't be after picking on him, Shamus. Think of all that poor Liam has been through."

"Oh, sorry. Sometimes I just plain forget about the *Dorn*."

Liam forced a smile onto his lips. "No need to be sorry. I guess I'll head down to the harbor and see who's hiring."

"Back to shoveling coal, is it then?"

"If someone'll have me. I might be considered back luck." Liam grabbed his coat and cap before opening the front door.

Jennie hefted the toddling Katie to her hip. "Don't fret yourself, Liam. Go on with you, now. We'll expect you for supper."

"So eager to be rid of me?" Liam said with a grin. "Wait until I've buttoned my coat before turning the lock, at least!"

As Liam rode the incline railway down to Superior Street, he struggled to control a rising sense of dismay. Ice-out had arrived, and he could no longer put off signing aboard a new ship.

The elevated electric car, twenty feet above the street, hummed and clanked along the twin rails. Close-set houses perched beside the track. The car was jammed with men, women and children alike. A chill breeze carried through the half-opened windows, bringing with it the unmistakable odor of coal-smoke. The smell reminded Liam of the ore boats waiting in the harbor. He blew out his breath; this wasn't going to be easy.

The car halted for its next stop. Liam sat in silence and reflected on his months with the O'Rourkes. He was grateful for Shamus' friendship and Jennie's cooking, the fun he'd had roughhousing with the boys, even the few times he paced the floor with baby Katie until she drifted to sleep on his shoulder. Everything spoke to him of home, and Liam was reluctant to leave.

Memories of Eleanor came to trouble him as the electric car quivered and rolled forward again. He withdrew the newspaper clipping from his pocket and gazed at her picture. Her expression was fixed, the picture slightly grainy, but there was no denying the fact that it was the same girl who'd treated him with such loving kindness back at the lighthouse.

Liam folded the clipping away, too ashamed to admit he'd actively avoided writing her. With the drift of days, his promise to return to Haven Point seemed less and less viable.

He'd conquered his desire for whiskey, but his soul was still wracked by guilt. Why couldn't he have saved any of his shipmates, not even Nathaniel? Was there a purpose to any of this, or was the pain he felt just another example of the affliction he was fated to bear?

Eleanor deserved better, Liam told himself. She deserved a sound-hearted man, not one tormented by such unrelenting demons.

"Next stop, Superior Street!" the brakeman announced. Liam queued up with the departing passengers. Once off the railway car, he walked the streets until he arrived at the waterfront.

The local fleets had all assembled in the harbor, more than one hundred ships strong. Black smoke billowed from their stacks as stevedores hoisted supplies to the decks. Sailors hung suspended on bosun's seats as they scrubbed and painted the steel hulls. In the past such sights had quickened Liam's pulse, but at the moment he felt strangled by doubt.

He trudged along the wooden docks, occasionally lifting his eyes to catch the name emblazoned on each dark hull. *W.H. Brookings, Empire City, James J. Hill*—Liam halted at one of the Oglebay Norton ships, the freighter *Batavia*. A man waved to him from the deck and shouted down, "Are you looking for work, sailor?"

Liam cupped his hands around his mouth and yelled, "Fireman!" Liam watched as the man descended the long stern ladder and jumped to the dock.

They shook hands together. "Martin Osskopp, second mate. How many years you worked the ore boats?"

"Five. I worked last season in the boiler room on the *William Dorn*."

Martin frowned. "The ship that went down with all hands last November?"

Liam nodded gravely. "Except myself."

The second mate lifted his cap and scratched his head. "I'm not sure the crew will like it. There's been strange stories passed around about that wreck."

"I seek no special treatment," Liam said, stone-faced. "Only a chance to earn a living."

There was a space of silence. "Well, come aboard and let's talk it over with the captain. He gets the final word on everything, you understand." Martin started up the ladder, but paused halfway when he realized that Liam hadn't followed.

Liam's feet were rooted to the dock. His hands gripped the ladder so tight his knuckles shone like gristle. Fear cramped his guts. Perspiration broke out on his body. Panic beat like flapping wings inside his mind; once again the screech of the wrecking ship filled his ears.

Ice-water bit into his flesh, the tempest's howled in his head. A cataclysm of water and steel and pounding waves, punctuated by the roar of the exploding boilers, blackness and despair dragging him downward. *I'm already dead*, Liam thought. It was only his shell that walked among the living.

"I cannot!" Liam cried. He jumped back from the ladder before sprinting away from the ship. He ran to the end of the lengthy dock, his heart galloping his chest.

He ran until the pain in his damaged toes slowed his gait. Liam stopped to vomit over the dock's edge, heaving out his fear and rage.

He was a failure, a coward. He didn't even have the nerve to climb aboard a ship, let alone sail her from port to port. How was he ever going to earn a decent living again? Once more he was beset by desperate thoughts; why not just end his life quickly and escape his unbearable shame?

Liam spat and wiped his mouth. *One foot in front of the other*, he thought, forcing himself forward. And so he walked, until finding himself near the Booth Fisheries office. A voice called to him from one of the nearby slips, saying, "MacLann? Aren't you the one called MacLann?"

This man was a big fellow, a Nordlander, dressed in a cable-knit sweater and oilskin trousers. Liam had seen him before, remembering the shape of the man's brow and the color of his hair and eyes. A cabin on the North Shore, wreckage from the *Dorn*, a glass of whiskey…"Nils Finnesgaard?"

"Then it is you!" Nils exclaimed as he came over to greet Liam. Liam felt a twinge of pain in his ribs from the crushing strength of Nils' embrace. "I'm pleased to see you again, MacLann."

Liam's despair began to lift. "What brings you to Duluth, Nils?"

"The fishermen, we all board in town over the winter and find work where we can," Nils told him. "But now we are readying for our return to camp. I have to arrange for all our supplies on credit, nets, groceries, even clothing."

"Credit?"

"*Jah*, it is the fishermen's way. We pay our debts at the close of the season from the money we make." Uncertainty touched Nils' expression. "But this year I'm not sure how much we'll earn, because I'm one man short on my six-man crew."

"One man short, eh?" A new possibility occurred to Liam. "What kind of fish do you take from the lake?"

"Herring in the spring, mostly, and lake trout later in the season. Two men to a boat, one to navigate and lift the nets while the other man picks out the catch." Interest shone in Nils' face. "You were a fisherman, once."

"Aye, a long time ago, off the western coast of Ireland. All the men in my family, my father, my grandfathers, down to the earliest chieftains of Inishmore."

"You should come live with us and fish, MacLann. That is, unless you have signed aboard a new ship?"

"No, I'm through with that," Liam replied. He clasped Nils by the arm. "When are you leaving for the North Shore?"

"The *America* sails tomorrow at eight in the morning. Think about my offer, and if you accept then be there with a steamer ticket in hand." Nils grinned. "What adventures we will have, if only you'll take the risk!"

Returning to the O'Rourke's home by way of the incline, Liam mulled over Nils' offer. Joining the Norwegians for the fishing season might help counter his humiliation at the *Batavia*. He felt a sincere regard for the Norwegians; Liam recognized himself in their stoic demeanors and humble natures. But going to Little Nesna would also bring him into contact with Eleanor, something he still wasn't certain he was ready for.

He thought over Shamus' advice. *If you're waiting for just the proper moment, you'll be an old man before it comes.* Was it simply a matter of waiting, Liam wondered, or had the time come to take the situation into his own hands?

Fleeting memories returned to him: the scent of Eleanor's hair, the soft richness of her voice, her clear, gentle eyes always watching him with concern. The way she'd surrendered to him that night on the beach, when his mouth had commanded hers and he'd drawn her close. *Eleanor.* Liam swallowed hard and wished he could speak with his sister Maeve before making his decision. But time was short, and Maeve was thousands of miles away.

"I'll talk to Shamus and Jennie, tonight," Liam murmured as he settled back in the railcar seat. "They'll know the path of wisdom, sure."

It was ten o'clock in the evening when the three adults gathered near the stove in the O'Rourke parlor. Jennie sat sewing a patch on her husband's trousers while Shamus smoked and read the newspaper. Liam stared at the glowing coals through the stove grate. Outside, a raw April wind moaned against the eaves, but inside there was only warmth and good fellowship.

Liam extended his legs toward the stove. Inside the grate, the coals glowed white with tiny licks of sapphire flame. Few things mattered as much to Liam as staying warm, and, at the moment, he felt very much like a lazy cat soaking up the stove's heat.

Shamus looked over the top of his newspaper and asked, "Did you sign aboard a new ship today, Liam?"

"No. I'll not be sailing on the freighters again."

"Will you be staying in Duluth, then?"

"Don't know." Liam's eyelids drooped slightly. "But someone did offer me a job on a fishing crew, up north. I'd be working at the fish camp just south of Haven Point."

"Will you go, then?" Jennie questioned.

"I think I might. But there's a problem." Liam squirmed in his seat. "I'm frightened of the water since the wreck."

Shamus laid his newspaper aside. "Then you must go, boyo, and face what you fear. You'll never feel right again until you do."

"Aye. But there's more." Liam sat silent, unwilling to elaborate.

Jennie drew her chair closer to Liam. "Is it Eleanor you're worrying over?"

Liam nodded, the words lost in his tightening throat. "I thought as much," Jennie said. "You think that because you haven't written that she won't stand the look of you again."

"And why would she? Eleanor probably thinks I've forgotten about her!"

"But you haven't forgotten her, Liam," Jennie said. "You care deeply for Eleanor."

Liam nodded, admitting to this truth for the first time. "But how can I face her, when I've turned my back on her all these months?"

"It's not too late, Liam," Shamus said. "If she's half the woman she seems to be, she'll give you another chance. And besides, how will you know until you actually talk to her again?"

Liam had no answer for this. Jennie picked up her darning once again, her expression serene. "When I was a girl in Ballyshannon, the old women used to say that there was another isle, just on the horizon, called *Hy Brasil*. Heart's Content. I'm guessing you'll find it, by and bye, though 'twon't be easy. Nothing worthwhile is easy, Liam, especially when it seems that you're on the downside of advantage. But if you have the courage, then anything is possible."

*   *   *   *

Eleanor worked alone in the upstairs bedroom, packing her trunk for the journey to Haven Point. The *America* was scheduled to arrive the following day, and then it would be a matter of hours before they were dropped ashore at the light station.

Bridget and David were listening to Adeline read a story down in the parlor. Adeline's voice drifted up the stairwell. Was it *Gulliver's Travels* this time, or perhaps *David Copperfield*? Eleanor used to love to snuggle beside Adeline and listen to her tell these stories over and over. But no more. She'd lost respect for her mother, though she was careful not to show it, for her father's sake.

Eleanor's thoughts traveled to the season ahead. This would, in all likelihood, be her last spring and summer at the light station. Either she'd purchase the cove or begin her new life in St. Paul with Uncle Casey and Aunt Regina. Change would come, one way or the other.

Eleanor thought about Regina and the one occasion she'd actually visited her in St. Paul. Eleanor had been much younger then, only eight at the time. Eleanor and Adeline had taken turns holding the infant twins on their laps during the journey. Eleanor remembered sitting beside the window and watching miles of countryside race by. They'd arrived at the train station, enormous and noisy and filled with a crush of people, and then Uncle Casey had taken them home in his carriage.

It was a modest house by Summit Avenue standards, but to Eleanor it had seemed like a castle. She recalled few details of the visit, save that Casey and Regina, childless, had thoroughly spoiled her. Candy treats, a trip to the zoo, a new flounced dress, and, best of all, a porcelain doll with real black hair. That doll now sat on Eleanor's highboy dresser in her bedroom back at Haven Point, a little worse for wear all these years later.

This was just one more thing Eleanor was looking forward to at the light station. The only item left to pack now was her hat box, and, as she retrieved it from the dresser, she decided to tally her savings, which were hidden inside.

At the bottom of the box lay Liam's pendant, its silver face staring up at her in the lamplight. Setting the box aside, she held the pendent in her palm and thought of Liam.

What had become of him? Why hadn't he written? Was he too busy carousing with the other sailors, maybe even visiting some of the women in the brothels? The thought sickened her.

Hearing footsteps on the stairs, Eleanor closed her fingers around the pendant. It was John. "The packing all done?"

"Yes," Eleanor replied, her expression guarded.

A frown slanted John's brows. "Something I should know about, Eleanor?"

"Nothing, Papa. It's nothing important."

"Wait now, no secrets." John held out his hand. Reluctantly, slowly, Eleanor brought her hand forward and opened her fingers. "I think I understand. Souvenirs from a wrecked heart, daughter?"

The look in John's eyes was so compassionate, so sincere, that Eleanor's resolve faltered. "I miss him *so* much, Papa," she whispered, tears smarting her eyes. "I didn't know it was possible to hurt like this, inside."

John drew her into his embrace. "That's what love is, Eleanor. Pain and fear and uncertainty, all bound by that madness we call hope."

"Will I ever see Liam again?"

"It's hard to say. If two people are destined to be together, nothing can keep them apart in the end."

Eleanor stepped away. "Oh, Papa, that's just a fairytale for little children."

"I'm not sure I agree with you. Call me old-fashioned, but I believe that one man and one woman are meant to love each other, only and forever."

"If I believed that were true for me and Liam, then I could bear anything that happens." Eleanor broke into embarrassed laughter as she dried her face. "What a spectacle I've made of myself!"

"About all you can do is wait to see what happens, but if you never hear from Liam again, he's a sorry fool. Now, I'd like nothing better than a slice of Mama's peach pie, so put your money box away and let's go down to the kitchen together."

CHAPTER 13

▼

When the steamship rounded the final rocky point, Eleanor saw that a field of ice still separated the *America* from the beach at Haven Point. The tower stood as it always had, a sentinel in the wilderness. Eleanor felt a familiar quiver of excitement. Reopening the light station each spring was always a thrill, even after all these years.

She heard the clanking of thick metal chain as the steamship cast anchor. Crewmen lowered a small supply boat from a set of davits on the starboard side. Down below, other crewmen began unloading the Thompson's baggage.

"Come along. It's time for us to go," Adeline said, herding Eleanor and the twins toward the stairs. Below, they climbed from the freight doors onto the ice, where John was loading their travel trunks into the boat.

"David, lend a hand," John said, grabbing hold of a line at the boat's bow. With help from two of the crewmen, they began to haul the small craft across the ice.

Eleanor followed at a slower pace, her shoes slopping through slushy puddles. The clouds overhead were milky white, with hints of pink on the horizon. A faint aroma drifted in the air, an aroma that reminded Eleanor of newly overturned dirt.

After a half mile of hard pulling, the men finally forded the beach. Winter flotsam and jetsam were strewn here and there: bits of twigs, pine cones, white gull feathers, the rotted remains of a birch tree. To Eleanor's surprise, all remnants of the *William Dorn* life-raft had been washed away.

The thought instantly brought back images of Liam, and Eleanor gazed at the spot where she discovered him the night of the storm, the spot where he'd said goodbye.

All her pent-up hurt to anger. Who was she to wait? She'd made clear how she felt about him their final night together. The bonds between them were broken irrevocably, as far as she was concerned.

Bridget came to join her. "You're thinking about him, aren't you?"

"I don't know what you're talking about," Eleanor answered, turning away.

"I know you are, so don't try to hide it. I've been thinking about Liam, too, ever since we started toward shore."

"What happened between us is over. I have no interest in what's happened to him since," Eleanor said brusquely.

"Mama will sure be glad to hear that." Bridget nodded toward Adeline, who was already climbing the path to the house. "She was worried all winter you'd find some way to run off to Duluth."

"And what would have been the point, since he evidently didn't care enough to write?"

"What's meant to be is meant to be. That's what Lars always used to say," Bridget told her, hefting the suitcase. "Come on, we'd better help Mama get the wood stove started, or we're in for a cold supper tonight."

"She'll want to start some bread rising right away in the morning," Eleanor agreed. "For the new assistant."

They began to walk upward along the path. "I can't wait to meet Mr. Russell," Bridget said. "What do you suppose he'll be like?"

"Hard to say. Every assistant keeper we've had has been so different from the others."

"I hope he can sing well and accompany me on the piano, if it suits him," Bridget said. By now they'd arrived at the front door. "Are you ready to go inside?"

Eleanor peeked through the window. The simple interior was home-like and inviting. "Yes," she said, "more than ready."

Eleanor, exhausted from laundering sheets and beating out rugs, overslept the morning the assistant keeper arrived. She opened her eyes and blinked, confused at the time. Sunlight shone brightly through the east-facing window. Despite the radiance, Eleanor's cold nose reminded her that true spring was still several weeks away.

Bridget's bed was already empty. Eleanor stirred; why had her mother allowed her to sleep so late? Just as she threw back the blankets, David opened the door. "Mama has breakfast ready. She says to hurry. Papa came in a few minutes ago to tell her that he'd sighted the *Amaranth*."

Eleanor jumped from her bed. "Tell Mama I'll be right down."

David closed the door, and then it was time for the unpleasant routine of dressing. Eleanor's corset felt especially binding that morning, and she cursed as she fastened the stays. "One day I'll burn this corset, just to spite Mama," she muttered, and then drew on her shirtwaist and skirt.

In the kitchen, Adeline stood at the stove. Fried eggs and hash browns sizzled in a cast-iron skillet. "Where are David and Bridget?" Eleanor asked.

"Down at the shore with Papa watching the tender ship come in."

Eleanor took her seat at the table. "Why didn't you wake me?"

"I looked in on you earlier, and you were sleeping so quietly I hated to disturb you." Adeline smiled. "Just like when you were a baby."

"Mama, please don't say things like that!"

"You'll always be my little girl, no matter." Adeline placed a heaping plate of food in front of Eleanor before taking her seat. "It *is* nice to be back, isn't it?"

"I guess so," Eleanor said. She took a bite and grimaced over the taste.

"We can make a fresh start, hmm?" Adeline continued. "Put away the foolishness of your silly crush on that Irishman?"

"If you say so, Mama," Eleanor said quietly. If only Adeline knew how little she cared for Liam just then. Eleanor pushed away from the table. "I'm going down to the beach to join the others."

Adeline frowned at the uneaten food. "I'll come with you, then, since you seem to be in such a hurry." They drew on their coats and hats before walking to the door. "I'm eager to meet Mr. Russell," Adeline said. "I have a feeling he'll make a favorable addition to our little clan here at Haven Point."

Lake Superior had discarded her alabaster robe of ice as she yielded to the warming air and strengthening sun. Large fissures gaped in her raiment, and it was through these breaks that the Coast Guard icebreaker, *J.D. Morant*, nosed ahead of the *Amaranth*.

The Thompson family watched the tender ship drop anchor. Before long the supply launch chugged through the gently rolling ice-cakes. John met them at the edge of the ice field, and then, along with the crew and the new assistant, helped drag the small boat ashore.

"Good to see you again, Thompson," Captain Krenshaw said. "I trust your family had a passably good winter."

"Everyone is well, thank you," John said. "I see you've brought my new assistant."

"Of course! Mr. Russell, come along then, no shyness allowed!" A tall young man dressed in a black keeper's uniform stepped forward. "John Thompson, allow me to introduce Assistant Keeper Cameron Russell."

Eleanor observed Cameron as he approached John, bearing a leather suitcase in hand. He seemed younger than the assistants they'd had in recent years, maybe twenty-two or twenty-three. His face was smooth with clean, handsome lines, and he had thick black hair cut short to the collar. Cameron's smile was reticent as he shook John's hand.

"Welcome to Haven Point Light Station, Mr. Russell. How was your journey?"

"Tiresome, but expeditious," Cameron replied. His eyes moved from face to face until they came to rest on Eleanor's. "Accommodations were more than adequate."

"Glad to hear it," John said, in a fatherly tone. "I hope the Lighthouse Board prepared you for what you'll find here, Mr. Russell. Life on the North Shore is a little more rugged than what you might be used to in Duluth."

"Oh, yes, well, my father has filled my ears with all the grim realities of an assistant keeper's lot since I agreed to the position."

"Your father?"

"Sumner Russell. Surely you've heard of him? Owner of the Zenith Steamship Company?" Cameron's smile broadened. "Didn't the Board inform you in the telegram?"

John's ears reddened. "No, they didn't," he said. "But it shouldn't matter too much, a least in regard to your duties. There's always a lot to learn your first season at a light station."

"Yes, I'm certain you're right." Cameron looked away, giving a distinct air of boredom.

Adeline stepped forward. "Adeline Thompson," she introduced, offering her hand to Cameron. "Why don't I take you on a little tour of the assistant's house, and then perhaps we can enjoy a cup of coffee afterward?"

"I'd like nothing more," Cameron replied. Eleanor watched as her mother led the new assistant along the pathway to the house before turning at the approach of a crew member. He was a short man with striking red hair.

"Miss Thompson?"

"Yes?"

"Miss Thompson, pardon, my name is Shamus O'Rourke. I was a guest at your house the last time our crew came ashore, back in December," he explained.

"Yes, I remember. Is there something I can do for you, Mr. O'Rourke?"

"I have a letter to give to you from a friend of mine." Shamus withdrew an envelope from his coat pocket. "'Tis from the big man himself."

Eleanor glanced up sharply. "Is it—?"

"Aye." Shamus pressed the letter into her hand. "He's not forgotten."

Eleanor slipped the letter inside her pocket and asked, "Where's Liam now?"

"At Little Nesna. The note explains everything." Shamus briefly touched her arm. "He's sorry for the delay in writing to you. He had a rough time of it over the winter. Still troubled by the shipwreck, poor man."

This hadn't occurred to her before, though it did help to explain his silence. Eleanor was about to question Shamus further when she was cut short by Captain Krenshaw's strident voice. "Keeper Thompson, we've brought lumber and nails to rebuild the dock, and a new glass window."

John, unloading supplies, answered, "Glad to hear it, Captain. We'll keep plenty busy with all the repair work."

Krenshaw fixed a hard look on John. "There's something else. Superintendent Greer sends word he'll be coming soon to conduct a full investigation regarding your actions after the wreck of the *William A. Dorn*."

Adeline and Cameron sat visiting over coffee in the kitchen when Eleanor and the younger children arrived. "David, Bridget, Eleanor, come join us at the table. Mr. Russell has been sharing the most interesting stories about life in Duluth."

"What's Duluth like, Mr. Russell?" David asked.

"A grand city, with buildings ten stories tall at least. There's a new hotel and an opera house, one of the fanciest built anywhere."

"And don't forget to mention the motorcars," Adeline said.

"Ah, yes, the motorcars." Cameron's tone grew expansive. "All the well-to-do gentlemen own them. They love to terrorize the carriage horses with their loud horns. My father owns several, and I've even driven one myself."

"What's it like? To drive a motorcar, I mean," Bridget asked.

"Rather like flying, I imagine. Perhaps one day you'll ride in one yourself."

"Not much hope of motorcars ever coming to the North Shore," David said. "The roads around here are just dirt trails."

"I can well imagine," Cameron said. "No individual of means would bother to attempt travel in such unpromising country as this, I can assure you."

Eleanor flushed over Cameron's comment, even as Adeline smiled and said, "My thoughts precisely. That's one reason we are sending Eleanor to St. Paul this coming autumn."

"St. Paul?" Cameron shifted his gaze toward Eleanor. "Why, you don't seem old enough to brave the travails of the big city just yet."

"I'll be twenty-one on my next birthday," Eleanor replied curtly. His patronizing tone had raised her hackles.

"Twenty-one. I see." Cameron rose from the table. "Off to help at the shore now. Don't want to create a bad impression on my first day."

In Cameron's absence, Adeline emptied the remains of his cup in the sink. "Mr. Russell seems a real gentleman," she said with a small sigh. "We can look forward to better times now."

Eleanor felt the outline of Liam's letter through the skirt. "Mama, I'm heading upstairs to the make the beds."

"Fine. I've got bread rising in the pantry and a venison roast that's ready for the oven. Mr. Russell will see that we're no different from city folk, that we're just as cordial and well-mannered."

Eleanor felt a surge of irritation as she mounted the stair. Why should they care a whit what Cameron thought about them? He was little more than a stranger, an outsider.

She didn't need his or anyone's approval. As far as she was concerned, Cameron Russell meant nothing at all.

Eleanor closed the bedroom door before taking a seat on the bed. Withdrawing the envelope, she stared at the name written across the front. Miss Thompson. *Sounds very formal,* she thought with a slight frown. Could this be the same Liam?

"Dear Eleanor," it began. Eleanor smiled, reassured.

Dear Eleanor,

I hope above all that this letter finds you in good health and spirits, and that you have not forgotten your best fellow and most ardent admirer. I have been living with kind friends during my winter stay in Duluth, chief among them the man who delivered this into your keeping. His name is Shamus O'Rourke, and he is a man whom you can trust.

Eleanor, I beg forgiveness for not writing sooner. I tell you now that I fell under the dark cloud of self-pity and strong drink, and would still be in such a low state if not for Shamus. Daily I pray for deliverance from the guilt I bear, and hope that you will allow me to see you once again.

Nils Finnesgaard has asked me to join his fishing crew, and I have accepted. I will work at Little Nesna this season with the goal of regaining my sea-legs and to honor the promise I made to you. If rejection is your choice, I will abide by that, for I know that I am entirely to blame.

You can find me at Nils' camp. I await your decision.

Most devotedly, Liam

She read the letter several times through and then stared at the final line. Liam wanted a decision. A decision to forgive his silence, to renew what had blossomed between them last December.

Eleanor placed the letter inside the envelope and then ran her fingers absently along its edge. She'd almost convinced herself that Liam no longer cared. How much easier to continue with the present course and redouble her efforts with her laundry business and her plans for the cove. But Liam's return had changed everything.

She didn't need him, she told herself. Everything she wanted she could accomplish by herself. Yet she realized it wasn't entirely true. He was the one person who seemed to believe her dream of the lodge was worth pursuing. Was Liam's faith in her worth more than her distrust?

Shamus. She must talk with Shamus at once about Liam. Eleanor dashed through the door and down the stairs, barely pausing long enough to grab her coat.

"Eleanor, where are you off to in such a hurry?" Adeline called after her.

"I'll be right back!" Eleanor answered, then hurried down to the beach, where, to her disappointment, the launch was already motoring its way back to the *Amaranth*.

Eleanor watched from the shore, crestfallen. She was concentrating so intently that she didn't notice Cameron's approach.

He scuffed his shoes against the rocks, calling her attention. "Have you lost something, Miss Thompson?"

"No, not really," she said. Eleanor studied Cameron's face, his green eyes fringed with dark lashes, his bold, arching brows, the arrogant tilt of his mouth.

"Perhaps you'd care to give me a tour of the tower, Miss Thompson?" Cameron suggested.

"I'm certain Papa will show you everything soon enough," Eleanor replied. She eyed him skeptically. "Have you ever worked at a lighthouse on the Great Lakes before, Mr. Russell?"

"Gracious, no. Never even stepped foot on a boat until today."

"Then why did you come?"

"For the challenge, mainly. Would it surprise you to know that I have often longed to escape my father's scrutiny? Or that I wish to connect with people who work for an honest living?"

"I guess I hadn't thought of that," Eleanor murmured, abashed.

"You'll learn many things about me, Miss Thompson, in due time. Now, if you'll excuse me, I'd like to unpack my belongings," Cameron said. He took a few steps up the pathway and then paused. "Don't you remember me, Miss Eleanor? Last summer when I was a guest at the Grand Hotel?"

Eleanor thought for a few moments. She recalled the lavish parties teeming with young people, both men and women alike. She had recollections of young rakes in dark suits and top hats, but never anyone specific. "I'm sorry, I don't," she confessed.

"Well, I remember you quite vividly. The hotel owner once boasted that you were the best cook's helper he had ever employed."

"That was months ago, Mr. Russell." Eleanor drew her coat more tightly around her. "Now, if you'll excuse me," she said before hiking the path alone.

Cameron's appearance at Haven Point struck Eleanor as peculiar, regardless of what he'd said about his reasons for coming. Tending a lighthouse was grueling and thankless, made more so by the fact that the pay for an assistant keeper was pitifully low. Why would a gentleman lower himself to such work, especially on the North Shore?

The fact that her mother had taken a liking to Cameron came as no surprise. Adeline was as transparent as the glass windows on the lantern-deck; undoubtedly she was already scheming to attract Cameron's interest in her eldest daughter. *Mama will have her work cut out for her*, Eleanor thought ruefully as she entered the house.

A rich, bored young man would find little to admire in someone like herself. That much she *did* remember from her days as a cook at the Grand Hotel.

*   *   *   *

"Tell us about your family, Cameron, and why you've come to Haven Point."

Everyone was gathered at the dining room table for the noon meal. Cameron had already finished his second helping of venison and stewed apples, and he dabbed his mouth with a napkin before answering John's question.

"My father, as you already know, owns Zenith Steamship," Cameron began. "Father built that company from the ground up, so to speak. My grandfather was a vessel master for many years, and he taught my father every aspect of seamanship and what it took to be a leader of men.

"Zenith Steam is one of the most prominent and profitable companies hauling cargo on the Great Lakes today. I've enjoyed a life of privilege since I was very young, but now my father is determined to teach me the value of hard work before I assume stewardship of the company's daily operations. I was offered a choice, you see: work as a deckhand on one of my father's ships, or serve a season at a lighthouse. Obviously, I chose the latter."

"I see." John took a bite of bread which was slathered with butter and raspberry preserves. "Why here? There are better-paying positions at other lighthouses, especially along Lake Michigan."

"Proximity to home. Mother didn't want me to stray too far." Cameron leaned back in his chair. "One season at Haven Point shall suffice, I would imagine. All I need do after that is bide my time and wait for the old goat to kick off before inheriting his financial empire."

John, who'd just taken another bite of bread, choked and had to quickly gulp from his glass of water to get it down.

Eleanor stared at Cameron with a mixture of wonder and disgust, and was about to say something disagreeable when Adeline chimed in, saying, "How simply marvelous! A man with your resources and talents, why, there's almost nothing you couldn't accomplish!"

"A point I hope to prove to one and all, madam," Cameron said with a slight nod toward Adeline.

"Well, if it's hard work you've come for, I'll dish it out in spades," John said. "We stand two six-hour watches, which vary in length through the change of seasons. Twice a week, weather permitting, you'll row the skiff up to Grand Marais for short supplies. The *Amaranth* makes a stop here about once a month, so the first order of business will be to rebuild that dock."

"I see." Cameron laced his fingers together. "Everything appears to be run in an orderly manner at Haven Point."

"Well, I do the best I can. Superintendent Greer makes a surprise visit twice during the season, and, if the buildings and grounds aren't kept in perfect order, we could both lose our jobs."

Adeline clucked her tongue and said, "Now, John, don't scare the poor boy!" She smiled at Cameron. "We do make time for fun once in a while."

"What sort of fun?"

"When it gets real hot in the summer, we head down to the beach and go swimming," Bridget replied. "We like to go on picnics, especially at the cove with the old cabin."

David added, "Better than that is the fishing. Papa and I like to take the skiff to his secret fishing spot and reel in a whole mess of trout, you wouldn't believe the size—"

"And what about you, Miss Eleanor?" Cameron interrupted. "What do you like to do with your free time?"

Eleanor laid her fork beside her plate. "I read. I sew and knit. But mostly I like to sit by the lake, alone."

"Alone?" Cameron said, brows quirked with interest. "How diverting! Perhaps you could show me what you see, sometime."

"Perhaps." Eleanor rose from the table. "Pardon me. I have some things to check on outside."

She carried her plate into the kitchen and placed it in the sink, thinking. In some ways Cameron seemed the perfect replacement for Lars: young, bright, educated, and articulate. But Eleanor would have preferred ten Lars Berglunds to one Cameron Russell. Cameron's artifice stood in sharp contrast to her memory of Lars' genuine warmth.

"It's going to be a long season," she murmured before heading out the door.

CHAPTER 14

▼

Eleanor sat at the vanity in her parents' bedroom, combing her long hair. Once combed, she gathered the hair up and pinned it into place, for she was in a particular hurry that morning. Closing the door on her sleeping father, Eleanor descended the stairs and went in search of Adeline.

She found her mother in the kitchen, mixing batter for pancakes. "Mama, I'm getting ready to row down to Little Nesna," Eleanor announced.

"It's a little early yet, don't you think? The fishermen haven't been at their camp long enough to have dirtied a great deal of laundry, surely."

"I'd like to get a start on things anyway," Eleanor said brightly. She didn't dare tell her mother the true reason behind her visit.

"But I thought you promised to row Cameron out to the cove today."

"I never made any promises. It was his idea, anyway," Eleanor said, slipping into her coat.

"Well, I must say, if I were in your shoes I'd much rather spend time in the company of a man like Cameron Russell than with those foreigners. I'm sure he longs for conversation with someone equal to his style and candor, and you, my dear, are the best we can offer."

"Since when am I supposed to act as hostess to Cameron?"

"Don't be uncharitable, Eleanor." Adeline dusted her hands on her apron. "You could learn a great deal about the social graces by just spending time with Cameron. The truth is, I think he's lonely."

"Cameron's hardly lonely. He seems to enjoy your long visits over coffee," Eleanor said as she reached for the laundry basket.

"And what's that supposed to mean?"

"Nothing, Mama," Eleanor said. "Don't look for me until after lunch," she added as she breezed out the doorway.

Adeline followed her out the door. "This stubborn streak of yours must end, Eleanor Ann Thompson! I won't have you speak that way to me in my own house!"

"I'm not listening!" Eleanor threw back. She was answered by the slam of the door.

Eleanor marched down the path, inwardly fuming. Adeline's pressures were growing unbearable. For her part, Eleanor had done her best to avoid Cameron, though she found this difficult with his frequent visits to the house. It wasn't that she disliked Cameron; rather, she wished to avoid the appearance of any favor on her part, especially in front of her mother.

Cameron was hard at work on the new dock when she arrived at the beach. It was a bright, clear day, with stray clouds scudding across the dome of blue sky. A stiff breeze drove the waves against the shore. There was a deeply organic smell in the air, the odor of thawing earth and the rot of damp leaves.

Cameron wore denim overalls and a light brown chambray shirt with a tweed cap. He finished pounding a nail and looked up. "Where are you off to, Miss Eleanor?"

"Today is laundry day, Mr. Russell. I do business with a fish camp just south of Haven Point."

"I see." There was a hint of disappointment in Cameron's eyes. "Perhaps we can take our little boating trip another time? I'm anxious to have a look at the cove Bridget told me about."

"Gladly, though there isn't much to see," Eleanor said. She gave him a conciliatory smile. "You probably find this wilderness quite dull, I'm afraid."

"You might be surprised by what I think." Cameron nodded toward the rolling surf. "Be careful out there, and make sure you have a lifejacket on board."

"I always do," Eleanor said, and then bent to place the basket in the bottom of the skiff. She pushed the vessel into the water, stepped inside, took up the oars, and began to row.

Eleanor thought of Liam as the skiff rose and dipped in the shallow waves. In the days since reading Liam's letter, she'd found it difficult to concentrate on anything else. She recalled every moment of their time together following the shipwreck: her care of his injuries, their long conversations, their passionate embrace on the beach. But all these memories were now tempered by her mistrust.

She wasn't the same girl who'd begged him to take her with him last December. The long winter in Grand Marais had opened her eyes, to the changes taking place in the lives of her friends and of how critical it was to keep forging her own path. The cove and her lodge were the only things that mattered, she told herself. Not her mother's dream of gilded domestic bliss, nor a sailor who was, in reality, little more than a stranger.

A new thought occurred to her; *what if Mama finds out that Liam has returned north?* Adeline might well forbid Eleanor's going to the fish camp and ruin any chance she had of buying the land. Was she risking her dream for the sake of a man she wasn't even sure she cared for?

Eleanor pulled hard against the oars. Soon, very soon, she would know the answer.

Little had changed at the fish camp from the winter before. The yard was still littered with boxes and barrels and spindly net-reels, while smoke drifted from the cabin chimney. Several men lay on their backs near the shore, slapping a coat of fresh paint on the underside of one of the Mackinaw boats. Eleanor craned her neck to see if either of them were Liam. But as the skiff nudged the dock, she saw that it was only Nils and his cousin, Sollie.

Nils scrambled to his feet. "Miss Thompson!" he called as Eleanor threw him the line. When the skiff was secured, Nils helped her up to the dock. "I wasn't expecting to see you for a few days yet. Though you are always welcome, of course," he added with a smile.

"It's good to see you again, Mr. Finnesgaard. Is Liam MacLann here?"

"*Jah*, MacLann is here," Nils replied, a twinkle in his eyes. "He's been waiting."

"Where is Liam now?"

"Chopping wood in the forest. Just follow the sound of the axe-falls and you'll soon find him."

"Thank you, Nils."

In the half-shadows of the forest, Eleanor picked her way through wet patches of mud and snow, weaving amongst the giant oaks, drawn forward by the steady *chop* of the axe. A bramble caught her skirt, and she yanked it free. Anxiety tightened her chest, and she moistened her lip, her mouth suddenly dry. Onward she went, until, skirting one last tree, she saw him.

Liam was dressed in green plaid and wool trousers, his hands tightly gripping the wooden handle of an axe. Liam's back was turned toward her, and for a moment she paused, riveted by the sight of him as he swung the axe deftly against the fallen tree.

Liam planted the axe deep and turned around to look at her. Surprise lit his face. "Girleen, you've come."

"Liam." She crossed the short distance to where he waited. Sweat glistened on his neck and arms, and his skin was dusted with tiny flecks of wood. He was breathing hard, his face flushed from exertion.

Eleanor stared at the russet and gold of Liam's hair, the gleam of his eyes, the smile spreading across his lips. He was taller and more robust than she remembered. "Ah, the sight of you makes me feel glad to be a man," he said. "So bonnie, even prettier than I recall." Liam reached out to touch her hair, but she drew away.

"What's the matter, Eleanor?"

She stared at him, unable to answer. The scent of him, wood smoke and sweat, surrounded her. Liam stepped closer, and her heart kicked in her chest. "Don't," she said in a low voice.

Confusion knotted his brow. "Girleen, say something, will you? Tell me why you've come!"

"I—I wanted to see if your injuries were healed," she stammered. "And that's the only reason I'm here now."

"The only reason? What about the things I told you in the letter?"

"What you said was very sweet, Liam. But I don't understand why you waited until now to write. I thought you were never coming back to the North Shore."

"That was my intent," Liam confessed. "But I couldn't shed the memory of you." He took her hand. "Can we sit and talk together?"

Eleanor sat beside him on the fallen log, fighting the impulse to flee. *Tread carefully*, she told herself, filled with misgiving.

"How was the winter for you?" Liam asked.

"There's not much to tell, really," she replied. "I cleaned houses, as usual. No school, of course, and I hardly saw anything of my old friends. Most of them have married or left town, it seems."

"What about the cove, girleen? Have you saved enough money to buy it yet?"

"Not yet. That's one of the reasons I'm still offering to do laundry for the men here at Little Nesna."

"Is that the only reason?" Liam asked, his hand tightening over hers.

"Please don't," she said, pulling away. "I'm not ready for that."

The eagerness in Liam's eyes dimmed. "You've not forgiven me, then."

Eleanor swallowed the rising lump in her throat before answering, "I want to forgive and forget, Liam, I really do. But I'm afraid."

"I know. I'm afraid too, sometimes."

She searched his face. "The *Dorn?*"

"Aye. Bad dreams of the shipwreck. Christ, Eleanor, I felt so alone. I wanted to die, I was killing myself nightly with bottle after bottle of whiskey." Liam shook his head. "'Tis thankful I am that Shamus found me when he did, or I might not be here today."

"I wish I'd known. Maybe I could have helped you."

"And what good would it have done, hmm?" he asked, his words edged with heat. "I was acting like a madman. I would have turned you out rather than show myself for the drunkard I'd become!"

"I'm not a child, Liam. I've dealt with much more difficult circumstances, as you well know!"

Liam sat in silence for a moment before saying, "Fair enough. It was selfish of me not to give you the chance. But maybe that's the real reason I accepted Nils' offer, to ask your help again." He paused, then asked, "Will you help me, girleen?"

Eleanor wavered. A part of her yearned toward him, toward his plea for help. "I don't know. The truth is, Liam, I'm not sure that you truly want to be helped." She stood then and began to walk away. *It had been a mistake to come,* she told herself. Best to let memories lie in the past, as they had before.

Liam caught her by the sleeve. "I was wrong to have treated you so poorly, girleen. I'll do anything to make things right between us again," he pleaded.

"It's too late, too many things have happened—"

"Just give me a chance," he said. "I want to prove to you the man I can be."

Damn his persistence, she thought. *Damn those beautiful eyes, that chiseled face.* Eleanor shrugged free from his grasp. "I need some time to think. You must be patient with me, Liam."

"Patient. Aye, that I can be, if you wish," Liam said. He wiped the sweat on his face with his sleeve. "I want to see you again, though. And soon."

Eleanor wrestled with her doubts. *It begins again, all of it,* a warning voice told her. Trouble would dog them both from this moment onward.

"Where?" Eleanor asked. "It can't be at Haven Point. And it can't be here; Mama's as tyrannical as ever, and she'd suspect something if I didn't return from my laundry run in the usual time."

"To hell with her anyway," Liam said, and Eleanor held back a smile. "It can't be during the daytime, anyway. Beginning tomorrow, we'll be out fishing from sunrise until after dark."

"What about the cove?" Eleanor suggested. "It's half-way between, though we'd have to meet very late, after Papa goes on watch and Mama's asleep. Midnight, most likely."

"Laundry day, then, aye. Whatever day you've come to the fish camp, that will let me know."

"All right. But what about your fear of the lake, Liam?"

A fleeting look crossed his face, a mixture of shame and apprehension. "I have to try," Liam said. "I owe it to my mates from the *Dorn.*"

His courage moved her. That part of him remained unchanged, thankfully. "Just be careful out there," she said in a soft voice.

"I'll try." Liam yanked the axe from the log. "Go along with you now. I've got a fair pile of wood to chop yet. Oh, and one last thing. Do you still have the necklace I gave to you?"

"It's back at the house. I can bring it when we meet, if you like," Eleanor said.

"Keep it as a measure of my faith, girleen," Liam said before returning to work, grunting as he swung the axe. Eleanor turned and hurried through the woods, intent on gathering the Norwegians' laundry at the camp.

Eleanor mulled over the details of their meeting as she rowed northward to Haven Point. Liam's physical presence had overwhelmed her. Everything he'd said and done left her in emotional disarray.

He'd seemed genuinely sorry for not writing. Maybe she should forgive him and offer him another chance. Yet what did Liam really mean to her? Those first few hours after his rescue had been filled with drama and emotion, and afterward, during his recovery, she'd been intrigued by the story of his difficult life. More than that, she'd responded to his suffering, to his feeling of isolation in the world.

Things were different now, of course. Liam was healed and living with the amiable Norwegians. He had no real need of her, save for his obvious attraction.

Her cheeks tingled with the thought of it. Liam MacLann was still as handsome and mysterious as ever, yet now her heart had changed. She wasn't going to act foolish or impulsive. If the two of them were going to build a relationship, it must be done on the basis of mutual friendship and respect.

But any future meetings might come at a price. What would her mother and father say if they found out she was sneaking off to see Liam at night? And what might yet happen if she allowed him back inside the circle of her heart?

"I wish I had someone to talk to about this," she murmured as the skiff drew near the light station. "I wish I wasn't so alone."

When Eleanor returned to the house, the Victrola phonograph player in the parlor was playing a concerto. Bridget looked up from the rocker as Eleanor entered the room, a look of pleasure on her face. "Where have you been?" the younger girl asked.

"Down to the fish camp for laundry," Eleanor replied as she undid her coat. "I left the clothes basket out on the step. Mama wouldn't appreciate the stink of fish filling her house, after all."

"No, she certainly wouldn't. I thought you were supposed to take Cameron out to the cove today."

"Another time," Eleanor said. "Where's Mama?"

"Over at Cameron's with a loaf of fresh oatmeal bread." Bridget rolled her eyes. "He'll gain ten pounds if he doesn't stop complimenting her cooking."

"You know how much she enjoys hearing his praise," Eleanor said. "It's really almost laughable the way she lights up around Cameron."

"Like the belle of the ball," Bridget agreed. "Where are you off to now?"

"Upstairs to fix my hair. The breeze off the lake made a mess of it."

"Let me help you," Bridget said, lifting the needle off the phonograph's cylinder before following Eleanor up to their parents' bedroom.

Eleanor sat patiently at the vanity while Bridget undid her chignon. "Boy, you weren't kidding," Bridget commented as she let Eleanor's hair fall to her waist. Bridget pulled a tiny twig from the dark strands. "What's this?" she asked, holding it out to Eleanor.

Eleanor tried to snatch it away, but Bridget wouldn't let her. "Something happened while you were at Little Nesna, didn't it?"

Eleanor weighed the wisdom of confiding about Liam. Bridget might tell Adeline, intentionally or otherwise. But she needed someone to talk to, and her sister was the only available person at the moment. "Yes, something did happen. I saw Liam at the fish camp. He's come north to work for the Norwegians."

"I knew it! I could tell the moment you walked in!" Bridget said as she began to brush and gather Eleanor's hair.

"You have to promise not to tell *anyone*," Eleanor said, looking hard at Bridget in the mirror. "Mama would throw a fit if she knew."

"Of course she would. She hates everything about Liam." Bridget twisted the hair into a tight knot before inserting the pins. "What about Cameron?"

"What about him?" Eleanor said. "I mean, what do you think of Cameron?"

"I don't think much of him, frankly. He's all talk and no heart, if you know what I mean. Mama adores him, of course. She told me that she has high hopes for the two of you." Bridget stepped back. "There. Good as new."

"Thanks." Eleanor touched her hair briefly before rising. "Do you promise not to tell?"

"What's there to tell? You've not agreed to elope with Liam, after all." Bridget peered at her sister. "Right? You wouldn't just run off with Liam without Mama and Papa's approval?"

"No. I couldn't do that." Below, the kitchen door opened and then closed. The two sisters glanced at one another. "Promise, all right?" Eleanor insisted

"All right, I promise." They headed toward the stairwell. "She's going to be unbearable about Cameron, you know," Bridget said in a half-whisper. "She can be very determined."

"So can I," Eleanor replied.

"Eleanor? Are you back with the laundry?" Adeline called from the kitchen.

"Yes, Mama," Eleanor replied. She winked at Bridget and they both stifled a laugh. "We'll be right down."

Later, as Eleanor placed the boiler on the stove, she felt grateful for Bridget's willingness to listen. They'd often clashed over the years, with Eleanor resenting Bridget's status as favorite child. But they remained sisters, even through the difficult times.

As Eleanor went to fetch the laundry basket, she paused on the front stoop and looked toward the lake. She and Liam had struck an awkward arrangement with agreeing to meet at the cove under cover of darkness. But there was no way to avoid it if she was to keep the peace at home.

A sense of failure clung to Eleanor; working at the Grand Hotel should have given her the strength to stand up to her mother's bullying. But instead she felt as ineffectual as ever.

Eleanor pushed these thoughts away as she returned to the house. It would be another week until she and Liam met face to face again. Perhaps, by then, her heart would feel more settled.

CHAPTER 15

▼

Ambivalence shadowed Eleanor all that next week. One moment she'd be wash-ing dishes at the sink and recalling Liam's touch, his voice, his plea to her. The next she'd be stung by the remembrance of the long winter with no word from him. To make matters worse, Adeline continued to extol Cameron's polish and *savoir faire*. Eleanor began to compare Liam's raw vibrancy and Cameron's sophistication, and this did little to help her growing sense of uncertainty.

Laundry day arrived, and with it the day of her next meeting with Liam. Eleanor ate little of her breakfast, then rushed through her morning chores with a carelessness that brought a stern look of disapproval from her mother.

The *Amaranth* was scheduled to deliver a load at the light station that after-noon. After the dinner dishes had been cleared and washed, Eleanor went to visit the shore and watch for the incoming ship from the cliff just south of the beach.

It was a sun-drenched day, unusually warm for that time of year. Waves bil-lowed lazily across Superior. The air was thick with the familiar spiced evergreen fragrance of jack-pines and Douglas firs. Eleanor felt her heart lift, as though coming alive again after the long northern winter.

John, Cameron, and David were already at the beach, adding the finishing touches to the new dock and boathouse. Eleanor paused at the foot of the dock to speak with her father. "The dock is even better than the one before, Papa."

"Thanks, Tomboy," John said with a smile. He nodded to the far end where Cameron was applying a final coat of paint to the boathouse eaves. "Cameron's done a terrific job, better than I would've expected from him."

"I'm glad to hear that." Eleanor watched as Cameron continued to work. "I had my doubts when he started here."

"He's shown a great deal of improvement. None of this is easy for him, you understand." John mopped the sweat from his brow. "The *Amaranth* ought to be here any time."

"I'm going up to the cliff to watch," Eleanor said. "May I borrow your scope, Papa?"

"It's in my coat pocket, over there on the rocks," John replied. "David and I are heading up to the house for a glass of lemonade. Let us know when the tender ship arrives, and keep a sharp eye open for the superintendent's flag."

"Of course, Papa."

Following a steep, narrow path, Eleanor climbed to the top of the cliff, where she sat on the warm, smooth rocks. She lifted her face upward, basking in the glow of the sun. Then, closing her eyes, she listened to the slosh and gurgle of water slapping at the cliff's base, far below. Gulls shrieked overhead.

A crunch of pebbles on the path. Eleanor opened her eyes and saw that it was Cameron. He was wearing denim overalls and a short-sleeved undershirt. "Do you mind if I join you?" he asked.

"If you like," she told him.

Cameron settled beside her on the rock and rested his elbows on his knees. His muscular forearms wore the sheen of sweat, which did not go unnoticed by Eleanor. Cameron removed his cap, then, and used it to wipe the back of his neck. "Whew, it's hot today."

"Yes. Unseasonably warm, really. Don't get too used to it, though. We'll probably have snow next week."

Cameron laughed. "Just like in Duluth." He picked up a stone and hurled it over the cliff's edge. "It already feels like years since I was home."

Eleanor peered at him. "No doubt you find living here most tedious."

"To the contrary, I've grown to like it more and more each day." Cameron spoke with uncharacteristic earnestness. "The fresh air and hard work have acted like a tonic on my nerves."

"Tell me, Mr. Russell, why would a man from a wealthy family feel nervous about anything?"

"Things are not always what they seem. I've been a constant source of disappointment to my father, I'm afraid. He's always telling me how useless I am, how I've never had to earn anything on my own." Cameron stared at his hands. "Is it my fault that I'm the only child in the family, or that mother spoiled me horribly?"

"Yet Zenith Steamship will be yours one day. That must be worth something."

Cameron shrugged. "Well, blood is blood, I suppose. You can't escape your destiny." He refitted his cap and continued. "Anyway, all of it seems far removed from my experiences here at Haven Point. I've grown to appreciate your family, Miss Eleanor. They've shown the greatest consideration. But I enjoy your company most of all."

"I'm no one of consequence."

"I wouldn't say that at all. You've a kind nature, Eleanor. I see it in the way you help your parents, in the time you spend with David and Bridget and in the work you perform daily. You're unique, Eleanor, a real treasure. The kind of girl a man grows fond of."

It was meant as a compliment, but to Eleanor it sounded contrived. "Surely you must have engaged the attention of some worthy young lady in Duluth, Mr. Russell," she said, trying to steer the conversation away from herself.

"Call me Cameron," he insisted. "Yes, there were a few. Silly girls, inconsequential bits of fluff, debutantes more interested in the frippery of opera night than in paying proper respect to their suitor." He slid a degree closer. "You're as unlike them as can be imagined. I've never known any girl with such spirit and dedication."

Eleanor's inner alarms were going off. "You speak too boldly, Mr. Russell. We are, after all, mere acquaintances."

"I'd very much like to change that, with your permission," Cameron said as he took her hand. "I'd like to offer you my friendship, Eleanor, and perhaps, in time, something more."

Eleanor gazed into Cameron's face. It was beautifully formed, smooth and unsullied by labor or care. His eyes darkened, and then he leaned forward into a kiss.

Eleanor froze as his lips brushed hers, and then she drew away at once. "You shouldn't have done that," she said.

"Why not? Pretty Eleanor. Does it bother you that I find you very attractive? Because I do, you know. Very attractive indeed."

Cameron's words caught her by surprise. What could he possibly see in her? They had absolutely nothing in common.

She was about to explain this to Cameron when she was interrupted by the distant moan of the *Amaranth*'s steam whistle. Hastily she rose and withdrew the scope from her skirt pocket. "Goodness, there she is," Eleanor said, collapsing the scope before beginning her descent from the cliff.

"Right on time," Cameron remarked. Eleanor, agitated, climbed down the steep path so quickly that she snagged the edge of her skirt on a protruding rock. As soon as her shoes hit the beach she hurried toward the house.

She found her family sitting in the kitchen. "The *Amaranth* has arrived," she announced breathlessly.

"Did you see the white flag?" Adeline asked.

"No sign of it, Mama."

"Is Cameron still down at the dock?"

Eleanor nodded. "Well, we'd best get down there, then," John said as he rose from the table. "Hopefully they've included some new baby chicks and a couple of piglets, or we'll be short on meat come next fall."

"Don't forget about Mama's seed packets," Bridget added. "We can start planting the garden soon."

After John and the children had gone outside, Eleanor opened the icebox and withdrew the lemonade pitcher. She poured a glass for herself, and took a long drink, trying to calm herself after the dash across the beach. As she placed the glass on the table, she realized Adeline was watching her.

"What's bothering you, daughter? You're white as a lily."

"It's nothing."

Adeline drew near and straightened Eleanor's collar. "You're worn out, and probably from the strain of all that rowing you've been doing. I'm going to speak to your father about putting a stop to this laundry business."

"Don't you dare, Mama! You know how much I need the money I earn!"

Adeline's eyes narrowed. "So be it. Ruin your health, it won't hurt me in any way. I just hope that Regina has better luck bringing you to heel next fall, for I've apparently failed in that regard."

Eleanor bolted out the back door. Why couldn't her mother just leave her alone?

She halted at the ridge. The *Amaranth*'s launch was already chugging toward the new dock, where Cameron, John, and the children stood waiting. Eleanor gave herself a hard shake and then continued down the path.

Cameron been unusually candid with her about his difficulties with his father and had also made clear his admiration for her. Eleanor closed her eyes for a moment and felt his lips again, the stir of his breath against her face.

Cameron was everything that Liam was not: cultivated, polished, and well-spoken. A man with a definite future awaiting him. And her mother had taken quite a liking to him, certainly. If Liam had not returned, might she have turned instead to Cameron?

Time alone with Liam would answer these lingering questions, once and for all.

Eleanor walked alone through the woods that night, a kerosene lantern swinging from her hand. She wore a heavy knit shawl drawn round her shoulders to ward off the chill night air. The narrow deer path took her over a low-cresting hill and then down into a tree-lined valley. An owl hooted, followed by the subsequent whir of flapping wings. A breeze whispered through the overspreading trees, the air was moist with the promise of an approaching storm.

As the path began to rise again, distant thunder rumbled across the sloping hills. Eleanor hurried along, eager to reach the shelter of the cove's fishing cabin.

Soon the sound of rushing water reached her ears, and she knew that she was close to the Aspen River. The path came to an abrupt halt at the edge of a ravine, where a flowing stream merged with the river's main body. It was swollen with the spring melt, jumping and tumbling in its rush to the lake. Eleanor forded the shallow river by using several large, flat rocks as stepping stones. She climbed up the far bank and then she made her way along the gentle slope which marked the upper reaches of the cove.

Even in the darkness, Eleanor saw the outlines of the cabin, and beyond a brightly burning bonfire near the shore. Her footsteps quickened in anticipation of finding Liam.

He was not at the bonfire, however. Eleanor held the lantern high, straining to see any sign of his Mackinaw boat. Yes, there it was, resting in the sand. But where had Liam gone to?

"Liam!" she cried, turning a circle.

"Girleen!" he answered within the cabin. Relieved, she rushed inside to meet him, but as she held the lantern out she was scandalized by the fact that he was only half-dressed.

"Gracious, Liam, what are you doing?" Eleanor asked, setting the lantern on the floor.

Liam stood drying his bare arms and chest with a towel. "You've seen me before with even less than this," he teased, smiling. "'Tis only that I wanted to wash off in the lake and rid the oily fish smell from my skin."

"You took a bath in the lake? Why, the water can't hardly be forty degrees!"

"'Twas a cold dip, sure. But I stood by the fire before coming in to dry off." He caught her up in his arms then and lifted her off the ground. "And you'll help to warm me, won't you?"

"I just might, if you'd stop squeezing the life out of me!" she told him.

Liam's mood shifted, and when he set her down again he sought a kiss. Eleanor tensed, though only for a moment. Her lips molded to his as they tasted one another with ease. Slowly he drew away, murmuring, "Very nice."

"It's the least I can do, considering the fact that you almost froze yourself for my sake." As Liam drew on his sweater, Eleanor glanced around the interior of the decrepit cabin. In the lantern's glow, she noticed that a portion of the roof had collapsed. "You might not stay dry for long, however, if it starts to rain."

"Ah, now, I won't allow it!" He lifted her from the waist and twirled her in a circle, raining kisses on her face and neck. Eleanor laughed, infected by his giddiness. Abandoning restraint, she leaned into his embrace, and she heard him groan, felt the answering tension in his body.

Liam's grip tightened momentarily, but then he released her. Eleanor drew back and peered at him. "Why did you stop?" she asked.

"Because I decided a while ago that we'd best go slow, or we'll end up doing something we might regret," he told her. "I don't want to rush you in any way, girleen. You're too important to me to do that."

This was unexpected. Eleanor followed Liam outside to sit on a log beside the bonfire. His arm circled her shoulders as they sat close together. Overhead, the blanket of clouds began to retreat, revealing black velvet sky cast with a net of gleaming stars.

Eleanor stared into the orange and yellow flames. "I thought it was what you wished," she said quietly.

"Sure and I do. But might it not serve us to be friends before lovers?"

"Mama once told me that men and women can never be friends."

Liam stiffened at the mention. "Whole books could be written about what that woman doesn't know," he said. "'Tis a heavy yoke you bear, girleen, to be related to that she-witch."

"You shouldn't talk about my mother that way, even if she is difficult." Then, anxious to change the subject, Eleanor said, "Tell me all you've been doing."

"Well, the life of a fisherman is almost worse than that of a stokerman. We rise at 3:30 AM, dress in three layers of clothing and rubber boots, launch the boats onto the lake, row twenty miles to the herring nets, then draw the nets up from the freezing water before picking them clean. Once that's finished, we return to camp, to gut the fish and chop them in half."

Eleanor wrinkled her nose and said, "How repulsive."

Liam grinned. "Then we 'bait on,' meaning that we thread the pieces of fish onto stiff, notched wire. We load the herring inside the bait boxes and carry them out to the Mackinaws. By 6:30 AM we're ready to row out to the hook lines, where we harvest the real money, the lake trout."

"And how long do you stay out after that?"

"Eight to ten hours." Liam chuckled at her look of astonishment. "So can you believe me when I tell you that I'm bloody well exhausted?"

"You poor man," Eleanor said, reaching over to touch his arm.

"'Tis no so bad, except for the part about riding in the boat all day. I'm still not overly fond of Superior."

"Has it gotten any better? Your fear of the lake, I mean?"

"Aye, some." Liam's eyes were fixed on the fire. "But everything's been quiet, with no gales or storms stirring. Can't say how I'll feel when the heavy weather rolls in." He stood and then added more wood to the fire. "It's thankful I am that my father and brothers aren't here to see my fear."

Liam held out his hand to Eleanor. "Join me, here, close to the fire." Eleanor shrugged out of her shawl and went to sit with him. He slid behind her, and began to caress the skin on the back of her neck, and she felt herself go limp at the gentleness of his touch.

"Have you written to your family in Ireland, Liam?"

"I wrote to Mam and Maeve both, just before I left the O'Rourke's. I won't be expecting a return letter for a month or two yet."

Liam began to massage her shoulders. His touch was a luxury, pure pleasure. "Tell me, why didn't you return to Ireland after the shipwreck?"

"I can never go back, Eleanor," he after some pause.

"Why? Because of the expense?"

"There was trouble back home before I left. 'Twould be folly to show my face among the islanders again."

Eleanor sensed there was more to the story. *Why won't he tell me happened?* she wondered. What was he hiding?

"Well, what about Graceville?"

"I did write to Uncle Tim Pat, to tell him about the wreck and that I was fine. He wrote back and asked me to come west and work on his farm. I never answered him."

"You might be better off with your family."

"I don't want to leave the North Shore, Eleanor. Everything that I care about is here." Liam spoke with quiet conviction, but his words melted Eleanor's heart. For her sake alone, it seemed, Liam was willing to remain in the northlands.

"Do you still have nightmares, Liam?"

"Aye, most every night. I try not to think about them during the day." Liam shook his head. "I don't know what's worse: the dreams of the wreck, or of Conall."

Eleanor shivered at the mention of Conall's name. She hadn't thought about that ghostly voice in months, yet the memory of it returned to her now with chilling intensity. "He's not at rest, is he?" she said, turning to face Liam.

"I should have saved him," Liam said, his words filled with bitterness. "Everything I touch turns to ruin, everyone I care for is harmed or taken away. And that's when I start thinking maybe it's wrong for me to be here with you now, girleen. I couldn't live with myself if anything bad happened to you because of me."

"Don't think that way, please," she said. "Would I be with you now if I thought you were some kind of danger to me?"

"No, I suppose not. But you have uncommon courage, girleen. Maybe more than I have myself."

Eleanor took up Liam's hand. "Let's shake off this gloom. I want to show you something." She led him back toward the cabin.

"What's this all about, now?"

"I'm going to take you on a tour of my lodge," she replied with a smile.

After retrieving the lantern from the cabin, Eleanor led Liam to a site overlooking the river. "Here's the entrance to the lodge. Guests will come inside and receive their room keys in the spacious lobby, which of course will offer a sweeping view of the lake." Eleanor stepped off several paces. "A massive stone fireplace, to warm visitors who venture up here for a winter retreat."

Liam watched her with interest. "A portico with *chaise lounges*, for reading or quiet naps," she continued. "A formal dining room, with the best cooking the North Shore can offer. Upstairs, on the second and third floor, guest rooms with comfortable beds and maybe even private washrooms." Eleanor gestured toward the river then. "I'll offer trout fishing and hunting, of course, and hire guides for excursions on the lake itself. Lawn tennis, horse-shoes, croquet, woodland hikes; any activity that pleases city folk."

"Girleen, you've grand ambitions," Liam said. "Tell me, after the lodge has been built, where do you intend to hire the help?"

"I'll advertise, if necessary. I can post the positions in the Duluth, Minneapolis and St. Paul newspapers."

"A sound plan." Liam drew close beside her. "But maybe there's someone who's already thinking about coming to work for you."

"Oh? And who might that be?" she asked with mock innocence.

Liam caught her in his arms. "I don't intend to be a fisherman forever."

"I thought you once said that you've no notion of making plans for the future."

"Aye. But a man can change his mind." Liam kissed her cheek affectionately. "Who knows, maybe I could even take a turn as assistant keeper at the lighthouse!"

"Assistant keeper," Eleanor repeated in a low voice. The reminder of Cameron cast a shadow across her thoughts.

Liam frowned as she squirmed from his embrace. "Did I say something wrong?"

"No, not exactly."

"Is there some problem with the new assistant?"

"Everything's fine," she replied. "He isn't quite as genial as Lars, but he performs his duties adequately."

"I see," Liam said. "What's he like?"

Eleanor struggled to form the best answer. "Worldly. Aloof. He's from a family with a great deal of money, born and raised in Duluth."

"'Tis a strange thing for a man like that to seek work at a lighthouse," Liam said. "Do you like him, then?"

"Like him? Well, I don't *dislike* him—"

"He's an educated man, hmm? Handsome, even?"

Eleanor's expression went flat. "I suppose you could say that. Honestly, Liam, I haven't really given Cameron much thought."

"Have you heard anything from Berglund?" Liam asked, changing the subject.

"Lars wrote to Papa last winter. He moved to his brother's farm in Iowa and is doing quite well. In fact, Lars spoke of a new sweetheart and even plans for a summer wedding."

"A lucky man." Liam draped the shawl around Eleanor's shoulders. "I owe him a great deal for helping to save my life."

"Lars deserves every happiness," Eleanor agreed.

Back at the shore, the two sat side-by-side again on the log. Liam stirred the fire embers with a long stick as Eleanor rested her head against his shoulder. "You've changed so much, Liam."

"Changed? In what way?"

"Not so rough around the edges. More soft-spoken."

"Aye, well, you can thank Jennie O'Rourke for that. She was strict with me about staying off the bottle and even talked me into coming to Sunday Mass with the family." Liam chuckled. "You'll have to meet her, Eleanor. You'd take a shine to one another, I just know it." Liam stifled a yawn. "I should be heading back to the fish camp now. I'll only get a few hours' sleep as it is."

"Same night next week?"

"If you're willing. Now, allow me the pleasure of rowing you home."

"I'll come, don't worry, and yes, you may take me home," Eleanor said.

Liam kicked sand over the remnants of the fire and then held the lantern high as he helped Eleanor into the Mackinaw.

As the boat cut through the inky darkness, water sluiced against the hull. Liam rowed in silence, which suited Eleanor. She mulled over their long conversation together. Liam was indeed a changed man; his time with the O'Rourke family had obviously shown him a different life. Beyond this was the surprise of his expressing an interest in working at the lodge.

In what capacity? she wondered. As a builder or boat-guide, perhaps? Or maybe as her husband?

Only once before had she ever thought about marriage to Liam, and that was the night he'd given her Maeve's necklace. What would it be like to be his wife? The thought of Liam joined with her in bed brought a rush of heat to her face. But what about his nightmares and his remorse for the past?

Such things might cripple a man forever.

CHAPTER 16

▼

"Happy twenty-first birthday, Eleanor, and may all your wishes come true!"

It was a late afternoon in June. Eleanor sat at the head of the dining room table, wearing a new white linen tea-gown, a gift sent from her Aunt Regina. Everyone had gathered together for the small celebration. A balmy breeze fluttered the window curtains, redolent with the scent of the lilac bushes blooming just beneath the sill.

Adeline had baked a birthday cake. A single candle burned atop the thick white frosting, and Eleanor watched the flame dance as her mother placed the cake on the table.

"Make a wish," Cameron insisted. He sat to her right, and she glanced at him momentarily before blowing out the candle.

"What did you wish for?" Bridget asked.

"She can't tell or it won't come true," David countered.

"Some wishes are meant be kept secret, anyway," Cameron said.

John left the table just then and returned with a bucket of ice cream that had been hand-cranked that morning. "Good thing the ice blocks are still holding out in the cellar. By this time next month we'll be out."

"Birthday girl gets to cut the cake," Adeline said, handing Eleanor the knife.

Eleanor cut while John scooped up ice cream with a ladle. "Well, Eleanor, now that you're all grown up, you won't have much use for your old Papa anymore," he teased.

"Please don't say that, Papa. I'm no different from yesterday."

"He's right, you know," Cameron agreed. "Time to put your childhood dreams aside and think about the future."

Eleanor arched a brow. "And what's that supposed to mean?"

"Don't be rude, Eleanor," Adeline said. "Cameron only meant that you can't just go on being your father's daughter forever."

"How does that concern Cameron?" Eleanor argued. She was sick and tired of her mother always favoring Cameron during their conversations.

"I didn't mean anything by it, Eleanor," Cameron said. "I was just seconding your father's opinion."

"Let's not have a row, Eleanor," Adeline said. "We should all show some consideration for Cameron's feelings, after the letter he received yesterday."

"What letter?" Bridget asked.

Cameron stirred his fork absently through the melting ice cream on his plate. "A letter from my betrothed back home. I made her an honorable offer of matrimony before leaving for this assignment, and she has refused me. She's taken with another man, it seems."

"Oh," Eleanor said. She looked at Cameron closely, unaware he had a serious attachment with anyone. "I'm sorry, Cameron. I didn't know."

His lips thinned. "I didn't want to mention it on your special day, because you think me rich and spoiled and have no feelings."

"That's not true," Eleanor said, stung by his open accusation. "I never said anything like that, Cameron."

Cameron tossed his linen napkin on the table. "None of that matters, anyway. No one cares about me, either here or at home." Cameron rose from the table and then strode through the kitchen door.

"Go after him, Eleanor! He needs you!" Adeline insisted, grabbing her by the arm and propelling her toward the door.

Stepping outside, Eleanor caught a glimpse of Cameron, just as he slipped into the fog house. Irritation prickled her; why such histrionics, especially on her birthday?

She found Cameron beside one of the air compressors. His back was turned to the door, and Eleanor approached tentatively. "Cameron, are you all right?"

Cameron turned, and Eleanor caught her breath, for tears clung to his dark eyelashes. "No," he said with an angry sniff, wiping his face with his sleeve. "But that's immaterial to you, Eleanor, since you hate me so."

"Hate you? Why on earth would you say that?"

"Don't act so innocent! I see it every day, the way you refuse my overtures of friendship, avoid my company, belittle my comments!"

Eleanor faltered. It was true that she often kept Cameron at arm's length, but *hatred*? "I didn't know that my friendship meant so much to you, Cameron."

"Then I guess I've been making a fool of myself, hoping—well," he added blandly, "I suppose you have no desire to open the birthday gift I bought for you."

Eleanor blinked. "You bought a birthday gift for me?"

"Here it is," Cameron said, withdrawing a small package from his coat pocket. It was wrapped in white tissue paper and tied with a burgundy-colored bow.

Eleanor fingered the package before tearing the wrapping away to reveal a tiny box. "Oh!" she exclaimed as she opened the lid. Inside was a cameo necklace, ivory against a field of black onyx. She cradled the necklace in the palm of her hand. "Cameron, it's beautiful."

"Do you like it?" he asked. "I wrote to my mother not long after my arrival here, asking her to order it."

Eleanor pooled the cameo back inside the box. "I cannot accept this," she told him. "It's much too expensive."

"I won't hear of it. Now, allow me." Cameron lifted the necklace and placed it around Eleanor's neck. The cameo came to rest on her skin just above the lace collar of her tea-dress. "You see? It fits you perfectly." With one finger he traced along the delicate gold chain. "So lovely, like the wearer herself."

They were standing very close. "Cameron, I—"

"You still don't understand how much you've affected me. I can't stop thinking about you, Eleanor." Cameron leaned a little closer. Eleanor gazed into his face, caught by the green-gray flecks in his eyes. "You're the most beautiful woman I've ever known," Cameron said. "If ever you were to come to Duluth with me, no lady could hold a candle to you, I swear it."

Eleanor stepped away. "I shall never leave the North Shore. My life, the life I've chosen, will remain here always."

"Would you leave if another man asked you, I wonder?" Cameron asked, his expression hardening. "Who is it that you visit, Eleanor, when you leave at midnight with lantern in hand? And where is it that you go? To your cove, the one you hope to purchase?"

Eleanor matched his cold tone with that of her own. "It's none of your business."

"Everything at Haven Point is my business," Cameron said. He regarded her calmly. "You won't keep your secret for very long."

"Oh? And what about your own secrets? Why didn't you tell me about the girl who wrote to you?"

"You wouldn't understand about Sophie, Eleanor. Our parents wished for us to marry since we were children." Cameron's glance dropped to his shoes. "Her rejection of my suit is just another failure on my part, I'm afraid."

"It might not be too late, Cameron," Eleanor said. "Perhaps when you return home next winter—"

"It's quite over between us. Sophie made that very clear in her letter." Cameron's expression brightened. "What's past is the past. I'd like to think that the future lies in another direction." There was no mistaking the implication of his words, and Eleanor felt a blush creep up her neck. "This is probably as good a time as any to invite you to a special July Fourth Dance, to be held in Grand Marais."

"A dance on the Fourth? Why haven't I heard of it?"

"I read the handbills when I rowed up to Johnson's Mercantile yesterday. There'll be food and games and music." A note of assurance crept into Cameron's voice. "I've already spoken to your mother, and she fully supports my asking you."

"I see," Eleanor said. She fingered the cameo absently. "I must speak to Mama before I give you my answer."

"Of course." Cameron lifted her hand to his lips. "Take all the time you need to think things over. I'm more than willing to wait."

When Eleanor returned to the dining room, Adeline was clearing away the table. "Did you speak to Cameron?" Adeline asked. "Is he all right?"

"He'll be fine, Mama."

Adeline's face smoothed. "Thank goodness! I was worried he'd decide to leave before—"

"Before what?" Eleanor demanded. The question hung between them. "Go on, finish what you were about to say!"

"Really, Eleanor, must I spell everything out for you?" She spied the cameo hanging around Eleanor's neck. "How lovely! Did Cameron give that to you just now?"

Eleanor clasped the cameo. "You didn't answer my question."

"Did you thank him?"

"No, because he didn't need to give it to me. I don't expect anything from Cameron."

"Well, I think he expects something from you, daughter. Can't you tell when a man is pursuing you? He moons after you in the most touching way. I'm surprised that you haven't noticed."

Eleanor smirked. "Cameron's not pursuing me, Mama. He just ended an engagement with another woman."

"Precisely the opportunity you need," Adeline said. She wrung her hands. "It could be accomplished with the greatest of ease. Offer him home-baked cookies, walk with him on the beach, read aloud to him in the afternoons. You could have him eating out of your hand if you wished!"

"I'm not certain I do wish it." Eleanor sat in a nearby chair with a huff. "This all feels so sudden."

"You didn't seem to think it so sudden with that Irishman last winter."

"That was different. Liam is different. He's—"

"Poor and uneducated and completely unsuitable. And I don't want his name mentioned in this house again, Eleanor. Do I make myself clear?"

Eleanor glared at her but said nothing. Adeline continued to stack the dirty dishes. "Has Cameron invited you to the dance yet?"

"Just now, when we were talking."

"And did you accept?"

"I haven't said yes or no," Eleanor replied. She gave her mother a searching look. "Apparently you've given your blessing, though I'm not sure why."

"Isn't it obvious?" Adeline drew a chair to sit in front of Eleanor. "You've told me on several occasions that you have no desire to live in St. Paul with Casey and Regina. So be it. But here, right under your very nose, is an attractive young man who stands to inherit a great deal of money! And, miracle of miracles, he's shown a strong preference for you, Eleanor! It's a golden opportunity, being handed to you freely!"

"How can you be so certain of his feelings, Mama? We've only known one another for little more than two months!"

"I'll leave that for you to discover," Adeline said. She lifted Eleanor's hand and gave it a pat. "Go to the dance with him, Eleanor. Enjoy yourself. Allow others to envy you in the company of such a handsome and eligible man."

Eleanor felt the weight of the cameo around her neck. Cameron had given it to her as a gesture of his good will. Perhaps she had judged him too harshly up till now. "I suppose I might. No harm can come from it."

"That's my good girl!" Adeline said. "I'll sew a new dress for you, something eye-catching. You'll be the center of attention, I promise!"

"It will just be enough, Mama, if Cameron and I can enjoy a pleasant time together." Eleanor rose from her seat. "I think I'll go upstairs and change."

"Take your time today, my dear, since it is your birthday," Adeline said. As Eleanor climbed the stairs to her bedroom, she heard her mother's happy humming.

Eleanor entered her bedroom and went to gaze out the window. Everything had unfolded with extraordinary speed: Cameron's emotional outburst, his gift of the cameo, and then his invitation to the dance. For the first time she felt her loyalties wavering. His attractive looks, his charm, his money: what girl wouldn't feel flattered by such a man's attentions?

But he wasn't Liam. Her Liam. Each time they met together she felt herself drawing closer to him. His companionship and their long talks together had become the highlight of her week. But there were moments when Liam grew silent and unreachable, causing her to doubt him once again. He was still wracked by nightmares, she knew, reliving the shipwreck over and over without resolution.

"It's just a dance," she told herself. Eleanor unclasped Cameron's neck and laid it next to the St. Brendan's medal, which was lying atop the highboy.

Two gifts, each as different from the other as the men who'd given them.

*   *   *   *

Liam and Nils were taking their lunch break inside the Mackinaw boat several miles out on the lake. Both men wore oilskin coveralls, their caps tilted back as they took their ease.

Seagulls flocked overhead, attracted by the occasional chunk of bread that Nils tossed aloft. Liam gazed at the shifting panoply of gray-bodied, white-and-black-winged birds, and he smiled at their aerial acrobatics.

The thirty-foot vessel was only half full with the day's trout catch. "The wind, she has vanished," Nils said. "Not much use checking the rest of the hook lines."

"Oh, aye, a dead calm it is," Liam agreed. "Maybe an afternoon off won't be such a bad thing."

"I think you're right," Nils said. He withdrew a round tin of chewing tobacco from his shirt pocket and stuffed a pinch of black weed between his cheek and gum. "Our take is ahead of where it was this same time last year, and I have you to thank for it, MacLann."

"Me?" Liam said, stirring.

"*Jah*, it is true. All last year, Gustav was already slowing down in his work. He'd come late to the boat in the mornings, then refuse to pull his share when we packed the catch in the fish house. It was worse when he started drinking." Nils spat an arc of tobacco into the water. "Having you on my crew is like having two Gustavs."

"Och, don't be saying that, now. More likely the weather's been fair and bonnie, that's all."

"Well, we have had good weather, that's true. But I'll be damned if you're not the best fisherman I've ever met. You practically *think* like a lake trout, MacLann."

"A man reads the signs. He gets a feeling about where the fish are feeding, where they'll come to the surface to sun themselves." Liam sniffed. "'Tis no great talent."

"I disagree." Nils took two pickled herring sandwiches from the basket and passed one to Liam. "Anyway, it already feels like you've been with us for years. One might even think you were a Nordlander," Nils added, a wry glint in his eyes.

"In a pig's arse," Liam threw back. He reclined a little as he luxuriated in the bright sunshine. He dipped one hand over the gunnel. Cold water played through his fingers.

Images formed in his mind. *Water, fluid and smooth, dark depths below, ice-water dwelling of the voiceless dead, Superior, Superior...*Liam jerked his fingers clear and sat up with a suddenness that made the boat lurch. Goosebumps raced down his arms and back.

"Something wrong?" Nils asked.

"It was here." Liam took a deep breath and then released it slowly. "The shipwreck. The *William Dorn* is below us, aye, and the remains of all her crew."

Nils' brow clouded. "How can you know? I thought you said that you couldn't see anything when she wrecked."

"I just know," Liam said. He rubbed his mouth. "I've seen things. Visions. Dreams. Christ, I've even talked to the spirit of my brother Conall, dead now these past five years!" He passed a shaking hand across his brow. "Sometimes I think 'twould have been better if I'd perished along with the rest of them."

Nils waited for a few moments before answering. "There is purpose for you here, now, MacLann. The men of Little Nesna need you. Miss Thompson needs you."

Liam started at the comment. "What does Miss Thompson have to do with anything?"

Nils gave a snort. "I may be a poor immigrant, but I wasn't born yesterday," he said, leaning himself forward slightly in his seat. "A blind man could see how you feel about her."

"You don't mind it so much, then, that I borrow the boat to go meet her?"

Nils shrugged. "You must do as you will. But when the trout season starts to slow, you should visit Haven Point during the daytime."

Liam's shoulders slumped. "'Tis not possible, for her mother's set against me. We must meet in secret."

"You're courting Eleanor without her parents' permission?" Nils asked. He shook his head. "My friend, that's unwise."

"We haven't much choice if I'm to see her at all."

"You need to earn the mother and father's respect, for Eleanor's sake," Nils said. He tossed the crust of his sandwich skyward for the gulls. "No more fishing today. We row for camp, then take an early supper and get some extra sleep."

Liam nodded, watching as Nils placed himself on the centerboard and lifted the oars. As Nils began to row, Liam gazed upward at the gulls still gliding overhead.

Nils' admonition had touched a raw nerve. Liam was beginning to chafe over the constraints of his midnight meetings with Eleanor. Why must he skulk like a thief in the shadows? What crime had he committed, save that he was a man without property or name?

But that was precisely why he'd come to America. To build a new life. To gain occupation and buy his own land. To put the past behind and forge a new identity, both Irish and American. And if that included marrying an American woman like Eleanor, then all the better.

It was time to stop hiding and openly declare his feelings to Eleanor.

"There's a letter for you, Liam. From someone named Mrs. Bryant in St. Paul."

Liam, returning from the Mackinaw, halted just inside the cabin doorway as Sollie came over and handed him an envelope. Liam looked over it before asking, "When did this come?"

"Mail bag delivery from the *America*, not long after you and Nils left this morning." Sollie returned to the pot atop the stove and took a quick taste of bubbling cooked beans. "Never been to St. Paul, myself."

"Nor have I," Liam said as he opened the envelope. He unfolded the letter and saw that it was from Nick Bryant's mother.

Liam had written to Sadie Bryant not long after his return to the North Shore, encouraged to do so by Nils. But Liam hadn't expected a reply of any kind.

It was a short letter, less than a page, and Liam read it at a gallop. Sollie, wiping his mouth after another taste of beans, asked, "What's it about?"

"Jesus," Liam whispered, crumbling the letter with his fingers. "I can't well fucking believe it."

"What's wrong?"

"You wouldn't understand," Liam said as he went to sit on his bunk. His earlier sense of optimism over Eleanor evaporated as Sadie's words blazed across his conscience: *"Though I praise God for your safe rescue, Mr. MacLann, it grieves me to wonder why you couldn't have helped my boy Nicky..."*

Liam found it hard to even swallow. "Poor woman," he muttered, clutching the ball of paper. Liam thought of the last time he'd seen Nick in the boiler room: the coal-blackened face, the rascal's grin, the story about the cook with the woman in his cabin. It all felt a lifetime ago, but in truth had been little more than six months.

"Is something wrong, Liam?" Sollie asked.

"A letter from the mother of one of my shipmates from the *Dorn*," Liam replied. "Nick Bryant was my best friend in the whole world."

"I see," Sollie said. He patted Liam's shoulder. "You're a lucky man to have had a friendship like that. Not many do."

Liam stared blankly past Sollie. "I miss the times we spent together, you know? Drinking and playing cards and getting into fights. No one knew how to have fun like Nick."

"He must have been a good man," Sollie said, then returned to the stove and ladled beans into a bowl. "Why not come and have something to eat, eh?"

"I guess I might," Liam said, taking a seat at the table.

"Good. And you'll have some coffee too," Sollie encouraged. He beamed as he filled a cup and placed it on the table. "Maybe we can play a round of cards later too, hmm, like you once did with your friend?"

"Maybe," Liam said before taking a bite of beans. They tasted delicious, savory with bacon fat and brown sugar. "You won't mind if I win, though?"

Sollie's eyes twinkled. "We'll just see," he said, filling a plate of his own. They sat together and ate in companionable silence, and Liam felt his grief lessen a degree.

Will it ever leave altogether? Liam wondered as he looked out the cabin window toward Superior. *Will there ever be peace for me in this life again?*

*   *   *   *

When Eleanor joined Liam a few nights later at the cove, she sensed immediately that something had changed. Liam seemed distracted and out-of-sorts, not even giving her a customary kiss of welcome. There was no bonfire, and a thick layer of clouds obscured the sky. Darkness pressed in around them.

She found him sitting on the cabin floor. "Why didn't you build a fire tonight?" she asked.

"Ah, well, I wasn't up to it."

Eleanor draped the shawl on the floor beside the lantern before sitting next to Liam. Eleanor touched him and asked, "What's wrong?"

"Nothing. Everything." Liam rose and began to pace. "Aren't you tired of all this, Eleanor? Don't you think it's time we told your family about the two of us?"

Eleanor drew her knees up and circled the fullness of her skirt with both arms. "What's happened, Liam? Why are you acting this way?"

"I got a letter a few days ago. From Nick Bryant's mother, who lives in St. Paul."

"Nick's mother? Why would she be writing to you here?"

"I sent a letter to Nick's mother and one to Captain Graling's widow. Nils said that it might help to ease the nightmares." Lamplight bathed the hard planes of Liam's face. "'Twas a mistake, I tell you."

"What did she say?"

Liam resumed pacing. "Oh, she was pleasant enough. Thanked me for taking the trouble to write, telling me what a good boy her Nicky had been, that she was grateful we were friends." Liam kicked at a pile of rotted shingles. "But 'twas the last part that tore at me. She wondered why I hadn't been able to save Nick. Seems she read the whole account in that newspaper story."

"But, Liam, I thought that story was only reported in the *Duluth News-Tribune*."

"'Twas what I thought too," Liam said, "but it must have been printed elsewhere." He pressed his palms to his temples. "My head aches with the fact of everyone knowing."

Eleanor rose to comfort him. "Liam, I'm sorry," she said. "I wish there was something I could say."

Liam took her by the arms. "You never answered my question. Why can't we make an open declaration? I want you to tell your mother and father about us, Eleanor."

"It's too soon," she answered. "Once I've bought the cove, and paid for the construction of a house—"

"And what if you cannot buy the land?" he interrupted. "What if someone else buys it before you, hmm? Is that the only plan you've made?"

"Why are you acting this way?" Eleanor asked, angered. "Don't you care about me?"

Her words vibrated in the air between them. "Aye," Liam whispered as his fingers dug into her flesh. "So much that it hurts, girleen." Abruptly, he began to kiss her.

His forcefulness upset her. "Let me go!" Eleanor cried, freeing herself. Her sympathy toward him vanished. "Why must you grab at me like some wild savage!"

"Is that what you think I am, eh? A savage?"

"No, but you can't just take what you want without asking!"

Liam's eyes narrowed. "There's something different about you tonight," he said. "As though—as though something lay between us."

Thoughts of Cameron flashed through Eleanor's mind. "I—well, if you must know, I am going to a dance in Grand Marais with the new assistant keeper," she told him.

"What? He's asked you to a dance?"

"Yes. Cameron gave me a nice gift on my birthday and asked very politely if I would accompany him to the dance." Eleanor met Liam's gaze squarely. "I've decided to accept."

"So, you'd two-time me just like that!" Liam said, snapping his fingers in her face. "A fine fool I've been, thinking that you cared for me the way I do for you!"

"Liam, nothing has changed! I consider Cameron a friend and nothing more!"

"I can well imagine what he thinks about you," Liam muttered. He walked to the door and stood, waiting.

"What are you doing?"

"Taking you home. 'Twas a mistake to come tonight."

"That's it? That's all you have to say?"

"I'm tired, girleen. I work my arse off all goddamned day. 'Twould be best to part now before I say something I'll regret."

Eleanor gathered the lantern and shawl before brushing past him. "Don't worry about returning me to Haven Point. I can find my way home well enough, thank you."

"Suit yourself," Liam said. They hesitated for a moment just outside the door, and Eleanor looked at him, awash in misery. She longed to reach out to him, say something that would heal this sudden breach. But without another word, Liam stalked off in the direction of the Mackinaw, leaving Eleanor to hike home alone.

CHAPTER 17

▼

Liam was in a black mood the next few weeks, unsociable with the Norwegians and given over to brooding by the shore. Nils did not ask him about it directly, but Liam could tell from the look in Nils' eyes that he guessed his troubles with Eleanor. Liam appreciated Nils' distance but secretly longed for advice. He was consumed by uncertainty. Who was this interloper, and why was Eleanor even considering him? Liam had plainly shown his feelings for her, and been the model of patience she'd asked him to be.

It seemed a cruel blow, especially since he'd begun to find his sea-legs again. But maybe he'd miscalculated when he'd pushed the issue of telling her parents. Maybe Eleanor still wasn't ready to stand up to her mother. Liam cursed his impatience and grew even more taciturn and withdrawn.

One night the men gathered in the cabin to play cards and drink whiskey. Liam watched them from his bunk, dour and unmoving. "Hey, MacLann, why not join us for a game?" Nils asked.

"I don't think so. I've no good luck these days."

"Well, take a nip of whiskey then," Nils said, holding out his glass.

"No, no," Liam said, waving him off. "Not tonight."

Sollie, who'd won the most rounds that evening, grinned and said, "What you need is the chance to get out and meet some new girls. We are all of us going to Marais for the dance on the Fourth, even Johan here—"

"Hell will freeze over before I show my face there," Liam said, and then rose from his bed and went to the table to pour a tall shot of whiskey. While the others watched, he downed it in one swallow. With a trembling hand he wiped his mouth before taking a seat.

"Maybe you should try to talk to Eleanor, Liam," Nils suggested as he dealt the cards. It was the first time Nils had spoken directly about Eleanor since his and Liam's lunch in the boat.

"There's nothing to talk about. She's going to the dance with another man, a fellow with looks and money, and so that's that." Liam pretended to examine his cards. "I took a chance and came out on the losing end, once again."

"It doesn't sound like she's thrown you over," Sollie said. "Miss Thompson is still young. But she also has a good head on her shoulders." The big Norwegian took a sip from his glass. "She'll come around to you again, in time."

"Well, I'm not the kind of man to just sit and wait. Either she wants me or no," Liam said. "A man must have his pride, after all."

"Pride will see you grow old with no wife or children," Nils admonished.

"That's what Shamus O'Rourke said to me." Liam folded his cards and handed them back to Nils. "I have no heart for the game tonight."

Back in his bunk, Liam reached beneath his pillow and took out the most recent letter from his Uncle Tim Pat, delivered via the *America* earlier that day.

The whiskey was making Liam's head swim, and it was a little difficult to make out the words in the lamplight. Something about Rose O'Malley.

> —*for you see, cousin Liam, that Rose has come all the way to America to settle in Graceville. And while it is true that she has not spoken of you directly, I know she has come because she wants you for her husband. A girl doesn't leave Inishmore and travel thousands of miles just to smell the posies somewhere new.*

Liam looked up from the letter. Rose O'Malley, his childhood sweetheart, had immigrated to Minnesota! Alone, it seemed, with neither kith nor kin. Was it possible that she'd come because of him, as Tim Pat suggested? Liam searched his dim memories of Rose, of their walks along the county lanes, their talks together about farming and fishing. Had her love for him run deeper than he'd suspected? He read onward:

> *It's time for you to leave the shores of Lake Superior and come home to your own people. Come back to Graceville, Liam boy. You'd make Rose the happiest woman and give your poor mother peace of mind.*

Liam reread the letter several times. Longing seized him, longing for the sound of his native Irish Gaelic, for the ease of being among those who understood him best. Rose would make a capable wife for him, he knew. Hardworking and devoted, she'd give him a child every year in due time. They could purchase land, raise up a brood of youngsters, grow comfortable together in the years to follow.

But Rose was not Eleanor. Only Eleanor knew of his pain, his torment of the unseen. How could he ever explain such things to Rose? Beyond that, he didn't love Rose and never had. Love. Was he in love with Eleanor, then? Was that why he ached for her and raged against her in his jealousy?

Liam realized then that he would have to fight for Eleanor, make her understand how much he needed her. This other man was of no consequence, no matter how handsome or rich. She belonged to him alone.

That night Liam slept better than he had for a long time, convinced in his heart that she would respond to him as he wished. Before the dance, he would speak to her and do his best to make her understand.

*   *   *   *

The morning of the Fourth dawned gray and heavily overcast. Eleanor, who'd sat up half the night while her mother put the finishing touches on her new dress, frowned at the rain-filled cast of the sky. "How typical," Eleanor said as she lay in her bed stared out the window.

There'll be other dances this summer, she told herself. Cameron would be disappointed, certainly. Adeline would be inconsolable. But what about her own feelings? Eleanor rolled onto her back, thinking. She'd softened somewhat towards Cameron since her last argument with Liam. The bitter memory of Liam's words at the cabin had steeled her resolve to go to the dance and enjoy herself with the assistant keeper. Cameron had behaved the perfect gentleman in the interim, complimenting her appearance and even bringing her bouquets of wild-flowers each morning.

But as the day of the dance had drawn closer, she'd begun to feel a sense of guilt about Liam. Liam had come north to work at the fish camp for her sake. He'd been kindly and respectful toward her during their midnight meetings. And now she was repaying him by accepting the attentions of another man. No wonder Liam had been angry with her.

Eleanor rose from her bed and went down to the kitchen, where she filled a glass of water at the sink. She went to sit outside on the front step, listening to the distant sound of waves sloshing against the shore.

She took a drink and gazed at the delicate tendrils of a dew-laden spider web stretched between the metal rail and the top step. The first drops of rain began to fall, fat and heavy. Out on the lake, the wind had already begun to whip frothy caps on the waves. Were Liam and the Norwegian fishermen out on Superior? Eleanor rose to her feet, the wind flapping her cotton gown.

"Lord, please watch over the men on the lake," she whispered. "Keep them safe from harm, each one."

*   *   *   *

Liam had been watching the leaden horizon since sunrise, filled with apprehension as the sky began to darken. Nils too watched as clouds crowded the horizon and then swept over the lake.

Rain began to pummel the Mackinaw, sheer curtains of water that quickly soaked the men. They sat at opposite ends of the vessel, with Nils manning the oars. "She's going to be a widow-maker," Nils said.

"Aye. Superior's fist will hammer us, sure," Liam agreed. His expression was stoic as the boat heaved with the rolling seas.

Huge waves built in rapid fashion. The men quickly drew in the trout net, plucking fish as fast as possible. Winds drove spray over the gunnel, adding to their general misery.

"Here she comes!" Nils shouted as they were slammed by the first great wave. It almost flipped the Mackinaw over, and Liam pitched into the piled nets. Cursing, he disentangled himself in time to face the next wall of water.

"We've got to tie the boat to the net buoy!" Nils shouted. "Keep the bow facing into the waves, or we're dead men!"

Dead men. The words echoed in Liam's thoughts as he lashed the boat's line to the net buoy. The buoy, anchored to the lake's bottom, was strong and flexible and would stretch with the motion of the waves. It was their only hope of survival.

Nils raised the spray hood to keep water from filling the boat's bottom. Liam grabbed a bucket and began to bail. Superior had become a boiling cauldron in the span of a few short minutes.

Liam shook with fear. With each sickening crest and downward plunge into the next trough, he was transported once again to the *William Dorn* life-raft. Bile rose in his throat, but he fought it down, determined to prove himself in the face of the storm.

It was a wild and violent squall. The wind whistled in the air, a harsh scream of fury. Lightning branched across the sky, followed quickly by a deafening boom of thunder. Time and again green water threatened to capsize them, but the two fisherman hung on grimly.

An hour passed. Liam, numbed and drenched, continued to bail. He was seized by hopelessness; how was this any different from shoveling coal aboard the *Dorn* during the height of the November gale?

Nils said nothing as they rode the tumultuous hills of water. Liam glanced at him from time to time, trying to emulate the big Norwegian's sense of calm. *That man's a lion on the sea*, Liam thought, and this steadied his own sense of panic.

"What about the other fishermen?" Liam yelled. "Do you think they'll make it through?"

"They damn well better! Those boats are worth more than their poor sorry arses!" Nils answered. Liam grinned at Nils' gallows humor. It calmed Liam's fear, and for the first time he faced fully into the wind.

I will not be broken, he proclaimed in his heart. *I am my father's son, a son of the sea, and I will not be broken.*

Liam inhaled deep and shook his fist at Superior. *I am Liam Joseph MacLann, and I will not be broken!*

*   *   *   *

Eleanor was sipping her coffee at the kitchen table when the storm hit Haven Point in earnest. Wind hurled against the windows, driving before it torrents of rain. Lightning rattled the windows. David, who'd been setting up his toy soldiers along the kitchen table, looked outside and exclaimed, "Would you look at the trees out there!"

Eleanor went to the window, awed and a little frightened by the wild lashing and bending of the branches. A single emerald leaf plastered itself to the pane, shorn from the old oak in the yard.

Adeline, who was mixing ingredients for a cinnamon coffee cake, spoke to Eleanor, asking, "Light the lantern, if you would. The sky's so dark you'd think nightfall was coming."

Soon the lantern's glow filled the room. "Will Papa or Cameron light the beacon, Mama?" David asked.

"Cameron will, most likely. And it wouldn't surprise me if he starts up the foghorn as well," Adeline replied. As though in answer, the foghorn's boom reverberated through the kitchen's interior. "Conditions must be terrible on the lake."

Eleanor said nothing. Anxiety gripped her over the fishermen's safety. The image of Liam being tossed about on the waves in the small open fishing boat stirred her to action. She took down her father's oilskin jacket and sou'wester hat from the peg on the wall.

"Where are you going, Eleanor?" Adeline asked.

"Out to the tower to see if Cameron needs any help."

Adeline smiled. "A fine idea. But come back before too long; the coffee cake will be ready shortly."

"I'll return in a little while," Eleanor promised as she turned the doorknob and stepped out into the storm.

Wind and water smacked her face. There was a keen to the air that reminded Eleanor of the great November gale, only now the sky wept rain instead of snow and ice. It was a prodigious drenching, the worst storm yet of the '06 season. Eleanor clutched the hat as she hurried toward the tower.

Once inside, Eleanor removed the dripping jacket and then tipped out the water from the hat's brim. She stood still for a moment, listening for any sound of Cameron. Silence answered her, easing her tension a little. She did not relish the idea of Cameron coming in just as she was searching for Liam on the lake.

As she began to climb the curving stairwell, she felt a peculiar vibration shake the brick building. Eleanor stopped at one of the windows along the stair. Below, combers boomed against the rock base of the tower. With each impact the tower quivered, and a needle of fear began to worm its way into her heart. The fishermen were riding those tremendous waves, with nothing between them and Superior's depths save the thin wooden planks of their boats.

In the light room, Eleanor saw at once that Cameron had indeed lit the beacon. She shielded her eyes from its piercing brilliance as the lens rotated with stolid regularity. Eleanor climbed to the uppermost lantern deck, hoping she might yet catch a glimpse of the boats on the lake.

Superior was crisscrossed with seething waves. Giant seas ran up to the shore and smashed violently against the land. Heavy rain had cut the visibility to almost zero, and Eleanor realized how foolish her initial hope had been. The fishermen were probably many miles out on the lake by now. But the act of standing there and praying for their safety brought her a measure of comfort.

From down below, she heard someone open and close the annex door. Eleanor listened carefully to the weight and tempo of the footfalls on the metal steps, trying to gauge whether it was John or Cameron. She frowned, unable to decide. "Papa?" she called, cupping her hands to her mouth. "Papa, is that you?"

There was no answer. Eleanor descended from the lantern deck as the echoing footsteps neared the door, where she and Cameron nearly bumped into one another.

Eleanor took a stumbling step backward. She stared at him, riveted by his expression. Cameron's eyes were dark with mistrust, and he loomed over her in a way that was almost threatening.

"What are you doing here?" he questioned.

"I wanted to see the storm over the lake."

"I see." Cameron's gaze pinned her. "And there's no other reason?"

"Why didn't you answer when I called?" Eleanor asked him, evading the question.

"I didn't hear you, what with the boom of the waves against the rock," Cameron replied. He touched her shoulder. "You're soaking wet, Eleanor. Really, for your own sake, I must insist that you return to the house."

"I'm fine, really. I want to stay a little longer."

Cameron shook his head. "Your mother warned me about your stubbornness, though I confess I've never seen it until now." He took her by the elbow. "Please, allow me to show you back to the house."

"No," Eleanor said as she jerked her arm free. Quickly she returned to the lantern deck.

Cameron climbed the steps to join her. "You're here because of *him*, aren't you?" he asked.

Eleanor looked at him sharply. "Who are you talking about?"

"The Irishman. I know all about him, about the two of you." There was a pettiness to Cameron's voice she'd never heard before. "I know what happened last winter, Eleanor."

"Who told you?" she demanded.

"Why, Adeline, of course." Cameron's usual poise had returned, and he smiled as he spoke. "Poor fellow, your Mr. MacLann. Quite pathetic, really. Losing friends and occupation in one fell swoop, then finding the girl of his dreams, only to have the door shut against him by her mother." Cameron's smile became a smirk. "Really, dearest, such a low-born creature is far below your worth."

Eleanor clenched her hands. "I am not your 'dearest,' Cameron Russell. And furthermore, you don't understand a single thing about Liam or what he endured! How dare you judge a man that you've never met!"

"Oh, I've met him all right," Cameron said, matching her heated tone. "Once, when I was up to the Mercantile in Grand Marais, he and a few of those prattling Norwegians were on hand to buy supplies. I asked the clerk who they were, and he explained what they did and where their fish camp was located." Cameron chuckled. "The mystery of your midnight travels has been solved, I believe."

Cameron's smugness was unbearable. "I should leave now," Eleanor said, trying to move past him.

He blocked her way. "Tell me, Eleanor, does your mother know about the Irishman?"

"What does it matter to you?"

"It matters a great deal. You're very important to me, Eleanor," Cameron added. "And I don't intend to lose you."

"I was never yours to lose," she said as she pushed past him.

Eleanor paused just outside the annex door and cast her gaze across the lake. The squall was passing, thankfully. For a moment she considered walking to the fish camp, to learn any news of how the fishermen had fared. But they might not be back before nightfall, and she wasn't even certain that Liam would be willing to talk to her.

One thing was certain; she was finished with Cameron. He was too pushy, too nosy by half. Despite her mother's hopes to the contrary, she needed to end the possibility of any alliance between herself and Cameron Russell.

*   *   *   *

The following night, Eleanor was awakened by the gentle rap of a stone on the window. Rising from her bed, she moved past the still-sleeping Bridget and opened the window sash.

Below, lighted by the moon, stood Liam.

Eleanor's heart jumped, and she leaned out a bit. Liam motioned for her to come down. She held up one finger to him, signaling that she'd be just a moment.

Eleanor felt a rush of both relief and excitement as she grabbed her flannel wrap. She descended the stairs as quietly as possible, avoiding the squeaky seventh step. Once outside, she drew the wrap more tightly around her to ward off the cool edge of the night air. The grass was damp beneath her bare feet. Crickets creaked and churred. Behind her, the beacon swept the night sky.

Liam ran to her, and Eleanor flew into his arms. He hugged her fiercely.

Safety. Assurance. Refuge. How could she have ever doubted Liam and all that he meant to her? "I'm so happy to see you," she whispered.

"Ah, you're like breath and life to me," he told her, clutching her once again.

"Let's go to the barn where we can talk in private," she said. Hand in hand, she led him across the yard.

Eleanor slid open the barn door. Chickens clucked in agitation, and as she lit the dust-coated lantern, she heard a soft grunt from one of the suckling pigs. Sacks of feed lay piled along the barn's wall, and Eleanor nodded for Liam to take a seat.

They snuggled close, arms entwined. "Did you go to the dance with that man yesterday?" Liam asked.

"I decided against it. To be honest with you, I do not care for his company much. In fact, I dislike him greatly."

Liam tightened his grip on her. "I'm glad to hear you say that, Eleanor."

"What happened on the lake during the storm, Liam?"

"'Twas as bad as can be imagined. The waves—" He shook his head. "Nils raised the spray hood to keep the water from coming in. I bailed like a madman for what seemed like hours. The fear was choking me, but Nils kept his head and helped give me courage. I made it through, as did all the others."

"Liam, that's wonderful news" Eleanor said. She lifted the lantern to his face and gasped. Liam appeared to have aged five years overnight, with dark circles puffing under his eyes. "It must have been so dreadful."

"Aye, 'twas. But I have my sea-legs back now. I no longer live in terror of Superior."

"Well, that's worth a great deal, surely." Eleanor brushed a strand of hair from his forehead. "I was so worried about you."

Liam gazed at her for a long while. "Girleen, I owe you an apology for the way I acted at the cabin that night. I was wrong to speak so harshly to you. And as for your parents, you must use your best judgment. I'll wait as long as you like, for you are my own heart, *a cailín mo chroí*."

Joy spiraled through Eleanor, though it lasted for only a moment. The barn door flew open, and then Cameron stepped inside.

"Who's there?" Cameron demanded. He was carrying one of John's hunting rifles.

"Cameron, it's just me, Eleanor," she answered, rising to meet him.

"I thought I heard intruders," Cameron said. He glanced past her toward Liam. "Oh, I see," he said. There was a jaded, angry look in Cameron's eyes. "A little rendezvous, Eleanor?"

Liam was on his feet now. "'Tis none of your damned business," he growled.

"Oh, it is my business, most assuredly. You still don't know who you're dealing with, do you?"

"I don't give a sorry shit who you are," Liam said. "I'm not afraid of you."

"You're nothing, nobody. A dead man." A smile twisted Cameron's lips. "You should have drowned with all the rest. Then you could have been a cherished memory instead of a broken, drunken excuse for a man. And a liar, to boot."

A tense silence enveloped the barn. Eleanor looked from Cameron to Liam and knew their confrontation would end in violence if she didn't intervene. "Cameron, I want you to go back to the tower," she told him as calmly as possible. "Liam came to talk with me and nothing more." Her glance darted toward Liam. "And I've decided that I'm going to tell Mama about the two us tomorrow, so that will put an end to any further secrecy."

"Then why don't you tell her the whole truth about Liam, hmm?" Cameron said. His cold gaze settled on Liam. "Have you told her, MacLann, about the real reason you left your home in Ireland? About the fact that you're wanted for murder?"

Eleanor stared at Liam. "Murder?"

"Yes, murder," Cameron said. "A sheriff, no less. A man of the law. How did you do it, MacLann? Did you cut his throat in the middle of the night, or shoot him face to face like a man?"

Liam's eyes were downcast. "You should know," he said hoarsely.

"Ah, yes. Well, I'll leave you to tell Eleanor all the details," Cameron said. He briefly touched Eleanor's arm. "I'll be waiting for you at the house, my dear, when this felon has left us to our peace."

Cameron disappeared into the darkness. Eleanor stood rooted to the ground. "Did you really kill that man, Liam?" she asked.

"Aye, I did." He lifted his face to her, and she read the misery etched across his features. "But I did it to protect my brother, girleen. They were going to take him away for killing one of the island informers, a man without honor."

"I don't want to hear about it," Eleanor said in a bleak voice. She felt stunned by the fact that Liam had been responsible for another man's death. Worse than this, however, was that he'd kept it from her all this time. "Why didn't you tell me sooner?"

"I wanted to, believe me, I did, but I didn't know how. I thought you wouldn't understand..." Liam's words trailed off. "I can't change what's happened, Eleanor. There's nothing more to say about it."

Anger blazed through her. "Nothing more?" she cried. "What other things about your past have you hidden from me? A wife or children, perhaps?" She turned her back to him. "Leave now, before I call my father."

"You don't mean that, girleen. Say that you don't mean it." Liam drew her around. "Eleanor, listen to me. Cameron Russell's not to be trusted. Why would he be digging around for information about me if he didn't have some reason for it?"

"No doubt Cameron felt he was trying to protect my family. I don't condone what he's done, but you should have told me about the murder long ago, Liam. You always treat me like a child," Eleanor said. She broke away, tears streaming down her face as she hurried from the barn.

"Girleen, please, don't send me away—"

"I can't talk about this right now. I want you to leave."

Liam hesitated, then said, "You're not the only woman in my life, you know. Aye, there's a girl that's waiting for me right now out in Graceville."

Eleanor halted. "Who are you talking about?"

"Rose O'Malley. A girl I knew from back home, my old childhood sweetheart. Uncle Tim Pat wrote to say that she's come all the way to Minnesota to live and work, and for other reasons." Liam said no more, though his words were heavy with implication.

"Go to her, then, for all I care, and good riddance!"

It was a mortal wounding. Liam, his face like thunder, disappeared into the night without another word.

There. It was done. She'd sent him away, this stranger, this murderer. Eleanor shuddered; how close she'd been to giving her heart to him and making the gravest mistake of her life.

Eleanor walked back to the house, where Cameron was waiting for her, the gun still poised in the crook of his arm. "Are you all right?" he asked.

"Yes. He's gone." Eleanor sniffed and brushed her hair from her face. "I never want to see him again."

"I'll make certain of it." Cameron propped the gun against the wall and then put his arm around her shoulders. "Poor Eleanor. He almost had you convinced, didn't he? I'm only sorry that you had to learn of such a terrible thing in this manner."

"Why, Cameron? Why did you go to all the trouble to dig into Liam's past?"

"It was Adeline's idea, frankly. She never trusted MacLann, not for a moment. Soon after our conversation about him, I telegraphed my father and asked him to investigate Liam. I received my answer a few days ago." Cameron began to stroke Eleanor's hair. "I only wish that I could've spared you the humiliation of learning about it this way."

"I'm going inside now," Eleanor said before stepping away.

"Of course. I should return to the tower as well." Cameron touched the brim of his cap. "If you need me for anything, let me know at once. I'm completely at your service."

"Goodnight, Cameron." Eleanor waited until he entered the light tower before turning to go inside. His forgotten rifle was still resting against the side of the house, and she went to bring it inside.

The cold metal sent a shiver through her. Would Cameron have shot Liam? There was no question of their jealous hatred toward one another. And how would Liam have handled the situation if their roles had been reversed?

Murderer. Liar. These words chilled her to the marrow. Liam deserved whatever fate awaited him.

Never again would she trust him. As far as she was concerned, Liam MacLann could go to the devil.

CHAPTER 18

▼

For the next few days, Eleanor drifted through the house like a ghost. She did her chores, helped Adeline when asked, and even spent extra time with David in the new tree house John had built. Outwardly, Eleanor maintained the pretense of a dutiful, loving daughter.

But her heart, her very spirit, had been shattered.

At breakfast Eleanor ate little, and she did her best to avoid noon meals altogether. The last thing Eleanor wanted was to subject herself to Cameron's watching eyes and solicitations. Though he'd acted supportive toward her after Liam's departure, she felt mortified by the entire episode and the role Cameron had played in it.

Sleep offered no refuge. Too often Eleanor was troubled by vivid dreams of Liam. She would waken and lay staring into the darkness, envisioning him in the arms of that strange woman, Rose O'Malley.

She'd made the right decision, she reasoned. How could she place her welfare into the hands of a murderer?

But still Eleanor grieved. Was a future without him, without his love and strength, worth the cost of her distrust? This question repeated itself endlessly, and Eleanor had no answer.

One night she was visited by a different dream altogether. Eleanor was a passenger on a southbound train. The vessel lurched forcefully from side to side as it barreled along at high speed. She wore a dark wool suit with a ruffled cream silk blouse, the cameo hanging round her neck. On her lap she clutched a leather travel bag, and she hummed to herself, only vaguely aware of her destination.

Her gaze wandered to the brass-fitted overhead luggage racks, leather seats, the rows of half-opened windows, where tiny cinder ashes floated inside and dusted the bench. Scenery flew by, and Eleanor noticed she could no longer see the lake. Superior had vanished.

She shifted in her seat as sweat dripped down her neck and back. Her corset felt especially tight. The air was suddenly close and hot, and she gulped for breath. She turned around to call for the porter, to request a glass of water, and it was then she realized she was alone.

A man took his seat beside her, a gentleman dressed in a gray-colored suit and wearing patent leather shoes with a black bowler hat. His knees pressed against hers in the confined space. He was staring fixedly ahead, and Eleanor was unable to see his features. But, as he turned, Eleanor's hand flew to her mouth. It was Cameron.

"Well, Mrs. Russell, how are you enjoying you train ride?"

"Mrs. Russell? I'm sorry, there must be some mistake. My name is Miss Thompson."

"No mistake." Cameron lifted her gloved hand to his lips. "We were married yesterday at the courthouse in Duluth."

"That's absurd," Eleanor said, snatching her hand away. "Will you please ask the engineer to turn the train around so that I can return to Haven Point?"

"You can never return. We are man and wife, as I intended from the beginning." Cameron reached for the cameo, fingering it with obvious pleasure. "You belong to me now, Eleanor."

"No," Eleanor said, trying to sidle away from him. But she was locked in place, unable to move, even as he tore the cameo from her neck and began to undo her buttons…

"No!" she shouted. It was early dawn, and Eleanor realized Bridget was standing beside her.

Eleanor stared at her sister, her heart beating frantically. "What—?"

"You're having a bad dream," Bridget told her. "You woke me up, and the sun hasn't even come out yet!"

"I'm sorry." Eleanor swept her mussed hair from her face. "It's just that it seemed so real."

"Well, I'm going back to sleep," Bridget said as she slipped beneath the covers of her own bed.

Eleanor lay back on her pillow and stared at the ceiling. Why such an awful dream, and why Cameron? This was her home, after all. Nothing could harm her here.

This decided her; it was time to set Cameron straight, once and for all. Tell him that she did not care for and that she never could. Just plain and simple, face to face, everything open and honest.

Eleanor drew the quilt over her shoulder and settled into the comfort of her bed. In the morning, she would speak to him.

But she would not get her chance that day. John came down the stairs at ten o'clock, brimming with energy as he entered the kitchen and announced, "David and I are taking Cameron out on the skiff to show him my secret fishing cove."

Adeline, who'd just placed the filled copper boiler on the woodstove, regarded him with folded arms. "And I suppose that means you won't return until late this afternoon, hmm?"

"That's right. With any luck, we'll bring back some lake trout to fry up for supper."

"You'll need more than luck," Adeline said. "Don't bother yourself with the fact that I wanted you to string a wire fence around the vegetable garden. I'm sure you won't mind when the deer and rabbits eat all the pea pods and cabbage leaves."

John frowned. "Well, I guess we *could* postpone it—"

"Never mind. Go on ahead with the other boys and have your fun." Adeline nodded toward a pile of dirty clothing and bed linens heaped in the corner. "The girls and I will keep busy with the laundry while you're away."

John left in a hurry. A few minutes later Bridget came inside and said, "The three of them went down to the beach with their fishing poles. How come they get to take a day off when we have to work?"

"Never mind," Adeline answered. She added more wood to the stove, then dabbed her forehead with the hem of her apron. "It's going to be a hot one today."

"If we finish before they return, maybe we could take a swim," Eleanor suggested.

"That does sound like fun, doesn't it?" Adeline said, a gleam of truancy in her eyes. She bent to scoop up an armload of laundry, and had just straightened her back when she paused and said, "Heavens! I forgot to ask Cameron for his laundry!"

"I can get it Mama," Bridget said.

"No, Eleanor can go. Hurry, so we can finish our chores and then take that swim."

"I'll be quick," Eleanor promised. Retrieving an empty laundry basket from the pantry, she went outside and crossed the yard to Cameron's house.

She knocked on the door to make certain he was gone. When there was no answer, Eleanor let herself inside.

The assistant keeper's house was as quiet as a tomb. Dirty dishes sat piled in the sink. Flies crawled over the remains of a half-eaten sandwich on the wooden table. A stack of newspapers lay beside the plate. Eleanor wrinkled her nose.

Lars had never kept it this dirty. Messy, yes, but not filthy. What was Cameron thinking? If the superintendent made his surprise visit now, this would surely be marked against both Cameron and John. Eleanor shook her head; she'd have talk to her father about this when he returned.

With slow steps Eleanor climbed to the second floor. A board squeaked beneath her foot as she touched the bedroom door handle, and she hesitated. "It's only laundry," she said aloud. "Don't be such a chicken."

Eleanor entered Cameron's bedroom and released her breath, unaware that she'd been holding it. The room was nearly the same size as her and Bridget's, with a brass bed, an oak dresser, and a small roll-top desk and chair. Eleanor wandered to the desk, where she noticed a silver-framed portrait of a dark-haired woman. Cameron's mother, undoubtedly. Eleanor brushed her fingers around the frame's gilded inlay, intrigued by the woman's high-collared satin dress, her stiff posture, her melancholy expression.

There was another portrait, this time of a much younger woman. The girl staring back at Eleanor was beautiful, with blonde hair, an oval face, and lips drawn in a pretty pout. A name was written in ink along the portrait's edge. It read *Sophie, 1905.*

Cameron's betrothed, perhaps? Eleanor, embarrassed about snooping into his personal life, turned away. She set to work at once, filling the basket with the shirts, trousers, socks, and underclothes that littered the floor.

Eleanor stripped the bedding next. As she lifted the pillow, something caught her eye. It was a folded newspaper clipping.

She reached for the clipping, and then paused. It belonged to Cameron, and reading it would amount to an invasion of privacy. But curiosity bested her.

It was Liam's story in the *Duluth News-Tribune.* A circle had been drawn around the picture of the two of them standing together, and her own name had been underlined.

Eleanor's hand shook. *Cameron...*

Downstairs, the door opened and closed, and then footsteps echoed on the stairs. Eleanor fisted the paper, and turned as Cameron appeared in the bedroom door. "What are you doing in here?" he demanded.

"Mama asked me to gather your things for washday."

"You shouldn't be in here. No one gave you permission to enter my room."

"I'm—I'm sorry," Eleanor stammered. "I thought that you and Papa and David had gone fishing."

"I decided against it at the last minute. I felt a terrible headache coming on." Cameron took a step closer. "What are you hiding there in your hand?"

"Nothing," she whispered, more frightened than she had ever been before. With the spryness of a cat, Cameron bridged the gap between them and grabbed her wrist.

"Let me go!" Eleanor insisted.

"Not yet." With his free hand, Cameron seized the clipping. "Have you guessed my little secret? I came to Haven Point because of you, Eleanor."

She tensed and pulled back. "You're hurting me!"

"Like you've hurt me?" Cameron said. He twisted her arm. "Don't think I haven't noticed your snubbings, the way you hold yourself apart from me, when you're the one who should be grateful!"

"I want nothing to do with you!" she cried.

"The situation is far beyond that, I'm afraid." Cameron kissed her, his lips crushing her mouth. Eleanor uttered a little cry, then heaved and struggled to free herself. But he would not release her.

Cameron shoved Eleanor against the wall and pressed himself to her. The stink of his sweat, and the mixture of coffee and tobacco on his breath, made it hard for her to breath. He pried her lips open and forced his tongue inside her mouth, hard and violent. Reacting instinctively, Eleanor jammed her knee up against his groin. Cameron doubled over with a loud grunt.

Eleanor twisted away and ran for the stairway. Cameron chased her down the steps and caught her arm just short of the kitchen door. "Wait Eleanor! Let me explain!"

She glared at him, her hair disheveled, her lips burning with the taste of his mouth. "Why should I listen to you?" she cried. "You're abominable!"

"It might seem that way, but you know, you made me very angry back there," Cameron said, his tone bordering on conciliation. "Please. Just have a seat and listen."

Eleanor hesitated. Part of her wanted to go running to her mother and denounce Cameron. Yet she also felt compelled to learn the truth about his coming to Haven Point. "You have five minutes," she said.

"More than enough." Cameron withdrew a chair and gestured for her to sit. She remained at the door.

"As you wish," Cameron said. He took the chair himself. "I read about you and the Irishman when the newspaper carried the story about the shipwreck. It was a stirring account, one that people in Duluth talked about for months afterward.

"I remembered you from when you worked at the Grand Hotel last summer. You were so shy and quiet that I was probably the only one of my companions who took notice. But even then I saw the woman you are. Patient. Unassuming. Guileless. A great beauty, though you didn't even know it at the time." To Eleanor's surprise, Cameron blushed. "I must confess that I was smitten."

Eleanor was struck speechless. How could he be talking to her this way after what had happened upstairs? "You're lying," she said. "You're just saying this so that I won't tell my parents about what you did to me."

"I'm not lying, I swear it," Cameron said. "I admired you from afar those few months, because of course I wouldn't dream of pursuing you." His usual smirk returned. "The heir of an empire daren't court the cook's helper."

"Then why come here at all?" Eleanor demanded. "Why lower yourself to the level of such 'common' people?"

"Because I couldn't forget you, Eleanor. And when I was given the choice to either go to sea or work at a lighthouse, I knew this was where I wanted to go. To be close to you.

"Hate me if you will. Vilify me to your mother. I probably deserve all of it and more. But know one thing; I would not have acted the way I did if you didn't drive me insane with desire." Cameron rose and drew near, and Eleanor flinched at his touch. "I want you, dear girl. Is that such a terrible thing?"

Eleanor stood on the threshold, trembling. Some of what he'd told her was logical, but she sensed there was more left unrevealed. "Why did you lie to us, Cameron?"

"I didn't think you'd believe me."

"It was still a lie. Just like with Liam." She threw the accusation at him, waiting to see his reaction.

Anger darkened Cameron's face. "I'm nothing like him! Eleanor, can't you see how different we are? I could offer you a life of wealth and security, and he has nothing!"

"I want nothing from you," Eleanor told him. Cameron was mad if he thought she'd consider him after what he'd done to her upstairs. "I'm going home now."

"It's not that easy, Eleanor," Cameron said. "Relationships are about reciprocity, are they not? Well, there's something I expect in return for keeping certain secrets and not naming names."

The measured chill in Cameron's words stopped Eleanor short. "What are you talking about?"

"An arrangement. You agree to be my lover for the remainder of the summer, and I won't have my father arrange for Liam's deportation to Ireland."

"You can't touch Liam! He's been in America for six years now!"

"Powerful men like my father can pull strings, you know. Make contacts in Washington, launch an investigation." Cameron's smile broadened. "Nothing is beyond my family's reach."

"I hate you!" Eleanor cried, a white fury pounding in her head. "I wouldn't give myself to you if you were the last man on earth!"

"Then perhaps another harsh truth will change your opinion." Cameron paused for effect. "Your father could very easily lose his job here if I were to trump up a damaging report to Superintendent Greer."

Eleanor's sense of outrage deepened. "My father has done nothing but try to help you!"

"True enough. A noble individual, certainly. But life is not always fair, is it?" Cameron ran a finger along her face; Eleanor swatted him away.

"That hurts me, you know?" he told her, eyeing her with a sullen air. "Don't act so virginal, Eleanor. I could do things for you, things beyond your imagining. Things that would bring both of us a great deal of pleasure—"

"I'd rather die," she told him flatly.

"Brave words, bravely spoken." Cameron gripped her chin. "But bear this in mind, Eleanor. If you do not comply with my wishes, I promise to make a full report to the superintendent detailing your father's 'irresponsible' management of Haven Point. Before I left Duluth, Jamieson Greer expressed grave concern over the failure of your father to search for survivors after the wreck of the *William Dorn*. He told me that some of the families who lost men in the shipwreck are considering pressing charges against John for criminal negligence."

Eleanor, her chest heaving, fled through the door. Cameron's voice followed her, saying, "Never forget, Eleanor, even for a moment, that I can destroy your father's career!"

Eleanor ran the short distance from Cameron's house to the lake, where she waded into the surf, fully clothed, driven by the desire to wash away the feel of Cameron's touch. Her body rose like a cork in the waves, and she did not stop until she was submerged to her chin. Tears overtook her in great gulps.

Thoughts careened through Eleanor's mind. Liam…Jamieson Greer…John Thompson…Cameron…"*I could do things for you, things beyond your imagining…*" Eleanor snapped her head towards Cameron's house, forcing herself to think. Her first reaction was to warn her father at once; it was conceivable that Cameron might even try to harm Bridget or David. The danger was too great for Eleanor to keep silent.

Yet Jamieson Greer was due to arrive any day now. As district superintendent, Jamieson would believe the son of the illustrious Sumner Russell, especially since Jamieson already harbored serious doubts about John.

Eleanor knew it would appear unseemly if John were involved with any effort to force Cameron's resignation. Maybe she ought to take up the matter herself and talk to the superintendent when he arrived. But then Eleanor's heart sank as she summoned a picture of Jamieson Greer: tall and forbidding, he often wore a frown when conducting his inspections. Jamieson would likely view her actions as an attempt to interfere with Lighthouse Board business.

Beyond that was the indelicacy of Cameron's demands. How could she explain such a thing to a man like Jamieson Greer, or even her own father? It was all so humiliating.

Eleanor's thoughts turned to Liam. She needed to send word to him of Cameron's threats. But maybe Liam had left the North Shore already. Maybe he'd gone to Graceville and joined Rose O'Malley, after all.

Decision hardened inside Eleanor as she emerged from the lake. She would find some way to deal with Cameron herself. No one else would have to know, and no one would get hurt.

If only she didn't feel so deathly afraid.

Not wanting to face her mother just yet, Eleanor entered the house through the front door, and then went straight up to her room to change and crawl into bed. Adeline came into the bedroom shortly after, her expression searching. But Eleanor rolled onto her side and lay staring at the wall, unwilling to meet her mother's gaze. A moment later, Eleanor heard the door click shut, followed by the sound of Adeline descending the stairs.

Every part of Eleanor ached. An ugly bruise discolored her wrist, her face felt swollen, and there was an unpleasant taste in her mouth reminiscent of Cameron's grasping lips. She'd lingered so long in the lake that she'd taken a chill, which left her shivering beneath her quilt.

Eleanor slept for most of the afternoon. When she opened her eyes, she listened for any sound of either her mother or sister in the house. *They must be out weeding the garden*, Eleanor thought. Her loneliness intensified even as her earlier resolve began to crumble.

Heavy footsteps on the stairs, and then she heard a knock. Eleanor sat up and answered, "Come in."

John opened the door. "Can I talk with you, Eleanor?" he asked.

Eleanor nodded. John took a seat beside her, the bedsprings protesting under his added weight. The familiar smell of him, of pipe-smoke and kerosene, reassured her.

"Is everything all right, Eleanor?" he asked.

She swallowed. *He must not learn the truth, at least not yet.* "I'm fine, Papa."

"I'm not sure I believe you. You haven't been yourself lately."

"I've had a lot on my mind, I guess. Private matters."

"Well, I sure don't mean to pry, but I don't like what's going on around here. There's tension between you and Cameron, thick as molasses."

"Cameron has shown a romantic interest in me, but I told him that we're not suited," Eleanor answered carefully.

"I'm glad to hear it. I'd rather cut off my arm than see you involved with a man like that." John smoothed his hands on his trousers. "Sometimes I think I ought to leave the Lighthouse Service and get a job down in Duluth, or maybe see if your Uncle Casey has something for me at his law firm."

"I thought the lighthouse was your life."

"It's the isolation. I think it's getting to all of us. Just look at your mother and the way she fusses over Cameron," John said. "I think she's just hungry for neighbors and regular company."

"But you love your work, Papa."

John shrugged. "It's just a job. There are other things a man can do to put food on the table and keep a roof overhead."

"What about your own father, and the way he was lost at sea?"

"Who told you about that?" John asked.

"Mama did. During the big gale last November." Eleanor leaned her head against John's shoulder. "Why didn't you ever tell us before?"

"A man keeps things inside, sometimes. And that's not the only reason I became a lighthouse keeper."

Eleanor looked at her father intently. "Superior."

"Yes, Superior. She cast her spell over me long ago. And if I can keep the sailing men on the lake safe, then I consider it a privilege to serve." John gave Eleanor a hug. "You'd best fix yourself up and come downstairs. David and I caught five fat trout for supper."

Eleanor gave him a tired smile. "You go ahead. I'll be down in a few minutes, Papa."

"Just promise that you'll tell me if something's troubling you, all right?" John said, pausing in the doorway. "You can trust your old Papa, you know."

If only it were that easy, Eleanor thought, even as her father left her alone to herself.

CHAPTER 19

▼

A heavy-hearted Liam sat alone on an overturned fish box, waiting for the *America* to make its scheduled stop at Little Nesna. Liam was dressed in his best clothes with his packed bag sitting at his feet. He kept glancing northward along the shore, both anticipating and dreading the steamship's appearance. He drew a sigh and tossed a rock into the water, where it made a deep splash.

He was glad to be leaving the North Shore and all the painful recollections that went with it. Wrenching memories of the shipwreck. The hope he'd once harbored for Eleanor. The resentment he felt toward her and Cameron after their argument that night in the barn. Eleanor obviously favored the assistant keeper with his looks, his money, his smooth talk. Wouldn't even stop to listen to Liam's side of the story or give him the chance to explain. Just tears and accusations and the door slammed shut in his face.

Graceville awaited, along with his Uncle Tim Pat and cousins, and, of course, Rose O'Malley. *What will she look like?* Liam wondered. She was but a girl of fifteen when he'd left Inishmore. Rose would be a fully grown woman now, and though she might not be the beauty Eleanor Thompson was, there were other things to her advantage. Rose already knew of the sheriff's murder and had chosen not to judge him. And she'd come thousands of miles for his sake. Surely that counted for something.

Yet time and again his thoughts returned to Eleanor. Would she marry Cameron Russell? Would he finally be the man her mother had schemed for all these years? Just the notion of Cameron with Eleanor made Liam clench his hands. Nothing would have given him greater pleasure than to smash that man's face and ruin his pretty looks.

No use in thinking that way, Liam told himself. It was the impulse toward violence that had gotten him into this mess in the first place. If he thought it was worth the fight, he'd have to battle this man using his intellect, not his fists. But Eleanor had made her choice. There was no room in her life for someone she didn't trust.

Liam felt in his coat pocket for the steamer ticket, purchased by Nils the day before in Grand Marais. Liam planned to stay one night at the O'Rourkes, to say farewell, before embarking on his long journey westward.

Nils appeared, hauling a torn trout net over his shoulder. "Do you mind if I wait with you?"

"No. I could use the company," Liam answered. Nils upended another of the fish boxes and took a seat before spreading the net down over his legs and feet. Using a length of miter cord, Nils began to repair the ripped net line.

Liam watched him in silence for a few minutes. "Can I help?"

"Here, take this extra needle. There's a tear on the other end," Nils replied. Liam made himself comfortable, facing Nils while he worked. His fingers moved without effort, seaming and tying.

"Ah, this reminds me of home," Liam said. "Me old Da' and all us boys would sit by the hearth at day's end and repair the nets. The line was a little different, you understand, but the technique is the same."

"It makes me think of Norway, too. The men would sit and work and talk about the fishing around the Lofoton islands, while my mother and sisters served bread and coffee." Nils looked at Liam. "I envy you the chance to see some of your family again."

"'Tis hard to believe that I'll be with them again in just a few days." Liam's fingers slipped and he cursed softly. "'Twon't be the same without Conall."

"But there will be much to attend to. Reacquainting yourself with old friends. Finding a place to live. Seeing that girl who's waiting for you." Nils nodded toward the lake. "And you can finally put the past behind you."

"Aye. Maybe the nightmares won't follow me to Graceville." Liam stared at his hands and then dropped the net. "Och, what am I doing? I should be saying farewell to the others!"

"Don't bother. They're all salting down the catch in the fish house. They know you're leaving, MacLann. They've known it for a while now." Nils continued to work the net. "We'll all miss you. And not just for the work but because of how much you've become a part of our small family here at Little Nesna."

Liam coughed back a small lump in his throat. "I'll miss the lot of you too. I'll be sure to write just as soon as I arrive."

Nils looked past Liam. "There's the *America* now," he said, piling the net beside the fish box. Liam grabbed his bag and rose to his feet.

The steamer advanced along the shore, trailing black smoke in her wake. Liam waved as the ship blew her steam whistle and lowered anchor. The clan of Norwegians emerged from the fish house and came to shake Liam's hand goodbye. He thanked them all and then climbed into one of the Mackinaws, where Nils sat waiting. They began to row toward the *America*.

As the shore receded behind them, a strange feeling swept over Liam, a great certainty that he was doing the wrong thing. But then he turned and stared at the ship, where several crewmen waited to help him board.

The first man passed down a packet of mail to Liam. "There's a telegram as well," he said. "For someone named Liam MacLann."

"Oh?" Liam asked, frowning. He opened the Western Union telegram and read the terse message, sent to him from Mrs. Edward Graling in Cleveland, Ohio.

Nils, watching him closely, asked, "Who's it from, Liam? What does it say?"

"'Tis from the widow of the *William Dorn's* captain, Matilda Graling." Liam's frown deepened. "Seems she's taking Zenith Steamship to court over them blaming her husband for the wreck. The trial begins in three days, and she wants me to testify."

"Where's the trial going to be?"

"Duluth." Liam stared at the telegram and then folded it in his hand. He looked from the waiting crewmen to Nils. He had only a minute to decide.

All the events of his life seemed to merge into this one moment. His boyhood in Ireland. The shooting. His escape to America. Conall's death. The wreck. Eleanor. Always running from his troubles, always searching for some new way to forget.

Captain Graling had believed in him, had wanted to train him up to a new position with added responsibility. Liam's stomach knotted. *No more running*, he told himself. It was time to stand and fight. He would go to Duluth and champion his late captain's honor, for his own sake and the sake of his dead shipmates.

"It seems I'm not going home to Graceville, at least for now," Liam said.

Nils' face broke into a smile. "Up you go," he said cheerfully as Liam stepped from the bobbing Mackinaw and through the steamer's freight door. Nils tossed in the bag, and then waved a hearty goodbye.

"Come back north after the trial is over, MacLann!" he called. "We'll be waiting for you!"

✳   ✳   ✳   ✳

Eleanor carried the burden of Cameron's threat as best she could, reminding herself that she'd chosen to bear her burden alone. Eleanor felt strong, proud of the sacrifice she was making, like the heroines in the magazine stories. But at night her dreams were filled with dark shadows and clutching hands.

Eleanor arose at dawn and walked down to the shore, the one place she felt safe from Cameron's hungry eyes. Gulls perched in near-silence on the cliffs. Mist drifted inland from the lake, shrouding the shore in fog. Eleanor stood on the smooth stones and allowed the surf to race up to the toes of her shoes.

The morning wore on, one hour, then two. Eleanor wandered the length of the beach as the warming sun pierced the mist. An ache of loneliness expanded in her chest, threatening to drown her. There was no solace in the lake, no consolation in the rush of waves. Liam was in all likelihood gone, and she'd been the one to send him away.

But at least he's safe, Eleanor told herself. The further he was from Cameron Russell and the North Shore, the less likely he was to come to harm.

Dread coiled through Eleanor at the thought of Cameron. His presence at the noon meal each day had grown almost unbearable. It wasn't hard to imagine what he was thinking, and his leer made her feel nervous and sick. But worse than this, Cameron had begun to take a belittling tone with her father.

Eleanor covered her face and cursed her foolishness. Cameron was a dangerous man, and her father deserved to learn the truth about him. She must speak to her father at once.

But as Eleanor turned for the house, she was stopped by the throb of an approaching ship's engine. A tall bow emerged from the shimmering half-light of the fog. Eleanor squinted to read the name painted across the steel hull. *Amaranth.* She frowned, for the tender ship wasn't expected for a few days yet.

A white flag flew from the main mast. Fear stiffened Eleanor spine, and she took off running for the house. Never had the distance seemed so long.

Eleanor burst into the kitchen, where Adeline was taking a pan of cherry cobbler from the oven. "My goodness, Eleanor, what's the matter?" Adeline exclaimed.

"Mama, Superintendent Greer is here!"

Activity erupted at the light station as the tender ship tooted its whistle from the harbor. Adeline, though visibly shaken, marshaled the troops like any seasoned general. "David, I want you to greet the boat at the dock. Bridget, go upstairs and make certain the beds are made and that everything's neat as a pin. Eleanor, help your father with his uniform and make sure he runs a comb through his hair. You know he always forgets." Adeline removed her apron and hung it on the wall. "I'll go knock on Cameron's door and make certain he's awake."

Eleanor hurried upstairs and threw open her parents' bedroom door. John sat up in bed and rubbed his eyes, still heavy with sleep.

"Papa, it's the *Amaranth*. Superintendent Greer has arrived for inspection," Eleanor said. John jumped from the bed as Eleanor took his black wool uniform from the closet.

"Don't look," John said. "Just give me my trousers first."

Eleanor passed them to him at arm's length, keeping her eyes averted. A few moments later John spoke to her, saying, "You can turn around now. Give me my shirt and coat."

She handed them over and then watched as he tucked in his shirt tails and buttoned up the front. "Good thing I polished these shoes the other night," John said. "I had a suspicion old Jamieson Greer would be paying a call soon."

"Still, it always comes as a shock." Eleanor fetched the lint brush from the top dresser drawer. She brushed the back of his coat while he pushed all the brass buttons through their holes.

The only sign of John's nervousness was his dampened brow. He slicked a comb through his hair, and then fitted his cap on his head. "It'll have to do," he muttered, shaking his head. "Where's your mother?"

"She must be at the dock by now. Mama was just over to Cameron's to make sure he was awake."

"Well, I hope he'll be ready for all this. Hell of a day to get caught sleeping." John straightened his collar and took one final look in the mirror. "Make the bed, daughter. I'm off to greet the superintendent."

Eleanor was the last to join the welcoming party at the dock. Bridget and David stood close beside Adeline, who was making pleasant small talk with Superintendent Greer. Tall and gaunt, Jamieson stared down his spectacles at Adeline. He wore a crisply pressed uniform and held a leather carrying case in his bony hand.

John and Cameron waited off to the side. Cameron held his mouth tight, and a frown line furrowed his brow. *So much for his usual smugness*, Eleanor thought.

The crew from the *Amaranth* was beginning to unpack the foodstuffs, boxes of kerosene and barrels of gas from the launch. Eleanor recognized Shamus

O'Rourke among them. He winked and tipped his cap, and she gave him a fleeting smile.

Jamieson's gaze passed over each family member before coming to rest on John. "Keeper Thompson, Assistant Keeper Russell. Yes. Well, let us proceed with the inspection."

The superintendent strode up the pathway toward the tower, with John and Cameron following close behind. Eleanor released her breath before wiping the damp tendrils of hair clinging to the back of her neck.

"Did you see Mr. Greer's eyes?" Adeline said. "Oh, he's not happy to be here today, no, not at all." The catch of fear in Adeline's voice unnerved Eleanor. "He'll dismiss your father for certain this time, we'll be forced to seek refuge with Regina—"

"Mama, calm down!" Eleanor said.

Adeline passed a hand over her face. "Yes, you're right," she said before hurrying Bridget and David to the foot of the dock. "Come along, the both of you, I need help setting the table. Perhaps we'll soften Mr. Greer's opinion with a generous serving of cherry cobbler and a cup of fresh coffee."

David balked. "I want to stay and help the men unload."

Adeline glanced from David to Eleanor. "You might as well leave him here, Mama. That'll mean one less body crowding the house," Eleanor said.

"Well, all right," Adeline said. David quickly joined the men as they hefted the freight toward the lighthouse annex.

Eleanor sought out Shamus. "How are you today, Miss?" the wiry Irishman asked.

"Things couldn't be worse," she replied. Eleanor drew Shamus to the side. "Liam has decided to return to Graceville. He's probably on his way their already."

"'Tisn't so, Miss. Why, I just saw him yesterday in Duluth!"

"Duluth!" Eleanor clutched Shamus by the arm. "What's Liam doing in Duluth?"

"He's been asked to testify at the U.S. Courthouse. Captain Graling's widow has filed a lawsuit against the Zenith Steamship Company. Seems they're blaming the wreck of the *William Dorn* on her husband. Something about Zenith Steam avoiding any lawsuits from the victims' families."

"How unfair to Captain Graling!" Eleanor said. "No one person was to blame, at least according to Liam."

"That's why Liam decided to testify," Shamus replied. "You should go to Duluth and find him, Miss. He seemed very upset."

"I said terrible things to him," Eleanor confessed in a low voice. "He's leaving because of me."

"Don't blame yourself, Miss. Everything's eating him up inside. But he'll do the right thing, if I know Liam at all." Shamus nodded and said, "Now, if you'll excuse me, I'd best get to work."

Eleanor grappled with Shamus' extraordinary news. How long would Liam remain in Duluth? Probably at least until the case was concluded. Was this the only reason for his delay in leaving, or was he also struggling with his decision to return to Graceville?

She turned and gazed southward. "*Go to Duluth*," Shamus had told her. Well, and why not? She was a grown woman, and had already been to Duluth several times before.

Eleanor's attention was drawn to the tower, where the superintendent and both keepers were passing from the annex to the fog house. *Oh hell*, she thought. There was just no time to think and make a clear decision.

Her father needed her, for his own trial had only just begun.

"And now, Keeper Thompson, we come to the matter of the shipwreck on November the 28th last year."

An hour had passed since the superintendent's arrival, and the men had gathered at the dining room table following dessert. Bridget had gone off to join David and the crewmen at the beach. It was just as well, Eleanor thought; what followed promised to be most unpleasant.

She and Adeline busied themselves clearing the table, moving between the dining room and kitchen with the intent of listening in on the conversation. Adeline brought in the coffee pot to refill everyone's cup. Cameron thanked her openly, then turned his eyes on Eleanor, who'd been the object of his undivided attention since the moment they'd entered the house.

Jamieson Greer, at the head of the table, rifled through his leather case and withdrew a pile of documents. He laid them on the table and then leaned back slightly in his chair, as though the paperwork was evidence enough.

John spoke. "I believe the relevant facts were detailed in both reports, sir."

"That may be so." Jamieson angled forward as he adjusted his spectacles. "But those reports don't quite explain everything."

"I'm not sure I understand what you mean."

"The Lighthouse Board has been contacted by both the Lake Carriers' Association and the Zenith Steamship Company in regard to this particular case. It seems several of the families who lost men aboard the *William A. Dorn* have been asking pointed questions. 'Why was there only one survivor?' they ask, and 'why were there no rescue efforts?'"

John cleared his throat. "When Assistant Keeper Berglund suggested that we take the skiff out and search for survivors, I spoke against the idea. I believed, and still do to this day, that conditions were far too hazardous for our safe return. I saw what the waves did to both the dock and the *William Dorn's* life-raft, and I judged it too risky to row out into the storm."

"Are you aware that some people have accused you of cowardice? Are you a coward, Keeper Thompson?"

A space of silence. "No, sir, I am no coward."

Jamieson tapped his pencil on the table. "I've also been informed that charges of criminal negligence may be pressed against you."

"Why?" John asked, exasperated. "There's nothing written about shipwreck rescues in the 'Instructions to Light-Keeper's' manual! What more do these people want?"

"Their loved ones are dead. They've been deprived of their companionship, not to mention their financial support. What should we tell them? That you were acting prudently instead of thinking about your duty?" The superintendent's tone turned reproachful. "You should have listened to your assistant and searched for more survivors from the *Dorn.*"

Eleanor, listening from the dining room door, clenched her hands, thinking, *The truth must be spoken, I will not allow Papa's good name to be dragged through the mud...*"That ship went straight to the bottom of Superior, and it was only through a miracle that Liam survived at all!" she cried. "My father did the right thing, and you have no right to say otherwise!"

Everyone stared at Eleanor. Her outburst was a breach in etiquette of the worst degree. John, ashen-faced, said, "I think you should leave now, daughter."

Without another word, Eleanor left the room.

Eleanor ran across the yard to the fog house. She pounded up the steps past the resting equipment before coming to a halt in front of one of the narrow windows overlooking the lake.

A clammy sweat had broken out all over her shaking body. She inhaled deep and then blew out her breath in one long exhale.

She'd done the right thing, she told herself. She had defended her father's integrity, though most likely it would work against him in the end. *Maybe Papa's termination is a foregone conclusion anyhow,* Eleanor thought.

Distant movement caught her eye. Down at the dock, David and Bridget were still helping the crew unload. Shamus was among them, and Eleanor watched as he spoke to David.

Shamus. Liam. Duluth. Suddenly every thought was focused on her need to go to Liam. Nothing else mattered, as long as Liam was still within reach.

Cameron breezed in through the entry. "I thought you might be here," he said as Eleanor took a few steps back.

"Leave me alone!"

"Not until I make sure you don't do anything stupid," he answered. "I hope you realize how pathetic you sounded back there."

Eleanor spat in his face. "That's what I think of your opinions! At this point I could care less if Papa is fired, just as long as we get away from you!"

"You don't really mean that, Eleanor," Cameron said, wiping the spittle away. "I have a wonderful new plan for us, anyway; I want you to come to Duluth and live there as my mistress. You can be free of that domineering witch of a mother, and I can keep you in great style." Cameron's voice was low, seductive. "Say that you love me, Eleanor. Come now, darling, I need to hear you say it. Say that you love me."

Eleanor drew back her hand and slapped Cameron hard across the face. "Why must you continue to hurt me?" he cried. "Everything I've done has been for us, for our happiness!" He clutched her tightly, his face pressed against her cheek as he whispered, "Don't shut me out, Eleanor. Please, don't shut me out."

Two shadows stretched across the cement floor. Shamus and David, their arms loaded with boxes of machinery oil, entered the fog house. "Here now, what's this all about?" Shamus demanded.

Cameron fixed a venomous eye on Shamus. "Miss Thompson and I were having a private conversation," he said, "and I would very much appreciate it if the both of you would leave now."

Shamus set his box on the work bench, a troubled, angry look on his face. "Eleanor, come over and stand with your brother," he said.

Eleanor did so at once. Cameron remained where he was, his posture tense.

"Private conversation, my arse," Shamus growled. "Taking advantage, most likely!" Faster than an eye-blink, Shamus swung out and struck Cameron in the face.

The assistant keeper fell to the floor, a jet of blood spurting from his nose. Eleanor drew an open-mouthed David back toward the door. Cameron climbed unsteadily to his feet. He wiped the gore from his face and said, "You hit me, you dirty Irish bastard!"

Shamus grinned as he raised both his fists. "Aye, I hit you, and I'll hit you again if you come anywhere near Miss Thompson!"

Eleanor closed her arms protectively around David. His heart beat wildly beneath the fabric of his shirt. Cameron, still dabbing at his nose with his coat sleeve, made one last appeal to Eleanor.

"Don't let them come between us, my darling. We don't need anyone else; just send them away and we can clear up this little misunderstanding."

Fury welled up in her chest. "I hate you, Cameron! I'll never stop hating you!"

"So be it," Cameron muttered before walking briskly from the fog house. Eleanor hurried to the door and watched his progress down the path and across the yard.

Suddenly, the unthinkable happened. John, Adeline, and Superintendent Greer appeared on the front step of the house. "Oh, no," Eleanor whispered. Now Cameron would surely take his revenge and speak directly against John.

Cameron joined the group, his hand held to his nose. From where Eleanor stood watching, she saw the look of shock on her mother's face. Everyone was staring at Cameron.

Brief words were exchanged, far beyond earshot. A sense of resignation stole over Eleanor as she turned away. If her father was meant to lose his job, there was nothing she could do to stop it now.

"He's going into his house," David said from her side. Eleanor looked again, and indeed Cameron had climbed the front steps and shut the door behind him. Eleanor's shoulders drooped with relief as her parents escorted the superintendent down to the dock, but then something about the situation jarred her. Why hadn't Cameron taken Jamieson Greer aside and filled the superintendent's head with his lies?

"Miss Thompson, are you all right?" Shamus asked.

"Yes, I think so. Thanks to you."

Shamus tussled David's hair. "I'm sorry you had to see that, lad."

"I'm glad you whipped him, Mr. O'Rourke," David said. "I've never liked Cameron. I wish he'd leave Haven Point."

Eleanor took her brother aside. "David, go down to the dock with Mama and Papa. I want to speak with Mr. O'Rourke alone."

David thrust out his chin. "I'm going to tell Papa what happened."

"David, you can't." Eleanor gripped her brother by the arms. "I'll tell Papa myself after the superintendent is gone. But you must let me handle this, David. You have to trust me."

David searched her face. "Cameron wants to hurt you, Eleanor."

"I won't let him. Please believe me." She kissed his forehead. "Go along now."

After David had gone, Eleanor motioned Shamus to join her in the shady lee of the building. Eleanor spoke to Shamus, saying, "I suppose you're wondering about what happened back there?"

"Aye, well, the thought did cross my mind."

Eleanor searched Shamus' friendly face and warm eyes. Could he be trusted? He was Liam's friend, so that counted for something. Shamus had defended her from Cameron without hesitation. And Liam had written of Shamus—"*He is a man whom you can trust.*"

She told Shamus her story, beginning with Cameron's arrival at Haven Point in April and ending with Superintendent Greer's visit that day. Shamus listened without comment, though the scowl on his face deepened when she told him about Cameron's blackmail scheme.

"Cameron expects certain things or else he'll destroy Papa's career and have Liam deported to Ireland," Eleanor explained.

"He's daft," Shamus said, kicking at a stone with his boot. "I doubt very much that Liam's in any real danger after all this time. But I must ask you, Miss, why didn't you say anything to your father, or send word along to Liam?"

"I was going up to tell my father this morning, but then the *Amaranth* came. I would have told Liam, but I thought he already gone."

"Ah, you poor *cailín*." Shamus' expression was sympathetic. "None of this has been easy for you."

"What I don't understand is why Cameron didn't pull Superintendent Greer aside just now."

Shamus shrugged. "'Tis hard to say. Maybe he's not the big man he wants everyone to think he is. Or maybe he's got something to hide himself."

Eleanor was electrified by the thought. "You're probably right, Shamus. Why else would someone with his background come all the way up north unless he wanted to avoid some sort of trouble at home?" Her heart tripped with excitement. "What do you suppose it might be?"

"Och, it could be any number of things, with a man like that. 'Twon't be easy to discover, though. But I think you should try, Miss. Cameron must leave Haven Point."

"Yes, the sooner the better," Eleanor agreed as they began to walk toward the beach. "You've been a kind friend, Mr. O'Rourke, both to Liam and myself. I owe you a great deal."

Shamus reddened. "Ah, Miss, go on with you, now." They paused at the ridge. "Go to Duluth and talk to Liam. I know that he's pining for you, no matter what he said before."

"I just might. But first I need to decide what to do about Cameron."

Shamus tipped his cap. "Good luck, Miss. Let me know if you need help with anything." Eleanor watched as Shamus hurried to the dock, where the crew and the superintendent were readying for departure.

Thank goodness the inspection is finally over, Eleanor thought. She hoped her father still had his job. But now what was to stop Cameron from doing something desperate? Eleanor sensed that he'd reached the end of his patience, and the thought of what might come next was more than a little unsettling.

She joined her mother and father at the dock, where John was bidding Jamieson Greer farewell. He was the last man to board the launch, which then slowly motored its way back to the *Amaranth*.

"Poor Cameron," Adeline said. "Such a terrible nosebleed. And what an awful time to have one, what with the inspection and all."

Eleanor ignored her mother's comment, turning instead to her father. "Did you lose your job, Papa?"

"Not this time," John replied. "I know for a fact that the Lighthouse Service is short on qualified men just now. But I will be on probation for a year."

"I'm so glad," Eleanor murmured, embracing him. She rested her face against the rough wool of his uniform, thinking that the time had come to tell him about Cameron. But not in the presence of her mother, who was unlikely to believe her accusations about Cameron until she had evidence to back up her suspicions, evidence that might very well be waiting for her in Duluth. It would be best to confide to her father in private.

Her conviction over traveling to Duluth grew stronger. Liam was there. Was the answer to her present dilemma there as well?

Eleanor recalled the photograph she'd seen of Cameron's mother. Maybe she could pay Mrs. Russell a visit and, with any luck, discover some way of disarming Cameron.

But before she did anything, she needed to tell her father the truth, preferably alone. "I'm thinking about taking a walk on the beach tonight, Papa. Would you join me? There's something I want to discuss with you."

"Oh?" he said, raising a brow. "How does nine o'clock sound?"

"Perfect." Eleanor gave him a peck on the cheek. "I'll see you then."

CHAPTER 20

▼

The sun had begun its slow descent when John joined Eleanor at the beach. The first star glimmered as darkness crept up from the eastern sky. "Sure is a pretty evening," John commented.

"Yes it is, Papa," Eleanor said as they strolled side by side. A sense of calm stole over Eleanor; surely her father would help her decide what to do about Cameron.

"So, Tomboy, are you going to tell me what's on your mind?" John asked.

"Yes. But I'm scared, Papa."

"Eleanor, you don't have anything to be scared about."

"Please, Papa, just listen." Eleanor took a deep breath. "Cameron—oh gosh, this is hard to say—Cameron's a bad person, Papa."

John looked at her intently. "I think so, too, Eleanor, but I want you to tell me why you feel that way."

"Cameron told me that he came to Haven Point because of my picture in the newspaper article, and because he knew of me when I worked for the Grand Hotel." Eleanor tried to steady the tremor in her voice. "Cameron says he's in love with me, but I can never love him back. I hate everything about him."

Suspicion gleamed in John's eyes. "Did something happen?"

"Cameron tried to hurt me, Papa, the afternoon that you and David went fishing. He's threatening to slander you to Jamieson Greer and have you dismissed if I don't give him what he wants."

"What?" Instant anger reddened John's face. "You say Cameron hurt you? Eleanor, did he—?"

"No, Papa. Almost, but nothing happened."

"Almost is too much. You go on up to the house. I'll take care of this, and I'll do it now."

"No, Papa, wait! If you harm Cameron, you'll lose your job. Besides, I have a plan."

"What sort of plan?"

"I'm going to Duluth to talk to Cameron's mother. I think our answer lies with her, somehow."

"It's a risk," John said. "But if you're set on it, I won't stand in your way. Beside," he added, "it'll keep that lying son-of-a-bitch away from you for the time being."

"There is one problem, though. If I can find a way to force Cameron to leave, you'll be short on help, at least temporarily."

"Well, how about Berglund? I don't think he'd mind coming north to help for a couple weeks. I could send a telegram from Grand Marais."

Eleanor blinked. Why hadn't she thought of Lars herself? "Of course! I'm sure Lars would come back if we asked him!" She threw her arms around John's shoulders. "Oh, Papa, you're a genius!"

"Hold on, now," John said with a laugh. "I don't know if he'll come for sure. But he's a good soul, Berglund." John grew serious again. "When are you planning on sailing for Duluth?"

"Tomorrow, if you'll take me to Grand Marais."

"I could do that. One thing concerns me, though. Do you have enough money for the trip?"

"More than enough. I still have everything I saved from my laundry business."

"But what about that cove, Eleanor? Won't this be a setback?"

It was true that the steamship ticket and the price of a hotel would be costly. But she had to do this for herself, her family, and for Liam. Nothing else mattered.

"Papa, didn't I tell you once that I'd always be your brave soldier?"

John started, then smiled and said, "You're right, Eleanor. I've always depended on you."

They continued walking. "What will we tell Mama?" Eleanor asked.

"Nothing yet, until we come back with proof. Just let me handle her in the meantime."

"Can we take the skiff to Grand Marais as soon as you wake in the morning, Papa? The *America* will be making her run down the North Shore tomorrow."

"Absolutely. Have everything packed and ready when I come off my shift at dawn." John draped his arm around Eleanor's shoulders. "I'm proud of you for telling me the truth."

"I love you, Papa."

"And I love you too, Tomboy. You ought to head back to the house now and get ready for bed. You've got a long couple of days ahead of you."

*   *   *   *

Liam stood at the ironing board in the O'Rourke's kitchen the following morning, trying unsuccessfully to smooth the wrinkles in his new trousers. Jennie, washing dishes at the sink, asked him, "How do you like your new suit?"

"'Tis fine," Liam answered from between clenched teeth, "if only I could press the bloody wrinkles out."

Jennie dried her hands on her apron. "Give over," she said, reaching for the iron. Liam, who knew better than to argue, gladly stepped back.

The boys came running through the kitchen, followed shortly by a toddling Katie. "Mind the door!" Jennie yelled as they bolted outside. Katie stood at the screen and cried in protest.

"There now, you don't want to go following those ruffians," Liam told her gently as he lifted her in his arms. She leaned out to squirm away, then smiled and grabbed hold of Liam's ears. He grinned as he sat with her at the table.

"Shamus was sorry he won't be home in time for the trial," Jennie said as she pressed the trousers. "Is it nervous you are, Liam?"

"Oh, aye." Liam bounced Katie on his knee. "Whenever I think about standing up in court, I break out in a sweat."

"You've no need to worry. Just tell the truth. That's all a man can do."

"You make it sound so easy," Liam said, smoothing his fingers through Katie's curls.

Jennie paused and set the iron on the cook stove. "It can be, Liam, if you think about it the right way. And it might just be the thing for helping what ails you."

"Aye, it might. The nightmares are as bad as ever, sure. Sometimes I think I'll never be rid of them."

Jennie sat across from Liam. "Is that why you were running back to Graceville, then?"

"One of the reasons. Beyond that…" Liam's voice trailed off as he shook his head. "There's no reason to stay."

"I think I understand. You had a row with Eleanor and now you think she won't have you." A ghost of a smile touched Jennie's lips. "You should have told her about the shooting long ago, Liam. No wonder she was upset with you."

"Eleanor would never understand. She doesn't know what it's like back in Ireland."

"Och, that's the sense of a man for you," Jennie said. "Liam, think for a moment. Of course she doesn't know about Ireland, but is that any reason to hide things from her? You have to help her understand, help her see why you left to come to America in the first place."

Jennie took up the iron again. "It hasn't always been easy with Shamus, you know, him being born here in the States. There's things he'll never understand about Ireland either. But I try to be patient, Liam. And that's what you need to do with Eleanor. Just try."

"I thought—well, it doesn't matter what I thought," Liam said. "Once the trial is over, I'm on my way back to Graceville. Eleanor Thompson will never hurt me again."

"And a good thing too, with such tender feelings as you seem to have."

"Woman, you've a fine, sharp tongue, and I'll be thanking you to mind your own business—"

Jennie cut him short with a laugh. "See? You still care for Eleanor, though you'll not admit it to yourself." She draped the trousers on the end of the ironing board. "The North Shore is your home, your future, Liam. Don't throw happiness away with both hands. Things might seem bad now, but I know this is where you're meant to stay."

Before Liam could reply, the boys barreled back inside. "Uncle Liam, Uncle Liam, come outside! We found some wee kittens under the porch!" Flynn exclaimed.

Liam glanced from Flynn to Jennie. "We're not done talking about this," he said.

"Go on with you now. Get a little sun on that handsome face of yours," Jennie teased in return. Liam threw her a dirty look before following the boys outside. While they showed him the mewling kittens, his thoughts drifted to what Jennie had told him.

Liam knew in his heart that she was right about Eleanor, but his pride was still smarting over the whole affair. He'd kept his silence about the shooting to protect her, he told himself. It wasn't in his nature to be deceptive toward her or anyone.

But maybe I am ashamed, he thought as he cradled a tiny calico-colored kitty in the palm of his roughened hand. He'd grown up in the shadow of oppression, and the disgrace of it still clung to him at times. Liam wanted to be a better man for Eleanor, someone she could feel proud of. Yes, that was the true reason he'd not told her everything from the beginning.

But there was little time or energy to spare for Eleanor at the moment. The court trial was set to start the next day, and he'd need all his wits and cunning to face the coming ordeal. Perhaps afterward, when things had settled, he'd make a last attempt to contact her and at least offer an apology.

He owed her that much, if nothing else.

*   *   *   *

Eleanor emerged from the Spalding Hotel in Duluth and stepped onto bustling Superior Street. Throngs of people crowded the street that breezy summer day: men in dark suits and bowler hats, women in trim walking-dresses with wide-brimmed bonnets, boys in knickers and girls in smock dresses. Streetcars clanged beside horse-drawn wagons and carriages, and there was even a newfangled motorcar, chugging and coughing up its foul exhaust.

Multi-story brick buildings rose on either side of the street, partially blocking the sunlight. Telephone and electric lines were strung from pole to pole, block after block. News boys stood on the corners and hawked the city's competing papers, the *Duluth Daily News* and the *News-Tribune*. Scents mingled together: the aroma of baking bread from a local bakery, roses from a window planter, the ubiquitous odor of horse manure.

Eleanor smiled to herself; Duluth was as grand and boisterous as she remembered. Wearing her tea-gown and sporting a new straw hat, she clutched a small handbag as she haled a horse-drawn taxi.

One came to a stop in front of her. "Where to, Miss?" the cab driver asked.

Eleanor had written the Russell's address on a slip of paper. "2029 East Superior Street," she said as she stepped inside the taxi.

"Fashionable side of town, eh?" the cab driver said, smiling.

"Yes." Eleanor settled onto the leather seat as the driver gave the reins a snap. Soon they were clip-clopping along the brick street, heading north.

Downtown slowly give way to the outlying neighborhoods, and Eleanor's stomach churned with nervous anticipation. What sort of person was Mrs. Russell likely to be? Haughty and reserved? Or perhaps more like the people she cleaned houses for in Grand Marais, who were generally respectful? Mrs. Russell's character wasn't the worst of Eleanor's problems, however; more daunting was the issue of how to broach the subject of Cameron's demands. Eleanor chewed her lip, perplexed. Had she done the right thing by coming here? The odds were against her learning anything of value. Likely Mrs. Russell would just turn her from their door, no wiser than before.

Eleanor touched Cameron's cameo. She'd added it at the last moment, thinking it might help convince Mrs. Russell that she was in fact the girl Cameron knew from the lighthouse. It was the first time she'd worn it since Cameron had given it to her on her birthday.

The cab drew to a halt in front of the Russell home. It resembled an enormous square, dressed with flared dormer gables and classical details. The two-story walls were built of sandstone blocks, giving the house an impression of indestructibility. It seemed just the kind of hulking, unimaginative abode Cameron's family would choose to live in.

"That'll be twenty cents, Miss," the cab driver told Eleaonr as she stepped from the vehicle.

"Would you mind waiting? Just in case they're not at home?" Eleanor asked. "I can pay you a little extra for your trouble."

"I don't mind waiting, Miss. Just take your time."

Eleanor listened to the sound of the cab driver's idle whistling as she stepped along the brick sidewalk. Her heart beat a frantic tattoo in her chest as she climbed the portico steps and approached the elaborately carved front door; *what on earth was she going to say to this woman?*

Eleanor grasped the brass knocker and gave it several firm raps. There was no movement on the other side, and, for a moment, she almost turned back. But then the door opened and an elderly man, whom Eleanor guessed to be the butler, greeted her. "Good day, madam," he said. "How can I be of service to you?"

"I would like to speak with Mrs. Russell, if she's at home," Eleanor said with what she hoped was the right mixture of confidence and studied politeness.

"Whom shall I say is calling?"

"Miss Eleanor Thompson. Tell Mrs. Russell that I am a friend of her son, and that I live at the lighthouse where he's employed."

The butler considered for a moment, and then held the door open. "Please wait inside while I announce you."

Eleanor entered with a small exhalation of relief. So far, so good. But now came the hard part; actually talking with Cameron's mother and learning if there was another reason for why he'd come to the lighthouse.

The entry was lavish and yet tasteful at the same time, with marble floors, an Oriental rug, and an Eastlake style coat-tree. A curving staircase with turned balustrades flowed upward to the second story, quite elegant in its appearance.

Eleanor turned at the sound of someone emerging from the adjoining library, half expecting Mrs. Russell. But to Eleanor's surprise she saw that it was her old friend, Gracie. Gracie's face lit up with astonishment when she recognized Eleanor. "Eleanor!" she exclaimed. "My goodness, what are you doing here?"

"Hello, Gracie," Eleanor said with a smile. The two girls embraced. "I'm here to see Mrs. Russell."

"Imagine that! I was just thinking about you the other day, and now here you are!" Gracie bubbled with the same effervescence that Eleanor remembered so well. "Tell me, how do you know the Russels?" Gracie asked.

"I'm acquainted with their son," Eleanor replied carefully.

"Oh. Cameron." Gracie took Eleanor by the elbow and drew her aside. "Where's he been all this time? Nobody has said a word since he disappeared last April—"

"Madam will see you now," the butler announced from the hall entry. Eleanor glanced quickly at Gracie before following the elderly gentleman through the hallway and into what appeared to be a breakfast room or solarium.

It was a pleasant, airy room. Gauze curtains waved in the sun, letting in the smell of the well-tended gardens beyond. Potted ferns bloomed in tropical abundance from twin ornamental planters. A yellow canary tittered in a hanging bamboo cage. The remains of raisin toast and sugared pears sat on delicate china plates atop serving the cart beside the door.

What was more interesting to Eleanor, however, were the large number of jigsaw puzzles. Several covered the table, all half-finished, while a few more could be seen atop the buffet. Mrs. Russell, a piece poised in her hand, didn't even look up when Eleanor and the butler entered the room.

"Madam, Miss Eleanor Thompson," he announced.

At last Mrs. Russell looked up. She was an exact semblance of the picture that Eleanor had seen in Cameron's bedroom that day. Short and plump in stature, Mrs. Russell's face appeared somewhat drawn. Strands of white ran through her black hair. A pair of spectacles perched on her nose, which made her appear even older. *She must have been a great beauty in her day*, Eleanor thought with a brief stir of pity.

Mrs. Russell, dressed all in black satin, rose from her seat and extended her hand. "I am Margaret Russell," she said. "Do come and have a seat while I ring for tea."

"Thank you," Eleanor said. She placed herself at the table and looked over the puzzle, a copy of a well-known work of art.

Margaret requested tea from one of her kitchen staff and then seated herself opposite Eleanor. "Forgive the mess," she said with an apologetic smile. "Hobbies, you know."

"Hmm." Eleanor watched her closely, trying to think of some way to broach the subject of Cameron. But Margaret did it for her instead.

"So," Margaret said, folding her hands in her lap, "you know my son, Cameron."

"Yes. He works at the lighthouse where my father is the head keeper."

"I see." Margaret leaned forward perceptibly. "Is Cameron well? He seldom writes, I'm afraid."

"Well enough." Eleanor swallowed, still uncertain of how much to share. "He's been working very hard, if that's what you mean."

"Ah, I'm glad to hear it," Margaret said with genuine feeling. "His father will be gratified as well."

"Is Mr. Russell at home?"

"Sumner? Heavens, no. Always goes down to the office before dawn."

They paused as tea was served. Eleanor lifted her cup and took a sip. "It's delicious," she said.

"Sumner's favorite flavor, naturally." Margaret settled back in her chair and gave Eleanor an appraising look. "Now, my dear, will you tell me why you've come to all the trouble to visit me today?"

Eleanor reddened. "I—that is, we—have been having some difficulties with your son."

"Difficulties? How do you mean?"

Droplets of sweat dripped down Eleanor's back. "It's difficult to say," she began. "Cameron has been quite persistent in showing an untoward affection for me—"

"I sincerely doubt it," Margaret said coldly. "He's engaged to be married as soon as he returns from his little north woods venture."

"Married?" Eleanor repeated. "To whom?"

"Sophie Hartley, heiress to one of the greatest fortunes in Duluth. You've been misled, Miss Thompson. Cameron and Sophie share a great affection, I assure you."

Eleanor was stunned by the news. She felt as though she were groping her way through a swirling fog. "I was told that the engagement had been broken," she said.

"I can hardly believe it, since the wedding is planned for this coming Christmas day." Margaret allowed herself a little smile. "He's played a ruse on you, my dear child. Nothing more."

Eleanor made no reply. Once again, Cameron had lied to her and to her entire family.

Margaret reached over and patted her arm. "There, there, don't take on so, Eleanor. It's quite obvious that you're taken with him. I must apologize on my son's behalf if he's toyed with you in any way. Cameron was always such a mischievous child."

The crack in the door, Eleanor thought. "Tell me about your son, Mrs. Russell."

"Oh, he was a bright little boy, full of energy and always asking questions," Margaret replied, her face glowing with reminiscence. "He was the constant center of attention, telling delightful stories and putting on little plays for our amusement. I'm afraid that we spoiled him terribly, his father and me. But he was always such a darling toward his mother.

"When Cameron grew older he was distracted by worldly pursuits, you know, socializing and attending balls with the eligible young women of the city. Sumner began to fear he'd be unfit to look after the interests of the company in his stead, and so insisted that he either work aboard one of the company's ships or at a light station. I was so relieved when Cameron chose the latter, especially after that nasty business during the great blow last November."

"Will Cameron take over the company operations when he returns?" Eleanor asked.

"Not at once, you must understand. Sumner wants to appoint him one of the vice-presidents, and then train him to the position." Margaret's expression was serene. "He'll take his father's place, as has been planned since the day he was born."

"I see." Eleanor finished her tea, then rose and extended her hand. "Thank you very much for agreeing to speak with me. You've cleared up a great deal of confusion."

"Think nothing of it, my dear," Margaret said as she rose to escort Eleanor. "You seem like a nice young lady, and I wish you all the best." Suddenly, Margaret noticed the cameo, and her dark brows drew together. "Where did you get that?"

"It was a gift from Cameron for my birthday," Eleanor explained.

"How strange. It was supposed to be for Sophie." Margaret quickly shook her head as they proceeded to the front door. "Give Cameron my regards, and tell him to write his dear old mother more often."

"I will." Eleanor watched Margaret Russell's retreat before fitting her straw hat on her head. She felt a keen sense of disappointment from the interview, having learned nothing about Cameron more than she already knew. He could still use his blackmail scheme against the people she cared for, and she was powerless to stop him.

"Eleanor!" a voice hissed from near the coat closet. Eleanor turned to see Gracie emerge from the shadows. "Come outside with me—there's something I want to tell you."

Eleanor followed her quickly out the front door and around the side of the house. The moment they were alone, Gracie paused and lit a cigarette. "Jesus, I've been dying for a smoke all morning," she said after taking a long drag. Eleanor smiled, remembering how Gracie used to filch cigarettes from the male waiters at the Grand Hotel.

"What's this all about, Gracie?"

"I overheard a little of what you were talking about with the missus. Old bitch," Gracie said with a sniff. "Anyway, she put on a first-rate acting job, that much I can say."

"How do you mean?"

"Oh, sweetie, you don't know the half of it." Gracie took another puff before beginning. "Cameron accepted that job at the lighthouse not just because Daddy wanted him to actually do some real work for a change. Cameron needed to avoid the little 'scandal' he'd caused here, at least until next winter."

Eleanor's mouth went dry. "What scandal?"

"The maid he'd been chasing around got herself in trouble. You remember Allison, don't you?" Gracie's green eyes rested on Eleanor expectantly. "She's pregnant with Cameron's child."

"Oh, God, poor Allison," Eleanor said. "Where's she now?"

"At a boarding house on the south side. I take the trolley to see her once a week. She's been sick as a dog the whole time and isn't due yet until September." Gracie tapped her ashes into the grass. "So much for the Russell's perfect son. If Sophie Hartley or her family ever knew the truth—"

"They'd call off the engagement," Eleanor said. Thoughts clicked in her head as she considered the possibilities. "How much of a scandal would it create, Gracie?"

"Oh, well, you can just imagine. These society snobs pin a lot on their reputations. It would devastate Mrs. Russell."

"Would Allison ever speak against Cameron openly?"

"I think she might. Why?"

"Let's just say that Cameron Russell hasn't finished causing trouble." Eleanor placed a hand on her friend's arm. "Can you give me the address where Allison is living? I need to see her at once."

"Sure. I'll write it down and bring it out." Gracie stubbed out the cigarette and then disappeared inside the house.

Eleanor thought about Allison's situation and shivered despite the sun's warmth. That could have easily been her, if she'd given in to Cameron's demands. But now, ironically, Allison's misfortune might provide the solution to fighting his threats. "If only Allison will agree to help," she murmured. Without her cooperation, Eleanor's plan to confront Cameron would fall to pieces.

Gracie reappeared. "Here you go," she said cheerfully, placing the slip of paper in Eleanor's hand. "Good luck to you. Tell Allison that I'll stop by again on Sunday."

"Thank you, Gracie," Eleanor said as they embraced. "I won't forget this."

"Don't worry about it. Just don't let that bastard walk all over you or anyone else."

"I don't intend to." Eleanor clutched the paper in her hand. "I'll write and let you know what happens."

The cab driver had indeed waited. Eleanor read the address from the slip of paper to him.

"It'll cost you extra, ma'am," he said.

"I'll pay whatever it takes," Eleanor answered.

As the cab continued onward, Eleanor thought about her meeting with Mrs. Russell and Gracie's news about Allison. The entire Russell family was a pack of liars, Eleanor decided. They'd do anything to cover over their son's deficiencies to protect their own reputation. No wonder Cameron acted without fear of consequence.

She gazed out the cab window at the tall buildings of downtown. Eleanor remembered that the Zenith Steamship trial was set to begin that day, having read in the newspaper that Liam was scheduled to give his testimony. Maybe after her visit to Allison, she'd return to the courthouse to watch the trial.

It was the least she could do for Liam, she told herself. He was going to need all the support he could get.

CHAPTER 21

▼

The boarding house where Allison lived was a plain brick dwelling with tall windows and a small flower garden in front. Allison, answering her door, exclaimed, "My goodness, Eleanor! How did you know to find me here?"

"Gracie told me," Eleanor said, embracing her friend. Allison returned the hug awkwardly, obviously embarrassed by her rounded abdomen. They faced one another, each unsure of what to say, until Eleanor asked, "May we sit inside? I need to talk with you."

"Of course. Come along, my room is on the main floor," Allison replied. Eleanor followed her up the steps and into what appeared to be a respectable room (if one looked past the bare furnishings and smell of disinfectant). Eleanor was shocked by Allison's appearance; her hollow cheeks, the circles under eyes, how lank her soft blonde hair was. The summer heat and the strain of pregnancy had taken their toll on Allison's fragile beauty.

They talked about trivialities for a short while until Allison bluntly asked her why she'd come. Eleanor told her the entire story about Cameron, and Allison listened to her with guarded wariness.

"What do you want from me?" Allison asked Eleanor at the conclusion.

"A letter stating who you are and what Cameron's done. I need proof of his indiscretion."

"So my reputation will be ruined along with his?" Allison demanded, her face growing flushed.

"Not if I can help it. This is only to frighten Cameron and make him leave the lighthouse." Eleanor took Allison's hand. "I'm sorry for what happened to you,

Allison. I wish there was something I could do for you now. But I need your help."

Agitated, Allison rose from her chair to wander the small room, her hands covering her abdomen. Eleanor waited, inwardly torn by the need to ask Allison to expose her personal troubles.

Allison returned to her chair, tears glistening in her eyes. "I loved him," she whispered. "I gave him everything."

"I know," Eleanor said, a lump rising in her throat.

"But I also know what he's capable of, and that he must be stopped." Allison went to her desk and quickly scratched out a letter. "Take it, for what it's worth," she said, folding the letter in half before handing it to Eleanor.

"Thank you, Allison," Eleanor said. "Please write after the baby's born."

Both women lingered at the front door. "I've always admired you, Eleanor," Allison said, wiping her eyes. "I wanted to be like you, so strong and brave. You never let anyone boss you around at the hotel."

Eleanor thought of her own failures, especially with regard to her mother. But instead of refuting Allison, she hugged her one last time and said, "It takes incredible bravery to bring a child into this world alone, dearest Allison."

Allison held Eleanor's embrace for long moments, and then released her. She waited until Eleanor stepped into the waiting taxi before waving farewell.

*   *   *   *

Liam, sitting between Mrs. Graling and her lawyer inside the courthouse, experienced an almost uncontrollable urge to sink into the floor. Opening statements were just being presented, but already Liam felt as though they'd been imprisoned in the stifling room for hours. He tried his best to listen and concentrate, but the only thing he heard was the whispering and speculation behind him.

Presiding over the case was the black-robed judge, a respected man who'd spent his early years sailing schooners on the Great Lakes. Liam hoped this meant he would listen to the case with true impartiality.

Matilda Graling nudged Liam's arm and gave him reassuring smile. Stout-figured, Matilda was tightly packed into her chocolate-brown silk dress, while her silvery-gray hair was swept beneath a sober hat ornamented with curving black feathers.

When Liam had first met Matilda on the courthouse steps, he'd privately wondered if she had the will to wage war against Zenith Steamship. All his doubts had vanished at once, however. "For Edward's sake, I intended to win," Matilda had told him firmly.

Liam stared at the defense lawyers and recognized many of the same men who'd questioned him at the Marine Board of Inquiry earlier that winter. They refused to meet his eyes, which angered him. "They think they're better than us common folk. Just like the damned English back home," Liam muttered.

He stole a look at the crowd gathered in the courtroom. Many people were watching him, the women especially. These were the widows of his drowned mates, and their faces spoke visibly of their grief.

Others were present as well, men of importance, including Zenith Steamship's president, Sumner Russell. Liam studied Sumner as he drew a comparison between father and son. Yes, they were the same, save for the fact that Sumner had graying hair and appeared thirty pounds heavier. Sumner shifted his glance in Liam's direction, and Liam caught his breath. Sumner's disdain was palpable.

Liam recognized many ships' masters in the crowd, captains who'd managed to bring their ships to safety through the storm. This was a critical case, Liam knew; if judgment went against the company, it would constitute a major embarrassment for the company and weaken its position in the face of recent efforts of the sailors to unionize.

Though Liam had not seen her, Eleanor was among those listening to opening statements. She sat near the back of the room, fanning herself in the heat. Liam's head and broad shoulders rose above those seated around him. Her heart went out to him, imaging how nervous he must have been feeling at that moment.

Movement from the side caught her attention. It was the *News-Tribune* reporter, Hudson Fairfax. He smiled and nodded, and she returned the smile.

The lawyer for Zenith Steam had concluded his opening remarks. Liam was summoned as the first witness, and, after being sworn in, took the stand.

After the formalities of identifying Liam for the record, Mrs. Graling's attorney approached him. "Mr. MacLann, I'd like you to take us back to the afternoon of November 26, 1905. The day the *William A. Dorn* departed Duluth Harbor with a payload of iron ore, bound for Ashtabula, Ohio. From your written statement, we know that you visited the pilothouse. You do remember that day, don't you?"

"Aye. I'd not likely forget."

"Describe what the weather was like, and what you observed."

"Well, everything was clear and calm. Unnaturally so, really. There was no wind stirring the waters, that much I recall."

"I see." The lawyer, handsome and affable, spoke to Liam as though they were long-time acquaintances. "Were the gale warning flags raised at the time of departure?"

"No, they weren't. As I testified at the Marine Board of Inquiry," Liam added with a glare at the Zenith Steam lawyers.

The lawyer smiled. "Just so. Now, tell the courtroom how you found the mood of Captain Graling and his mates when you later paid a visit to the pilot-house."

Liam looked at Matilda, who sat watching him intently. "The men were relaxed and looking forward to the end of the season. Especially the captain. He mentioned how eager he was to return home to Cleveland to see his wife and grandchildren."

"Was there anything else unusual or out of the ordinary?"

Liam thought for a moment. "I remember the wheelsman commenting on how high the barometer was. As far as we could tell, there was only clear sailing ahead."

The lawyer strolled over to where the jury was seated. "Did you hear that, ladies and gentlemen? 'Clear sailing ahead.' Apparently, Captain Graling made his decision to sail based on the best available information. According to this witness' testimony, Captain Graling acted with sound judgment. His decision to sail was in no way negligent, contrary to Zenith Steamship's claim." He nodded to Liam and said, "Thank you, Mr. MacLann."

The defense lawyer approached the stand. Liam took his measure of the man, who had the look and smell of a rat about him.

"Mr. MacLann, wasn't it true that the ship's holds were grossly overloaded prior to sailing?" the lawyer questioned.

"I wouldn't say they were grossly overloaded. The ship was riding heavy, sure, but not dangerously so."

"How much over the safe limit was she loaded then, Mr. MacLann? One ton? Two?"

"Och, I don't know for certain. Maybe ten tons over."

"Ten tons," the lawyer repeated gravely. He shook his head. "Ten tons extra can wreck havoc on a ship when she's pounded by wind and waves. It could mean the difference between reaching shore safely or splitting apart and sinking to Superior's bottom."

"Objection, your Honor," Matilda's lawyer protested. "Speculation on the part of the prosecutor."

"Sustained." The judge gave a slight nod. "You may continue."

The lawyer returned to his questioning. "Mr. MacLann, would you say that Captain Graling knew that the ship's holds had been overloaded?"

"Aye, that he would have. There wasn't much the Old Man didn't know about his own ship." This brought a smattering of laughter from the crowd.

"I'm afraid this is no laughing matter," the lawyer said. "Twenty-eight men are dead because of what happened during that gale." Properly rebuked, the crowd fell silent.

"Again, I ask you, was the Captain aware of the situation?"

"He was. But almost every trip we rode heavy, especially toward the end of the season. It was well-known among the men that Zenith Steam expected all their captains to overload, to increase the profit ratio."

This brought a murmur from the crowd. The judge tapped his gavel and called for order. The lawyer advanced, his eyes narrowing, his expression more rat-like than ever. "That may have been the rumor among the crew. But was it ever a posted policy? I mean, did you yourself see it stated anywhere that the captain was expected to unsafely overload his ship?"

"No, but—"

"That will be all, Mr. MacLann."

Liam, who'd been growing angrier by the moment, gripped the chair arms with his hands. "Now, don't be twisting my words around in that fancy way of yours! Everyone bloody well knew that's how the company operated. They underpaid their sailors, especially the deckhands and stokers. They expected us to sail out in heavy seas, whether it was safe or no, to deliver their freight on time and keep to tight schedules. The men were accounted last in their list of losses, and now my friends, good mates all, are drowned and will never be seen again!"

"I repeat, that will be all, Mr. MacLann," the lawyer said, more forcefully this time.

"That will not be all!" Liam pounded the wooden rail with his open palm. "Captain Graling was one of the finest masters I ever sailed with, and I trusted my life to him! To say that he was reckless is a lie, no, worse than lies! My shipmates died honorably, in the face of a storm no man should have survived!" Liam pointed at Sumner Russell. "You need to make changes, pay the men more and build the ships stronger! You owe them that much, for the love of Christ!"

"Objection!" the head defense lawyer thundered.

"Sustained." The judge glared at Liam from beneath bushy white brows. "You will refrain from speaking and step down from the witness stand, Mr. MacLann."

Liam grunted as his strode from the box. He trembled with rage. Flopping heavily beside Matilda, he sat for long minutes and stared at his hands. A sense of doom settled over Liam as his anger sifted away. He'd failed again, losing his temper like that. Now everything he had said in Graling's favor would probably be disregarded.

The following witnesses were either sailors who'd been on the other ships during the storm, or technical experts arguing the merits of ship design and load-bearing capacity. Liam passed a hand across his forehead, his mouth dry as a sandbar. What he needed more than anything was a drink of water.

Quietly excusing himself, Liam passed through the double doors and into the hallway. The air was much cooler, and he stood for a moment, breathing deeply. *Ah, that was better.* He went in search of the drinking fountain, where he bent down and took a long, blissful drink. Already his mood was beginning to lighten. He stood and wiped his chin, and when he turned around he saw Eleanor.

At first he just stared in surprise. She stood looking up at him, her face shining with admiration.

"Girleen, what are you doing here?"

"I came to listen to your testimony, Liam. I thought it was important for me to be here."

"You came all the way to Duluth just to hear me talk in court?" he asked, amazed. "How did you find out about it?"

"Shamus told me when the *Amaranth* stopped at the light station, the day before yesterday."

Once again, Liam was struck dumb with silence. She was radiant, as fresh and lovely as an ocean breeze. His heart contracted; how easy it would be to reach out and touch her, beg her forgiveness. But then he stopped himself and asked, "Is that the only reason you came?"

"Well, I *did* have other business to attend to—"

"What other business? Something to do with that man, that assistant keeper?" Liam accused, his jealousy flaring.

"In a manner of speaking, yes. But it's not what you think, Liam—"

"I'd rather not think of it, or of you, or of anything that happened between us," Liam muttered, pushing past her. It had been there for him again, just for a moment, that sense of connection between them. But he beat it down fiercely, stomped it into the dust.

"Liam!" Eleanor walked after him, and he slowed, still pulsing with hurt.

"What the hell do you want from me?" he asked

"I—I just wanted to tell you how marvelous you were on the witness stand. I'm so proud of you for standing up to those men and telling the truth. You're the bravest man I know, Liam."

Misery pierced Liam. She was so earnest, so sincere, that for a moment he almost believed her. "Thanks," he said before turning again for the courtroom doors.

"Will you leave for Graceville after the trial is over?" Eleanor asked in a small voice.

"Aye, that I will. I have the train ticket in my pocket. Once things are tied up here, I'll be leaving directly."

"I wish the best for you then," Eleanor said. "I hope you will take a few happy memories with you from the North Shore."

"A few. We had some good times together, and that was all. That was all you ever meant to me, Eleanor. Don't hang onto something that was never real to begin with." Liam turned his back and then slipped through the doors. He cursed the need to say these things to her. But it was for the best; she was still obviously involved with that other man. A clean break was what they both needed.

Liam felt weak with exhaustion, both from his battle on the witness stand and his unexpected meeting with Eleanor. He took a deep breath and then went to sit beside Matilda.

He hoped with all his heart Eleanor hadn't seen his face. Because if she did, she would know that he had told a lie to her worse than anything said by those Zenith Steamship lawyers.

∗   ∗   ∗   ∗

Eleanor stared at the courtroom door in Liam's wake. Why must he always jump to conclusions, why must he always feel so suspicious about her? Yes, she should've tried to explain the situation with Cameron, but not here, not in some public hallway. A tear spilled over, and she brushed it away. If only Liam knew how much she hated Cameron…but it was useless. He was leaving to rejoin his family in western Minnesota. There was nothing to hold him here on the North Shore, apparently.

She took a seat on a nearby bench, overcome with fatigue. It had been an extraordinarily long day already: first the interview with Mrs. Russell, followed by the visit to Allison, and now this disappointing encounter with Liam.

Eleanor kept Allison's letter safely hidden in her handbag. She took small comfort by imagining the look on Cameron's face when she finally confronted him with the truth.

Someone spoke to Eleanor, asking, "Miss Thompson?"

It was the reporter, Hudson Fairfax. "Mr. Fairfax," Eleanor said. "How good to see you again."

"And you as well," Hudson said with a smile. "May I sit with you for a moment?"

"Of course." Eleanor made room for him on the bench. "I saw you in the courtroom."

"Yes. Covering the story for the newspaper, naturally." Hudson nodded toward the courtroom doors. "You've kept in touch with Mr. MacLann, then?"

"Yes. His testimony today was quite moving."

"Magnificent. He'll make wonderful press," Hudson said with a grin. "A hero for the working man."

"He'd deny that, you know."

"That makes what he says more believable. I still receive letters from readers who want to know what happened to the both of you. That story resonated with a great many people."

Eleanor found this hard to believe. "We just did the best we could, Mr. Fairfax."

"Some folks would disagree with you, Miss Thompson." Hudson withdrew a business card from his pocket. "Here's the newspaper's address. If you need anything, *anything*, just contact me, and I'll be glad to help." He rose and shook her hand. "I'd best get back to the trial. Good day to you, Miss."

"Good day," Eleanor said before glancing over the business card. Another stroke of luck; certainly, Hudson would help her if she needed to expose Cameron's scandalous story to the public. It would add the necessary starch to any warning she would give to Cameron after her return to Haven Point. Yes, with Allison's letter and the reporter's contact, she held the key to turning Cameron's threats against him.

As Eleanor rose and prepared to leave the courthouse, she cast one last look at the courtroom doors. Liam was still inside, probably listening to more testimony. She flushed as she recalled his stirring speech on the witness stand; for the first time, Liam had stood his ground and not run from trouble.

If only she weren't in such a hurry to return home and deal with Cameron, she thought. There might have been a chance to wait for Liam and try to reconcile their differences.

But now there was no chance. She needed to accept the fact that, however painful, Liam would never be a part of her life again.

*   *   *   *

To Eleanor's dismay, it was Cameron who met her when the *America* dropped anchor in the harbor outside of Haven Point the next day. He sat watching her from the skiff, looking especially disgruntled. The steamship crewmen passed down Eleanor's suitcase before helping her into the seesawing boat.

"Thank you!" she called as the crew closed the freight door. Eleanor tried her best to avoid making eye contact with Cameron. He dipped the oars into the water, took a few strokes, and then asked, "Well, Eleanor, did you enjoy your little adventure in Duluth?"

"I did." Eleanor turned to face him. "It was *most* interesting."

"I see," Cameron said. "And did it have anything to do with Jamieson Greer's inspection the other day?"

"Yes. But the exact reason is my business alone."

"I can well imagine the reason. I saw the newspaper article about the Zenith Steam trial. I know that MacLann was there to testify." Cameron gripped the oars more tightly. "No doubt you went running to him with all your misfortunes."

"I saw Liam, yes. But not because of you or anything that you've done or said." Eleanor glared at him from across the skiff. "You might think that you frighten me, Cameron, but I'm not afraid of you any longer."

Cameron's rowing slowed. "Something's happened. Who did you see when you were in Duluth?"

"I'm tired, Cameron," Eleanor said, unwilling to bandy with him any longer. He rowed without comment in the direction of the shore, where John stood waiting on the dock.

"Did you find everything you need?" John asked, offering a hand up to Eleanor.

"Everything and more." She touched her handbag and gave him a knowing look.

"I understand." John's face broke into a smile. "Well, Eleanor, I'm real glad that you're home. We all missed you."

"Even Mama?"

"Well, that's hard to say. She was mad as hops that I wouldn't tell her where you'd gone or why."

"We'll soothe her ruffled feathers, don't worry," Eleanor assured him. Father and daughter walked together up the path. "I'm just glad to be home, Papa," Eleanor said. She meant every word.

Duluth might have its charms, but the North Shore was where her heart belonged.

"Papa, look! It's the *America!*"

Another week had passed. Eleanor, wringing laundry outdoors in the tub, looked over to where David was pointing from the tree house. John, at the woodpile, swung his axe through a length of birch before pausing to stare out at the lake, where the *America* had dropped anchor.

It was a sultry afternoon, the air so humid it was like breathing through a wet towel. John wiped the sweat dripping down his face and said, "Someone's coming across in one of her rowboats, and I think I recognize Lars Berglund in the bow."

Eleanor's heart raced as she hurried to the ridge. By now, the *America's* small boat had arrived at the dock, and yes, it was indeed Lars. "Lars!" Eleanor called joyfully, waving. In the distance, the tall Swede returned the gesture and shouted a greeting.

A young woman climbed up beside him on the dock, suitcase in hand. Broad and buxom, the young woman's flaxen hair shone in the bright sunlight. She was dressed in light blue homespun, and her golden braids were twisted into a thick knot.

David came up beside Eleanor. "Go tell Mama and Bridget that we have visitors," she told him. "And then tell Cameron as well."

Lars and the young woman climbed the pathway from the beach. Lars had changed little since the previous December; his kindness was evident in his jaunty expression, his easy, loose-limbed gait, the relaxed set of his shoulders.

"Berglund!" John exclaimed, stepping forward to greet his former assistant. "How are you these days?"

"I'm well, sir, thank you," Lars said, his eyes sparkling. The woman appeared nervous, and Eleanor smiled, hoping to help ease her anxiety.

"Welcome back to Haven Point, Lars," Eleanor said. She turned her attention to the young woman, "You must be Mrs. Berglund."

"I am." The woman stepped forward and offered her hand. "My name is Anja."

"Pleased to meet you," Eleanor said as she gave Anja's hand a brief shake. "I'm Eleanor Thompson."

A smile spread across Anja's round face. "I have heard so much about you, Miss Thompson, and about Haven Point. I'm so glad to be here."

"Thank you both for coming," Eleanor said with feeling. Her gaze shifted to Lars. "Are you ready for this?"

"I am," Lars replied, his expression sharpening. "More than ready."

Adeline and Bridget came to join the group. Adeline, flustered, stared round-eyed at Lars and his wife. "Gracious, Mr. Berglund, what a surprise to see you here today!"

"It's good to see you again, Mrs. Thompson," Lars said. He circled an arm around his wife's shoulders. "I'd like you to meet my wife, Anja."

"Wife?" Adeline, her jaw gaping, peered at Anja for a few seconds, and then recovered her composure. "A pleasure to meet you, my dear."

Anja curtsied and turned a bright shade of red. Adeline glanced from their faces to the suitcase sitting between them, and then asked, "Are you planning to visit for very long?"

"Well, ma'am, that kind of depends," Lars said. He took his hat in his hands and was about to speak when Cameron emerged from his house. All eyes turned toward him, and Eleanor watched as he advanced a few steps and then paused.

Adeline, who must have sensed the tension, frowned and asked, "What's wrong? John, tell me why Lars has come."

Eleanor took her mother's arm and said, "Mama, I want you to invite Anja up to the house for a cup of coffee. Please, Mama."

Adeline drew up short. "I'll not move an inch until you tell me what's happening."

"Please, Mama, just go to the house for now. There's something we have to do, something unpleasant. Trust me this once, Mama. I promise to explain everything later."

Adeline looked toward John. "It's best," John said. With a jerk of her chin, Adeline turned and stalked toward the house. Anja stood a little off to the side, wide-eyed and unmoving.

"Bridget, why don't you escort Anja up to the house, help Mama entertain her," Eleanor said.

"It would be my pleasure," Bridget said in her most grown-up voice.

David ran up just then, with Cameron a few paces behind. Eleanor quickly took David aside and whispered, "Go up to the house with Bridget. I need you to make sure Mama doesn't interrupt what's about to happen."

"Oh, all right," David said, dejected. "But you have to promise tell me what happened later."

Cameron waited until David left before confronting Lars, asking, "Who the hell are you?"

"I was the assistant keeper last year," Lars answered. His face had closed in a hard, determined set. "And, God willing, I'll be the assistant yet again before this day is over."

Cameron laughed. "What gives you the right to just waltz in here and demand your old job back?"

"I think you've given him every reason, Cameron," John said gruffly.

"There's nothing to discuss," Cameron said, jabbing a finger in John's chest. "I was appointed by the Lighthouse Board, and my father serves as chairman of the Lake Carriers' Association. You're mistaken if you think you can force me to leave."

A white flame of anger blazed to life inside Eleanor. "Cameron," she said, "my father knows the truth. About everything."

Cameron's expression went blank. Agonizing seconds crawled by. "It doesn't matter," Cameron finally said. "No one tells me where to go or what to do."

"You're wrong, Cameron." Eleanor withdrew Allison's letter from her skirt pocket, where she'd kept it since her return from Duluth. "Here's all the proof I need of what kind of person you really are."

"Give me that," Cameron said, snatching for the letter. Lars grabbed his arm, however, and gave it a savage twist.

"I can read it aloud, if you like," Eleanor said. "It's from your lover, Allison."

"Let me go," Cameron snarled, wrenching his arm free. "That woman's nothing more than a liar, a whore."

"You're the liar, Cameron," Eleanor said. "Gracie told me what happened, when I went to Duluth visit with your mother."

"My mother?" Cameron stared at Eleanor, incredulous.

"Yes, your mother. I know all about Sophie Hartley and the wedding. I also know that one of the reasons you came to Haven Point was because Allison was pregnant with your child. Because of the possible scandal."

"You—you wouldn't dare!" Cameron sputtered, his face bloodless.

"In a heartbeat." *Now for the killing blow.* "I met up with Mr. Fairfax, the *News-Tribune* reporter, at Liam's trial. He gave me his business card before we parted." Eleanor held that out for Cameron to see as well. "I'm sure he would love to hear every detail of your affair—"

"Enough!" Cameron cried. Murder gleamed in his green eyes, but both Lars and John stood between him and his quarry. "What is it you want?"

"You must leave Haven Point immediately. Lars and my father will row you up to Grand Marais, and you can catch the *America* to Duluth the day after. You will tender your resignation at once to the Lighthouse Board. And you will promise never to bother Liam MacLann." Eleanor folded her arms decisively. "If you do not meet those conditions, I will have no choice but to expose you to public scrutiny."

Cameron looked from one stony face to another. "It seems I have no choice in the matter, now does it?"

"Let's get your things packed, Cameron," John said. "We'll take you to Marais when you're ready."

Cameron began to follow John, but then stopped and glared at Eleanor. "You think yourself so smart, don't you? You think you've beaten me. But you haven't, you know. I'm going to marry a rich and beautiful woman, and you have no one. MacLann is gone and won't be coming back. You'll be all alone."

"Eleanor won't be alone," Lars answered, placing a hand on Eleanor's shoulder. "She has family and friends who care for her, and that's more than you'll ever have."

"See it that way if you like. But you won't forget me, Eleanor." Cameron smiled. "You'll never forget."

Eleanor turned away. It was true that she would never forget Cameron, or his lies, or how much she despised him.

Superior spread before her. A freshening breeze was blowing inland, sweet with the smell of lake water. Eleanor filled her lungs and then exhaled; she felt cleaner already. Soon Cameron would be gone for good, and with him the nightmare of fear and uncertainty that had been dogging her for weeks.

Eleanor turned to Lars and said, "I want to thank you for coming, Lars. I hope the money I sent was enough to cover your traveling expenses."

"More than enough. I'd have come sooner if I'd known how bad things had gotten here." Lars looked at her with a mixture of fondness and concern. "Are you going to be all right, Eleanor?"

"I will be, especially now that Cameron is leaving. This has been a dreadful summer."

"Cameron's worse than your father described in the telegram." Lars shook his head. "Cameron Russell ought to be horse-whipped."

"He'll never bother us again, and that's all that matters," Eleanor said. Her face softened as she glanced toward the house. "Anja seems a like a wonderful girl."

"She is." Lars said it simply and without reserve. "We're suited to one another. Both from good Swedish stock," he added with a grin.

"I can't wait to get to know her," Eleanor said. Lars offered her his arm, and they strolled toward the house. When they reached the back door, Eleanor paused and said, "How am I ever going to explain all this to Mama? She was so fond of Cameron, so carried away by his charms."

"Just tell her the truth, Eleanor. Even she has to accept that Cameron is a bad person."

"You don't know how stubborn Mama can be," Eleanor replied.

"Oh, don't I? Remember, I lived here for five years, Eleanor. I probably know better than anyone."

As they mounted the steps, Lars paused and asked, "What ever became of Liam? I thought the two of you would be engaged by now."

"He's left the North Shore and will be returning to Graceville, last I heard. Liam was never really happy here. Too many bad memories from the shipwreck."

"A shame. He really loved you, Eleanor."

She searched Lars' face. "Do you think so?"

"As near as I can tell," Lars said, and then opened the door for Eleanor. Inside, Anja was smiling and nodding over something Adeline had said. *Such an engaging, pleasant girl,* Eleanor thought. Just the kind of wife that Lars deserved.

With Lars at Haven Point, it would feel almost like old times.

CHAPTER 22

▼

The trial was over, the verdict rendered, and Matilda Graling had come to the O'Rourke's house to share the news with Liam.

"Well?" Liam asked, alone with Matilda in the parlor. "What did they say?"

"They ruled in our favor." A smile broadened across Matilda's face. "One of the jury members told me afterward that your testimony was the key factor in their decision."

"Saints be praised!" Liam cried, swooping her up in an unceremonious hug. Matilda laughed and hugged him back briefly before insisting that he set her down.

"A woman my age can't bear this much excitement," Matilda teased, and then smoothed her dress. "I'm grateful for all you've done, Mr. MacLann. My husband's good name has been cleared, and now the families of the crewmen will be free to pursue their lawsuits against Zenith Steamship." She sniffed and dabbed her nose with a scented cloth. "I wouldn't be surprised if the company tries to reach a settlement before any further legal action is taken."

"I hope the families will get something out of this, some security," Liam said. "'Twill help them face the future without their men."

"No day is ever easy after the death of a husband or father. But money does help lighten the burden." Matilda's demeanor grew more business-like. "Which brings me to the other reason for my visit today. I have something I wish to give you in return for your invaluable help."

Liam frowned. "You don't owe me anything, Mrs. Graling. I've done my duty. I couldn't count myself a man if I hadn't."

"That's beside the point. I know you've suffered a great deal since the shipwreck. Please allow me to offer you a portion of my husband's estate." Matilda pressed an envelope into Liam's hand. "Edward would have wanted it."

Liam peered into her face for a few moments, and then nodded. "Me thanks," he whispered. "God bless you, Mrs. Graling."

"Goodbye, Mr. MacLann. May the future bring you bounty and good fortune. Heaven knows you deserve it." She shook his hand and then departed.

Jennie and the children, who'd been hanging on every word from just inside the next room, flew to Liam's side the moment the door closed. "Open it Liam! I'm dying to know how much she gave you!" Jennie cried.

Liam's hand trembled as he tore open the envelope. He read the amount written on the check, and then read it again.

Jennie's hand flew to her mouth. "Jesus above, Liam! Why, 'tis a king's ransom!"

"Aye," Liam said faintly. "More money than the whole of my family could earn in a lifetime."

Patrick, impatient, tugged on Liam's sleeve and asked, "How much is it?"

"Three thousand dollars," Liam replied. "I am wealthy man."

"*Three thousand* dollars!" Jennie exclaimed. "Think of it! Liam, you'll never have to work another day in your life!" She gave Liam a hearty hug. "Ah, were that Shamus was here now to share the news!"

Liam began to wander around the parlor, his knees weak, his thoughts scattered. "I—I don't know what to do, Jennie girl. I haven't the first idea what to do with all this money."

"You should buy a castle!" Flynn insisted.

"No, a big boat to go sailing on the lake!" Patrick countered.

"All well and good, boys, but Liam should start with another fine suit to match the one he bought for the trial," Jennie suggested. "A man of means needs to look the part."

"You're right, as usual," Liam said with a chuckle. He stared out the window and wished mightily that Shamus was on hand to counsel him. But the *Amaranth* wasn't due home for several days yet. "Maybe what I need is a good stretch of the legs to mull things over."

"A grand idea. I'll pack a few sandwiches and you can take them up to the city summit. 'Tis a fine view of Superior from up there."

"Can't we go with Liam, mother?" Patrick begged, staring up at Jennie with earnest eyes.

"Ah now, leave the poor man alone. The last thing Liam needs is the two of you pestering him." Jennie disappeared into the kitchen and returned a short while later with two sandwiches wrapped in brown paper. "Take your time, Liam. There's much for you to decide."

"Aye. I'll be back before nightfall," he promised. Liam fitted on his cap and stepped out the front door, breathing deep the summer air. Humming the tune to an old sea shanty, Liam headed in the direction of the incline railway.

A short while later, Liam disembarked the railway and then walked for a mile or so westward along a portion of road known as the Boulevard. Parties in horse-drawn carriages passed by, stirring up clouds of dust in their wake. Liam listened to the lively chatter of the men and women, some laughing, some sitting arm in arm. Liam should have felt happy as well. But their merriment only served to deepen his sense of isolation.

He left the road and struck across the wooded countryside. The land continued to rise, the grass and earth giving way to black basaltic outcroppings. Wild-flowers sprang from the rocky hillside, while the air was alive with buzzing insects. Pine scent filled Liam's nose, the smell of pitch heavy in the warm sunlight.

At length he found what he was seeking, a singular rock, massive and tabular and just right for stretching out on. Liam climbed up and then lay on his back with knees bent and his hands locked behind his head. He stared at the blue roof of sky. A stiff breeze raked the clouds along at a steady clip, the stray wisps swept far out across the lake.

Liam sat up for a moment and gazed at the distant harbor. It was lined with dozens of steamships, all appearing absurdly small in the distance. Tiny columns of black smoke rose from their stacks, and Liam heard the thin wail of a distant whistle. *The ships sail day and night*, he thought. Day and night, month after month, year after year. Empires built on the risks hazarded by common sailing men.

He lay back again and closed his eyes. The great irony of his present situation was not lost on him. The wreck that had almost taken his life had now granted him an enormous boon. Three thousand dollars was an astronomical amount. He should be happy; he should be ecstatic. Why, now he could return to Graceville in style and marry Rose O'Malley as soon as possible. But not even this thought cheered him.

Voices from the past echoed in Liam's thoughts. His father Joseph, in their *curragh* on the sea—"Strength is born of character, *mo buachaill*. The staunchest heart can accomplish miracles."

Nick Bryant, aboard the *Dorn*—"I'm always telling everyone you're the luckiest man I know!"

Jennie, the night before he returned to the North Shore—"Nothing worthwhile is easy, Liam. But if you have the courage, then anything is possible."

Nils, in the cabin at Little Nesna—"The man who lives when all others are lost is hallowed, sanctified. A second chance. Don't waste it, MacLann."

Shamus, on the porch as they stared out over the city at night—"I can't imagine my life without Jennie and the children, and nothing would keep me from that happiness."

Lastly, the voice of Conall, in the dream-vision aboard the lifeboat—"A future of great possibility awaits you. Do not shirk your duty, nor despair of love."

"Conall," Liam said as he shifted atop the rock. Suddenly, he felt a chill caress his skin, and he opened his eyes to see Conall sitting only a few feet distant.

Liam sat up quickly. "Hello, brother."

"Liam-boy." Conall was just as Liam remembered from their days together, with one great difference; there was a shimmering cast to Conall, a transparency that set him apart from the living.

"Why have you come to me?" Liam asked. He wondered if he'd lost his mind completely.

"I'm here because I'm needed. Because your heart aches. Because you can't see the plain truth in front of you," Conall answered.

Liam stirred. "Ah, you always thought you were the boss of me in the old days. When are you going to let me run my own life, hmm?"

"When you can stop making such a mess of things. When you stop running away. When you stop acting like such a horse's arse." Conall smiled, and Liam began to relax a little.

"Why are you going back to Graceville, Liam-boy?"

"You know why. Because Uncle Tim Pat needs me. Because of Rose. Because—well, and why should I stay? What the hell do I have to keep me here?"

"Open your eyes! You have friends that care about you, good people like the O'Rourkes and those fine Norwegians. You have enough money to buy a bit of land like you always wanted. And there's a girl up north who's broken-hearted you're leaving."

"What happened with Eleanor is over. She's chosen another man—"

"Don't be so sure. Things are not always what they seem."

"Jesus, there you go again, talking in riddles!" Liam said. "Just straight out say what you mean!"

"The man in question is gone. There never was anything between them. She's only ever loved you, from the moment she found you on the beach. And if you can't accept the truth of it, then you're welcome to a life of regret without her."

Liam cocked his head, trying hard to think. This was all so bewildering, so difficult to comprehend. "Answer me this, then; *why me?* Why was I saved from drowning?"

"You've known it all along, Liam-boy. You knew it when you testified in court on behalf of your shipmates. You know it now." Conall stood and brushed his hands on his trousers. "Their lives were worth something, Liam. Be deserving of their sacrifice. Live on in the way that would have made them proud, that will honor them. It's the only way you'll ever find peace."

Conall's outline began to flicker and grow faint. Liam stood and said, "You won't be coming to me again, will you?"

"No. You've no need of me. You'll find your way. I must go to the place prepared for me." A look of love came into Conall's face. "One day you will join me, though 'twill be many years from now."

Tears filled Liam's eyes. "I will never forget you, *dearthár*, or the things you've taught me."

"Follow your heart, Liam-boy. That's the only path to happiness." Conall faded and disappeared, leaving Liam alone with tears streaming down his face.

Wind from the lake breathed over Liam, nearly snatching his cap away. He dried his face and then stood staring out over the lake. Superior. It stretched away into vast distances, to Wisconsin and beyond until it merged with the horizon.

Had he been so wrong, after all? Had he been longing for home, when in truth he had been there all along?

Slowly, ever so slowly, Liam's uncertainty began to sift away. He faced north, gazing past the rolling hills. Beyond the tossing sea. Beyond the barriers between the past and the future.

Liam jumped down from the rock. He felt twenty pounds lighter than when he'd climbed up. The brightness of the day filled his heart, and as he walked he began to whistle.

He couldn't wait to tell Jennie O'Rourke his decision.

*   *   *   *

It was early in the afternoon on July the 28th, and Eleanor was preparing to deliver the latest load of clean laundry to Little Nesna. In her pocket she carried two objects: the St. Brendan's medal given to her by Liam, and the cameo necklace from Cameron. Each morning when she rose and dressed, they stared back at from atop the highboy. She'd begun to think of them as relics of the past, painful reminders of what might have been, both for better and for worse.

Down at the boathouse, she placed the laundry basket inside the skiff. Eleanor made certain the life jacket was on board, and was about to climb into the boat when she was interrupted by a call from Bridget.

"Eleanor!" Bridget came walking quickly down the path with a tied bundle in her hand.

"What's wrong?"

"Nothing's wrong. Anja just wanted to be sure that you took these to give to the Norwegians." Bridget gave her the sack. "Swedish butter cookies."

Eleanor peeked inside and smiled. "They look delicious, just like everything Anja bakes."

"Lars better watch out, or she'll turn him into a fat old man before his time," Bridget said with a laugh. "They do seem content together, don't you think?"

"Yes. It already feels like they belong here, like this is where they should stay. But I suppose it's only a matter of time before the Lighthouse Board sends a new assistant keeper."

"I hope that doesn't happen for a while yet. But at least anyone else will be better than Cameron Russell."

"And good riddance, too." Eleanor looked toward the house. "Mama's still having a hard time accepting what happened, even after I showed her Allison's letter."

"I feel sorry for Mama. She wanted to believe that Cameron was really in love with you, and that you'd marry and be rich. He was the answer to all her dreams for you," Bridget said. Eleanor held back a smile; her baby sister was sounding older and wiser than her fourteen years. "Say, Eleanor, what did you do with that pretty necklace Cameron gave you for your birthday?"

Eleanor felt inside her skirt pocket and withdrew the cameo. "I was planning on tossing it into the lake, far out from the shore." She offered it to Bridget. "Why don't you take it?"

Bridget turned it over, running her fingers across the face. "You won't mind if I wear it once in a while?"

"Not at all." Eleanor gave her sister a smile. "It'll be a reminder of how close we all came to disaster."

"But what about the other necklace, the medallion from Liam?"

Eleanor held it aloft. "I was thinking I might visit the cove and bury it on the beach. There are memories there…" Eleanor shook her head. "I'd better get going before the wind is too strong."

"Hurry back. Anja is cooking a special supper to mark the end of their first week here," Bridget told her. Eleanor stepped into the skiff and took her seat on the centerboard. Sliding the oars through the locks, she began to row out onto the lake.

The skiff glided easily through the waves. Light glittered off gently rippling swells that rolled onward to purl against cragged headlands and shores. A golden glow shown off red-hued cliffs crested with stately pines and endless stands of hardwood forest. Gulls sallied from the embankments to glide across Superior. Basaltic boulders lay tumbled and piled below the surface. Like a vision come to life, the North Shore's grandeur surrounded Eleanor, further anchoring her to this place of timelessness and beauty.

As she rounded the final headland before the cove, Eleanor was surprised to see a Mackinaw boat resting on the beach. It was a vessel whose markings she did not recognize. Her surprise turned to astonishment when she saw that someone had made repairs to the cabin, and that smoke was rising from chimney.

"Oh, no," Eleanor groaned. Someone else had purchased the land! An iron band squeezed her heart. It couldn't be true, it just couldn't be! After all her hard work, the dreaming and planning: this was the crowning blow.

Who could have done this? *Probably someone from one of the cities to the south*, she thought bitterly. Someone undeserving of such a treasure as her cove. She fought back a rising sense of despair. Well, it was done and over with. Maybe it was best to just keep rowing toward the fish camp and then discover later who'd paid for the land.

Eleanor dipped the oars and took a few half-hearted strokes, then stopped. She owed herself the truth, she realized. She would meet this new owner herself.

Soon the skiff's bow scraped against sand and rock, and Eleanor climbed over the gunnel, soaking her shoes in the rushing surf. Quickly she hauled the boat ashore and then stood panting beside it, gathering her courage to knock on the cabin door. What would she say? She imagined the absurdity of the conversation that would follow—"Hello, I'm Eleanor Thompson, thank you so very much for purchasing this property and destroying my dreams."

With slow steps she climbed the sloping hill and paused before the door. There was no sound or any movement from inside the cabin. Again she deliberated, wanting more than anything to run back to the boat and forget she had ever come. Just as she was about to turn back, the door opened.

It was Liam.

Eleanor stared at him, disbelieving. But then Liam smiled and said, "Hello, girleen."

"What on earth are you doing here?"

"I've been living here for about a week." Liam's smile deepened. "I've spent all that time making the cabin weather-tight, so I'll be comfortable come winter."

"But why? I thought you had decided to return to Graceville!"

"A man has a right to change his mind," Liam said. "You know that I always had a hankering to buy myself a spot of land."

"*You* bought the cove? Why? Where did you get the money?"

"Come in here with me, Eleanor," Liam invited. "I'll explain everything."

Inside, the roof had been patched and the rotten floor-boards replaced. The log walls had been chinked and sealed, while sunlight streamed through two brand-new glass windows. There was a small cook stove, bed, table and chairs, icebox, dry-goods, and two lanterns.

"Have a seat," Liam said as he drew out one of the ladder-back chairs. Eleanor did as he asked, and then watched Liam slide a small wooden box from beneath the bed. He rummaged through its contents and withdrew a folded newspaper article. "Read for yourself," he said, sitting down across from her.

Eleanor read the headline of the *News-Tribune* article: "Zenith Steam Ruling in Favor of Captain's Widow: Sole Survivor's Testimony Key to Victory." She looked at Liam. "Oh, Liam, how wonderful! It must be a relief to know the jury believed what you had to say."

"Aye, I won't deny it. But the best part is that the families of my shipmates should be taken care of financially because of this. I heard from Shamus that Zenith Steam has announced they will settle all claims out of court."

"That still doesn't explain where your money came from, though."

"Mrs. Graling gave me a generous gift from her husband's estate. A check for three-thousand dollars, to be exact."

"Three-thousand?" Eleanor repeated. "I can't believe it!"

"Nor could I, at first, though I've already been hard at work spending it. The day after I deposited the check, I sent a telegram to Uncle Tim Pat in Graceville.

I told him that farming just didn't interest me. I sent another letter to Rose O'Malley, a short one, wishing her well and telling her that she'd best not wait for me. I was sorry to hurt her, poor Rose, but it was best to be leave no misunderstanding."

"And so there really is no reason for you to return to Graceville," Eleanor said. "But then why did you buy the cove instead? There's land for sale all over, not just here."

"Isn't the reason obvious? I bought it for you, girleen."

"For me? But why?"

"Take a walk with me. There's something I want to show you."

Eleanor followed Liam out the door and across the beach to a trail cut through the densely packed woods. Eleanor stared at his back as he led the way, still struggling to accept reality of his presence.

The path began to rise until it opened onto a bare cliff-top, where a wide vista opened before them. Eleanor turned her face into the wind for the moment, smelling Superior, tasting the breeze. When she turned to back to Liam, he was watching her and smiling.

"All right, now, tell me why you've brought me here," Eleanor insisted.

"Look and see." Liam pointed to the trunk of a nearby aspen, where he'd carved the words, "Liam loves Eleanor."

"I do love you, girleen, with all my heart," Liam said as he drew her into his arms. "I knew it the day I learned about the verdict, when I went to think alone about my future. I know it was wrong of me not to tell you about the shooting, and I'm sorry for it. But 'twould be worse to let what we have together slip away. I never want to lose you again."

Eleanor gazed at Liam's face, at every precious line and curve. A feeling inside her expanded and grew. He *was* the one she'd dreamed on all these years, heroic yet passionate, a man who would stop at nothing to win her.

"Oh, Liam," she whispered before pressing her lips to his. He kissed her hungrily, her cheeks, her eyelids, her chin. His lips traced down her neck, igniting a whirlwind of desire inside her.

"Girleen, girleen, I've waited day and night for you to come," Liam said hoarsely. "Do you forgive me?"

"I do, and I understand," Eleanor replied, running her hands through the waves of Liam's hair. He kissed her again, harder this time, and she gave herself over to the need that blazed between them.

With great reluctance, Liam released her. "There'll be time for that soon enough," he said with a wolfish grin. "But I've something I need to tell you first."

Eleanor waited, breathless. "I want to give the cove to you, free of any obligation," Liam began. "I'm asking you to marry me, Eleanor, but if you decide against it, I'll just sign the land over to you. And I'll even give you the money to help get started on the lodge. But it's up to you. You can stay as you are, a woman of independence, or marry me and become my wife."

Eleanor gazed at Liam, overwhelmed by his generosity. She didn't have to marry him, she told herself. She'd proven her own resourcefulness and ability to persevere. But she was reminded once more that, in many ways, Liam MacLann was still in exile, a man without a home.

That decided her. "Why can't I be a woman of independence *and* a wife?" Eleanor said, half-teasing.

Liam's eyes widened. "Is that your way of saying yes?"

"Yes, Liam," she said. "Yes, I will marry you and become your wife. I love you, Liam. I have since the moment I saw you."

With that he embraced her, his arms squeezing her tight. "You've made me the happiest man, Eleanor Thompson," he said. "And I'll do my best to return the favor, I swear it."

Together, they wandered to the cliff's edge, where they could see the cove curving off to the distance. "I'll have to hire some masons and carpenters to really get a start on the lodge," Eleanor said. "Are you certain you're ready for all the hard work ahead?"

"I've some folks in mind to help. Shamus and Jennie told me they'd like to leave Duluth and come live up here with us, once we have the room."

"Maybe Lars and Anja could stay on and help us too," Eleanor suggested. She smiled at the quizzical look on Liam's face. "Cameron has left Haven Point for good, and Lars is standing in as interim keeper. Anja and Lars were married just last month in Iowa."

"I see. Is Anja a good woman?"

"The sweetest I've ever met. And better than that, she can cook like a dream. Anja Berglund would be perfect for running my kitchen and dining room."

"You should ask them both at once," Liam agreed. "In the meantime, I can still help the Norwegians at the fish camp, at least until the lodge really begins to take shape. Your dream will come true, Eleanor. I'll make damned well sure of it."

"I want you to come home tonight so that we can tell my parents," Eleanor said before planting a kiss on the tip of Liam's nose. "I'll never hide my feelings about you again, I promise."

"'Twouldn't do you much good. I won't be staying away like I did before." Liam grinned. "And I'm thinking your mother will take a different view of me now, with a tidy sum of cash in my bank account." He took her hand and said, "Do you realize that the shipwreck was nine months ago on this day, exactly? What does it mean, do you suppose?"

"I'm not sure that it means anything, but I do know one thing." Eleanor withdrew the St. Brendan's medal from her pocket. "I want to give this back to you."

"You don't want it?" Liam asked, crestfallen, as she slid the medallion over his neck.

"I want you to keep it, Liam, to remind you of Ireland always."

"Thanks," he said. Liam gazed deep into her eyes. "Ah, I remember the first time I ever saw you, girleen. You were asleep in the rocking chair beside the bed. I thought that I had died and gone to heaven, because you were as beautiful as an angel."

"Oh, you're just saying that because I've agreed to marry you."

"No, no I'm not," Liam said, growing serious. "You were both shadow and light to me those first few days. I lost my heart to you then, though I was too stubborn to know it."

"Why Liam, you sound just like a poet!"

"A bit of the Irish charm, you might say." Liam's arms were around her once again. "Have I told you that the nightmares about the wreck have all ended? Since my last day in Duluth, I've slept as soundly as a wee babe every night."

"Do you know why?"

"I understand at last why I was saved. I'm here to tell their story. To keep the memory of my shipmates alive. Nick Bryant, Tom Gustnor, Ransom Hoyt, Allen Wright, Nathanial Klassen, Captain Graling, all the crew: I must make certain no one ever forgets their heroism that night on the lake."

"I think you're right, Liam," Eleanor said softly. "You must keep their memory alive."

"I intend to, girleen, don't worry." Suddenly Liam swept her into his arms. "Shall I carry you off to our castle, my queen? 'Tis a small one for now, sure, but one day 'twill be as grand as you imagined!"

She giggled. "By all means, brave knight. But allow me the pleasure of walking there myself." As Liam set Eleanor down again, she gave him another kiss and said, "I never want this end, Liam."

"I'll never stop loving you, girleen. You're mine, my very own." They walked together, hand in hand, eager to begin their future together.

The rush of waves filled Eleanor's ears, thunderous music from Lake Superior's distant past. The emotion that had grown in Eleanor now burst and overflowed. Certainty. Contentment. Home. Yes, more than anything, Liam was now her home.

It can never end between us, Liam, she whispered in her heart, *for you will always be my dream.*

978-0-595-38642-0
0-595-38642-3

Printed in the United States
58597LVS00004B/1-102